Praise for Wilkie Martin's *unhum*

'Madcap tales'

'Cult following for his wacky boc
they are entertaining'

'I enjoy how silly everything is'

Jo Ann Hakola
The Book Faerie, bkfaerie.blogspot.co.uk

'This author has become one of my favourites'

Anders Mikkelsen
Koeur's Book Reviews, koeur.wordpress.com

'Had me giggling'

Carol Siewert
book reviews forevermore, clsiewert.wordpress.com

'It reached my quirky sense of humor'

Carolyn Injoy-Hertz
Reviews & recommendations, carolyninjoy.wordpress.com

'Very much the funny man's Sherlock Holmes'

Scarlet Aingeal
Scarlet's Web, scarletaingeal.booklikes.com

'An amusing fantasy take-off on Sherlock Holmes and Watson'

Nancy Famolari
Nancy Famolari's Author Spotlight,
nancyfamolari.blogspot.co.uk

'I liked Inspector Hobbes and The Blood from the word go. It hit the road running with more double entendres than a Carry On film'

Brett Hassell
Amazon UK Top 50 Reviewer,
Amazon USA Top 1000 Reviewer,
Amazon CA #1 Hall of Fame Top 50 CA Reviewer

unhuman

I
Inspector Hobbes and the Blood

II
Inspector Hobbes and the Curse

III
Inspector Hobbes and the Gold Diggers

IV
Inspector Hobbes and the Bones

V
Inspector Hobbes and the Common People

Also by Wilkie Martin
Razor
Relative Disasters

As A. C. Caplet
Hobbes's Choice Recipes

Children's books as Wilkie J. Martin
All in the Same Boat
The Lazy Rabbit

Inspector Hobbes and the Bones

unhuman IV

Wilkie Martin

The Witcherley Book Company
United Kingdom

Published in the United Kingdom
by The Witcherley Book Company.

British Library Cataloguing in Publication Data.
A catalogue record for this book is available from the British Library.

ISBN 9781910302026 (paperback)
ISBN 9781910302033 (kindle)
ISBN 9781910302040 (epub)
ISBN 9781910302057 (hardback)
ISBN 9781912348541 (large print paperback)
ISBN 9781912348060 (audiobook)

1

The man walking past the coach stop had his raincoat hood pulled low against the morning drizzle, but I barely noticed him until he punched me on the nose. Fearing another blow, I cowered and covered my face, and by the time I felt safe enough to look up, he was sauntering away as if nothing had happened. I blinked away tears and spluttered meaningless sounds of shock and outrage while warm blood dripped between my fingers. Eventually, I managed to construct a coherent question.

'Why?'

If he heard, he ignored me.

I mopped up some of the gore with a ragged tissue from my coat pocket, and, as the pain kicked in and rage grew, considered the possibility of pummelling him into the ground. I'd even got as far as taking a tentative step after him, when a big black Mercedes with tinted windows drove by, splashing me with filthy, slushy water. It pulled up next to the man, who got in without looking back and was driven away, leaving me infuriated, if more than a little relieved, since I've never really been a fighter, and he'd looked a solid, muscular sort of bloke. Instead, I shook my fist and exorcised my frustration and temper by shouting insults, though not too loudly in case he heard. In all the excitement, I forgot to note the car's number plate, a practice my friend Inspector Hobbes of the Sorenchester Police had tried to instil in me when I used to help with his more difficult cases.

Much had changed since those days. I was married and had become, I hoped, a better and more confident person. Other than what had just happened, no one had hit me since my marriage to Daphne, but two years had passed and she was leaving me, which hurt far more than a mere bloody nose. I turned around, hoping for one last glimpse, but the National Express coach with her aboard had already pulled out of sight onto the Pigton Road. On impulse, I reached for the smartphone she'd given me for Christmas, but what was the point? She was heading for the airport, and there was no way she could come back to comfort me, even if she'd wanted to. I'd just have to cope, and get used to being alone again.

I realised I hadn't spoken with Hobbes for at least a couple of months, though, now and again, I'd spotted his vast ugly frame loping along The Shambles in the town centre, and had been reassured to see him out there, fighting crime and setting the world to rights in his own bizarre 'unhuman' fashion. Feeling suddenly lonely, I decided to pay him a visit. Lunchtime, I thought, would be good, because he'd almost certainly be home then, and I'd stand an excellent chance of a free meal. My mouth started watering at the mere thought, as anyone who'd been treated to the cooking of Mrs Goodfellow, his brilliant, if eccentric housekeeper, would understand. The only trouble was that I'd only recently breakfasted, and would have to wait until one o'clock.

Pulling myself together, the soggy tissue still pressed to my dripping nose, I turned towards the office, where I had to look in from time to time in case they were missing me. I crossed the road, heading towards The Shambles, and five minutes later entered the *Sorenchester and District Bugle's* front door, inhaling the familiar scent of printers' ink and stale coffee as I trotted upstairs to the main office. Phil Waring, the editor, as elegant and well-groomed as ever, was speaking to Basil Dean, a grizzled old hack, whose strange left eye was already aimed at me while the other concentrated on his computer screen.

'Hi, Andy,' said Phil. 'All right?'

I nodded.

'What happened?'

'Someone punched me,' I said, 'but it's nothing.'

'I'm glad to hear it.'

'Umm ... when I say nothing, it's actually incredibly painful, but I'll be okay.'

'Excellent.' He turned back to Basil. 'Okay. We'll run the one about the university rugby team's unprecedented success as it is, but are you sure about the weather one?'

'It's based on the Met Office's long-range forecast,' said Basil, whose accent still marked him as a Liverpudlian, though he'd lived in the Cotswolds for over forty years. 'I'm always a bit sceptical about this sort of thing, but it does look as if we're in for a right good deluge, like, and with all that snow still in the hills ...'

Disgruntled by their lack of sympathy, I headed to the gents and examined my battered hooter in the mirror. It wasn't as bad as I'd feared. It had already stopped bleeding, appeared as straight as ever, and wasn't nearly as sore as it might have been. I was still baffled by why the guy had attacked me, for I couldn't think of anything I'd done to provoke him, and I hadn't even recognised him. Perhaps I'd just had the misfortune to meet a random nutter, as had happened now and then, though it had usually been the more systematic ones that worried me. However, there was nothing I could do about it, so I decided to put it from my mind and get on with writing my review of Bombay Mick's Indian restaurant. I splashed water onto my face, wiped away the blood stains, dried myself and returned to the office.

Phil had recruited me as the food critic, giving me a second chance at the *Bugle,* and my career had been going comparatively well. I believed I'd become accepted and reasonably respected by my colleagues, which had never been the case during my previous stint. This time, despite only being a part-timer, my name, Andy Caplet, appeared regularly on bylines, and I was enjoying the work. It took me out and about and gave me an opportunity to sample a wide variety of foods and locations. Mostly, it was the eating that was the best part, even if no restaurant I'd visited had yet reached Mrs Goodfellow's culinary standards.

The previous week I'd reviewed Big Mama's Canteen. Big Mama was a large and formidable woman, though welcoming enough, and the place had been neat and friendly. I'd given it a favourable write-up, saying that it was an appealing little place, where I'd enjoyed some fine dishes and where the house Barolo had left my palate singing. I'd even submitted the piece, plus a courtesy copy to Big Mama's, via my smartphone, which, given my technophobic tendencies and awkward fingers, had been a miracle.

While my computer booted up, I made myself a mug of instant coffee, before sitting down and bashing out my piece. It was rather easy since Bombay Mick's food had been nicely spiced and tasty, unlike its rival, Jaipur Johnny's, where everything had been over-spiced and burnt, forcing me to write a real stinker, but only after a period of confinement in the bathroom with a nasty case of the Jaipur trots. After an hour or so, I finished my five hundred words and emailed it. I checked a few things, got up to leave, and was putting on my coat when Phil called me over.

'Thanks for the review,' he said. 'It reads well. And I've got a bit of news for you. It seems your articles have come to the attention of some influential people.'

'I'm sorry,' I said. 'What's wrong with them?'

He laughed. 'Nothing. In fact they like them and you're going to be syndicated in both *Sorenchester Life* and *Cotswold Hodgepodge.*'

'That's great,' I said, relieved not to be getting a bollocking, aware that old habits and thought patterns still lurked in dark corners of my mind, though Phil was nowhere near as terrifying as Editorsaurus Rex Witcherley, the previous editor. Plus, since I'd once saved Phil's life, I figured he would never be too nasty.

'It'll mean you get paid a bit more.'

'Brilliant! Thank you,' I said. 'Right, I'd better be off. See you.'

I bounced downstairs in a state of mild euphoria, wishing there was someone to share my good news with, for I'd never before had a pay rise. Looking back, I'd never deserved one since my early career had been one long chain of largely self-made disasters. What had changed me was meeting Hobbes.

I stepped out into The Shambles, deciding it was still too early to direct my feet towards number 13 Blackdog Street, where he lived, and recalling the first time I'd visited there in my capacity as deputy stand-in crime reporter, when I'd been nervous of his reputation. Since then, despite episodes of terror, pain and horror, my life had improved beyond measure.

A woman shouted. 'Look out!'

A black Mercedes mounted the pavement and sped towards me, forcing me to dive headlong into the entrance of Grossman's Bank. The car drove away, jumping the red light, and turned into Pound Street.

'Are you okay?' the woman asked, running towards me as I sprawled.

She was young and pretty. In fact, she was beautiful, and her soft green eyes were expressing concern. She was dressed in something fluffy that emphasised her attractions without being at all slutty.

'Umm ... yes, I think so,' I said, getting to my feet, almost oblivious to the stares of the bank's customers, and enchanted by a whiff of her perfume. 'Thank you for warning me.'

'It looked deliberate,' she said, frowning and pushing

back her long blonde hair.

'You mean someone was trying to run me over? Why would anyone do that?'

She shrugged. 'Who knows? Are you sure you're all right? My name's Sally.'

'Andy. I'm fine, and I'm sure it was just an accident. No one would have any reason to hurt me.'

'I suppose not.' She hesitated, biting her lip in the most fascinating and charming manner. 'Look, Andy, I don't normally do this sort of thing, but can I treat you to a coffee?'

I knew I shouldn't, but I hesitated and was lost. 'Umm ... okay.'

'Shall we go to Pinky's?' she asked. 'I hear that's good.'

'Umm ... why not try that one?' I pointed down the road.

'Café Nerd? What's it like?'

'I've never been in, but it might be brilliant,' I said. 'Anyway, it's closer.'

The truth was that Pinky was Daphne's best friend, and although having a coffee with a ravishing young woman who'd just saved my life was entirely innocent, for some inexplicable reason the idea of her seeing us together was making me feel guilty.

'Fine,' she said, taking my arm.

I was sure every passer-by was staring at us and thinking bad thoughts about me, so I was glad to get inside Café Nerd. It was nothing to write home about, being a bland, white plastic sort of place, with walls plastered in posters from comic books, but it looked comfortable enough.

'What would you like?' I asked, reaching into my pocket.

'Put your wallet away,' she said, squeezing my hand. 'This one's on me.'

'Very kind,' I said. 'In that case, I'll ... umm ... have a cappuccino.'

She ordered from a smiling young guy with a red bowtie

and I managed to lead her to a booth in the corner, out of sight of the front window. I took off my coat and sat down by the wall, expecting her to take the seat facing me. It was disconcerting when she slid along the bench by my side, and despite my budging up as much as possible, she came a little too close. Not that it wasn't pleasant, but I think I'd have preferred more space, and I was baffled why she was gazing into my face with those alluring green eyes.

'It's not a very nice day,' I said, wishing I'd given myself an escape route, and trying to fill an uncomfortable silence.

At least, I found it uncomfortable, but, Sally appeared quite relaxed. I tried to match her, and might have succeeded had she not touched my knee.

'Did you know,' she murmured, 'that you are a most attractive man?'

'Me? Come off it. I'm nothing special.'

'Oh, but you are, Andy.'

I think I blushed and was only saved further embarrassment when the guy came with our drinks.

I grabbed my cappuccino, and took a gulp. It was scalding hot, but I forced it down, guessing she wouldn't be much impressed if I spat it all over the table, and it did at least give me a few moments to think, though I couldn't think of anything.

'Gosh, I was thirsty,' I said, fighting off the pain and putting down the cup.

'So I see. You strike me as the sort of man who knows what he wants and how to get it. It makes you extremely desirable.'

'Does it? I'm flattered, but I've got to tell you I'm married.'

'So? We're only having a coffee. What's wrong with that?'

'Nothing, I suppose, but ...'

I gulped as her hand strolled on fingertips a little higher up my thigh.

'What harm can it do? Besides, you're not your wife's property are you?'

'Well, no. Not as such.'

'You're not her chattel. You're a free man.'

'Yes, of course, but ...'

'And I'm a free woman.' She paused and nibbled her lip again.

It was a most charming little habit.

'I'm normally very shy,' she said, 'but you're so sweet and so very handsome ...'

With no further warning she threw her arms around my neck, pulled herself even closer and kissed my lips. Taken aback, I didn't stop her. I doubt I could have, though I knew it was wrong, and, indeed something about the whole experience felt weird. Even so, I let it happen. The small part of me that enjoyed what was happening, that was flattered, over-rode any guilt and suspicions and somehow, I was kissing her and she was in my arms, her body warm and soft, her scent enchanting but discreet. The whole café lit up for an instant.

'Thanks, mate, that'll do nicely,' said a gruff male voice.

It was all over in a flash. Sally broke from my embrace, slid from the bench and walked straight from the café without a backward glance. The man who'd spoken was stout and balding with a long grubby mac, his nicotine stained fingers holding a camera. He took a few more snaps of my shocked face, glanced at the screen, grinned and turned away.

'What are you doing?' I asked, looking around and feeling confused.

'Taking photographs,' he said over his shoulder. 'Thank you for your cooperation.'

'But why? What's going on?'

'Doubtless all will be made clear shortly. Nice to have met you, Mr Caplet.'

'How do you know my name? Who are you?'

He waved and walked out.

Determined to extract more information, I grabbed my coat and started for the door.

'Excuse me, sir,' said the waiter, blocking my path. 'You haven't paid for your coffees.'

'She said she'd do it.'

'She didn't.' He glanced at a paper bill in his hand. 'That will be five pounds and fifty pence, sir.'

'For two coffees? You've got to be joking.'

He pointed to the sign above the counter. 'All our prices are clearly displayed.'

I glanced up and coughed up, pleased to have the cash, which was still somewhat of a novelty. When I eventually got outside, I looked up and down The Shambles, but Sally and the photographer had gone. To my mind, the whole incident had all the ingredients of a set-up, particularly since he'd known my name. It must have been, and they were intending to blackmail me, but why? I wasn't rich or anything. However, I feared I'd find out all too soon, and there was nothing I could do but wait.

2

I decided to head for Blackdog Street, although it was only eleven-thirty and still far too early for lunch. I expected Hobbes would be out policing, but Mrs Goodfellow would probably be home and I had no doubt she'd offer me a cup of tea in exchange for a chat. By then I really was thirsty, having been too occupied to take more than just the one gulp of super-heated cappuccino. Deep in thought, wondering about the odd stagnant taste in my mouth, but back to my normal self, I strolled up The Shambles, avoiding the market stalls in the middle where I was well known as a sucker. I passed the stately old Cotswold-stone church and waited for the lights to change so I could cross the road into Blackdog Street, feeling as if I were going home, because I'd lived there for several months when Hobbes took me in after I'd accidently burned down my flat and lost my job. It was only then, aged thirty-seven, that I felt my adult life had begun, and that everything before had been a sort of pupation, a period when I'd achieved almost nothing other than survival. Those days were gone and I'd emerged like a butterfly from a pupa to enjoy the fruits of adulthood. Well, maybe not a butterfly, but I had definitely emerged from darkness into light and things had been going so well.

As I waited, a black Mercedes with tinted windows approached in the midst of a stream of traffic. A rifle barrel pointed from the back window, and I turned to run. There was a sudden sharp pain in my left buttock and I fell forwards with a cry.

'Are you all right, mate?' asked an innocent bystander.

'I've been shot,' I said, numb with horror, except in the buttock area.

'Where?'

'Just here.'

'No, where are you hurt?'

I pointed at my bottom.

'Ooh! I bet that smarts. Who did it?'

'I don't know and it's not important. Call an ambulance!'

'Why?'

'What do you mean why? I've been shot!'

'You'll get over it. It'll sting and you might get a little bruise, but it's nothing to get so worked up about.'

And then the unfeeling, heartless swine just walked away.

I touched the spot, expecting blood, but there was none. However, my probing fingertips located a small hard lump stuck in the fabric of my trousers. It turned out to be an air gun pellet that had passed right through my coat and jacket but not through me. A little ashamed, if still sore, I got to my feet and, seeing the lights had changed and the traffic had stopped, hobbled across into Blackdog Street, heading for the terrace of old stone houses at the end. When I reached number 13, I limped up the three stone steps to the glossy black front door with its shining brass knocker, and reached into my pocket for my key, which wasn't there. Of course it wasn't, because I'd given it back after moving in with Daphne. I reached for the doorbell.

'Hello, dear,' said a familiar high quavering voice that made me jump.

Although I looked down the grille into the cellar, up at the windows, and down the street, I couldn't see her. 'Hello, Mrs Goodfellow. Umm ... where are you?'

'On the roof, dear.'

Dressed in a red cardigan and skirt, and a matching headscarf, she was leaning over and waving with no visible means of support. My stomach lurched to see such a frail old woman in such a precarious place.

'Why?'

'The old fellow reckons we're in for torrential rain and gales, so I'm making sure the tiles are all safe and secure and that the gutters are clean.'

'But it must be really slippery up there with all this drizzle. I don't think you should be doing it at your age, and especially in this weather.'

'Far better to do it now than in a gale, dear. That really would be dangerous, and what's my age got to do with anything?'

She had a point, I suppose, but I wasn't happy.

'Nearly finished,' she said, 'so if you give me a moment, I'll come down and let you in. It's nice to see you.'

Arms outstretched for balance, she slid along, squatted, scooped up some gunk with a trowel and threw it into an old sack. Then, looking like a diminutive Santa who'd been on a strict diet, she slung the sack over her shoulder and trudged up the tiles to the summit.

'I'll be with you in a minute,' she said and disappeared.

A minute later, the front door opened.

'Come in, dear. How are you?'

'Fine,' I said, stepping into the neat, if faded, sitting room. With its homely flowery wallpaper and slightly tatty furniture, it looked comfortingly familiar and unchanged, and I started drooling at the aroma of something rich and savoury that was cooking, and which almost, but not completely, overpowered the feral odour I associated with Hobbes.

'You don't look fine,' she said, peering up into my face. 'Have you been fighting? And you've got a bit of a limp.'

'Well, actually, someone punched me on the nose, and then someone shot me in the bottom with an air rifle.' I showed her the tiny pellet and sat down carefully on the sofa.

She laughed. 'Do you want me to take a look at it?'

'No, not really,' I said, ignoring her callous attitude,

though I knew how kind she'd be if I'd genuinely been hurt. 'How are you?'

'Very well.'

'And Hobbes?'

'The old fellow's much the same as always. He'll be back for his dinner at one o'clock. Would you care to join him? It's nothing special, just mutton chops.'

'If you're sure there'll be enough, then yes, please.'

'That'll cheer him up. He's been a little bit down since ... since he had to deal with something nasty.'

'But, he often deals with nasty things – he's a policeman.'

'Of course, but this was out of the ordinary.'

'I can't remember seeing anything too bad in the *Bugle* ... or do you mean that killing in Barnley?'

'No, dear. That was just a drunken fracas that got out of hand when a silly argument became a punch-up. A young man fell, hit his head and died. It was sad and unpleasant, but easily solved. No, I gather it was far, far worse.'

'What then?'

'He hasn't talked about it. All I know is that something happened on Hedbury Common, and that it was not a normal police case. I'm glad I don't know any more. Would you like a cup of tea?'

'I would,' I said, unsure whether to be upset at missing out on the action, or relieved I'd been spared.

'I'll go and make one. Do you like celeriac dauphinoise?'

'I expect so.'

'Good, then make yourself at home.'

'Thank you. Umm ... is Dregs out with Hobbes?' I asked, missing the big, black delinquent dog who, though he'd once terrorised me, had become a firm friend.

'He's out courting some bitch, and I'm not sure when he'll be back.'

She went into the kitchen, leaving me with just the latest issue of *Sorenchester Life.* I took it from the coffee table and flicked through, more interested than normal now my reviews would be in it. It was a sure sign I was rising up the social standing, since the glossy magazine was clearly designed for posh people, and largely featured posh people. I'd sometimes wondered why Mrs Goodfellow ordered it, for she was anything but posh and Hobbes was ... Hobbes.

Most of the magazine struck me as rather pointless, particularly a long, boring piece about the university rugby team's unexpected recent run of success, but one article about a prize pig called Crackling Rosie grabbed my attention. It wasn't that I was especially interested in pigs, although she looked to be a fine specimen of the Sorenchester Old Spot breed, but because her owner was a local man called Mr Robert Nibblet, better known to me as 'Skeleton' Bob. Bob was the skinniest man in Sorenchester, and widely known as a spectacularly unsuccessful petty criminal and poacher. The police largely tolerated his unlawful activities, since the fines and compensation he had to pay dwarfed the proceeds of his crimes. He'd won Crackling Rosie when bowling for a pig at St Stephen's Church Fete, and was now claiming to be on the straight and narrow. I laughed out loud, for, although it was possible I'd grown old and cynical, I had little doubt he'd be back in the crime pages of the *Bugle* soon. A voice in my ear made me jump.

'Here's your tea, dear,' said Mrs Goodfellow, and placed a mug on the table.

I nodded, shocked as always by her abrupt appearances. How she could move as quietly as a cat was beyond me, but then, compared to Hobbes who, when he wanted, could be quieter than a mouse in felt slippers, she clumped around like a rhinoceros.

'Thank you,' I said when I'd got my breath back. She'd already gone.

The tea was delicious and fragrant, and when I'd drunk

it, I considered offering my help in the kitchen, though my culinary skills, unlike my appreciation of them, were not great. However, I had learned an awful lot from Mrs Goodfellow and most of my recent efforts had turned out reasonably edible, unlike many of Daphne's. Although I'd never told her, and never would, she was almost as bad a cook as my mother, who'd even been known to devastate tinned soup. My palate had of course been spoiled by the delights Mrs Goodfellow had bestowed upon my unworthy plate and, although Daphne had undoubtedly been the best thing that had ever happened to me, I'd still experienced occasional nostalgia pangs for life at Hobbes's, especially when meal times were approaching. It occurred to me that I had so much to thank the old girl for; without her, my appreciation of good food would never have developed, and I would never have been able to do my job.

The front door swung open.

A vast figure in well-polished black boots, baggy brown trousers and a flapping gabardine raincoat stood framed in the doorway. As he pulled the door behind him, his eyes scrutinised me from beneath a tangle of dark, bristly eyebrows, and his ugly face broke into a display of grinning yellow teeth.

'Andy! What a wonderful surprise,' said Hobbes. 'Are you staying to lunch?'

I got to my feet and shook the hand he was proffering. It was as hard and as hairy as a coconut and made mine feel as small and weak as a baby's.

'Yes,' I said. 'Mrs Goodfellow invited me. I hope that's not a problem?'

'Of course not. How are you?'

'Apart from being punched on the nose, nearly run over, and getting shot at from a car this morning, I'm fine.'

He chuckled. 'I'm glad to see you've still got your taste for adventure. Take a seat and tell me about it.'

I sat back down and recounted the events of the morning, leaving out the kissing part, and let him examine the pellet that I'd kept in my pocket. When I'd finished, he looked thoughtful.

'It seems someone is out to intimidate you.'

'Or kill me.'

'Shooting you in the backside with an air rifle pellet does not count as an assassination attempt.'

'What about trying to run me over?'

'Then why did the girl warn you? I'm interested in her role in this, but doubtless everything will become clear in good time. Have you annoyed anyone recently?'

'Not that I can think of.'

'Have you written any particularly scathing reviews?'

'No ... well yes, a couple of days ago at the start of my curry house special, but it's not been published yet.'

'I remember one from a few months back,' said Hobbes. 'It was about The Italian Job in Hedbury. That was a stinker, though from what I've been told, accurate.'

'I suppose so,' I said, gratified he'd actually read it. 'Do you think they might be behind the attacks?'

He scratched his jaw with his thumb, producing a sound rather like someone sawing a log. 'It would seem an overreaction, but some of these restaurateurs and chefs can be rather precious and thin-skinned. Do you remember what happened to your predecessor?'

'The Fat Man? Do you mean when Featherlight dangled him from the church tower to make him apologise, after a bad review.'

Len 'Featherlight' Binks, the landlord of the Feathers, the most disreputable pub in town, claimed to have once been an army chef and prided himself on his cooking, despite what it did to his customers. Oddly, the pub maintained a loyal clientele and was so shockingly awful that it attracted tourists looking for an experience. For a fair number, their experience ended, for one reason or another, in the hospital.

'Dinner's ready,' said Mrs Goodfellow.

'Thank you, lass,' said Hobbes and smiled as the shock of her voice launched me from the sofa.

It was always the same, but I knew I'd forgive her as soon as I'd started to eat. Hobbes ushered me into the kitchen, which was just as I remembered, and we took our places at the well-scrubbed wooden table in the middle of the red brick floor, as the old girl dished up. The aroma was so delicious I'd already picked up my knife and fork before remembering that Hobbes always said grace, a habit imposed during his far-distant childhood. Trying not to fidget, I waited until he'd finished.

Although I'd had a slight fear that memory had built up her powers too high, that she'd only seemed so brilliant in comparison to my mother's dreadful concoctions, along with the abominations from the Feathers and the Greasy Pole, and that my recent fine dining might have spoiled me, the first morsel made me realise just how foolish my concerns had been. She was, quite simply, the best cook I'd ever known, and by such a distance I wondered if I'd been far too generous in most of my reviews. Indeed, many of the restaurants I'd assessed as excellent now seemed merely adequate, for her mutton chops, slow cooked in a rich tangy sauce were a taste of heaven, the celeriac dauphinoise was fragrant and substantial and the sautéed leeks worthy of their own paragraph of effusive praise at the very least. As usual, Hobbes and I ate in reverential silence until our plates were clean.

'That was delicious,' said Hobbes as she came to clear up, and I nodded, fearing an emotional breakdown if I tried to say anything.

'How is Daphne?' asked Hobbes, when the old girl had served us tea in the sitting room.

'Fine, I think.'

'That's a strange answer,' he said, tipping sugar into his mug and stirring it with his finger.

'She's gone away.'

'Where to?'

'Egypt. She left this morning.' I glanced at my watch. 'I expect she'll be on the plane by now.'

'Is she on holiday?'

'No, she's got a secondment on an archaeological dig. Apparently, they think they might have discovered a lost city beneath the sands, but she didn't know where, because it's all secret to protect it from grave robbers.'

'That sounds interesting,' he said. 'If it weren't for all the camels, I'd like to go back there some time.' He took a huge slurp from his mug.

'I didn't know you'd ever been,' I said and took a tiny sip of tea. It was still scalding.

'It was after the Great War.'

'Why?'

'I was sent to sort out a rogue anubis.' To my surprise, he shuddered.

'What's one of those?'

'A so-called mythical creature, and that's all I'm prepared to say. It was not a happy experience ... for either of us. Besides, it was where I developed my camel allergy.'

Since I'd long ago learned that he could not be persuaded to say more than he wanted, I dropped the subject, just adding it to the pile of mysteries. I'd once believed my slow realisation that he was not strictly human, that he was, in fact, 'unhuman', had been his greatest mystery, but, since then I'd learned such snippets of his history that mere 'unhumanity' seemed almost unremarkable.

'What are you doing these days?' I asked, changing the subject.

'Surprisingly little since a nasty case up on Hedbury Common before Christmas. Yesterday, I investigated some petty vandalism in Stillingham, but it didn't take me long to nail the culprit, a fifteen-year old lad who'd got bored and smashed some windows. I've had a word with him and I doubt he'll be any trouble now.'

'That's good,' I said.

'It is for the public, but it's not very exciting for me. Still, I'm sure something will turn up soon. It usually does.'

3

Hobbes finished his tea and got to his feet, saying he was heading back to the police station. Having decided to tag along, I was soon in the once familiar position of scurrying behind, breathing heavily, and trying to keep up with his long, lazy lope. When we turned into Vermin Street I was suddenly and unexpectedly enveloped in a big black dog.

'Get off!' I said, wrestling with Dregs who, having not seen me for a while, was determined to make up for lost time. I was delighted to meet him again, despite his long wet tongue. In addition, I was rather proud he'd failed to knock me to the ground, as he'd done so many times before.

'Have you finished courting for today?' asked Hobbes.

'What?' I said, taken by a sudden fear that he'd heard something.

But he was talking to Dregs, who wagged his tail and contrived to look smug.

'Should he be out on his own?' I asked.

'I doubt it, but he insisted.' He paused and looked down the road. 'Hallo, 'allo, 'allo, what's going on here then?'

A spaghetti-thin man in a threadbare jacket and stained trousers, tears rolling down his bony face, was running towards us shouting. 'Mr Hobbes! Mr Hobbes!'

'Calm down, Bob,' said Hobbes. 'Whatever is the matter?'

'It's Rosie,' said Skeleton Bob as he drew near. 'Some swine has murdered her.'

'Rosie who?' asked Hobbes, frowning and reaching for his notebook.

'Bob's prize pig,' I said. 'It was in *Sorenchester Life.* I forgot to tell you I'm going to be published in *Sorenchester Life!*'

'When did this happen?' asked Hobbes.

'This morning,' I said. 'Phil Waring told me.'

'Thank you, Andy, but I was asking Bob.'

'It must have happened overnight, Mr Hobbes. I went to feed her this morning and there she was, dead. Murdered! She was such a sweet pig.'

'Tell me what happened,' asked Hobbes, who to his credit was still looking concerned.

'Someone must have broken down the wire around her yard and attacked her in her house. There was blood all over and she was dead. Stabbed I reckon. She was a lovely animal.'

'Most unpleasant,' said Hobbes. 'Have you informed the police yet?'

'We don't have a phone because we couldn't pay the bill. I had to walk and I've only just got here and I'm really tired.'

'But your cottage is only five miles out of town. It shouldn't have taken you more than an hour and a half,' I said.

'I had some things to deliver,' said Bob. 'I have to do them all on foot since they took my van away. They reckoned it wasn't roadworthy.'

'I heard you drove it into a pond,' said Hobbes.

'Yes, but I could've got it out.'

'I also heard it had no brakes and that all four tyres were as bald as eggs and that there was a big hole in the floor.'

'But it still went like a bomb.'

Hobbes smiled. 'I'll give you a lift home and take a look at the crime scene. My car's at the station. Do you fancy a trip out, Andy?'

I nodded and he led the way down Vermin Street and through a dank and mossy alley, before we reached the back of the police station where his latest ridiculously small car, a rusty Nissan Micra, was parked. Bob and I had to cram into the back since Dregs preferred riding up front. The engine started.

'Hang on,' I muttered.

The car hurtled through town, Hobbes ignoring red lights and road signs, until we hit the main road to Bob's place where he could really crush the accelerator. Although Bob whimpered occasionally, I, acting on the principle that ignorance was bliss, screwed my eyes closed and thought happy thoughts until we'd stopped. Hobbes's driving hadn't got any better, though in fairness he never had accidents unless he meant to, when presumably they should have been called deliberates.

'Where's the crime scene?' he asked, getting out and looking around at the red brick hovel and the chaotic yard that was littered with rusting metal and nameless junk. Dregs, to his chagrin, was not allowed out and moped in the car. At least he was spared the drizzle.

'Behind the cottage,' said Bob. 'It's not a pretty sight.'

'No, it isn't, but I expect new windows and a lick of paint would help,' I said.

Bob frowned. 'I meant the crime scene. It's in the orchard.'

He showed us round the back, which involved an undignified scramble over what might, in a previous existence, have been a tractor. Although the so-called orchard contained a number of bare trees, they didn't look likely to bear fruit, and I'd have guessed they were sycamores. However, the pig run in the corner looked well kept, apart from the broken wire fence and the bloodied carcass. She'd been a big pig. Hobbes glanced at me.

'I remember the routine,' I said. 'I have to stay back ... or should I say sty back?'

'No, you shouldn't.' He was already in the pig run, looking, poking and sniffing.

If anyone had asked me, I'd have said the only smell was pig.

Kneeling down, he examined Crackling Rosie and the muddy ground. He nodded as he got back to his feet and leant into the brick pig house, a solid structure about the size of a medium-sized garden shed.

'Yes,' he said. 'Rosie is certainly dead, and your surmise that she was killed is entirely justified. However, I don't believe the culprit was human.'

'D'you mean aliens did it?' I asked, and was ignored.

'You see,' Hobbes continued, 'there are two sets of trotter prints.'

'Two?' said Bob. 'But I've only got … I only had the one.'

'And Rosie's wounds appear to have been caused by tusks, so I believe she was attacked by a wild boar.'

'I thought they were extinct in this country,' I said.

'They were,' said Hobbes, 'but some were brought back in collections, and, of course, a few escaped and bred. I wasn't aware of any around here, but there would appear to be at least one.'

'Are they dangerous?'

'Apparently,' said Hobbes, with a glance at Rosie. 'However, the occasional ones I've met have been quite charming.'

'What are you going to do about it?' asked Bob, still tearful. 'She was a lovely pig and didn't deserve to be murdered by a fence-crashing boar.'

I sniggered and Bob stared at me, nonplussed, looking forlorn in the increasing drizzle.

'I will report the incident,' said Hobbes. 'Perhaps I'll track down the culprit and assess the risk to the public.'

'Do you think it might attack someone?' I asked.

'Possibly,' said Hobbes, 'and it might cause a road accident.'

'I guess it's likely to be a road hog,' I said.

Hobbes acknowledged my little jest with a nod, but it soared way over poor Bob's head.

I wished I'd thought to bring an umbrella since my tweed jacket, as absorbent as kitchen towel, was growing heavier, and stinking like Dregs did before it was necessary to give him a bath – a wild and messy procedure.

'I'm ruined,' said Bob. 'I was banking on breeding from her and now I'll have no money coming in at all. How will I pay the bills? How will I eat?'

'At least you'll have bacon,' I said, trying to help him see the bright side.

He burst into tears.

'That was a little tactless,' said Hobbes. 'Cheer up, Bob. I'll ask your wife to make you a cup of tea.'

'Fenella isn't home. She said I was spending too much time with Rosie and that I had to choose between the two of them. I couldn't, so she walked out and went to stay with her mum.'

'I know how you must feel,' I said. 'My wife's just gone to Egypt.'

'You don't understand,' said Bob, his head in his hands. 'She'll come back now Rosie's gone.'

Hobbes led him into the house, sat him down on a stool, made him a pot of tea, and left him to sob as we returned to the car.

'Where are we going?' I asked once I'd broken free of Dregs, who'd scrambled over the seat to take a good long sniff at my jacket.

'To the Wildlife Park,' said Hobbes. 'It's possible they've lost a boar, though I don't remember seeing any there.'

'There were some guinea pigs in the petting zoo,' I joked. 'Perhaps it was one of them?'

'Despite the name they are not actually pigs, and they're far too small to be a threat to a porker like Crackling Rosie. I do recall Red River Hogs there, but I think it unlikely that the park would let anything escape. However, they might have some information about them.'

I sat back, closing my eyes, as he stamped down on the accelerator. Now and again car horns blared, but I remained blissfully ignorant as to the cause.

After a few minutes, we slowed and turned and I risked a look. We were approaching the Wildlife Park by way of a long driveway between fields. Last time I'd gone there, it had been on a glorious summer's day with hundreds of visitors, but the car park was empty now, and even the fields appeared deserted, though I did eventually spot a morose bunch of Bactrian camels sheltering under a tree.

A notice board next to the narrow green ticket booth bore the message: Have we got Gnus for you! Moving into pastures gnu, our gnu herd of wildebeests!

Another board read: Visit our South American bird collection and meet the rhea of the year! See how our Peruvian Pelican's bill holds more fish than his belly can!

The attempts at humour made me suspect they were the work of Mr Catt, the director.

A well-wrapped man emerged from the booth, holding up a gloved hand, and approached the car. Hobbes opened the window.

'Two adults, is it?' asked the man.

'Police business,' said Hobbes, showing his ID.

The man rolled his eyes and tutted. 'I've been freezing my arse off all day and the first visitors turn out to be cops. It was a complete waste of my time coming in!'

'Cheer up, sir,' said Hobbes. 'At least you'll be paid.'

'I bloody won't. I'm a volunteer.'

'You must love animals,' I said.

'Used to, until the blasted giraffe started pissing on me from a great height.'

'Sorry to hear that, sir. Where can we find Mr Catt?'

'In the aquarium.'

'I hope he brought his towel,' I quipped.

'Thank you for your help, sir,' said Hobbes, ignoring me.

He parked the car and we headed into the aquarium, where it was pleasantly warm, and lit only by the soft glow of fish tanks. Mr Catt, a chubby, red-faced little man in a dishevelled safari suit, was staring into one of the smaller tanks that was home to a variety of brightly-coloured little fish, some with torn fins. A young woman in blue overalls and thick glasses was standing on a step ladder, trying to scoop up a small orange and white fish that kept darting into a big greenish globby thing.

Mr Catt turned as we approached. 'Mr Hobbes,' he said, 'good afternoon.'

'Good afternoon, sir,' said Hobbes, saluting.

'You find us trying to trap a clown fish, *Amphiprion percula.'* He nodded at the woman. 'This is Annette. Annette's essential for catching fish.' He chuckled.

'What's wrong with him?' I asked, as Dregs, an avid observer of wildlife, sat and stared.

'Percy is looking green around the gills, and has been attacking all the other fish, apart from Derek the domino fish, *Dascyllus trimaculatas,* who he won't allow to move away from him or the anemones.'

'Is that unusual?'

'No,' said Mr Catt, giggling like a silly kid. 'Clown fish like to keep their friends close and anemones closer.'

'Most fascinating, sir,' said Hobbes, 'but we're here on business.'

'Of course, Inspector. How may I be of assistance?'

'Do you keep any wild boar?'

'*Sus scrofa?*' said Mr Catt, shaking his head. 'Why do you ask?'

Hobbes explained.

'Very sad,' said Mr Catt, 'but, no, we don't have any in our collection. However, it was only a matter of time before they reached this part of the world, and from what you said it sounds like there may only be the one so far. It'll be interesting if they start breeding nearby. That could cause a lot of problems.'

'What sort of problems?' asked Hobbes. 'Are they likely to attack the public?'

'They're normally afraid of people, so attacks are quite rare, but possible in certain circumstances. They are, however, quite likely to go for pet dogs if they feel threatened, and they've been known to spook horses, causing riders to fall. In addition, they can cause traffic accidents, and since they're so big, hitting one at speed is likely to be extremely serious. They can also create mayhem on farmland and in gardens.'

'Yes!' cried Annette, having finally trapped Percy. She transferred him into a polythene bag of water and climbed down.

'Oh, well done!' said Mr Catt. 'Plop him in the holding tank and I'll take a look when I'm finished here.'

As she turned to go, Mr Catt glanced at his watch and called after her. 'And then would you go to the office? Our *Latrodectus hesperus* is due for delivery in five minutes.'

'What's that?' I asked.

'A black widow spider for our arachnid collection. It proved difficult to source her until we looked on the web.' He sniggered as Annette walked briskly away, shaking her head.

Not being a fan of creepy crawlies, I shuddered. 'Aren't they poisonous?'

'I doubt anyone's tried to find out, because they don't look very appetising. They are, however, venomous, if that's what you mean, though they rarely bite humans, and their bites are hardly ever fatal.'

'Fascinating,' said Hobbes, 'but where is a boar likely to live?'

'They prefer mixed woodland but can exist in a variety of

habitats, provided there is sufficient shelter and adequate food and water. Are you going to do anything about it?'

'I might have to. Mr Nibblet was most upset. Is there any reason why the boar attacked Crackling Rosie?'

'Hard to say. It could have been territorial; sometimes a pig won't accept other porcines in its boardom.'

'What?' I said, puzzled.

'A king has a kingdom. Therefore, a boar has a boardom.' Mr Catt explained, smirking. 'I thought everyone knew that.'

'Umm ... are you sure?'

He shrugged and continued. 'It might have been a fight over food, or it's just possible that it's an unusually aggressive specimen.'

'A psycho killer?' I suggested.

'Could be,' Mr Catt agreed.

There was a small glass box with a perforated lid in the corner that I only noticed when something thin and brown, partly hidden by twigs, moved inside. 'What's that?' I pointed, a little nervously, fearing it might be a snake.

Mr Catt walked over, picked up the box and showed me. Inside was an insect with an evil wedge-shaped head, bulbous eyes, and with spiky front legs held out in humble supplication. 'This little beauty is a Chinese praying mantis, *Tenodera sinensis.* She's waiting to be introduced to her soon-to-be-late husband. The females tend to devour the males during the very act of copulation, so her husband is not long for this world. But what a way to go, eh!' He sniggered.

I was grateful for having been born human.

'Is that all?' asked Mr Catt.

'I believe so,' said Hobbes. 'Thank you.'

'A pleasure, as always, Inspector. I'd better get on. I must see what is ailing Percy, and I have to check on one of our carp who keeps hiding away.'

'It's probably just a little koi,' I said, grinning.

'No, he's a silver carp, *Hypophthalmichthys molitrix,*' said Mr Catt seriously, 'and rather a fine specimen. Good afternoon, gentlemen. When I've finished in here I need to check on our bipolar bear. My work is never done.'

The rain was heavy as we ran back to the car.

'What next?' I asked as we got inside. 'Are you going to hunt it down?'

'No. We'll head back to town,' said Hobbes. 'It would be difficult, not to mention unpleasant, to go on a wild boar hunt in this rain, and, besides, you're not really dressed for outdoor activities.'

'That's true,' I said, pleased he'd noticed, though slightly disappointed, since hunting with Hobbes was an exciting, if occasionally terrifying, experience.

Still, the weather was really horrible, and I'd grown accustomed to comfort, warmth and stability since marrying. I didn't regret the marriage, not at all, even though I'd admit to days when I'd missed the visceral thrill of being out and about with Hobbes. If everything was running to plan, Daphne would be flying south-eastwards across Europe and would soon be crossing the Mediterranean to Egypt. I hoped she'd do well, for I'd not forgotten her excitement at being offered the chance to use her archaeological skills on a new site. And yet, I wasn't happy she'd chosen to be so far away, particularly as I didn't know how long she'd be there.

Hobbes dropped me off outside our flat, the one Daphne had bought when she first moved into town, and coincidently the one I'd previously lived in until I'd accidently burned it down. Since I'd caused so much damage, the whole building had required refurbishment, with the result that it was far smarter than it had been in my solo days. Really, I'd done everyone a favour.

'If you have any more trouble with attackers,' he said before driving away, 'then call me. This sort of thing is prone to escalation, and I would advise taking care for the immediate future. I'll see if I can find out what's going on, because I can't have members of the public attacked and you are my public. Mind how you go.'

I poked in the number to unlock the building's door, and went inside, a little shaken by what he'd said, for in my naiveté I'd decided the worst had already happened. The idea that there might be more attacks had simply not occurred, and, as I trotted upstairs and opened our front door, I began to worry again. Why had the guy taken photographs of Sally and me? Had she really liked me, or had she just been toying with my affections? I feared the latter, though not as much as the prospect of being blackmailed.

I made myself a drink, sat down in the kitchen, and thought that Hobbes might have had a point in suggesting some disgruntled restaurateur held a grudge against me. That could explain the punch on the nose, and the Mercedes intimidation, but a blackmail plot, if that's what it turned out to be, seemed far-fetched. After all, what could anyone expect to get from me? I wasn't rich, had no possessions of great value, and wasn't in a position of any real influence. The whole thing seemed so unlikely. Perhaps I'd misinterpreted the whole incident. Maybe Sally had been the target and I'd merely been collateral damage. However, this shaky hypothesis collapsed since I had to admit that young women were not normally so smitten by my manly charms that they flung themselves into my arms. I would have to wait and see, though it was an unhappy thought that any day I might receive an envelope with photographs, and a letter made up of words clipped from newspapers, if that's how it was still done. The only good I could see in the situation was that Daphne was away, and I hoped I could sort things out before she returned, for there was no denying the photos would be what the press always called 'compromising'.

The rest of the afternoon I frittered away on her old laptop, scaring myself when reading of possible terrorist activity in Egypt and, although it was probably nowhere near where she'd be, I couldn't stop worrying. She'd insisted that any threat was negligible, and it probably was, but I still fretted and intended to continue fretting until she was safely home.

In the early evening, I ate baked beans on toast, watched some telly and went to bed. Although I took a book, I became sleepy almost at once and, having turned off the bed-side light, fell asleep.

4

When I surfaced from a plunge into deep sleep, rain was battering the windows and the wind was howling. It was nearly four o'clock, and clamping pillows to my ears didn't drown out the din, which, even in my dozy state, struck me as unusual as our flat was triple-glazed and we could usually hear nothing of what was going on outside. I gave up on getting back to sleep, mooched into the lounge, and pulled back the curtains.

I could see little out in the blackness other than frills of rain rippling down the window, until a lightning flash lit up a world of wind and water. Almost simultaneously, thunder roared like an artillery bombardment, or at least like I imagined an artillery bombardment might sound. The weather forecasters had got it about right for once, though if anything they'd underestimated the storm. Yet, warm, dry and safe inside, I found it all quite exhilarating, until the window shattered.

All the lights blinked out and something bashed into me, sending me flying across the room. Although I don't think I quite lost consciousness, I was stunned, winded and discombobulated and it must have taken several minutes before my brain engaged a gear and worked out that I was on my back, pinned down by a crushing weight. The storm had become deafening, rain was in my face and I was shivering and goose pimply, pyjamas not being adequate for the occasion. It took another couple of minutes before I worked out that one of the massive old trees in the communal garden had come down and smashed through our flat. Wriggling free wasn't easy because of the smooth, wet, laminated flooring, and it took several minutes of grunting and groaning before I got a grip on Daphne's heavy oak sideboard and pulled myself free. The manoeuvre tore my pyjama bottoms in two lengthways, and as I stood, they fell around my ankles, exposing me to the elements.

After a rummage, I unearthed a small torch in the sideboard and turned it on. The tree had not only smashed through the window, but had also knocked in a large chunk of the wall, and, to judge by the broken tiles, part of the roof. I was covered in scratches, grazes and bruises, but these, and losing my pyjama bottoms, seemed a small price to pay for having escaped. It could have been so much worse, but I wondered what Daphne would think when she reached camp and phoned me. If she could, when our phone was somewhere under the tree.

I heard shouting and, thinking I might be able to help or fetch help, ran to the front door, opened it, stepped boldly into the hallway, before retreating in a bashful panic, realising in a flash of lightning that I wasn't presentable. Besides, it seemed sensible to ensure I was adequately dressed for the storm. Turning back, I clambered over the tree's dripping branches towards our bedroom, and shoved open the door. I came within a whisker of plunging into a gaping void where the floor had been, but, somehow, my grip on the door handle stayed firm and allowed me to haul myself back to safety, my heart pounding, my insides squirming.

The outside had come inside, and vice versa, and our bed and all our things were downstairs on our new neighbours' flattened flat. They'd only moved in a couple of weeks earlier, and I hadn't even met them. I shouted down, but got no response, and feared I never would. The situation was clearly far worse than I'd imagined, but the gust of wet wind around my nether regions reminded me that I was in no state to parade around. Yet, since all my clothes, not to mention the wardrobe that had contained them, were now downstairs, I was nonplussed until I remembered Daphne's dressing gown. She kept it on a hook behind the bedroom door, and, unless it had blown away, it might still be there. Groping around the back, terrified of the drop in front, I found it at last and jiggled it loose. Although it was sopping wet, small and pink, it was far better than nothing.

I put it on, tied the cord, and scrambled back over the branches to the hallway, where Mrs Rodgers, a large and normally cheerful divorcee of indeterminate age, and Mr Hussain, a slight, bald man in his late fifties, were talking in her doorway. Both were holding candles. Both gaped when they saw me.

'D'you know what's happened?' asked Mr Hussain.

'A tree came down,' I said. 'It's smashed up our flat and our bedroom floor has fallen on top of the new people below.'

'Aubrey and Hilda Elwes?' said Mrs Rodgers, her eyes widening. 'That's awful.'

'Have you called the emergency services?' I asked. 'My phone's gone.'

Mr Hussain shook his head. 'No, we had no idea what was going on.'

'I'll do it now,' said Mrs Rodgers and disappeared into her flat with Mr Hussain tagging behind.

'I'll see if anyone needs help,' I said, though I doubted they could hear me.

I ran downstairs, where a tall, slim young man was banging on the Elweses' front door, shouting at the top of his voice. He turned his torch on me when he heard my approach. I thought he looked vaguely familiar, and suspected he might be a neighbour.

'A tree's smashed into the building,' he said, looking panicked. 'I can't get a reply from Aubrey and Hilda.'

'Our bedroom's fallen on them. Mrs Rodgers is calling the emergency services.'

'Do you think we should break in?' he asked.

'Umm ... good question. If they're hurt, they may need our help quickly. I'll do it.'

Filled with unusual bravado, I charged their front door, only to bounce off like a tennis ball. Groaning, I sank to my knees, and rubbed my shoulder.

'Or we could wait for help,' he said.

'I wish I'd thought of that.' I got back to my feet.

Although he carried on banging and shouting, no one else appeared, and I began to fear other flats had been destroyed. I ran to the next front door along and pounded on it.

'Are you all right in there?' I cried, but there was no response.

'You're wasting your time,' said the young man. 'That's my place, and I'm here.'

'Oh, right. I think I'll take a look outside.'

'Okay, but hadn't you better adjust that ... thing you're wearing?'

I retied the cord, using a double knot, ran to the block's back door and opened it. As I stepped out, a shrieking wind nearly blew me back inside, and might have done had the spring-loaded door not slammed. The night air was so full of rain it was a struggle to even breathe, and my puny torch barely made a glimmer in the blackness. Hunched against the storm, clutching the dressing gown, I stumbled and groped my way through the communal garden until there was a lull in the wind. It gave me the opportunity to run, but, unfortunately, I ran into something that knocked the wind from my lungs, as it knocked me onto my back, where I lay stunned for a few moments with rain pouring up my nose. When my lungs re-inflated and my head cleared, I tried to stand up, but struck my head and fell back, moaning. By the feeble glow of my torch, I saw I'd again been flattened by the tree. My teeth were chattering and, although sense told me to concede defeat and to retreat into the dry, a tiny seed of resolve was growing. Getting back to my feet, I forced myself onward, battling the elements, imagining myself a hero such as Scott of the Antarctic, though memories of his tragic end were not encouraging. Onward I went, through branches and twigs, getting scratched and battered, until I reached a massive hole in the wall containing a huge chunk of tree. I scrambled into what had been the inside.

'Hello?' I yelled. 'Is anyone there?'

There was no reply.

'Mr and Mrs Elwes, are you all right?'

'If you mean us, then yes,' said a soft male voice from behind. I assumed it was Mr Elwes.

Two figures appeared in my torchlight.

'What have you done to our flat?' asked a hooded woman who was almost as tall as the man at her side.

'Me? Nothing.'

'Where's it gone then?' Her voice was sweet and sounded amused.

'The tree came down on it.'

'I wondered what it was doing there,' said Mr Elwes. 'We were out.'

'In this?' I gestured at the weather.

'Why not?'

'It's horrible.'

'Or exhilarating,' said Mrs Elwes.

I shook my head, and shivered, thinking there were some odd folk about. 'I'm getting really cold and I'm going back inside. Mrs Rodgers is calling for help.'

'Okey dokey,' said Mr Elwes, who did not sound much concerned.

Above me I could hear something moving, as if it was sliding. For a moment I wondered what it might be, and then it hit me.

5

I could smell hospital, and a familiar voice was asking how I was feeling. Despite a dull, throbbing headache, I opened my eyes to see a thin lad in a white coat, with a stethoscope around his neck.

'Dr Finlay,' I said, and shook his hand.

He nodded. 'Indeed. You haven't been in for ages. Nice to see you again.'

'Thank you ... umm ... what happened? What am I doing here?'

'You received a nasty blow to the side of the head from half a roof tile. It was lucky your neighbours were there to rescue you, because I gather the rest of the roof collapsed moments after they got you out.'

'No, that can't be right. I went to rescue them ... I think. Umm ... things are a little blurry.'

'That's perfectly normal with a concussion.'

'Another one? Why me?'

Dr Finlay shrugged. 'Wrong place at the wrong time. Now, I have a few questions...'

'Fire away, doc.'

'Do you know your name?'

'Of course.'

'Well, what is it?'

'What's what? Who are you? ... Only joking. I'm Andy ... Andy Caplet.'

'Excellent, and how are you feeling?'

'Fine, apart from a bit of a headache, and I'm a little sore here ... and here.' I felt around and wasn't surprised to find a bandage on my head.

'Excellent. How many fingers do you see?'

'Eleven. Including the finger of fudge in your top pocket.'

'Very amusing. It's a snack for later ... if I'm not too busy.'

'That's a point. I'm feeling rather hungry. What time is it?'

'Twenty past ten,' said Dr Finlay after glancing at a wall clock.

'Really? How long was I out?'

'No more than two minutes after the tile hit you, according to your neighbours, but longer after the second incident.'

'Second incident?'

'You were lying on a trolley in triage awaiting initial assessment when you decided you needed to visit the bathroom.'

'Oh, yes,' I said, as memory juddered back into focus. 'I really needed to go. What happened?'

'According to Nurse Dutton, you leapt to your feet, ran around frantically, tripped over that rather fetching dressing gown you were wearing, and head-butted the reception desk. You were in and out of consciousness for over an hour then, but you appear fine now.'

'I rather think I am. I've been told I've got a thick skull. By the way, was anybody else hurt? In the flats I mean.'

'Just you.'

'Good. Umm ... do we get fed soon?'

'Not until lunchtime, but you'll be out before then. We'd normally keep you in longer for observation, but the density of your cranium is well known to us, and, anyway, we're full and need every available bed.'

'But there's a tree in my flat! Where will I go?' As full recollection came back, I was gripped by a sudden panic. 'And I've got no clothes!'

'Don't worry,' said Dr Finlay. 'We contacted Mrs Goodfellow who'll be bringing something for you to wear.'

A massive surge of hope washed through me; if the old girl was involved everything would turn out all right.

'She'll be here before twelve o'clock, and suggested you could stay with them while you sort things out. I have other patients to see now, but someone will be with you in a few minutes to run through a bit of paperwork and then, assuming you're still feeling well, you're free to go. Nice to meet you again. Keep safe. Bye.'

'Bye, doc. I'll give it a try.'

Despite his youthful appearance, Dr Finlay had treated me several times in the past, but when Daphne had been around I'd gone unscathed. Left to my own devices, I'd managed to stay out of hospital for less than a day. I hoped she'd have a good laugh when I told her, but how was I going to tell her when my mobile was in the Elweses' flat and the landline and my laptop must have been smashed by the tree? The plan had been that she'd text or email me when she'd reached camp, but that was clearly out of the question. I supposed I could do the contacting, because I knew it was possible to get my email on another computer, but I had an awful feeling I'd need a password and I hadn't a clue what mine might be, since Daphne had set up my account. All in all, it seemed I wasn't doing a great job of coping.

As soon as I was free to go, Mrs Goodfellow, clad in a daffodil-yellow rain cape and green wellingtons, stomped into the cubicle, lugging a battered leather suitcase.

'Hello, dear,' she said. 'I've brought you some clothes.'

'Thanks,' I said, taking the case, and leaning down to receive a kiss on the cheek. 'It's been a difficult couple of days.'

I explained how I'd got there while I turned my back and dressed, glad to rid myself of the totally inadequate – and draughty – hospital gown.

'That's a nasty-looking bruise on your bottom,' Mrs Goodfellow remarked. 'Was that where you got shot, dear?'

I nodded and pulled up my pants. Although she'd seen me naked often enough and there should have been no need to feel bashful, I still was. Embarrassment was a concept she seemed unable to grasp. However, as I'd expected, all the clothes, including a fabulous tweed jacket, fitted as if bespoke, though they'd formerly belonged to her errant husband, who'd last been heard of setting up a windsurfing school in Bali, called Washed Up. His previous enterprise had been a naturist colony on Tahiti, until the authorities clamped down and he could bare it no longer. When I'd finished dressing, I noticed she'd brought a gabardine raincoat and an old pair of black wellies.

'Is it still raining?' I asked.

'Worse than ever, dear. It's wild out there. Trees have come down all over, roofs have blown off, there are already some floods, and now the river looks like it's going to burst its banks. The old fellow's helping with the evacuation and is worried the rain is turning into a drownpour.'

'D'you mean a downpour?'

'No, dear. It's getting so bad there's a risk to members of the public.'

'I just can't imagine the Soren bursting its banks. It's such a placid little river.'

'But not today, and it has flooded in the past. About thirty years ago it filled our cellar with six inches of filthy water.'

'That must have been unpleasant.'

'It was, though we weren't the worst affected by far. The houses across from Church Fields were flooded three feet deep and had to be pumped out!'

'Well, let's hope it stops soon. I'm ready now. Shall we go?'

'Yes, we'd better. I've still got his dinner to prepare. Would you like to join us?'

Had there not been a number of sick and injured people about, I might have whooped for joy. Instead, I smiled and said, 'I'd love to. Thank you.'

She led me through the A&E department towards the exit. 'You can use your old room if you'd like, until you've sorted out somewhere else. The old fellow reckons your block of flats is structurally unsound and will have to be demolished.'

Although I'd assumed the tree must have caused a great deal of damage, I'd barely thought about the consequences. I was, or rather we were, homeless, and although for me the flat had just been a pleasant place to live, for Daphne it had represented a whole new life, a break from the past after the loss of her first husband, whose bones Dregs and I had once stumbled across.

'Oh, dear,' I said, inadequately. 'I suppose I'd better go round and see if I can salvage anything ... after we've eaten of course. '

'You can't, dear,' said Mrs Goodfellow. 'No one is allowed in. It's too dangerous.'

'It's a disaster then. I guess it'll be tricky to find anywhere good to live when all our neighbours are looking for places as well.'

As we reached the exit, the old girl unfurled a large umbrella that just seemed to appear in her hand, and stepped out into the storm, which was at least as bad as it had been in the night, if not quite as dark, and I was dressed more appropriately. It was not surprising that hardly anyone was walking, and that even traffic was scarce. Those few cars and vans that were out were crawling along, their wipers going full tilt. Water sluiced off every surface, drains overflowed, the roads were already ankle deep and it was a struggle to even walk with gale force gusts threatening to blow me over, though Mrs Goodfellow, snug beneath her oversized umbrella, seemed to have no problem. I put it down to her diminutive size, since the wind obviously couldn't be bothered to knock her about when it had me to batter, though how she managed to stop the umbrella from blowing away or turning inside out was a mystery. Blackdog Street was a little uphill from the hospital and I was gasping like a heavy smoker in a marathon when we reached number 13, and she let us in.

'Wow!' I said, as she closed out the weather.

She nodded. 'It's worse than ever. I hope the old fellow's all right. He doesn't swim too well.'

'I thought he did everything well, and I've seen him diving for eels.'

'Not everything, dear. He doesn't like to be out of his depth.'

'I'm sure he'll be fine,' I said, delighted to discover something at which I might best him. It wasn't that I was such a great swimmer, but Daphne had given me lessons and I'd become confident in water, as long as it wasn't too cold or too deep.

'I'd better get on with dinner, dear. I'll do something substantial, because he'll need it, and I expect you're hungry, too?'

'I certainly am. I didn't have any breakfast today ... and I only had beans on toast last night. What are you cooking?'

'Smoked haddock soufflé with herb champ.'

'Marvellous,' I said, although not entirely sure what herb champ was.

However, it had always been one of the delights of the old girl's cooking that, although she had a set of particularly wonderful dishes based on the seasons and whatever turned up in the shops, her repertoire was seemingly endless. She had no need of cookbooks or scales, and I'd sometimes watched her at work, noting every ingredient and how she treated it. Since moving in with Daphne, I'd attempted my own versions, and on the whole, the results had not even come close to the originals, though they'd mostly been tasty enough for Daphne to declare me a good cook. Compared to her, I probably was.

I relaxed by watching the end of a black and white cowboy film on the telly. It turned out to be rather a good one. Westerns had once been a bit of a no-go area until Hobbes persuaded me to watch a few, and I discovered there was something brave and spirited in the best of them, while the landscapes were often breathtaking. He'd visited the American West back in the sixties and I think he enjoyed the familiarity.

The front door opened, bringing in rain and the chime of the church clock striking one. Hobbes nodded at me, shook out his coat, hung it on the bullhorn coat rack in the corner, and closed the door behind Dregs, who, soggy but exuberant, insisted on drying himself on me. Hobbes ran upstairs to wash his hands, returning just as Mrs Goodfellow announced in a loud voice from behind my ear that dinner, as he typically called lunch, was ready.

Had I not been pinned down by the dog, I would have leapt from my skin. As it was, my alarmed twitch threw him off and onto the rug, where he blinked and looked confused, clearly wondering how he'd got there, but giving me the chance to escape. The aroma of smoked haddock as I entered the kitchen was mouth-watering.

'How's things?' I asked when Hobbes took his seat.

'Not good. If this rain keeps up, and I think it will, the Soren will burst its banks this afternoon. The environment people don't think it will cause much of a problem, but I'm not convinced. The trouble is there'll be so much run-off from the hills, and the ground is already saturated.'

'Here you are,' said Mrs Goodfellow, placing plates in front of us.

Hobbes, dismissing his worried frown, smiled, thanked her, and said grace before giving his full concentration to the soufflé and the champ, which turned out to be mashed potato with green herbs and a pool of melted butter in the centre. It was a treat, and, since I realised it would re-calibrate my appreciation of good food, I suspected the next restaurant I visited professionally would suffer in comparison. We ate, as ever, in silence and, as usual, Mrs Goodfellow disappeared. I assumed she took food, but I couldn't remember ever seeing her do so, other than tiny tastes to ensure a dish met the mark.

Yet, as soon as we'd finished, she was back to receive our praise, to clear away the plates and to start washing up. Hobbes was extremely well looked after, as I'd been when I'd lived there, and I had to admit that moving in with Daphne and having to share the household chores had come as a real shock. Neither of us had found the transition easy. I didn't think I was completely to blame, since I'd been spoiled, firstly by my mother, and then by the old girl. In between, I'd lived a bachelor's life with a bachelor's disregard for housework of any kind other than what was absolutely essential.

'I'm afraid I'll have to forego my cup of tea,' said Hobbes, getting to his feet. 'I must get back to work. I fear there'll be serious flooding.'

'Can I come along?' I asked, looking forward to an afternoon of excitement.

'No,' said Mrs Goodfellow. 'You've had a head injury and must take it easy for the rest of the day.'

'But ...'

'Doctor's orders,' she said.

'I don't remember that.'

'Which just goes to show why you need to take it easy,' she said, giving me her stern look.

'I'll see you later,' said Hobbes, chuckling as he left the kitchen.

'But what am I going to do all afternoon?' I asked.

'I think you should take a nice nap,' said Mrs Goodfellow.

'I don't want one.'

'You'll do as you're told, young man!'

And so I did. I went upstairs, undressed, put on a pair of blue striped pyjamas, and got into the bed I'd once called my own. The sheets were crisp and white and held a delicate fragrance of lavender, but I wasn't tired. After about five minutes, the old girl brought me up a mug of tea. I inhaled the aroma and sipped. No one could make tea like she could, but as soon as I'd emptied the mug, the dull headache that had been bothering me receded and I became incredibly sleepy. I lay down, pulled up the blankets and closed my eyes. The last thing I heard was rain battering against the window.

6

Still fuzzy with sleep and convinced I was home in bed with Daphne, I rolled over for a cuddle, only to experience a moment of apparent weightlessness and confusion before I smacked onto floorboards. It was too dark to see and, as I got up, struggling to remember where I was, I turned the wrong way, stubbed my toe against something hard, and flopped back onto the bed with an oath. I groaned and cuddled my foot, finding it a poor substitute for a wife, and a painful reminder that she'd gone away and that I was back at Hobbes's. My watch showed it was six o'clock, meaning that supper, as he called his evening meal, would be ready in half an hour. The fact helped soothe the pain.

I found the light switch, dressed and opened the bedroom door, wondering why there was no sound, other than wind and rain on the windows, and, more importantly, why there were no cooking aromas. A horrible idea that I'd missed supper and had slept right through until morning had to be put to rest, so I rushed downstairs. The house felt deserted, and I re-checked my watch, and even turned on the television news, but both pointed to the conclusion that it really was just after six o'clock in the evening. The only times Mrs Goodfellow had not cooked Hobbes's supper were when she'd gone on holiday or to a dental conference, and I'd been hoping for some really comforting food. I felt I needed comforting. Ideally, I'd have liked to talk to Daphne, but hadn't yet worked out how and, anyway, I wasn't much looking forward to telling her my news.

It was not a great story. Left alone, I'd been punched, been nearly run down, made myself liable to blackmail, been shot in the buttock, lost the flat, and I suspected, most of our possessions, had been in hospital, and was now back as a guest at Blackdog Street. Although I didn't think any of it had been my fault, and it could all have happened to anyone, I feared it wouldn't sound too good. In addition, I didn't quite believe the part about none of it being my fault, for I had to concede that the blackmail incident, if that's what it proved to be, might have been partly down to my folly. I should have thanked Sally for her warning and just walked away, but I'd always found it hard to say no to a pretty face – not that I'd had many opportunities to say it.

However, I'd always prided myself on an ability to prioritise and, even with the guilt circling in my head, it struck me that food and drink was my most urgent need, and, although I hoped Mrs Goodfellow would return soon, I thought I'd better have a contingency, just in case. I decided to visit Heaven, a new bar and restaurant that had recently opened on Rampart Street. This would mean I'd get a meal, I could persuade them to forward the bill to the *Bugle*, and I'd get paid for writing about it. In the circumstances, it didn't seem a bad idea.

My stomach rumbled, time passed, and I fretted as six-thirty marched towards seven when I gave up and hit the road to the restaurant, which was only about a ten-minute stroll away. Suitably clad for such a short walk, I opened the front door and looked out, still hoping to spot the old girl coming back. I didn't, and I couldn't see anyone out, though there were sirens and shouts in the distance. Rain was still teeming down and the road was a river, with the last of the snow piles sinking like doomed islands. It was only after I'd shut the door behind me that I remembered I didn't have the key anymore. I tried to convince myself that it would not be a problem, because Hobbes and Mrs Goodfellow would certainly be back by the time I returned. Almost certainly.

I jumped down the steps and turned right, heading for Goat Street before veering left onto Rampart Street. As I walked, I noticed how deep the water in the road had become, and realised it would be tricky to cross without filling my shoes. The wellies Mrs Goodfellow had given me were behind the door at Hobbes's, though they might as well have been in Siberia for all the good they could do. I kept going, hoping there'd be somewhere to cross dry-shod, but I was out of luck. With filthy brown water starting to spill across the pavement, it became clear that if I was going to get anywhere, I'd do so with soggy feet. I took the plunge at the junction, gasping as icy water gripped my toes and despite emptying my shoes on the other side, I squelched with every step.

As I was climbing the three steps to Heaven, its front door opened and a skinny young man in a white shirt and black bowtie looked me up and down.

'You're not the sandbag guy, are you?' He sounded disappointed.

'No, I'm here to eat, though I don't have a reservation. I hope that'll be all right?' I glanced inside, reassured by the absence of diners.

'I'm sorry, sir, but we've had to close.'

'Why? I'm really hungry.'

'It's the flood, sir,' he explained as if to an idiot.

'Flood? It's only a bit of rain spilling over.'

'With respect, sir, it isn't. The Soren has burst its banks, Colonel Squire's lake is overflowing, water is pouring into town – can't you see it? It's still rising.'

'So, that's why you want sandbags.'

'Yes, but so do loads of other people, and there may not be any left. It might be too late for us anyway, because there's already water running into the kitchen.'

'Well, I'm sorry to hear that, but ... umm ... do you know if anywhere else is still serving food?'

'I don't, sir, but we're not the only place having to shut the doors tonight. Good luck, and come back when we're dry.'

I sloshed away, my stomach growling like a famished bear. The Bar Nun was also closed, as was Big Mama's, Jaipur Johnny's, Thai Po, and even my last resort, The Leaning Tower of Pizzas. Many businesses and houses were already sand-bagged and, as I turned away, hoping for better luck elsewhere, I wondered where the fire brigade had got to.

I found them around Pound Street and Ditch Lane, where they were pumping out basements and cellars, trying to flush the waste down drains that were already overflowing, while all sorts of people struggled to build dams. The water was around my ankles, but I'd reached the stage where it seemed I had no option but to press on.

'Hello, dear! Are you feeling better?'

Mrs Goodfellow, clad in her yellow cycle cape and wellington boots, was among the workers. As she spoke, she tossed a sandbag to the next guy in the team, who I recognised as Kev the Rev, the church curate.

'Much better,' I said. 'I wondered where you were. Is Hobbes here?'

'He was, but he went to help with the evacuation on Spittoon Way and Dribbling Lane and around there. Church Lake is overflowing, the river's pouring out across the land, and some folk are in real difficulty. What are you doing out?'

'Actually, I was looking for somewhere to eat,' I said, ashamed. 'I hadn't realised things were so bad. Umm ... can I help?'

'I wouldn't worry, dear. We've nearly done as much as we can for now. I'm sorry I haven't had time to make supper, but, as you can see, it's all hands to the pumps.'

'In that case, I'll see if I can help Hobbes.'

'I'm sure he'll be delighted to see you up and about. Dregs is with him.'

I splashed towards Dribbling Lane, which, from what I could see, might, more accurately, have been renamed

Torrent Lane. By then the flood had reached my calves and, despite my heavy tweed trousers, I was shivering and my feet had lost all sensation. I was up to my knees when I reached a mass of miserable people huddled beneath the strange, open-sided pillared building that Hobbes reckoned had once been part of a medieval hospital. Hobbes himself waded into view, with a tubby middle-aged woman on his shoulders and a child beneath each arm. Dregs followed, looking embarrassed, probably because of the basket of kittens in his mouth and the bedraggled tabby cat riding his back. Despite his fierce appearance, he could be quite a softy. He took his passengers into the shelter and sat back and watched them.

'Good evening,' said Hobbes, grinning, water dripping off him. 'Are you here to help, or are you just sightseeing?'

'I was looking for food, but I'll do what I can.'

'Good man. I'll put Mrs Harrison and her children into the dry, and then you can help rescue the Vernons.'

He carried the woman and the children to safety, spoke with them for a few moments, his voice soft and reassuring, and came back to join me.

'How are you with boats?' he asked.

'Umm ... I've never had much to do with them since I was a kid. One overturned and I got stuck under it. Why?'

'We're going to need one to reach the Vernons at the end of Hairywart Close.'

'The big house in the hollow?' I asked, following as he loped towards Church Fields.

He nodded. 'But, the hollow is now a pond, and water is already lapping the bedroom windows.'

'Umm ... where are we going to get a boat?'

'Church Lake,' said Hobbes, maintaining a pace that meant I had to jog.

'Aren't they only there in summer?' I asked, breathing

hard.

'That's when they're for hire. The rest of the time they're stored on the island.'

'But, won't the island be under water?'

'Of course,' he said, turning towards the lake, 'but I expect the boats are floating.'

'How will we reach them?'

'I have an idea,' he said, 'though you might not like it.'

'What?' I shivered – not because of the icy water lapping my thighs, though that didn't help, but because I'd had previous experience of ideas that he thought I might not like.

'You can float out and retrieve them.'

'Me? On what?'

'On an emergency lifebuoy.' He turned to grin at me.

'But, the water's freezing, and I'm already half-frozen.'

'Then the exercise will warm you up.'

'Why can't you do it?'

'I'd give it a go if you weren't here, but I suspect the lifebuoy might not support me, and I don't float well.'

Though unconvinced, I kept following him down the slope, the icy water taking my breath away as it lapped my groin. His plan was clearly crazy, and anyone in his right mind would have just walked away, but for some reason I knew I was going to do it. When we reached the lifebuoy, a ring about an arm's length across, he pulled it from its mounting and held it out.

'There are two ways you could do this. You could either put it over your head and shoulders and swim, or you could sit in it and paddle. Take your pick.'

I had a flashback to when the Caplet family was enjoying, if that was the word, a week's holiday in Devon, and when Granny Caplet had given me a little spending money. I'd not known what to do with it, until I fell in love with a little inflatable canoe in the beach shop. Though Father said it was a silly toy for a seven-year old, it was a ship to me, and I planned to explore distant islands where I'd find exotic beasts, friendly natives, and, of course, pirate treasure. I remembered the pungent aroma of vinyl, the effort to inflate her, and the run to the sea to launch her. Granny's money had not quite stretched to a paddle as well, but I reckoned my hands would make a reasonable substitute. Not being a fool, I decided to make myself familiar with how she handled before attempting any oceanic crossing, and so I paddled parallel to the shore, a few feet out. Everything went really well for a minute or two, and my confidence grew until a big wave picked me up, carried me up the beach and tipped me out face first into the sand. The worst part had not been the pain, or hearing the big kids laughing, but seeing my vessel bubbling and hissing from a gash in one of the tubes. That was the end of my nautical adventures for, despite sticking a plaster over the rip, I could never afterwards get it to stay up.

'Are you still there?' asked Hobbes.

'I was just thinking,' I said, almost as excited as I'd been back then. 'I'll sit in it and paddle with my hands, like I used to. Umm ... I can't see the island.'

'I strongly suspect it's beneath where those trees are poking through,' he said. 'The boats are stored on the other side.'

'It looks quite a long way.' I peered into the night, shivering, and on the verge of changing my mind. 'I'll freeze my butt off.'

'Then you'd better move yourself, and quickly,' said Hobbes. 'Don't worry, butts may freeze, but they don't usually come off.'

Not having really expected sympathy, I decided to get it over with as soon as possible. 'Okay, but could you help me aboard?'

He scooped me up and plumped me down right in the

middle of the ring. For a horrible moment I thought I was going to drop right through or capsize, but a helping hand from him and some severe muscular exertion on my part allowed me to balance.

'Off you go,' he said, shoving me in the right direction. 'Be careful, and don't take any unnecessary risks.'

I nodded, gritted my teeth and set off like a hero, wobbling through the darkness, awkward and ungainly, but paddling with all my might, though my craft, particularly its keel, was not exactly streamlined. Progress was slow, my shoulders were soon aching, and my hands were numb, but the warmth from the effort meant hypothermia seemed a little less certain.

'You're doing well,' he said. 'You'll soon be there.'

I didn't waste breath on a reply but kept paddling until the trees were in reach. As he'd said, the boats floated just behind, but he'd not mentioned that they'd be upside down and tied together in a line. I tried to release the first one, but, unable to see much, finding the knots tight, the rope soggy and frayed, and my fingertips numb, soft and squidgy, I made no progress. I nearly gave up, but the heroic flame that had sparked up had not yet burned out, and I thought I might as well have a go at the next boat along. By a miracle, and with the assistance of some severe muttered swearing, a knot parted and I had my prize, or rather prizes, because I had no way of getting rid of the first boat. Yet, it was far too cold to dither, so I looped the rope around the lifebuoy and headed back, taking the long way round the trees, trying to avoid entanglement. Upside down boats are neither manoeuvrable nor streamlined, so progress was painfully slow, and my shoulders and stomach muscles were soon burning. I'm not sure I would have made it, but, as soon as I'd cleared the trees, I began gliding forwards, riding on a bow wave and leaving a wake. Hobbes was hauling me in with the lifeline.

'Well done,' he remarked as I came alongside.

'No problem,' I said and levered myself out, thinking the worst was over.

But it was yet to come.

As my feet touched bottom, there was a sudden eruption. Filthy, foaming water was everywhere and, I was dragged under, spinning around as if in a whirlpool. Blind panic and good luck brought me back up, gasping with the cold.

'What was that?' I cried, grabbing the lifebuoy, though I was already standing.

Hobbes didn't reply. In fact, there was no sign of him. Fearing he'd also been sucked under, I groped around in the black water for what seemed like an age, and was despairing until Dregs arrived at a gallop. He dived underwater, like a bear hunting salmon, but bobbed up again almost immediately. Then, he swam out a little, plunged and disappeared. I was just starting to believe I'd lost him as well when he broke surface like a hairy submarine with Hobbes's coat collar in his teeth. A moment later Hobbes himself appeared. He scrambled to his feet, coughed up half a pint of water, and patted Dregs on the head.

'That wasn't much fun,' he said, shaking himself like the dog. 'Are you all right, Andy? You look as if you've just seen a ghost.'

'Yeah ... umm ... it's just that I found something down there. It ... umm ... felt like ... I don't know.'

'Where?'

I pointed.

He came towards me and started groping around in the murky water. 'I can't feel anything.'

However, Dregs, who was enjoying the time of his life, dived again and surfaced almost immediately with what looked horribly like a human skull in his mouth.

'Not again,' I said.

7

'Give,' said Hobbes, and took the skull from the dog's mouth. He ran his hands over the dome, and sniffed. 'It's human, but there's no meat left on it.'

'Now what?' I asked, staring at him with horrified fascination.

'I'll put it back for now, since it's not a fresh one. The dead will have to wait until the living are safe. Would you still like to help me rescue the Vernons?'

To my surprise, I nodded, though what I really wanted was warmth and dryness and a total absence of skulls. Most of all, with my body running on empty, I wanted ample supplies of hot, delicious food. I feared I'd soon succumb to cold or famine, and that I'd fall in when I fainted through lack of sustenance. In my mind's eye I pictured fishes gnawing at me as I sank into the slime, leaving my bones to roll in the deep alongside the skull we'd found.

I said none of this to Hobbes who, having untied and righted the boats, had launched himself into the first one, with Dregs scrambling in after him.

'You'd better take the other one,' said Hobbes.

I hauled myself aboard and watched him lean forward, fiddle under his seat for a pair of oars and slide them into the rowlocks.

'Follow me,' he said. 'And quickly.'

He set off, with Dregs sitting in the bow like a figurehead. I groped for my oars, but couldn't find any. Instead, there was a single long pole, and it struck me that my boat was not the same as Hobbes's, in that it had a flat bottom, didn't have a pointy bit, and had a platform at one end. I stared, dumbfounded, for a moment before realising I'd got myself a punt, a vessel with which I'd had no experience. However,

Father had once dragged me along to a dentists' conference in the days when he was still trying to interest me in the dark arts, and I'd watched students mucking around in them on the river. That would be sufficient knowledge, or so I hoped.

I tottered towards the platform, and wobbled there a while, gripping the pole like a tightrope walker, certain disaster was approaching fast. Yet, I didn't fall in, and when I'd set one end of the pole firmly down in the mud, everything became much more stable and I felt almost secure. Of course, merely balancing successfully was no good to anyone. I had to follow Hobbes, shoving my boat along with the pole without losing it, or falling in, and although spectacular failure and ignominious splashdown seemed imminent, it wasn't quite as difficult as I'd imagined. When I pushed, the punt slid forward, and I soon discovered how to use the pole as a sort of rudder. I went after him, and, despite the occasional lurch, I didn't fall. The rain was still teeming down.

My progress, though slow, was steady, and I made it to the Vernons' house, where Hobbes was already helping the family to escape through a bedroom window. Between us, we took all eight of them aboard, and headed back. Soaked to the skin, I shivered all the way, but, despite feeling light-headed with hunger, nothing went wrong.

I was glad to reach land, where Mrs Goodfellow and other kind people helped us into the shelter of the old hospital building. Kev the Rev had magically organised hot drinks and blankets, and the mug of hot, sweet coffee was just what the doctor would have ordered. I held it in both hands, making the most of its warmth as I sipped, and after a while my teeth stopped chattering, and I was able to devour some biscuits. Still, I'd had enough of being heroic and just wanted to be warm, and to have proper food set before me. Fortunately, I didn't have long to wait before

Hobbes decided we'd done all we could and led us home.

'I'm sorry, lads,' said Mrs Goodfellow on the way, 'but I haven't had time to cook.'

'You've been very busy,' said Hobbes. 'Perhaps we can get a takeaway?'

'I'm not sure anywhere will be open,' I said, my voice slurred as if I'd had a few too many lagers.

'There's no need for takeaways,' said the old girl with a sniff. 'I can throw a stir-fry together using Sunday's leftover pork, and it shouldn't take more than a few minutes. How would that suit you?'

'Just fine,' said Hobbes, and I grinned like a condemned man whose reprieve had just come through.

The pavement along Blackdog Street was mostly submerged and a number of houses had sandbag dams that were holding back the waters. Others, ours included, had water pouring through the grates into their cellars.

'There's nothing we can do for now,' said Hobbes with a shrug. 'Let's get inside. And quickly.'

It was wonderful to be out of the weather, and even better to immerse myself in a hot bath, though, with supper already cooking, I wallowed for no more than ten minutes before emerging, glowing with the warmth. I dried off, wrapped myself in a heavy old dressing gown and hurried downstairs, led by the enticing aroma of stir-fried pork with onions and ginger.

Unfortunately, supper wasn't quite ready, so, after Mrs Goodfellow had re-bandaged my head, I perched on the sofa and drank more hot sweet coffee, trying to be a model of polite restraint and patience until Hobbes, having showered and changed, joined me.

It looked like being a grand end to a trying day, until the phone rang.

Hobbes picked up the receiver.

'Inspector Hobbes,' he said. 'How may I help you?'

He listened for several minutes, saying nothing except for 'Yes, Ma'am,' just before he replaced the receiver.

'That was Superintendent Cooper,' he said, looking grave. 'The dam at Fenderton Mill is about to collapse and it's serious. I'm going over there now.'

'You won't be able to drive in these floods,' I pointed out.

'No, so we'll have to pick up the boats again.'

'We?'

'If you're up for it.'

Like an idiot, I nodded. 'Let me finish my coffee and get dressed.'

'Quickly,' said Hobbes. 'When the public's in peril, there's no time to lose.'

Any sensible person would have backed down, mentioning that he was exhausted, recovering from concussion and hypothermia, and that he'd already been quite heroic enough for one day, but my crazy mouth, having gulped down the coffee, overrode any sense left in me and said something stupid I'd once heard in a film. 'Let's get ready to rock and roll!'

He seemed to get my meaning and I ran to my room where there was scuffling under the bed and a strong smell of wet dog. However, Dregs, evidently suspecting a dastardly plot to get him in the bath, stayed where he was while I dug out warm clothing and waterproofs, preparing myself for action. I could still have backed out, my excuses being reasonable enough, but I'd been missing excitement since my marriage, and a part of me wanted to be involved. Besides, if people were at risk, I should help, and do something to make Daphne proud of me. Of course, I really should have been trying to establish communications with her, but I had to admit that a small part of my brain thought that a little worry might do her good, and might teach her not to be so dismissive of my concerns. I tried to pretend I wasn't being childish, but didn't quite convince myself.

I jogged downstairs. 'I'm ready to go as soon as I've put my wellies on.'

Hobbes was already in his coat, his only concession to bad weather. I sometimes wondered if he only wore it so Mrs Goodfellow wouldn't nag him about catching a chill, though he did find the pockets useful for holding his notebook and pencil. I pushed my feet into my boots and was ready to go.

As soon as Hobbes opened the front door, Dregs bounded downstairs to join us. Then he saw the weather, put the brakes on and scarpered back upstairs. I didn't blame him. I just hoped he'd stay under my bed and not get in it, or bury a bone under the pillow as he'd once done.

We stepped out into the street and away on our mission of mercy, with Hobbes striding at a pace I struggled to match, especially as we were splashing through calf-deep water. A vicious cold wind fired heavy volleys of rain that stung my face, and by the time we reached Dribbling Lane I was already breathing hard. I'd half hoped the boats had gone and that I'd have another excuse to chicken out, but they were still sheltered beneath the roof of the old building. The people, though, had gone. I hoped they were somewhere safe, warm and dry and that they'd had something to eat.

'Do you want the punt again?' asked Hobbes, 'or would you prefer to change?'

'Umm ... do you think we'll need both of them?'

'We might.'

'I ... umm ... suppose I'll take the punt.'

We launched our vessels, climbed aboard and set off towards Fenderton, Hobbes rowing at a frantic pace and, though I really put my back into it, the heavy old punt was, at best, a sedate craft and I soon fell behind. Still, I couldn't help notice that his technique was open to improvement, since much of his effort went into lifting the boat, almost pulling it clear of the water before it crashed down with a massive splash. If he'd only managed to get all that power into forward motion I'd have lost sight of him in seconds.

It was strange to be floating between houses, and the feeling grew as I reached the inland sea where there'd been Fenderton Road and fields on the previous day. The street lights were still working, casting orange reflections and shadows on the dark waters, making me imagine I was on the coast, though fortunately there were no real waves. I just kept punting, maintaining my balance, letting my mind wander, and keeping warm with all the exercise.

'Wotcha, Andy!' said a high-pitched voice, seeming to come from about water level. 'Mind the current ahead.'

I came within a flea's whisker of overbalancing. It was Billy Shawcroft, the dwarf, a good friend of Hobbes's and mine, who was in a kayak.

'Hi,' I said, as he drew alongside. 'What current?'

'The river's still there, you know, though you can't really see where it starts. It's running fast, but if you give yourself a mighty shove now, you'll make it across. Careful, though, because it'll hit you hard, and you'll need to keep your balance.'

I did as he said, feeling the sudden punch of the river thrusting me sideways. Had he not turned up, I reckon I'd have gone in, but he had and I didn't. Not quite.

'Where are you off to?' he asked when I'd reached still water.

'To Fenderton. The dam is collapsing and I'm going to help.'

'I'll come, too. I've just been helping out at the butchers down The Shambles. Most of their meat has washed away in the flood – it was a bit choppy down there. Is that Hobbesie splashing ahead?'

'Yes. He left me with the punt. I didn't know you were a kayaker.'

Billy smiled. 'I love to get out on water, and I built this myself, because the ones in the shops are all for big people like you.'

Although I'd never considered myself big, being only of average height, I could see his point of view. Little in modern life was designed for small people, yet he was a cheerful guy and adept at overcoming the many difficulties that were thrown at him. He gave the impression that he could do anything, and was certainly a man of no small ability. I'd soon come to understand why Hobbes always treated him with the utmost respect.

'I'll go on ahead and catch up with him,' he said, 'in case anyone is in immediate danger. See you.'

He set off, powering through the flood like a shark, leaving me floundering in his wake. It only took him a few minutes to pull alongside Hobbes, and he must have passed on some words of advice, because Hobbes was soon rowing like an Olympian. Within a minute or two they'd both passed out of sight into the gloom. I kept going, despite a blister growing on my right hand, and it must have taken me half an hour to reach the outskirts of Fenderton which was almost unrecognisable. A few minutes more and I caught up with Hobbes, who was hauling a bedraggled man aboard his boat to join four other people hunched miserably in the middle.

With a powerful thrust on my pole, I went alongside. Had Hobbes not put his arm out and stopped me, I would have smacked into a wall.

'What can I do?' I asked.

'The dam's gone, so use your eyes and ears, and if someone's in trouble, pull them out. Keep your centre of gravity low so you don't overturn.'

'Then what?'

He pointed up the slope. 'They'll be safe there. It's where I'm taking these good people.'

After he'd rowed away, I heard a cry for help and spotted a man waist deep in a torrent roaring down the hill. On his shoulders was a small child in a red raincoat.

'I'm coming!' I yelled, turning the punt towards him.

As he nodded, he lost his footing and went under. I pushed along, taking care to avoid the worst of the flow, while moving as fast as I dared. The man bobbed up, spluttering and gasping, and looking around helplessly for the child. A sick, helpless feeling welled up in my stomach and only a massive exertion of will stopped me panicking, for I knew that if I thought about it too long, I'd confuse myself and dither. The kid needed rescuing quickly if it was to have any chance, and that meant keeping in control of myself and the punt, and acting immediately. So, without any kind of plan, I pushed off, crouching on my platform and peering into the turbulent, shadowy waters, hoping for a glimpse of red. The flow swept me towards what were normally water meadows, and the glimmer from the Fenderton street lights began to fade with every second.

Within too short a time I was in near darkness and beginning to despair. Then there was a splash to my left and, maybe, a hint of red. I flung myself to the side, nearly overturning, and plunged a hand into the water. To my amazement I felt something, grabbed it and held on. It was the kid's coat, and the kid was still in it. When I hauled him aboard, for he turned out to be a boy of about three or four years old, he took one look at me and began to scream. Taking my coat off, I covered him, and strained my eyes searching for the man, his father I supposed, though I could barely see anything other than streetlights receding into the distance.

I shouted without response, except for an increased volume from the kid up front, whose screaming was already getting on my nerves and not helping in any way. No doubt he'd had a shocking and unpleasant experience, and I was trying to be sympathetic, but it was no way to carry on in an emergency.

'Stiff upper lip, old chap!' I said, with no effect whatsoever.

The punt had begun bucking, rolling, shaking and picking up speed towards the bright lights of town and I guessed we'd drifted into the Fenderton Brook, its normal sluggish flow now a churning nightmare. With a lurch of horror and panic, I realised I had to get us out before it joined the river, but when I reached for the pole, it had gone. Dimly, I remembered a splash when I was rescuing the noisy, ungrateful brat up front, who didn't seem to care that we were helplessly adrift. I quickly discovered that swearing didn't help, but the worst thing, something that nearly sent me into a panic, was that I had a horrible feeling that the brook joined the river just before the road bridge near the end of Dribbling Lane. With the height and ferocity of the waters, I really couldn't imagine us getting through there in one piece. In desperation, I knelt and paddled, my hands pulling frantically, but I might just as well have tried to propel a battleship with a button.

I could now make out the course of the river, streaked with white foam where it was smashing into the bridge, and I guessed the arch below was completely submerged. We were cannoning towards it far too quickly, and there was nothing I could do to prevent a smash. I was going to be broken, or drowned, or both, and so was the boy.

'Help!' I yelled, my voice loud, though cracking with fear.

There was nothing else I could do, though I didn't really expect anything. However, a woman appeared on the bridge.

'Are you all right?' she asked.

Even in the midst of terror, I thought it a stupid question. Did I look as if I was all right? However, it was not the time for sarcasm.

‘No,’ I shouted above the river’s roar, ‘and I have a child with me.’

‘Then you should be ashamed of yourself.’

I bit down on a waspish response, lurched to the front end and picked up the kid, which at least stopped him screaming, though it started him kicking me in the stomach.

The bridge was horribly close.

‘I’ll throw him up.’

‘You can’t. I’ll drop him.’

‘No, you won’t.’

‘What’s his name?’

‘Don’t know.’

‘Then what are you doing with him?’ Her voice was sharp with suspicion.

There was no time left.

‘Ready?’ I screamed.

8

The woman, looking shocked, nodded, the punt bounced and rolled, and I lifted the kid above my head. Despite receiving a kick in the teeth for my efforts, I launched him and felt the woman take his weight just as the punt smashed into the bridge and disintegrated. For an instant, I glimpsed her white face and blue hair as she dragged the boy to safety, and then the river had me. The shock of the cold water was dreadful, as was the immense violence of the current. Everything went dark and I knew I was under the bridge, desperate to breathe, though all around was water, cold and blackness. Hard things struck from all sides and I was tossed around like a leaf in a gale, sure I was going to die. Just to add to the fun, the bandage around my head started to unravel and wrap itself around my throat, threatening to strangle me. It was, at least, an alternative to drowning.

Incredibly, my face came up into air, and I was gasping and sobbing, knowing I'd made it through in one piece. I was shooting feet-first towards where the bank would normally have been and when a tree root came into view, I grabbed it, held it, and rejoiced in its strength and solidity, using it to haul my battered body into relatively placid, thigh-deep water and safety. The woman was standing on the bridge clutching the wriggling boy to her chest, and shouting at me, though I couldn't catch any words. I was just pulling myself clear, and thinking of heading back to Blackdog Street for a well-deserved meal in the warmth, when I glimpsed something shooting from under the bridge.

It was a man, face down and limp. The river thrust him across to the far bank, where there were no roots, just a rough stone wall against which the waters crashed and foamed. I called out, but he didn't even twitch. I looked for help, but there was none, and, I knew I was his only hope, assuming he was still alive. Having no option, though unsure whether I'd survive another immersion, I plunged back in.

The current struck. It ducked and pummelled me, and I couldn't reach him, until I had a brainwave. I lassoed him with a loop of my bandage, pulled us together and turned him face up. After that, I was effectively stuck, with one hand keeping his head above water and the other grasping the wall. There was no chance of dragging us back across the churning Soren to relative safety, and I knew if I tried that we'd both be swept away, like the shattered debris of my punt. From what I could see downstream, where there were other bridges, our chances of surviving would be negligible, but if I stayed put, I doubted I'd be able to cling on for long. I was shivering so much the whole world seemed to be shaking as the cold leached the last strength from my body. Within minutes it was all I could do to keep both our faces above water. Then the man coughed and groaned, and the knowledge that he was alive kept me hanging on for a little longer. Still, the end seemed very close.

'Chin up, Andy.'

It was Hobbes, and I clung on with renewed hope, the last of my energy and determination kicking in. He was rowing towards us and, though he now looked like he knew what he was doing, I still wished he'd do it faster.

As he drew near, he jumped in, the water reaching his waist. He waded towards us.

'Careful,' I cried, my voice taking on a weird vibration as my teeth chattered, 'it gets deep.'

As he reached the river, his boat was swept away and he went down, the dark waters closing over his head. I feared he was lost, and was on the verge of despair when his hands grabbed my waist, lifting both me and the casualty from the water, and carrying us back across the current. With a powerful surge, he reached the shallows, and his head burst into the night. I felt the blast of air as he exhaled. He stood still for a moment, sucking down a great lungful of air, his face eerily pale in the sodium light, still holding us in his great arms.

'Thank you,' I said indistinctly over the chattering of my teeth.

He pitched face forward into the water, spilling us. Keeping tight hold of the man, I groped hopelessly for Hobbes, who'd sunk without trace and would surely have been a goner if Billy hadn't turned up, handling his kayak as if it were part of him. Powering towards the spot where Hobbes had sunk, leaning so far over it was incredible he didn't capsize, he plunged his stubby arms deep into the water. Then, somehow, he was dragging Hobbes's head and shoulders across the deck, and, although his kayak listed like a torpedoed ship and he was only able to paddle on one side, he dragged him up to the bridge. Though exhausted and chilled to my soul, I followed, hauling the semi-conscious man with me, until I could put him down. Remembering enough of my first aid course to check he was breathing, I rolled him into the recovery position, reassured by his moans.

I helped Billy pull Hobbes clear of the water, but when we laid him down on his back he wasn't breathing. Fearing the worst, I dropped to my knees, but Billy dived head first into his abdomen. Hobbes coughed, a plume of water shot from his mouth like a fountain, and he spat and sat upright, looking dazed. Billy rolled off, and got to his feet a little unsteadily, rubbing his head, and I was nearly in tears.

'That,' said Hobbes, following a long cough, 'was not as much fun as it might have been. I really began to think I wasn't going to make it. That current is strong. How is the casualty?'

'Moaning and throwing up,' said Billy.

'Good,' said Hobbes, still breathing heavily, but pushing himself onto his feet. 'I'll take a look.'

He knelt at the man's side, checking him over. 'It's Nathan Pegler. He should be fine, but I suppose I should get him to hospital.' He glanced at me. 'I saw what you did. It was brave. You saved his life, as well as the boy's. Well done.'

Since praise from Hobbes was almost as rare as dogs on unicycles, I was taken aback. Then, realising what I'd actually done, I basked in a warm glow of satisfaction; it was the only warm thing around.

'Inspector, I demand that you arrest that man!'

The woman who'd caught the boy walked towards us holding him by the hand. Her voice, shrill and grating, was aimed at Hobbes.

'Which man, madam?' asked Hobbes.

'That one,' she said, pointing at me.

I recognised her severe face and the blue hair poking from under her headscarf, as well as the glare she was aiming through horn-rimmed glasses. Unfortunately, we'd met several times before and her opinion of me was, to say the least, unfavourable.

'He's a bad lot,' she insisted, 'and I should know. I've caught him thieving.'

I cringed, because I couldn't deny it. She had once caught me in the act of pilfering a pamphlet from the church, and although I'd had a particularly good excuse, needing the information in it to save Hobbes from a terrible fate, she'd never forgiven me. Her distrust and dislike had multiplied after I accidently hit her in the face with a dead rat. Ever since, whenever we met, she'd keep her gorgon glare on me until I'd slunk away, and, since she frequented the church in the centre of town, I'd done a great deal of slinking and slipping away down backstreets and alleys to avoid crossing her path. At least she wasn't carrying her umbrella, which she'd once used to beat me, and I realised she didn't need it. The rain had stopped at last.

'Mrs Nutter,' said Hobbes, his voice hoarse but patient, 'that was all in the past and has been explained. What's he done this time?'

'He's been gallivanting on the river in a stolen punt – and I know it's stolen because it belongs to Mr Nelson, my neighbour, who runs them – and he's been putting this little lad at risk. If you want my opinion, I don't even believe the child is his, so you should arrest him for kidnapping as well.' She glared at me. 'Is he your son?'

'Umm ... no ... but ...'

'He admits it, Inspector. When are you going to arrest him?'

'Mrs Nutter,' said Hobbes, 'I have no intention of arresting him.'

'Then, I shall inform your superiors.'

'Madam, I have no superiors, just some people who get paid more.'

I was a little surprised at his bold statement, but, knowing Hobbes, it was probably just a statement of fact. It did, however, shut her up for the moment.

'Andy was rescuing Pegler junior from the flood,' he continued. 'I saw what he did, and I must also commend you, Mrs Nutter, on a most fine catch in difficult circumstances.'

'Oh. Thank you, Inspector,' she said, mollified. 'I couldn't let the poor boy down.'

'Of course not. Now, I need to attend to Pegler senior. Would you be so good as to look after the boy for a minute?'

'Of course,' she said, all smiles.

Hobbes glanced at Billy, who was ensuring Mr Pegler was comfortable, or at least as comfortable as he was likely to be after being immersed in icy water and lying on a bridge. 'Would you mind heading back to Fenderton and inform Mrs Pegler that her husband and son are safe, and that there is nothing to worry about, but that I'm taking them to the hospital as a precaution?'

Billy nodded, returned to his kayak and paddled away. Though he was one of the most capable people I'd ever met, his diminutive stature often led people to treat him like a child. It had taken me a while to realise, and he still sometimes surprised me. He was a good man in a crisis, as Hobbes often remarked, though, of course, not without faults; sometimes he drank too much, and he had a reputation as a card sharp, although no one, not even Hobbes, had ever caught him out.

'How are we going to get them to the hospital?' I asked.

'I'll carry them, but I'd suggest that you head straight home and take a hot bath. This water may be contaminated and there have been warnings of rising pee levels and worse. You'd better take my key in case the lass is out again.'

He handed it to me and I splashed homewards, shivering and close to exhaustion, but, for once, pleased with myself. He passed me at a gallop on Spittoon Way, with Mr Pegler in his arms and the boy perched on his shoulders, urging him on as if he were a pony.

At last I reached Blackdog Street, where I was surprised to see a number of people messing about on air beds and inner tubes, making the most of the flood, even though others were still pumping out basements or building barriers. There was no sign of Mrs Goodfellow outside, which I hoped suggested she was home and that food would be available. My hunger pangs had not gone away, and the thought of eating intensified the emptiness.

I walked inside to be a greeted by a massive smelly dog hug, while a whiff of cooking made the world feel right, though I was a little surprised to already be thinking of there as home again. It reminded me that I should get in touch with Daphne, and that I ought to find out what was happening with the flat. However, I put such thoughts to the back of my mind and, fighting off Dregs, hurried into the kitchen.

'Hello, dear,' said Mrs Goodfellow with a cheerful smile. 'You look wet and cold. Have a quick bath, and by the time you get down your supper will be ready.'

'Thanks,' I said. 'It smells fantastic.'

'How's your head? Do you want it bandaging again?'

'No, it'll be fine.' I hurried to the bathroom.

By the time I was clean, dressed in my pyjamas, and ready to eat, Hobbes was already at the kitchen table, wrapped in his dressing gown, kitten slippers on his feet, a massive mug of steaming tea in his fist.

'You took your time,' he said. 'Let's eat.'

He rattled off the most rapid grace ever, and we unleashed ourselves on stir-fried pork in a most delicious tangy sauce and served with a mountain of fragrant rice. The hot, spicy food almost made up for all the privations and suffering of the day.

'That was fantastic,' I said when my belly was as tight as was decent. 'What was it called?'

'Stir-fried pork and stuff,' said Mrs Goodfellow. 'I just threw in what was available, and I'm glad you liked it.'

'Praise from a food critic,' said Hobbes with a smile, 'is praise indeed.'

The old girl blushed and grinned her toothless grin. 'I'll clear up and make you boys another pot of tea.'

However, I was too full to even contemplate adding more to my stomach. Warm, and relaxed, I began to feel very sleepy.

'How are the Peglers?' I asked, forcing my eyes to stay

open.

'Very well. There was nothing much wrong with the boy, and he was happy to be reunited with his mother. Mr Pegler had a touch of hypothermia and a minor head injury, but was fully conscious and feeling much better when I left.'

'Good.' I said and, giving up the struggle, took myself straight up to bed. Although I had an idea I should be doing something, it didn't keep me awake for long.

9

Although my sleep was long, it was not especially peaceful. I kept dreaming of Daphne, certain I had something important to tell her, but she was too far away and, although I tried to reach her, something always blocked my way, and by the time I'd dealt with it she was even more distant, becoming at last a tiny dot on the horizon. My final desperate attempt to catch her was thwarted by Sally, who was pounding a drum and forcing me to dance to her beat.

When I began to surface, rising from dreams into the grey light of a new day, the drumming continued, but it was only when I heard Mrs Goodfellow open the front door that I worked out someone had been knocking. I sat up in bed, yawning, stretching and listening.

'Hello, dear,' said the old girl. 'What brings you here so urgently?'

'Have you heard anything from Andy?' asked a woman.

It was Daphne's friend, Pinky.

'Yes, dear. He's upstairs in bed.'

'So, he's here. I've just had a frantic phone call from Daphne, wondering why she couldn't get in touch, and when I went round to their flat it had been destroyed. I thought he might have been killed. Is he all right?'

'He's fine.'

'Well, that's good, I suppose, but why didn't he call her?'

'He was rather busy.'

'Too busy to send an email, or Skype her, or use a telephone? I don't believe it.'

By then, I was out of bed, in a clean shirt and underpants, and pulling on a pair of trousers, buttoning them up as I galloped downstairs. A little more caution would have been advisable, since my bare feet skidded on the steps and I bounced to the bottom on my bottom.

'Hi,' I said, getting up with a light laugh, as if my pratfall had been just a jolly little jape, though it had actually hurt quite a lot, and I could feel I'd have a bruise or two to add to my collection.

'Andy, what were you thinking of? Daphne's distraught, and I've been worried, too.' Though Pinky frowned, her big blue eyes expressed concern.

'Sorry.'

'Is that all you can say?'

'Come in, dear,' said Mrs Goodfellow.

Pinky came in and sat with me on the sofa.

'Would you like a cup of tea? Or a coffee?' asked Mrs Goodfellow.

'No, thank you,' said Pinky. 'I can't stay long. I've got to open the café.'

'I'd like a cup of tea, please,' I said.

Mrs Goodfellow hurried away and I smiled at Pinky, who was dressed in her trademark pink trouser suit, with a low cut pink blouse. She'd lost a little weight I thought, and looked beautiful, and I had to force myself not to stare, though she'd always been too pretty to ignore.

'How are you?' I asked.

'Never better, but Daffy's worried sick. She reached camp yesterday and has been trying to contact you ever since. She saw about the floods online. You should have let her know you were well.'

'But, I lost the computer and the phone and my mobile when the flat was hit.'

'There are other computers and telephones,' said Pinky, frowning. 'You could have come to us. Sid wouldn't mind you using his laptop, or you could've tried that new internet place you wrote about.'

'Gollum's Logons? I suppose I could've, but I was in hospital with a head injury.' I pointed to the lump, although it was no longer evident, 'and then I was rescuing people from the flood.'

'You must still have had a few minutes!'

Overwhelmed by a sudden shame, I hung my head, knowing I could have made time had I really tried, and that a peevish, childish part of me was sulking, wishing to hurt her because she'd gone away. Also, I had an idea that I was already struggling without her, which did nothing to raise my self-esteem.

'I'm sorry,' I muttered again.

'It's no use apologising to me. Call her now.'

'Umm ... but I don't know her number. You see it was in my mobile, and I hadn't written it down, and I can't remember her email.'

I knew I must be coming across as pathetic and incompetent, and that was without admitting that I'd also forgotten my own logon. After all, once Daphne had set me up, I hadn't needed to remember.

'I'll write the camp's number and her email down for you,' said Pinky in a voice she might have used to an imbecile.

She took a notebook and pen from her pink handbag, scribbled on it, tore off the leaf and handed it to me. The paper, too, was a delicate shade of pink, and the only thing that surprised me was the black ink. I thanked her.

'I've got to open the café,' she said, getting up.

'How is it?'

'Fine. Sid put down sandbags, and nothing got past.'

'How are the floods?'

'Not quite as bad today, though everywhere near the river is still awash. I must go.'

Mrs Goodfellow, who'd just reappeared and placed a mug of tea before me, opened the front door.

'Call her,' said Pinky as she left.

'What should I do?' I asked Mrs Goodfellow after she'd

shut the door.

'Call her. Use our phone.'

'But won't it be the middle of the night there?'

'No, dear, it'll be approaching midday. Egyptian time is only two hours ahead.'

'Can I have some breakfast first?'

'No.'

I grabbed the phone, dialled and waited, hoping she'd be in.

'Hi,' I said when I heard it picked up. 'I'm really sorry I haven't called, but the flat's been knocked down by a tree, and I was in hospital with a head injury, and then I was rescuing people from the flood, but I'm all right now. How are you? I love you.'

'Thank you, sir, I am well, but who is speaking?' asked a man with a strong Egyptian accent.

'Oh ... sorry. My name is ... umm ... Andy.'

'Ummandi? I do not know you, sir. Why you say you love me?'

'It was a mistake. I don't really.'

'Why not? What have I done?'

'Nothing. I thought you were my wife.'

'I not your wife! I married already.'

'I know ...'

'How you know I married?'

'I didn't ...'

'Then you lie!' He was sounding really pissed off.

'No ... umm ... me make big mistake ... me think you my wife,' I said getting flustered, and knowing I needed to remain calm, and to explain myself clearly. However, panic getting the better of me, I slammed the phone down.

'She wasn't in,' I said.

Mrs Goodfellow gave me her stern look. 'Try again, dear,' she said, crossing her spindly arms across her sparrow chest and tapping her foot.

I did as I was told. Had I not, she might have refused to feed me.

This time when someone picked up, I waited for a response.

'Hello?' said Daphne.

'It's me.'

'Oh, thank god! Where've you been? I've been trying to call you since last night, and you haven't answered my emails.'

'I've had a few ... umm ... problems.' I told her of my misfortunes, leaving out any mention of Sally. Other than my heroic rescue of Mr Pegler and son, it was a sorry tale.

'I see,' said Daphne. 'So you're back at Inspector Hobbes's. Well, at least that should keep you out of mischief for a while. But what's going to happen with the flat? Have you called the insurance company?'

'Not yet,' I admitted. 'As I said, I've been rather busy.'

'Well you'd better, as soon as possible.'

'Umm ... okay ... who are we insured with?'

'All the details are on the computer ... That's not much help is it?'

'Not much. Even if I can find it, I suspect it's smashed or flooded.'

'Never mind. The insurer is The Pigton Insurance Company. Mr Sharples helped me arrange it, so he may be able to help.'

'Oh, good. I'll go round and see him some time.'

I rather liked Sid Sharples, the manager of Grossman's Bank, and an old friend of Hobbes. We'd got to know him quite well since Pinky had moved in with him shortly after she'd turned up in Sorenchester. The fact that he was a known vampire did not appear to bother either of them, and I tried not to let it bother me, though I could never quite relax in his company without the assistance of alcohol.

'Yes,' said Daphne, 'and you'll have to find some place for

us to live. You can't keep imposing on the inspector and Mrs Goodfellow.'

'I know, but it's not a good time at the moment. Half the town is under water and loads of people will be looking for some place to stay while their homes dry out.'

'Fair enough, but don't leave it too long.'

'I won't. How are you?'

'I'm great. This dig looks like it's going to be fascinating. Mahmoud's been showing me around and I'll start work properly tomorrow.'

'Who is Mahmoud?'

'Professor Mahmoud El-Gammal. I told you about him. He's the leader of the excavation and was the one who found the tomb of Rameses the Idiot ten years ago. Don't you remember?'

'Yes, of course,' I said, as if I had the first clue who Rameses the Idiot was, though I vaguely remembered hearing the name. I suspected he was an ancient Egyptian. 'Is it hot out there?'

'Like you wouldn't believe, and it's still winter. Mind you, I could believe it last night – it was literally freezing. You should have seen the stars though. They were brilliant, and so many of them.'

'Great. How's the food?'

'Not too bad. It's mostly been beans and flat bread so far, which is tasty enough and quite filling. I expect you've had better, though. Could you send Mrs Goodfellow out here?'

I laughed.

'Anyway,' she said, 'I've got to go. Mahmoud's in a bad mood. He received a crank phone call a few minutes ago.'

'Oh ... umm ... so they get that sort of thing in Egypt, too. Who'd have thought it? Right in the middle of the desert. How strange!'

'So, it was you, Ummandi,' she said with a chuckle. 'I won't tell him. Goodbye. I'm glad you're all right. Love you.'

That was it. The phone went dead and I was left with so much I wanted to say, specifically that I loved her and missed her, and though it was a cliché, it was true. I really was much better with her than without her, despite the good food at Hobbes's, and, of course, the excitement.

'Is everything all right?' asked Mrs Goodfellow.

I nodded, too emotional to risk speaking.

'I'll get you some breakfast. Would a full English suit you?'

I nodded again and replaced the receiver as she returned to the kitchen. A couple of minutes later, the mouth-watering aroma of bacon infiltrated the sitting room and I felt ready to start the day. Indeed, I was almost back to my normal self when she called. I went through and, having demolished the contents of the enormous plate she set before me, still found room for a couple of slices of toast and marmalade.

'Thank you,' I said as I finished the last crumb. 'Where are Hobbes and Dregs?'

'They left early. The old fellow said they had something to attend to from yesterday.'

So much had happened since then that, incredibly, I'd forgotten the horror of what I'd found. I told her about it.

'I wonder if it might have anything to do with the old abbey,' she suggested. 'You know, the medieval one that got knocked down.'

'I don't know much about that. Was it one of those that Henry the Eighth got rid of?'

'Yes, dear.'

'So, that might mean the skull came from a medieval monk,' I said, relieved, since ancient remains held little of the horror of recent ones.

'I don't know, dear. I expect we'll find out soon enough.'

'I expect so, but I think I'll take a stroll down there and see what's happening.'

It was a bright cold morning and the church clock was striking ten. The pavements were no longer awash, though the road still looked like a canal, and the streets sounded eerily quiet, despite plenty of townsfolk going about their business. It was a while before I realised this was down to the lack of traffic noise. I turned towards The Shambles, which was comparatively dry, and headed down the narrow alley at the back of the church, passed through the old graveyard, and into Church Fields. The lake looked at least three times bigger than normal.

The long lanky form of Constable Poll and a petite figure in white were talking together outside a tent on a grassy knoll above the water level, while Hobbes, fully dressed, was up to his waist in the lake. Dregs was doggy paddling by his side. They exchanged glances and ducked beneath the surface. When they popped up, Dregs began barking excitedly.

'There are more,' said Hobbes, and dived again.

He came up holding a pair of long bones and handed them to the woman in white before plunging back into the flood.

Constable Poll, who'd always struck me as far too friendly and easy-going to really be a police officer, nodded as I approached.

'What's up, Derek?' I asked.

'The inspector's found some sort of collapsed vault and has been fishing bones out all morning. We've already got remains from at least sixteen individuals, according to Doctor Ramage. By the way, have you met Doctor Cynthia Ramage, our new forensic pathologist?'

'Pleased to meet you. I'm ... umm ... Andy.'

She turned to face me and smiled. She had short dark hair and big brown eyes, and would have been rather attractive, had she not been mummified in those baggy white overalls.

'Are the bones from the monks at the old abbey?' I asked, hoping to appear intelligent.

'Probably not,' she said, 'since some appear to be from women and children.'

'So, what are they doing here?'

'I don't know yet, but I have a suspicion that there might have been an ossuary, or bone house, on the site. Or it's just possible we've stumbled upon a medieval plague pit.'

'So the bones are old?'

'They appear so.'

'I ... umm ... suppose it's hardly likely they are the results of a modern massacre.'

'I think we might have been aware of one of those,' said Constable Poll.

'Derek is right,' she said. 'The ones so far have the appearance and fragility of old bones, though I'll have to test them back in the lab to be quite certain.'

'So why is Hobbes bothering with them?'

'Because we can't just leave them out in the open,' said Poll. 'It's best to collect them before the floods go down and the public and dogs and wild animals can get at them, especially if it was a plague pit. Can you imagine what might happen if there was still infection?'

'I thought the plague came from rat fleas,' I said.

'The spread of the Black Death can be blamed on rodent fleas,' said Cynthia, 'but there was more than one type of plague, and people of those times were prone to all sorts of nasty illnesses. I'll learn more when I've got them back to the lab, but I'm ninety-nine percent convinced they'll prove of more interest to the archaeologists than to the police. Still, it makes a change.'

'There's a whole one in the drain,' said Hobbes.

'What do you mean?' I asked.

'A complete human body. I'll bring it out.'

He plunged again, emerged and began walking

backwards towards us, his arms around the torso of what had once been a man. The corpse was dressed in a grey suit and white shirt with a red and white striped tie.

'He can't have been dead for all that long,' said Cynthia as Hobbes laid him gently on his back at the waterside.

Though pale and bloated, the body was intact and the features were quite recognisably those of a middle-aged man, a little chubby, of less than average height, with short greying ginger hair and a wide bald spot on the crown.

'He was a monk,' I said, fighting a wave of nausea. 'I thought there weren't any round here anymore.'

Hobbes, dripping wet, examining the body, looked up, puzzled. 'What makes you say that?'

'His hair's cut like a monk.'

'It looks more like male-pattern baldness,' said Cynthia, squatting at his side. 'Besides, he's wearing a modern suit.'

'Sorry,' I said. 'I was getting carried away by history. What do you think killed him? Did he drown?'

'It would appear that he died before the flood,' said Cynthia.

'This may have had something to do with his demise,' said Hobbes, turning the head to reveal a horrible swollen gash around the temple. 'It's not a pretty sight.'

Constable Poll's loud vomiting started me off. Otherwise, I might have been all right, although my legs felt as if the bones had been replaced by wet spaghetti, and my head was swimming like a tadpole.

'Yes, indeed,' said Cynthia. 'Exposing the brain like that would cause instant unconsciousness, and, without urgent treatment, death would follow very quickly.'

'What caused the wound?' asked Hobbes. 'An axe?'

'It was certainly caused by a blade, but it would appear a little too narrow for an axe. A machete, maybe?'

'I see what you mean. Let's see if he has any identification.' Hobbes folded back the man's jacket, reached inside and pulled out a soggy leather wallet.

'What's in it?' I asked as curiosity overrode the nausea.

'A wad of bank notes and credit cards,' he said, unloading the contents. 'The credit cards are all current and in the name of Mr Septimus Donald Slugg. Aha! There's also a driving licence. It appears Mr Slugg lived at 10 Umbrage Crescent, Tode-in-the-Wold.'

'That'll be useful,' I said.

'It might well be,' said Hobbes. 'For the present, I'll work on the assumption that the information is correct and that this photograph is of the deceased. The features, as far as I can tell, match. Doesn't he have tiny ears?'

Cynthia nodded, and then looked thoughtful. 'I might know something about him.'

'Go on,' said Hobbes, looking up.

'Wasn't he that politician with the long hair and the green eyes? The one who said he wanted lots of new development in Sorenchester? The guy who formed the Sorenchester Needs Improvement Party? The SNIP? He seemed charismatic and persuasive when he was on television, but his ideas didn't make much sense when they were spelled out.'

'I remember,' I said. 'No one voted for the SNIP.'

'Actually,' said Hobbes, 'I believe that was Mr Solomon Slugg, who lives in Fenderton.'

'Yes, you're quite right,' said Cynthia. 'And do you remember when he got drunk and someone took photos of him lying face down in a bed of lettuce? What was the headline in the *Bugle?*'

'A Slugg in the Salad,' I said, nodding as the pictures came to mind.

'Yeah, that's it, and the article claimed he was more Slugg than Solomon. His campaign rather fizzled out after that.'

'Completely,' I said. 'Mind you, his manifesto was so ridiculous I doubt many would have voted for him anyway.'

'If anyone had bothered to read it,' said Cynthia. 'It's an odd name, though.'

'The surname is certainly unusual,' Hobbes agreed, 'so I think it possible that our Septimus was related to him.'

'I'd have thought almost certainly,' I said.

'But not necessarily, since there's little to suggest a family resemblance. Mr Solomon Slugg, as I recall, was tall, whereas Septimus is rather short.'

He pulled a dripping mobile phone from his pocket, poked a few buttons and frowned. 'I've flooded it again.' He turned to Constable Poll. 'Derek, I'd be obliged if you'd call Superintendent Cooper and let her know what we've found. And, Andy, since this now appears to be a crime scene, I'm going to ask you to step away.'

'Oh, yeah ... right,' I said, disappointed, but familiar with the procedure. 'What about Dregs?'

'He knows how to behave.'

A thought stopped me as I was turning away. 'Umm ... would you mind if I wrote a short piece about this for the *Bugle?*'

Hobbes thought for a moment. 'I can't stop you doing what you want, but from a police point of view it would be helpful if you would hold off for a short time, so the news does not alert the culprit.'

'Can I report about the old bones, then?' I asked, willing to do what he said for the sake of friendship, though a crime scoop would have been a massive boost to my career.

'Again, Andy, I'd prefer that you didn't for the time being.'

'OK,' I said, frustrated, though proud of myself for having even thought about writing an article. I suspected I'd missed a whole lot of news during my first stint as a reporter, when I'd been too focussed on myself to use my eyes and brain for the newspaper. On one occasion, I'd failed to notice that a bus had lost control and demolished a shop front, even though I must have stepped through the rubble when I was hurrying to a dog show. 'Editorsaurus' Rex Witcherley, my editor at the time, had not been impressed, especially when I told him the dog show had been cancelled. He'd been even less impressed when the reason for the cancellation emerged: there'd been a rabies scare, a fact I'd not considered newsworthy. Looking back on those times, I'd been less a newshound and more a short-sighted lazy lapdog, and had been incredibly lucky the Editorsaurus had kept me on for so long. But that was all in the past. With Phil Waring at the helm of the *Bugle,* I believed I might succeed, despite only being a part-time food critic.

Having carried the mortal remains of Septimus Slugg into the tent, Hobbes waded back into the flood, where Dregs was in hot pursuit of a passing coot.

10

I walked to our flat, or what was left of it, intending to see if anything was worth salvaging, but found it surrounded by a chain-link fence and signs warning of imminent collapse. Looking at the wreckage, it seemed incredible that everyone had got out without serious injury, for even the parts that hadn't been flattened looked ruinous.

As I walked around the perimeter, a quick movement caught my eye. Someone was scrambling about in the debris of our flat. My first thought was looters, and I reached into my pocket, intending to call the police, before remembering that my mobile was somewhere amidst all that rubble, if it had survived. The intruder was a tall, slim woman with long dark hair and a strikingly beautiful face. She looked up and waved.

'Andy, how are you?'

Hers was a soft, mellifluous voice with a musical lilt, and although I didn't recognise her, there was something familiar.

'Umm ... I'm fine ... and you?' I asked, playing for time, hoping for inspiration.

'Very well, thank you,' she said, stepping gracefully from the debris into the garden. 'How is your head?'

'Umm ... much better. What are you doing in there?'

'It's our flat.'

Inspiration struck. 'Mrs Elwes?'

'Hilda, please.'

'OK, Hilda. The sign says it's dangerous.'

She shrugged, a most graceful movement, and smiled. 'What's life without a little danger?'

'Safe?'

Her laugh was tuneful, almost angelic. 'I suppose it is, but a safe life is not an exciting one, is it?'

She gazed at me, rarely blinking, her green eyes so bright and alluring they made me nervous, though I could have stared into them forever.

'Probably not,' I admitted. 'How did you get in?'

'Over the fence. It's quite easy. Are you going to join us?'

'I don't know. I'd like to have my mobile and my laptop, but they're almost certainly smashed, so it may not even be worth looking.'

'Was your laptop the shiny red one?'

'Yes, have you found it? I also had a white smartphone.'

'I'm afraid your laptop is beyond help, but Aubrey found your mobile and it appears undamaged. Would you like him to fetch it for you?'

'If it's not too dangerous.'

'It's not dangerous at all. I'll ask him to bring it over. We found your wallet as well.'

She stepped back inside and a moment later, a tall elegant, well-dressed man with long hair that looked good on him emerged and walked towards me.

'Hi, Andy,' he said, smiling as he approached. 'More conventionally clad than last time.'

'Last time?' I said. 'Have we met?'

'Of course. We had a nice long chat while we were waiting for the ambulance. Don't you remember? I'm Aubrey Elwes.'

'No. Well, not much.'

'At least your head came off better than the tile. That smashed into a million fragments. You seemed all right at the time, apart from a small cut.'

I shook my head. 'It's almost a complete blank. We talked after the accident?'

'Yes, and you were most informative on the subject of aubergines. We had no idea they were so fascinating. Do you grow them?'

'Aubergines? No, but … umm … I have a friend who does.' It was one of Hobbes's hobbies, and although he had talked about them on occasion I hadn't realised I'd taken much in. 'I'm sorry if I rambled on.'

'Not at all. Hilda and I are always grateful for new knowledge, whatever the source. We also learned quite a bit about Egyptology. How's Daphne?' He handed me my wallet and mobile, squeezing them through the links.

'Thank you. She's fine. She's reached the camp and has been familiarising herself. She starts work tomorrow.' It was odd and disconcerting to be chatting to this man, who was, to all intents and purposes, a stranger.

'Have you found a place to stay?' asked Aubrey.

'Yes, I'm staying with a friend.'

'Inspector Hobbes?'

I nodded.

'I expect all this flooding is keeping him busy.'

'It is, and things are going to stay busy because …' I ground to a halt, aware I'd nearly said too much to this friendly man, who already knew more than I was comfortable with.

'Because of what?'

'Because he found something interesting. That's all I can say. It's police business, of course.'

'Of course. Well, nice to catch up with you, Andy. I'd better go back and help Hilda tidy up.'

He strolled back to the wreck of the building, leaving me dazed, confused and slightly unnerved – not an unfamiliar sensation, except for an added dimension of weirdness. He'd treated me as more than a mere acquaintance, almost like a friend. The fact was that I'd never been good at making friends, although I'd acquired a few after meeting Hobbes, and a few more after marrying Daphne. The trouble with the latter ones was my certainty that the thing they most liked about me was her. Still, why should I worry about being befriended? I was doing all right today, and it was nice to have my phone back, not to mention my wallet, which I checked, was still full of money and credit cards.

Lunchtime was not far away, and, having cash in my pocket, I decided to treat myself to an aperitif before returning to Blackdog Street. I turned along Spire Street and headed towards Mosse Lane and the Feathers, where Billy worked behind the bar. For reasons I'd never fathomed, he seemed to enjoy it there, and had proved astonishingly loyal to Featherlight, the landlord, whose short temper and violent outbursts had become a tourist attraction for reckless visitors.

As I drew near, I was surprised the old pub had a new door and double glazed windows. Featherlight was not known for his improvements, though he had once put down decking in the backyard in the hope of creating a beer garden. Although it had been a complete failure because he'd hadn't bothered to put tables or chairs out there and had neglected to water the potted plants, it did provide a useful area for guests to recover consciousness.

Featherlight himself, bloated, multi-bellied, and wearing a stained vest and shorts, was standing in the doorway behind a barricade of sandbags, glowering at the floodwater as if he longed to punch it.

'Good morning,' I said cheerily.

'What's so good about it, Caplet?'

'Well, it's not raining.'

'Didn't I ban you?'

'Umm ... no, I don't think so.'

'I'm losing my touch then.' He spat into the water. 'Do you reckon I can advertise my beer garden as a riverside terrace now?'

'Umm ... probably not. I think the floods will be gone soon.'

'Oh well, it was just a thought. Will your good lady be

joining you?'

'No, she's in Egypt.'

'A reasonably safe distance. What on earth does she see in you? It beats me.'

'To be honest, it beats me too.'

'Well, you're punching above your weight with that one, you lucky bastard.'

'True,' I said, pleased to find him in one of his affable moods.

'Enough of your blather. Are you coming in to spend money?'

'I thought I'd have a pint.'

'Well stop wasting my time, get inside, and don't splash unless you want to feel the business end of my boot.'

I stepped into the familiar fug, a heady mix of sweat, stale beer, old tobacco, bad cooking and years of engrained filth, the latter persisting despite Billy's best efforts. During quieter periods he could often be spotted hard at work with various patent cleaning products, and although he'd made little impression on the overall seediness, the last environmental health inspection had rated kitchen hygiene there as adequate, a colossal improvement. There'd been a time when I would sometimes eat there, and, somewhat to my amazement, I'd survived without any major internal horrors, although I suspected I'd been served spicy cat stew at least once.

My feet felt sticky on the greasy greyish floor covering that, according to the old-timers, had once been a carpet, and I felt strangely at home with the nicotine-stained walls and ceiling. I'd read how some modern establishments used a similar colour of paint in an attempt to make them look old and lived in, but the Feathers was the genuine article, and it had taken generations of heavy smokers and shoddy cleaning to produce the authentic effect of squalor, misery and degradation. Furthermore, the colour scheme was still developing, since Featherlight consistently ignored the smoking ban. No one, to my knowledge, had challenged him about it since a tourist, a huge, shaven-headed guy, had demanded that he stop smoking when serving food. To start with, Featherlight had merely ignored him, and it might have stopped there had he not coughed his cigarette butt into the man's curry. Courteously for Featherlight, he had immediately dug it out and put it back in his mouth, but the tourist, leaping to his feet, showing himself to be even taller than Featherlight, had insisted on a replacement meal. Featherlight, who has never appreciated that sort of thing, having asked him to sit down and shut up, though not quite as politely, had pushed him back into his chair. The tourist had sprung up again like a jack-in-a-box and punched Featherlight on the jaw. To everyone's surprise, Featherlight had not hit back immediately. Instead he'd invited him to step out the back.

The subsequent brawl had lasted as long as it took for the posturing tourist to get his guard up and to land on the decking. He turned out to have been an aspiring cage fighter who'd been looking for an opportunity to test his skills and gain publicity. Rumour had it that he gave up martial arts on regaining consciousness, and had to live on soup for six months. Since then, Featherlight had led a comparatively peaceful life, which was good for the over stretched resources of the local A&E, if not so good for Mrs Goodfellow's tooth collection.

'Wotcha, Andy, what can I get you,' said Billy's voice from behind the bar.

I leant over to see him polishing a glass.

'Hi,' I said. 'A pint of lager, please.'

He walked to a pump, climbed on to an upturned bucket and began to pour my drink.

'How's business?' I asked.

'Good. Despite the storm, most of our regulars checked in

last night, and we had a number of displaced people as well. The sandbagging has prevented any real flooding, though the cellar is somewhat damper than usual. We got off lightly. Some folk really had it rough.'

I nodded and fiddled in my wallet for the money, apologising for its dampness as I handed it over and took my glass.

'Cheers!' I said.

'Cheers to you too,' said Billy. 'By the way, I've got something to tell you.'

'What?'

'Skeleton Bob came in a few minutes ago. He was scared and bedraggled and reckoned he'd had to flee his cottage on an airbed because a huge, fierce grey creature was approaching through the flood. He reckoned it was a hippopotamus or something, and that it must have escaped from a zoo.'

'Was he drunk?'

'I don't think so. I think something had really scared him, so I tried to call Hobbesie, but couldn't get through.'

'He's drowned his mobile again.'

'I'm worried Bob'll do something daft.'

'Dafter than usual, you mean.'

'Yes. He was wittering on about borrowing a harpoon.'

'Where from?'

Billy shrugged. 'I've no idea, mate, but he seemed convinced he could get one. You'd better warn Hobbesie.'

'There are other policemen, you know. You could always have called the police station.'

'I could've, but most of the cops aren't as sympathetic to Bob and his ways, and he'll do almost anything to avoid them.'

'Anything except not breaking the law. Never mind, I should be seeing Hobbes at lunch, though he's very busy. The fact is I found something in the flood yesterday, and, well, it seems to have become a crime scene.'

'What sort of thing?' asked Billy.

'I can't say. It's ... umm ... police business, and there's a press blackout.' If I exaggerated, it was only because I was showing off.

'Was it in Church Fields? I saw something going on there when I came by.'

'I can't say,' I said. 'It's an official secret.'

'It sounds interesting then.'

I nodded and took a big slurp from my glass. 'Hey, what's up with the lager?'

'Nothing. It's the same rubbish as usual.'

'But it's good. There's none of that vinegary aftertaste.'

'Maybe it's because I cleaned out the pipes,' said Billy. 'The boss was in court last week and I took the opportunity to run the cleaner through them three times. I'm not sure anyone had bothered this century, and I'm not saying there was all sorts of horrible gunk came out, but it now takes me half as long to fill a glass, and people have started enjoying their beer. Even the boss didn't complain when he had his breakfast pint.'

I took another long, slow pull on my glass. 'Surely it's his job to clean the pipes.'

'Are you trying to tell me how to run my pub, Caplet?' Featherlight's great hand landed on my shoulder like a side of beef, and spun me round.

His face had just a hint of the stormy tint that was an early warning of violence.

'No,' I said, cringing, although he'd never hit me since I'd become friends with Hobbes. It wasn't that he was frightened of Hobbes, or anything as mundane as that. In fact, he was just about the only person in town who wasn't scared to face his wrath. I'd been puzzled for years until I'd discovered the reason; Featherlight was as 'unhuman' as Hobbes.

'You'd better not. Now, drink up and get out before I boot you out.'

Gulping down the remains of my lager, I removed myself from harm's way.

11

As I walked back to Blackdog Street, I felt as if I was going home, even though I'd only lived there for a relatively short time as a temporary non-paying guest, and had been away for a couple of years. It did, however, lack the one ingredient that would have made it perfect, which was Daphne.

Thinking of her, I checked my mobile, and was ashamed to see she'd made nineteen attempts to call me. Although there'd been genuine difficulties and obstacles, I could and should have tried harder to let her know I was safe, and check that she was well and happy. She really should have been my priority. Still, as Featherlight liked to say, there was no use crying over split lips. I was back in contact, and all was well, apart from the loss of our flat and most of our possessions, and that thing with me and Sally.

The Sally problem kept running through all my thoughts, bringing a constant nagging horror that I'd soon receive a mysterious and sinister letter, unless blackmailers had moved to more modern methods like texts or emails. I both hoped and feared I'd find out really soon and that I'd sort everything out before Daphne returned. I felt how I imagined a criminal might feel after being found guilty but before sentence had been passed; full of fear yet dreaming that the judge might yet be lenient. Of course, my case was entirely different as I hadn't really done anything wrong, though, unfortunately that wasn't how it would look. I dreaded Daphne's response should she ever see the photographs. What if she refused to believe my perfectly reasonable explanations and pleas of innocence? What if she convicted me on the evidence? Deep down I believed her to be amazingly tolerant of my faults and foibles, and I was deeply in love with her, as I hoped she was with me and I wasn't sure I'd be able to manage if she walked out of my life. Yet, despite knowing her as well as anyone might expect, I couldn't guess how she'd respond. At such times I really needed to talk to someone, such as Hobbes or Mrs Goodfellow, but I was far too ashamed.

When I got in, Hobbes and Dregs were already home, cleaned and dried. The good thing was that Dregs, having just been bathed, was in a subdued mood when he greeted me, and not inclined to rough me up or give me a good licking. Hobbes was on the sofa, doing the *Bugle's* Cunningly Cryptic Crossword, a task he seemed to enjoy, though it rarely took him longer than ten minutes. I was lucky if I worked out one clue in a week, though I could usually manage a decent stab at the concise version.

He finished, put the paper down and looked up. 'How was the Feathers?'

'Quiet and dry. Umm ... how did you know I'd been there?'

'The place has a unique aroma, and the grubby patch on your left elbow shows you leant on the bar.'

I glanced at the brown smudge on my sleeve. 'Umm ... did you find any more bodies?'

'If you mean fresh ones, then no, though there are still plenty of bones to be retrieved. There appears to be quite a spacious chamber down there, and I've advised Superintendent Cooper to call in a diving team to take a proper look. Doctor Ramage has taken Septimus Slugg's remains back to her lab, and the other recovered bones, which she still believes are hundreds of years old, are resting in peace in my office for the time being.'

'Couldn't you have just left them for now? I mean, what harm could come to them?'

'You'd be surprised what people will do sometimes, and don't forget there are ghouls about.'

He meant real ghouls, not just ghoulish humans. I'd had an alarming experience with a couple of them shortly after I'd first met him and was still disgusted that such creatures were allowed to live in town. Yet, so long as they didn't break the law too obviously, and didn't leave opened graves, he tolerated them, pointing out that the only real harm they did was to old bones, which they'd grind into ghoul hash. I was amazed they hadn't found these bones before, for they had an extraordinary talent for locating them.

It was then I remembered to tell him what Billy had said about Skeleton Bob.

'I'd better go and see him,' said Hobbes. 'I was thinking I ought to check up on him anyway. He was rather distraught after the loss of his pig.'

'How will you get there?'

'By boat, but since we broke the ones we used yesterday, I'll have to get another ... I know, I'll ask Sid if he still has his canoes. He won't mind lending me one.'

Though I knew Sid Sharples was a vampire, I hadn't known he was a canoeist as well. Mind you, I also hadn't known he flew a black micro-light until he buzzed me one afternoon in Ride Park, nearly causing heart failure.

'Dinner's ready,' announced Mrs Goodfellow, nearly causing heart failure, and making me reflect that life can sometimes be a series of repeating patterns.

I headed into the kitchen and sat down, soothing my strained nerves as Hobbes said grace. The food was excellent, even though it was just an egg and cheese salad. I'd not been a great fan of salads until I'd tried one of the old girl's, since never before had I realised that cucumber could be so fragrant, that lettuce could be so crisp, and that tomatoes could be so sweet. Besides, she had a way with boiling eggs and I was always a sucker for the nutty, crumbly Sorenchester Cheese, especially when taken with a dollop of her prize-winning pungent pickle. I was a very contented Andy by the time we'd finished and were back on the sofa, drinking tea. Hobbes made a phone call to Sid.

'D'you fancy a canoe trip?' he asked when he put the receiver down.

'Yes, why not?' I gulped down as much of the scalding liquid as I could before grabbing my coat and rushing out with him and Dregs.

We paid a quick visit to Sid's lock-up where Sid, unusually short, paunchy, balding and affable for a vampire, helped us take down a big red fibreglass canoe that had been slung from the beams. I helped Hobbes carry it down to the junction of Dribbling Lane and Spittoon Way by not getting in his way. He set the canoe down on the water, and we prepared for the voyage. Taking a paddle, I scrambled to the front, with Dregs, tail wagging like an old seadog, sitting himself in the middle. Then Hobbes plumped himself down in the back. The canoe pivoted, his end plunged, and mine rose, nearly catapulting me out, and leaving me high and dry. I grabbed the side and looked over my shoulder as Dregs slid backwards and raised me even higher.

'This will need a little re-organisation,' said Hobbes whose backside was within a whisker of the water line.

I splashed down as he sprang out.

'Right, I'd better take the middle, Dregs had better sit at the back, and you might as well stay where you are.'

Although Dregs was reluctant to take up the inferior position assigned to him, Hobbes insisted, and within a couple of minutes we were on our way to Bob's place, and I believe I made a contribution to our progress, though most of it was down to Hobbes, who seemed far more at ease in a canoe than he had been in a rowing boat. I said as much.

'I once spent some time in British Columbia,' he said, 'and found that canoes were often the best way of travelling any distance, though they weren't fibreglass in those days.'

'What were you doing out there?'

'Hunting a fugitive wendigo.'

'Were you on secondment?'

'No, it was a special assignment.'

'Did you catch him?'

'I caught *her* and I still have the scars to remind me.'

He would say no more, which was infuriating since I still wanted raw material so I could write about him. My original plan had just been to draft an article. Later, I thought I'd get a book out of him, and by then I was wondering whether a series might be possible. Unfortunately, though I'd picked up some amazing details, I was certain many of the really fascinating parts of his story remained locked up in that great ugly head of his. As far as he was concerned, the present was far more interesting than the past and only now and again, usually when he'd dredged up an old memory relevant to a current case, would he let slip an intriguing hint of old times.

Instead of giving in to frustration, I decided to make the most of the trip and to treat it like a jaunt. We took the direct route to Bob's, crossing flooded fields, gliding through submerged copses and over hedgerows and walls. It was quite pleasant, despite my worries about the beast Bob had spotted, but, other than a fierce-looking swan and some water-logged sheep gathered on a mound, I saw nothing to alarm me. After about twenty minutes we approached Bob's cottage, which, despite being in a relatively raised position, had water lapping the perimeter fence. A small brown dog, splashing around the edge, woofed, sparking a barking match with Dregs.

'Ahoy!' cried Hobbes's foghorn voice when we were a hundred metres or so away.

Bob's head poked round the side of the house. 'Hello, Mr Hobbes.'

'Good Afternoon,' said Hobbes. 'Permission to land?'

'Granted,' said Bob, his grin displaying despicable dentition.

Seeing the small dog walk up to us, its tail wagging like a propeller, and thinking I'd make myself useful, I grabbed the painter Hobbes had laid along the bottom of the canoe, and stood up, expecting to step into calf deep water.

'Not yet,' said Hobbes, a fraction too late to stop me.

I went in with a splash and a deal of astonishment, going under as if I'd stepped into the deep end of a swimming pool. Coming up, spluttering with the shock of sudden immersion, I swam, puzzled that the little dog was still walking at my side. Its movements were perhaps a little stiff.

'Hold on,' said Hobbes as I grabbed the painter.

I was expecting him to pick me up, not to tow me behind like hippo bait, but after a moment or two my feet touched the bottom and, like an idiot Robinson Crusoe, I dragged myself onto dry land. Bob tied the canoe to a fence post.

'Why did you throw yourself in?' he asked as Hobbes and Dregs stepped onto dry land.

'I didn't think it was very deep. I mean, that little dog was walking around without any problems. I don't understand it.'

Bob guffawed. 'That dog is a Stillingham Stilthound.'

'A what?'

'You heard,' he said, grinning from ear to eternity.

'I've never heard of such a thing.'

'That's because the working dogs have become quite rare,' said Hobbes, who was also chuckling. 'They were originally used for duck hunting in the days when they'd flood the water meadows around Stillingham every winter.'

To illustrate his point, the dog strolled ashore and greeted Dregs. It was a sturdy little animal with wooden stilts attached to powerful legs. Dregs looked up at him, seemingly as amazed as I was.

'Stumpy is staying here a while. He belongs to my old mate, Jake, who's having to dry out his house,' said Bob.

'Would that be Jake Custard, the council's flood expert?' asked Hobbes.

'That's him.'

'Is he all right?'

Bob nodded. 'He's bearing up, but will be better when he can move back home and have his dog back.'

'Good,' said Hobbes. 'Now, tell me about your mysterious sighting.'

'Oh, that,' said Bob, his face turning as red and shiny as a cricket ball. 'I was mistaken.'

'Were you drunk again?' I asked, shivering, dripping, and grateful for a sliver of sunlight that had broken cover to emit a tiny hint of winter heat.

'No, it was a mistake anyone could have made.'

'Robert Nibblet, what have you done this time?' asked a breathless woman's voice from inside the cottage.

'Nothing really,' said Bob, suddenly looking as pale as a white mouse, a nicotine-stained finger to his lips, his eyes pleading.

'Your wife's back,' I said. 'When did she return?'

'This morning, when I was in town,' said Bob.

'But, how did she get here?' I asked, with a gesture at the floods.

Hobbes, chuckling for a reason that escaped me, clamped his hairy hand across my mouth.

'Good afternoon, madam,' he said, as Fenella Nibblet filled the doorway. 'Just a routine visit.'

'Thank you,' Bob mouthed.

'Oh, is that all? I feared he'd been up to his old tricks again. It would be just like him to mess things up when I'm away,' said the spherical Mrs Nibblet, squeezing through the doorway and rolling from the house, wearing a close-fitting orange onesie that made her look like an enormous animated pumpkin.

'Delighted to see you again,' said Hobbes, releasing my mouth and snapping off a smart salute.

She nodded. 'So why are you here?'

Bob shook his head almost imperceptibly.

'There were just a couple of details I wanted to clear up regarding the attack on Crackling Rosie,' said Hobbes, with what must have been his attempt at a pleasant smile.

'Well don't waste too much time. That Rosie was a menace, but at least she'll make some good sausages.'

'Don't,' said Bob, with a sob. 'She was a lovely animal.'

'She was a lump of vicious lard,' said Mrs Nibblet.

'Well, so are you,' he retorted.

For a moment he stood there, angry and defiant, until realisation of what he'd said dawned. Mrs Nibblet directed a storm-force glare at him, and he attempted a smile. It came out as a grimace.

'What did you say?'

'It was just a joke, my dear, just a silly joke.'

Then, his nerve broke, and he fled, with his wife in hot pursuit, the pair of them bringing to mind a bowling ball chasing a skittle. Dregs and the stilthound, both barking excitedly, joined in the fun.

'What will she do to him?' I asked as they vanished around the side of the cottage. 'Do you need to protect him? I mean to say, she must be three times his weight.'

'More than that,' said Hobbes, 'and if there was a chance she'd hurt him I would, of course, intervene. However, as they've been married for over twenty years and Bob has survived entirely unscathed, I think he's safe. At heart, and despite appearances, Mrs Nibblet is a kind and loving wife, though many might consider him a most provoking husband.'

'There again, his survival might say more about how fast he is on his feet,' I suggested as Bob emerged from the other side of the cottage, having opened up a five second gap on Fenella, whose beetroot face was clashing horribly with the onesie. Dregs and Stumpy the stilthound were keeping up, their tails wagging as if this was the game of the century.

'Possibly,' said Hobbes, 'but Bob reckons her bark is worse than her bite.'

'Has she ever bitten him?' I asked as Bob headed for the dark side of the cottage.

'Not to my knowledge. And now she's using her brain.'

Mrs Nibblet had stopped running and was lying in wait at the corner of the house, breathing so heavily I could hear her from twenty paces. When Bob, bug-eyed like a rabbit, reappeared, she made a grab for him, but he ducked and slipped through her arms. Then, mystifyingly, and much to Hobbes's amusement, he carried on running round the house. She seized him on her second attempt.

'Robert Armstrong Nibblet,' she said, holding him by the scruff of the neck as if he were a naughty puppy, 'you apologise. You apologise now!'

'I'm sorry, dearest. Truly I am,' said Bob, squirming. 'Please forgive me.'

She glared for a long moment, before hauling him towards her and giving him a hug. I was just starting to fear she was crushing him, like a python crushes a deer, when she let go. He stepped back to breathe and when he grinned at her, she smiled back. The dogs, seeing the excitement was over, returned to splashing about in the water.

'I wish all domestic disputes were resolved so happily and quickly,' said Hobbes.

'And so entertainingly,' I said.

'Indeed. Let's leave the happy couple to their own devices. Get in the boat. Are you cold?'

'Yes. Especially now the sun's gone back in.'

'You'd better cover yourself with this,' he said, taking off his gabardine mac. 'Come here, Dregs.'

With a lingering look of regret for the breaking of a new friendship, Dregs hopped aboard, taking up his position in the stern. Hobbes shoved off with his paddle.

When we'd gone some distance, he began laughing.

'What's so funny?'

'Bob's hippopotamus.'

'Yeah, that was strange. I thought you'd question him about it. Umm ... what do you think he saw?'

'Mrs Nibblet coming home.'

'That's a bit unfair,' I said. 'I know she's rather a large lady, but no one would mistake her for a hippo ... and, anyway, didn't he say the beast was grey?'

'He did.'

'Well it can't have been her then. She was in orange.'

'I take it you didn't observe what was hanging on the washing line next to the airbed?'

'No, but what's that got to do with anything?'

'Everything.'

'What was it then?'

'A jumbo-sized grey wetsuit ...'

A glance over my shoulder proved he wasn't joking.

'... which I strongly suspect is hers. It certainly isn't Bob's – he'd be able to fit all of him into one of the legs.'

'Why would she have a wetsuit?'

'For scuba diving. Bob once mentioned she'd joined the local club.'

'There's a diving club in Sorenchester?'

'The *Sorenchester and District Orcas.* I had a try-dive with them once.'

'Really? What happened?'

'Firstly, they couldn't find any kit to fit me, and secondly, I sank, even when I shouldn't have. But never mind that, let's get you home and then I'll get back to work.'

Digging the paddle in, he sent us skimming across the water. Dregs sat at the back, his nose raised into the wind, his tail thumping. I expect I would have enjoyed the ride, too, had I not been so cold.

We were just approaching the outskirts of Sorenchester, cruising between parallel lines of Cotswold stone, where the tops of the inappropriately named drystone walls bordered a lane, when Dregs began barking. Hobbes stopped paddling and we drifted to a standstill next to a man who was chest deep in water, and breathing heavily.

'Are you all right, sir.'

'I'm just taking a breather. I'll be glad to get back home though. This water is not exactly tropical, is it?'

'No, sir,' Hobbes acknowledged, 'it isn't. Would you like a lift?'

'Thank you, but I'm on my bike. I'm training for the Tour of the Cotswolds and my schedule is all out because of the awful weather.' He glanced at his watch. 'I really should be going now.'

'Enjoy your ride,' said Hobbes, speeding us away.

Looking back, I could see the man peddling, or paddling, hard but not exactly moving at high speed. 'That's dedication,' I said.

Hobbes nodded.

'Though some might call it lunacy,' I continued.

'Possibly, Andy. It's all down to results. If he does well, it will be called dedication. If he doesn't it will be lunacy.'

When we'd reached dryish land, Hobbes and Dregs returned the canoe, allowing me to head straight home for yet another hot bath and change of clothing. The clean clothes remained something of a mystery, for they would always be ready, neatly folded and laid out, whenever I needed them. Even better, my filthy wet clothes would vanish and then reappear a day or two later, magically cleansed of all dirt and hurt, pressed and ready to go. I suspected Mrs Goodfellow was responsible, but had never caught her in the act, though one day I intended thanking her and judging her reaction to test whether my Sherlockian intellect, having eliminated the impossible, had come up trumps.

Hobbes and Dregs returned for a cup of tea before heading back out to check on developments at the bone site. Feeling warm, clean and drowsy, I took the opportunity for a quick nap. When I awoke it smelt like it was almost supper time, which was no bad thing, though I felt groggy and headachy as the sleep cleared.

I was at the table, willing and ready, when Mrs Goodfellow served up creamy fish chowder that, besides being utterly delicious, seemed entirely appropriate with all the water about. Just for a moment I'd had a slight worry that she'd managed to hoik the fish out of the street, but, since some of it was smoked haddock, I relaxed. Although it was obviously impossible for her to surpass herself with every meal, she seemed to manage it. I wished Daphne could cook half as well as her, though I'd have been just as happy if I could. I'd really missed the old girl's food, despite all my visits to restaurants. Even the best ones lagged way behind and I couldn't always choose the best, as Phil insisted that I visit all sorts of places. A few, with all due respect, stank: some literally so. On the bright side, the truly appalling ones were rare and made me appreciate the others.

Another admirable aspect of the old girl was that, unlike certain so-called celebrity chefs, she never got flustered or swore, though I'd once heard her mutter something that might have been unladylike when a starling fell down the chimney, blundered into the kitchen and belly flopped into the magnificent trifle she'd spent several hours working on for an old folks' supper. If it had been me, that bird would have breathed its last where it floundered. Since it wasn't, she dug it out, leaving behind a perfect sooty impression of every feather, washed it under the tap, dried it with a hairdryer and released it. Only then had she turned her attention to a replacement, somehow producing a superb Eton Mess just in time for Hobbes to deliver it to the church hall. Where she'd found strawberries in December was beyond me, though I'd occasionally speculated that she had magical powers. The truth was more mundane; she was simply outstanding at what she did and knew every shopkeeper, farmer and gardener who had whatever she required.

When we'd finished eating, and Hobbes and I were drinking tea, I asked how his investigations were going.

He thought for a while. 'The situation is not at all straightforward. I've had to inform the duty sergeant and call in other detective resources because of the murder of Mr Septimus Slugg. However, preliminary tests have confirmed that most of the other bones date from medieval times.'

'Most?'

'It turns out that not all of them are so old.'

'What do you mean?'

'The divers discovered an intact male skeleton this afternoon. It was still showing fragments of clothing, as well as something you wouldn't expect on a medieval corpse.'

'What?'

'A digital watch.'

'Wow,' I said, stunned. 'So that does make it recent.'

'Indeed,' said Hobbes. 'The watch in question is a mass produced Casio, and the model dates from the late nineteen eighties.'

'So that's when he died?'

'That is the earliest possible date, though, of course, he might have worn the watch for many years before his death.'

'Are there any indications what killed him? Was it another murder?'

'It would appear so. Dr Ramage pointed out some skull injuries that suggest he'd been bludgeoned. Besides, it's clear he didn't stick himself down there.'

'But I don't understand where all the bones are coming from.'

Hobbes sighed. 'That remains to be determined. However, I have spoken to Mr Spiridion Konstantinopoulos …'

'The local historian,' I remarked. 'I saw one of his books once.'

'He informed me that there are no records of any plague pits around the town and he agrees with Dr Ramage that the old bones were probably in an ossuary, or charnel house. That fits in with the discovery of the large chamber. It is, of course, underwater now, but it would normally have been underground.'

'Does that mean the killer knew where it was and hid his victims there?' I asked.

'It's a possibility, though I doubt it. It's more likely that the killer, or killers, dumped the bodies in the old culvert that runs alongside. Apparently, that was what collapsed under us and knocked down the ossuary wall.'

'It was a most unpleasant experience.'

'It was, but it may have been fortunate in that something was revealed that someone hoped would not be revealed.'

'Do you think the bodies might have blocked the culvert? Could that be why the flooding was so bad this time?'

'It wouldn't surprise me.'

'I wonder who did it and why?'

'So do I, and I intend to find out,' he said with a sudden grin.

'Good … can I come with you?'

'I expect so. At least for some of the time.'

'Excellent,' I said, and though I was genuinely delighted, a timid, or sensible, part of my brain was, as usual, screaming 'no!' Sometimes, my newly acquired courage astounded me, but mostly it scared me. Yet, investigating crimes with Hobbes always made me feel more alive, even when it left me half dead. The paradox had long puzzled me.

'Of course,' he continued after a slurp of tea, 'investigation will be tricky until the roads are clear. I really need to see Mr Solomon Slugg.'

'Couldn't you just phone him?'

'I could, but then I'd be unable to see him.'

'Or smell him?' I suggested.

He nodded and changed the subject. He always seemed a little reticent about his unusual abilities, but it had been the way he sniffed out clues at crime scenes that had given me my first inkling that he wasn't quite human.

That evening we stayed in. I watched the telly, while he read the paper. It was barely nine o'clock when he yawned and went up to bed. His yawn set me off, too, and I crashed out only a few minutes later. This time, so far as I could remember, I enjoyed a dreamless sleep.

12

Next morning, I sat alone at the table as the old girl ladled porridge into my bowl. The house was really quiet.

'Where are they?' I asked.

'Out. Somebody telephoned in the middle of the night.'

'I didn't hear anything.'

'I'm not surprised. You looked exhausted and you slept like the dead, except that you were snoring.'

'I didn't know I snored. Do I do it often?'

'Only when you're asleep, dear.'

I concentrated on eating my porridge, still amazed how she could transmute it into haute cuisine, and remembered the distasteful grey, lumpy mess Mother used to slop out, a sludge that was barely palatable even when laced with golden syrup. Nowadays, I looked forward to getting my oats, even though it meant I'd missed out on some other delight. I'd learned to accept whatever was on offer, and to await further delectation.

I'd just scraped my bowl clean and was wondering whether there was space for anything else when Dregs burst into the kitchen, heralding the return of Hobbes, who was looking rather bedraggled. He poured a mug of tea and took a big slurp.

'That's better,' he said, and spoke no more until he'd drained three further mugs and had spooned down a titanic volume of porridge.

Dregs, who'd lapped up a bowl of water, sprawled beneath the table and was soon fast asleep, twitching, and kicking my feet at odd intervals.

'Did you have an interesting call-out?' I asked, having restrained my curiosity for as long as seemed possible without bursting.

'Yes,' said Hobbes, buttering a slice of toast, 'but it was puzzling.'

'Who called you out?'

'Superintendent Cooper.'

'She must have been working late.'

'No, she was in bed when Sergeant Dixon phoned, and she decided she needed to call me.'

'What was it about?'

'A report had come in concerning intruders at a house in Fenderton.'

'One of the flooded ones?'

'No, one on the hill. However, I needed to borrow Sid's canoe again to get there, though the waters have receded quite a lot.'

'But why did she call you? It sounds more like a job for the ordinary police ... the ones in uniform that is.'

Hobbes applied marmalade to his toast and ate it slowly, while I waited.

'That would normally be the case. However, the house is on Elphinstone Road ...'

'So?'

'... where a number of very distinguished and wealthy people live.'

'So, they get special treatment? That's not fair.'

'Of course they don't get special treatment, but the house in question belongs to Mr Solomon Slugg.'

'I see,' I said. 'So you got to talk to him?'

'No, I didn't, because he wasn't there. No one was.' He scratched his chin, his fingers rasping on his morning stubble.

'Who made the phone call then?'

'According to Sergeant Dixon, the caller did not give his name and hung up abruptly before he could be questioned.'

'So how did he know where the call came from?'

Hobbes laughed. 'Andy, you really are a luddite! The

number was recorded and Dixon looked up the address. When he saw whose house it was, he called the superintendent. He's a bright one is young Reg.'

I nodded and turned to Mrs Goodfellow. 'Is there any more tea?'

'I've just made another pot, dear.' She carried it over and refilled our mugs.

Beneath the table, Dregs was snoring gently.

'Did you find anything?' I asked and took a sip of fresh tea.

'Only the mysterious disappearance of Mr Solomon Slugg.'

'Do you think he's been kidnapped?'

'It's a possibility. The back door had been left open, and someone had been in the house recently.'

'How did you know?'

'There was fresh mud on the floor.'

'Umm ... couldn't that have been Solomon? He might have opened the door and fled.'

'That wouldn't explain it.'

'Unless he ran out and back in and back out again. Perhaps he forgot his coat or something?'

Hobbes nodded and drained his mug. 'Good try, but there were two sets of muddy prints going in and out, and I'd suggest one of them was made by a woman.'

'Well, maybe he had a female friend round, and they both forgot something.' I was starting to think my reasoning was getting a little far-fetched.

'I'll keep an open mind, but, since someone telephoned about intruders, I would suggest that intruders are more likely, don't you agree?'

'Yeah, you're probably right. Was there any sign of a struggle?'

'There were signs of a hasty departure, but there was no blood, or any other damage.'

'Had the back door been forced?'

'No,' said Hobbes, 'but there were a few tiny scratches around the keyhole that might suggest lock picks. I don't often see them used these days, but this was an old-fashioned lock, and if I'm correct someone made a very neat job of it.'

'So the big question is, who did it?' I said, pleased with my insight.

'Or, more importantly, where is Mr Solomon Slugg?'

'Oh, yeah. There's that.'

'I'll go back later, have another nose around, and see what turns up. Now, I'm going to get myself neat and tidy.'

He finished his tea, marched upstairs and shortly afterwards I heard his heavy duty electric razor at work, followed by his yells as he stood under the dangerously powerful shower. A few minutes later, he returned, fully dressed and ready to go.

'Right,' he said, 'I'm off to work.'

'Can I come?' I asked, hoping.

'I'm going into the station to do paperwork, and to see if there's any new information on the bodies. I don't suppose that will interest you very much, but I intend to head up to Mr Slugg's place afterwards. I'll look back in here before I go, so if you'd like a trip out, then you'd be most welcome.'

'That'll be great,' I said, as he left.

Shortly afterwards, having pulled my feet from under Dregs, who'd somehow contrived to lie across them in his sleep, I took a look outside the front door. The floods were definitely going down, and other than hoses pumping filthy water into drains that now seemed prepared to take it away, things looked reasonably normal. The sun wore only a thin film of gauzy cloud, and there was, maybe, a hint of warmth in the air, a reminder that spring was not so very far away. There was still little sign of moving traffic, and I wondered how many vehicles had survived the deluge. The worst thing was the foetid stench of sewage.

I went back inside and telephoned Daphne, who, to my delight, was in the office, and in a sparkling mood, fizzing with enthusiasm about what she'd seen and done, and what was happening. The dig, she said, had uncovered a number of interesting artefacts, one of which was possibly unique and might point to the existence of a previously unknown Pharaoh. I formed the impression that the team was hoping for something to rival the tomb of Tutankhamen. She laughed off my concerns about a possible curse, and despite knowing my fears were silly, anything seemed possible since I'd fallen into Hobbes's world. I reserved the right to worry.

Afterwards I was unsettled and lonely, feeling every one of the thousands of miles between us, and despite her being the one in a strange land, I was the one who seemed to be struggling, and although we'd parted with statements of love, I feared she was enjoying herself far too much. What if she found so much fulfilment and excitement out there that she never came back? After all, what could I, a part-time journalist in an insignificant Cotswold town, offer a dynamic, fascinating and lovely woman like her? She was bound to meet someone quite different to me, someone like Professor Mahmoud El-Gammal, who was, I convinced myself, tall, slim and handsome, with dark seductive eyes and exquisite manners. I sat on the sofa, growing morose and self-pitying until Dregs woke up and bullied me into taking him for a walk.

We used the park's Hedbury Road entrance, which was above flood level. Looking back down the slope towards town, the fields were still mostly under water, and the church tower appeared to rise above them like a lighthouse. I let the dog off the lead to run and bark and sniff. The ground squelched with every step, making me glad of my

Wellington boots, but Dregs's tail was wagging in ecstasy, for cold, preferably muddy, water held none of the horrors of a bath. It was sad really, because he was dirtying his undercarriage so much that Mrs Goodfellow would insist on dunking him straight into the tub when we got back. Still, since he'd never worked out the link between getting filthy and ending up in the dreaded bath, he was perfectly content for the time being. I followed his meanderings, daydreaming about the allure of the other women I'd met recently, and wondering why I couldn't quite bring the charm and beauty of Sally and Hilda to mind when it was so easy with Pinky and Dr Cynthia, and Daphne, of course.

'Oi, Caplet!' Featherlight's harsh voice smashed through my reverie like a sledgehammer through a fruitcake.

'Good morning,' I said.

'Good morning be damned. Shift your arse and take a look at this.'

'What?' I asked.

'Shut up and I'll show you.'

He turned away, his bellies following a moment later, and headed for the trees, walking with a slight forwards lean, his arms at his sides as if pushing a heavy wheelbarrow. I couldn't help remembering Mother's advice about not following strange men into the woods, particularly as few were as strange as Featherlight. Still, he was obviously in a benign mood by his standards and I was likely to be quite safe. Besides, I had Dregs to look after me, which he could do if he felt like it.

After a brisk and muddy walk, we reached an overgrown stone quarry that had become a convenient place to tip old junk, and scrambled down a slimy slope. After skirting the murky puddle or pond in the middle we reached the far end where Featherlight called a halt. Dregs, who was running a little ahead, sneezed and retreated, his hackles rising.

'What's up?' I asked.

'See that?' said Featherlight, pointing at a perfect circle of flattened crushed grass about the size of the old vinyl long-playing records Hobbes occasionally played. In the middle was a star within a hoop made of split twigs.

As I stepped forward to examine it, Featherlight's heavy hand clamped onto my shoulder and dragged me back.

'I wouldn't do that if I was you, Caplet,' he said.

'Why not?' I asked, wondering why a bit of rustic tat worried him so much.

'It's dangerous.'

I laughed. 'Come off it! It's just a corn dolly, or something.'

'Even a mutton-brained numbskull can tell it's not a damned corn-dolly,' he growled.

He really did growl, like a huge angry dog, except there were words in it. The only other person I knew who could do such a thing was Hobbes, though he usually required something serious to tip him into angry mode. Featherlight's temper, however, was like a mantrap with a hair trigger: the slightest incident could set it off. I'd known him long enough that I should have known better, and I did know better, but some reckless impulse overrode sense and I tried to wriggle free. The next thing I knew, I was dangling by my collar from a branch, my feet kicking helplessly, while a purple-faced Featherlight roared improbable anatomical abuse into my face. When my wellies slipped off, Dregs bounced up to lick my feet, pleased to join in this jolly game.

All things considered, I'd got off lightly, and Featherlight, whose rages tended to be short, if often painful to anyone within range, was back to relative affability.

'That thing is dangerous, you wazzock,' he said.

'Fine,' I said. 'I believe you, but what is it?'

'It's a sign of trouble. Tell Hobbes.'

'I will, but what sort of trouble?'

'Bad trouble. Big trouble. Trouble with a capital T.'

'But why?'

'Ask Hobbes. I'm busy.'

'OK ... umm ... but before you go would you mind letting me down?'

It testified to his good mood that he deigned to unhook me.

'See you,' I said, as he stomped away.

'Not if I see you first.'

I put my boots back on, despite Dregs's best efforts, and considered picking up the star thing as soon as Featherlight was well out of sight. For once, caution, or maybe an inkling of unease, got the better of me and I turned for home.

When we got back to Blackdog Street, Hobbes was fiddling with the car.

'I'm just going to see Mr Slugg,' he said. 'Do you still fancy coming?'

Without thinking, I nodded and a moment later I was getting into my accustomed place in the back seat, with Dregs making himself comfortable in the front.

'D'you think the roads are clear enough yet?' I asked.

Hobbes shrugged. 'We'll soon find out. The car should be fine. Billy came round and dried out the works, so it runs all right, but I apologise that it's still somewhat damp inside.'

Somewhat damp was the understatement of the year, for he could have grown rice in there. Fortunately, he'd covered the seats with sheets of polythene, which, despite keeping my backside reasonably dry, were as slippery as wet fish. I belted up, expecting that we'd soon be hurtling along Blackdog Street. However, I was surprised that he drove with such care that I felt it reasonable to keep my eyes open and see how he was avoiding puddles and ensuring he never splashed anyone or created a wash that might flood houses. We continued at the same sedate pace as we turned left by the church onto Pound Street, headed onto Spittoon

Way and carried on towards Dribbling Lane, which was still awash, though nowhere near as deep as it had been. Unfortunately, the main road to Fenderton, slightly raised above the flooded meadows, was dry. He put his foot down.

I closed my eyes, clinging to the door handle, and despite my seatbelt, I slid from side to side and back. At last we turned and I opened my eyes for a moment, seeing that we were on Uphill Way, ascending at such a speed my ears popped. A few moments later we slowed down and I could breathe again and look around.

'Here we are,' said Hobbes, bringing the car to a stop on a broad gravelled driveway in front of an old-fashioned wooden garage set in a small, slightly unkempt garden. 'Let's see if Mr Slugg's in. I hope he is, because I'd really like a word with him.'

We got out of the car and I tried not to show how shaken I was, for my tolerance of his driving, though probably still better than most, had lessened since I'd been away. Dregs, left behind, moped.

We were outside a medium-sized house that looked in good nick, though the paintwork was a little tired. Hobbes strode up to the solid, heavy-looking front door and pressed the doorbell. An electronic Big Ben chime sounded within the bowels of the house, and then, besides Dregs bounding around in the car, there was silence. After a minute or so, Hobbes tried again. Then he knocked so hard a lesser door might have burst open.

There was still no reply.

'He's not in,' I said when Hobbes showed no sign of movement. 'Perhaps the intruders kidnapped him.'

'I suspect not,' he murmured, with a glance at a tiny security camera on the wall above.

'Umm ... now what?'

He took out his warrant card, held it to the camera and rang the bell again.

There was still no reply.

'Are you going to knock the door in?' I asked.

'Of course not.' He shook his head. 'Although I would like to talk to Mr Slugg, there's no immediate urgency. He is not suspected of anything and Superintendent Cooper takes a dim view of shattering doors without due cause. I should know.'

'So what happens next?'

He shrugged. 'We could go home and have a cup of tea.'

'Is that all?' I'd been hoping for a bit of excitement and felt let down.

We returned to the car, reversed from the driveway and headed downhill. After a few seconds, he stopped and parked by the kerb.

'Why have we stopped?'

'Because I heard movement inside the Slugg residence.'

'From here?'

He chuckled. 'No, when we were outside.'

'It might not be him,' I said. 'It could be his dog or something.'

'If it was a dog it would have barked, and besides I heard the television being turned off, which is not something dogs generally do. Therefore, I conclude someone is home.'

'Perhaps they aren't dressed yet,' I suggested.

'Perhaps,' he said, 'or perhaps somebody doesn't wish to talk to me. I think I'll try a surprise visit, and this time Dregs can come.'

We got out, closing the doors quietly, and, having sneaked back up the road, ducked behind the shoulder-high privet hedge surrounding Mr Slugg's garden.

'There, you are,' said Hobbes, peering through the foliage. 'I told you someone was home.'

A tired old chap wearing tinted glasses, and with long grey hair down to his tweedy shoulders, was looking from the large downstairs window. He turned away.

'Stay out of sight, and wait,' said Hobbes, 'I'm going in.'

He took a few steps back, sprinted forwards, hurdled the hedge and landed on all fours on the front lawn, looking like an ape in a raincoat. His knuckles grazing the grass, he jogged towards the window, knelt below it, and gave a low whistle. Dregs, who'd been sitting patiently by my side, leapt up and, barking his big head off, galloped round the hedge towards him.

Mr Slugg returned to the window, frowning and presumably wondering why a large, clearly mad dog was bounding into his garden.

'Dig!' Hobbes whispered.

Still barking, Dregs began digging on the lawn, his tail a blur of excitement. After a moment, the front door opened and Mr Slugg thundered forth, clutching a heavy wooden walking stick.

'Clear off!' he yelled, brandishing his stick like a sword and charging at Dregs, who stopped digging long enough to dodge a vicious blow that left a deep dent in the lawn.

'I'd be obliged if you would leave the dog alone, sir,' said Hobbes, stepping in front of the doorway.

'I'll have you as well,' said Mr Slugg, turning and rushing Hobbes, who ducked under a scything swipe.

'That's enough of that, sir.'

'Get out of my garden,' bellowed Mr Slugg, his face red, the veins in his neck sticking out like firehoses.

'I would appreciate a few minutes of your time, sir.'

'Clear off!'

He aimed another wild whack at Hobbes, who deflected the blow with his forearm, which threw Mr Slugg so far off balance that he fell nose-first into the wall.

'Are you injured, sir?' asked, Hobbes, his voice full of concern.

Mr Slugg groaned and rolled onto his back, his nose pumping blood. Hobbes confiscated the stick and handed him a clean white handkerchief.

'That must be painful, sir. Let me help you inside. Come on, Andy.'

Lifting the moaning casualty over one shoulder, he carried him into the house, dropping him gently onto a large black leather sofa. Mr Slugg, the handkerchief at his snout turning bright scarlet, groaned. We were in a comfortable living room, with two matching armchairs, a vast television on the wall, an impressive iron stove that was throwing out a tremendous heat, and a small bookcase filled with old paperback thrillers. The walls were covered in the sort of wallpaper that looked as if someone had hurled small splats of porridge at it before painting it a dull beige, and the carpet was thick and brown, reminding me of the tasteless soup I'd enjoyed, if that was the word, at Gollum's Logons. There was a faint stagnant odour in the house.

Hobbes stood back and saluted. 'I'm Inspector Hobbes of the Sorenchester Police, as you well know, having seen my ID. These are my associates, Andy and Dregs.'

'Andy's a ridiculous name for a dog,' said Mr Slugg with a sneer.

'I'm Andy,' I said.

'Don't I know you?' asked Mr Slugg, fixing his gaze on me.

'I ... umm ... don't think so.' For some reason, I wished he did.

He shrugged.

'I'd like to ask you some questions,' said Hobbes, 'and I'd like you to answer them, if that's all right, sir?'

'It doesn't seem as if I've got any choice, does it?' said Mr Slugg.

'Of course you do, sir. You don't have to answer, but if you don't, or don't to my satisfaction, I will have to get you to talk by other means, which you may find rather less easy.'

'A threat eh? Let's get it over then.'

'Not a threat, sir, just a fact. Firstly, may I have your full name?'

'No, firstly, what's all this about, Inspector? I haven't done anything.'

'Then you have nothing to worry about. Your name?'

'Solomon Slugg.'

'Thank you. And this is your residence?'

'Yes.'

Mr Slugg's voice had changed, becoming relaxed and mellifluous, while his pleasant smile made him appear at least twenty years younger. In fact he was nowhere near as old as I'd first thought, and was actually tall, slim and rather aristocratic in bearing. Now he'd stopped being aggressive, he seemed like a nice chap, the sort of hearty fellow you could enjoy a pint of lager with.

'Do you know Mr Septimus Slugg?' asked Hobbes.

'Mr who?'

'Septimus Slugg.'

He sighed. 'Unfortunately, Inspector, I do. He's my brother, though I haven't seen him in ages.'

'Why's that, sir?'

'It's not my fault. The truth is that he borrowed money off me – rather a lot of money – and has never seen fit to repay it. Not that I'd care if he'd made any sort of effort, but he was always a dead beat.'

'I'm sorry to hear that, sir,' said Hobbes, looking sad.

'Though, of course, I regret the estrangement, I'm better off without him in my life. But, why are you asking? What's he done this time?'

'I regret to inform you, sir, that we believe he is dead.'

'I'm not surprised. I suppose it was the drink?'

'It appears he might have been murdered.'

Mr Slugg shrugged. 'Well, I can't say I'm too surprised. I feared he'd come to a bad end one day. He always used to prefer low company and I'd guess he probably owed money to one of his so called mates who killed him for it. How did it happen?'

'I'm afraid that a person, as yet unidentified, struck him with a weapon.'

Mr Slugg shook his head. 'Poor Septimus. Oh, well.'

'Are there any other relatives we should inform?' asked Hobbes.

'No. Not any more, as far as I know.'

'You had other siblings?'

'No, it was just the two of us, and our parents are long dead.'

'Fair enough,' said Hobbes, looking thoughtful.

'I hope you catch the culprit. Do you have any leads?'

'Not yet, sir, but your information might narrow the field down a bit. You wouldn't happen to know the names of any of the low company he used to keep?'

'I'm afraid not. I purposefully kept myself free of that kind of association. A man in my position can't afford to have dirty little secrets, so I've always done my best to keep myself squeaky clean, and completely free of scandals.'

'Except for that time you got photographed when you were drunk and face down in the lettuce bed,' I said, butting in and receiving a frown from Hobbes.

'I was not drunk,' Mr Slugg said, anger in his voice, his face reddening and scowling for a moment. He pulled himself back together. 'On that occasion I was taken suddenly ill at my smallholding and collapsed. It was a shabby trick to photograph me and make political mischief of my misfortune. I'm certain those photographs ruined my campaign. I could have done so much good for this area.'

'There are all sorts of low tricks in politics, so I'm led to believe,' said Hobbes, a portrait of sympathy.

'I'm sadly afraid that is true, Inspector. However, I have always tried to play straight, though it would appear that honesty and integrity are not much valued these days.'

'You may be right, sir. Before I go, would you happen to

have any photographs of your brother?'

'No. I disposed of them. I do not like being reminded of my younger days, which were difficult through no fault of my own.'

'All right, sir. Would you happen to know where he lived?'

'As I said, I have had nothing to do with him in ages.'

'That's not a problem, sir.'

'Let me tell you frankly, Inspector, that I'm not sorry he's dead. I never wished him any harm, but if the fool managed to get himself hit on the head by a billhook, then I'm really not surprised. You may think I'm being callous, but you didn't know him. He was a wrong'un from birth. We were always so different that I could hardly believe we were related.

'Now, if that's all, Inspector, I have a busy day.'

'That is all,' said Hobbes. 'We'll be off now and thank you for your co-operation. Andy, Dregs, come along. Goodbye, sir.'

Turning away, he led us from Mr Slugg's house, shutting the front door behind him, and took us back to the car.

'So, did you get any useful information?' I asked.

'I believe I did,' said Hobbes and started the engine.

'What? Because I didn't get much from it. He seemed a nice chap.'

'Didn't he just?' said Hobbes, driving away. 'However, several interesting points came up that I will pursue. The first is to discover what's frightening him.'

'He didn't seem frightened to me. Just rather angry until you explained what was happening.'

'Then why didn't he answer the door? And why did he have that heavy stick to hand?'

'He might need it to walk. He is getting on a bit you know ... or perhaps he isn't ... he was much younger than I first thought.'

Hobbes glanced over his shoulder at me. 'He didn't need a stick when he ran from the house. Besides it was weighted with lead at the business end.'

'Like a weapon?'

He nodded.

'Why didn't you arrest him for attacking you?'

'No harm came from it, except to his nose. Hold on!'

As we reached the bottom of the hill and he turned the wheel, launching us into the main road, I slid across the seat and smacked my head against the side window. It was at such times that I especially wished I was safe with Daphne. I closed my eyes and wondered what she was doing, what treasures she was unearthing, and whether she'd find as many bodies as we had. At least that would be something to brag about next time I was being browbeaten by her intellectual colleagues. I reckoned I'd easily out-skeleton most of them.

13

As we were heading back towards town, Dregs suddenly leapt up and started barking and Hobbes stamped on the brake. I was mighty pleased the seat belt was so sturdy.

'There, I suspect, is Bob's murderer,' said Hobbes.

'What? Who? Where?' I asked, opening my eyes and slightly below my coherent best.

'There.' He pointed ahead.

Crossing the road was a huge brown, bristly beast with a brush of long dark hair standing upright along its back, as if it were sporting a Mohican. It turned to stare at us through a pair of pale, piggy eyes, giving us a good view of three-inch long tusks and alert, erect ears. Had I been foolish enough to get out and stand beside it, I reckon its shoulders would have reached up to my chest.

'The murderer?'

'Of Crackling Rosie,' said Hobbes. 'He's a big one.'

'Huge!' I said, awestruck and more than a little scared.

'He looks like he could do a lot of damage if he chose to, though Mr Catt reckoned they are shy creatures, and that it's unusual to see one out in the open during daylight hours.'

'It's probably hungry,' I said.

'Probably. This road will become busy soon, so I ought to make sure piggy doesn't get in anyone's way.'

'What are you going to do?'

'Arrest him. Stay here.'

Although I'd feared he'd say that, I didn't think it would be a good idea. I opened my mouth to comment, but he'd already gone, leaving me with a highly excited dog.

'Now my lad,' said Hobbes, taking a step towards the boar, 'you are going to cause an accident if you keep wandering into the road like that.'

The boar grunted and took a step back. Hobbes took another step forward. The boar took a further step back. The sequence continued for thirty seconds or so, the distance between them remaining the same, though the interval between steps grew shorter. Then the boar turned tail and fled into the meadow by the Soren, splashing through the dark waters, with Hobbes pounding along behind. Despite his bulk, he was all muscle and had a most impressive turn of speed. Much the same could have been said of the boar.

Dregs, who'd ceased barking, was watching intently, alert and whining, clearly wanting to be part of the chase. Hobbes put on a spurt and dived, grabbing for the boar, just as it jinked sideways. He made an enormous splash as he stretched his length in the water and sank from sight. The boar kept running, heading for the river, where it jumped in and was swept away in the rapid current.

Getting back to his feet, and shaking himself like a dog, Hobbes made a move as if to follow, shook his head, and turned back to the car.

'He got away,' I said, amazed, having developed a massive respect for his hunting abilities.

'I noticed.' He got back in and took his seat with a squelch.

'I didn't think he would,' I said.

'Nor did I, but he zagged when I expected him to zig, and when I saw he'd taken to the river I realised I couldn't catch him. Not this time anyway. All I got was this.' He held up a few hairs. 'I nearly had him by the tail, which would be nowhere near as much fun as catching a tiger by the tail.'

'Have you ever done that?'

'Just the once. I wouldn't care to repeat the experience.'

He started the engine, the car leapt forward, and we were soon heading back into Sorenchester, which still looked like the Cotswolds' answer to Venice. Gondolas wouldn't have looked out of place, though the waters had receded even since we'd been out.

'Where are we going?' I asked. 'Home?'

'To see if Dr Ramage has discovered anything new.'

Dr Ramage, looking incredibly young and pretty even in ugly white overalls that could have made her look like a snowman, was in her office, typing into an old-fashioned computer. She smiled as we entered, not appearing to notice that Hobbes was leaving puddles wherever he went. Dregs greeted her enthusiastically.

'I'm glad you're here,' she said.

My heart leapt, until I realised she was addressing Hobbes. I berated my heart for inappropriate leaping, since I was a happily married man, and it had no business leaping for other women, no matter how gorgeous.

'Is there anything new?' asked Hobbes.

'A couple of things. Firstly, I can confirm the majority of the bones are medieval.'

Hobbes nodded.

'Secondly, the recent skeleton was a man, probably in his late thirties. He was shorter than the average height, and had received a severe blow to the back of his head, fracturing the skull.'

'Was that the cause of death?' asked Hobbes.

'Such an injury would undoubtedly cause immediate unconsciousness and would probably be fatal unless the victim received immediate medical attention, and even then …'

'Clearly he did not receive immediate medical attention,' said Hobbes. 'I think I can work on the premise that he was unlawfully killed and disposed of.'

'Another point of interest,' said Cynthia, 'is that the state of the medieval bones indicates they'd been stored in a dry environment until very recently, whereas the modern skeleton came from a wet one.'

'That's ridiculous,' I said, 'since they all came from the same place.'

'Not at all,' said Hobbes. 'It confirms that the old bones were kept in the ossuary, assuming that's what it is, and the new ones had been stuffed into the culvert that runs alongside. The flood waters probably pushed them along to where we found them.'

'That's how I see it,' said Cynthia.

'Was there anything else of significance with the old bones?' Hobbes asked.

'Not really. I'll put all the details down in my report. And now to the cadaver.'

'Septimus Slugg?' I said.

She nodded and led us to the lab, the stench of which, a hint of putrefaction along with some pungent chemical, nearly turned my stomach. It would have done once.

The bones of the full skeleton were laid out on one metal table, and the body of Septimus was covered up on another. As she pulled back the sheet, I turned away, though not quickly enough to avoid a glimpse of bloated greyish skin.

'The body had been immersed in water,' she said, 'though I'm not precisely sure for how long. I would estimate for at least a month, but it might have been up to two months, because if he'd been hidden there in December or January, the cold weather would have helped preserve the soft tissues.'

Hobbes grunted acknowledgement and she continued. 'He was definitely killed by this blow to the head, and I can confirm the wound was made by a machete, or something very similar. In addition, there are these injuries to the arms. As you can see, there are three cuts to the left ulna from the same blade that caused the head wound, as well as a deep slash across the right palm.'

'Suggesting he tried to defend himself,' said Hobbes, sounding grave.

A horrible flutter passed through me as I imagined the pain and fear of the poor man's final moments. I wondered who would do such a thing, and why. Murder was uncommon around Sorenchester – Hobbes didn't approve of it – but it was clear a killer was on the loose. I was glad Daphne was well out of it.

'Mr Slugg,' Cynthia continued, 'despite being a small and slightly built man, was healthy at the time of the attack and might have put up quite a struggle.'

I heard her pull the sheet back up and turned around, trembling and breathing hard.

'Thank you, Dr Ramage,' said Hobbes, touching his forehead in an old fashioned salute. 'That was most illuminating. Is there anything else I should be aware of?'

'Not yet, Inspector. I have a couple more tests to perform, but I've given you the gist. I'll probably be able to finalise my report today.'

We said goodbye and re-joined Dregs, who we'd left in the corridor on account of the bones, although it was unlikely he'd have done anything to really embarrass us, because, like me, he'd become a gourmet since his introduction to the delights of Mrs Goodfellow's cooking.

'Now what?' I asked, fighting against Dregs's severe licking, and fearing I'd soon be as wet as Hobbes.

'Home. I need dry clothes and I could do with some grub. Visits to the mortuary always give me an appetite.'

He grinned, so it was likely he was making a joke. I chose to believe so.

14

Following an exceptionally fine chicken pie with fragrant buttered greens and leeks, I was sitting on the sofa, drinking tea. I remembered what Featherlight had said in the park and told Hobbes, treating it as something of a joke, until I noticed his serious expression and gave him the full details.

'Are you absolutely sure it was a seven-pointed star?' he asked.

'Umm ... yes ... pretty sure ...'

'It couldn't have been eight-pointed?'

'Does it really matter?'

'Yes. If it really was seven, then we might have a problem.'

'What sort of problem?'

'A nasty one. Sup up your tea, because you'd better show me where it is.'

Two minutes later, my tongue slightly scalded, we were marching towards Ride Park. Dregs was leading the way until we reached Keeper's Cottage, a small house backing onto the park, where he gave us a quick, apologetic look, leapt the wall and disappeared into the back garden.

'Where's he off to?' I asked.

'I expect he's courting again,' said Hobbes. 'He'll join us when he's done.'

No one else was in the park and the sun was drawing a faint mist from the sodden ground. No birds were singing and I was nervous, though I couldn't work out why. I tried to ignore the feeling and concentrated on the task in hand, making only one tiny navigational error by taking us into the woods a little too early. The detour did have one good outcome in that Hobbes spotted a set of boar prints, though they were several days old. Moving on, I soon found the quarry and the trampled circle of grass.

The star thing had gone.

'It was here,' I said, 'and Featherlight saw it, too.'

'I believe you,' said Hobbes, dropping to his knees, examining the area, and sniffing a great deal.

'The ground's too wet,' he said a few moments later.

'So you can't discover anything?'

'Beyond the obvious, no.'

'What's the obvious?'

'Clearly two people made the ring a few nights ago, probably the same night as the storm. The only visitors after that were you, Featherlight and Dregs and one other person, until a number of children came here later. I imagine they found the star and took it.'

'I suppose all that was evident,' I lied, 'but Featherlight reckoned the star thing was dangerous, though he wouldn't say why. Do we need to find those kids and warn them?'

He shook his head. 'Children by their nature would not be at risk.'

'What risk could there be from a star made from twigs?'

'None as such,' said Hobbes, 'unless they were spiky or poisonous ones, but since it was made of hazel ...'

'You never even saw it, so how can you possibly know that?'

He pointed to a bush on the edge of the grass ring. 'This is hazel, and these twigs were cut with a razor-sharp blade.'

'What does that mean?'

'That someone has a sharp knife, and knows the proper way to prune. Can you see how the cuts slope slightly downwards from the buds?'

I nodded. 'But I don't understand why Featherlight was worried.'

'I do,' he said. 'I think I need a word with him.'

He got to his feet, apparently oblivious to the sogginess

of his knees, and set off towards the Feathers, and since I could barely keep up with him, I had no breath to waste on questions.

The Feathers looked much the same as last time, except for the ambulance outside and the bloodied man who was limping towards it, supported by a paramedic.

'Hallo, 'allo, 'allo,' said Hobbes, 'what's going on here, then?'

'This unfortunate gentleman received an injury to his head when the dartboard fell on him,' the paramedic explained.

'Is that correct, sir?' asked Hobbes.

The man, a burly lout, nodded and groaned as he stepped aboard the ambulance. The doors closed.

'Do you believe him?' I asked, 'because I certainly don't. He had far too many injuries.'

'I believe a dartboard may have been involved at some point.'

We entered the Feathers, where Billy was helping an elderly table back to its legs, while Featherlight, grinning broadly, was hanging up the dartboard, the metal rim of which showed a head-sized dent. A handful of customers, seeing Hobbes, tried to appear as if their drinks were of immense interest, while totally failing to look cool, relaxed and as if nothing out of the ordinary had happened.

'Good afternoon,' said Hobbes.

The customers turned around, feigning surprise, and he was greeted by over-enthusiastic messages of welcome. Billy looked up, which was his default position, and Featherlight grunted.

'Make sure that dartboard is secure,' said Hobbes. 'They can inflict a lot of injury when they fall on somebody ... apparently.'

'It did fall on him,' said Featherlight.

'After you'd punched him three times?'

Featherlight glowered. 'That's a lie ... it was four times.'

'Four? I only made out three sets of knuckle prints on his face. Are you losing your touch?'

Featherlight grinned, displaying his horrible, discoloured teeth. I'd thought Hobbes's were bad enough, though they were always clean, except after he'd crunched up a raw bone.

'It was definitely four,' Billy piped up. 'A quick one to the belly, followed by three to the head.'

'What's this all about,' asked Featherlight. 'I did nothing wrong. The bloke came here looking for trouble, and I gave him some. It's what we in the business know as giving the customer what he wants. He'll live and he didn't complain, did he?'

'He did not,' said Hobbes, 'but I'd appreciate a bit more restraint in future. Casualties from your establishment put a strain on an already over-burdened health service. Superintendent Cooper asked me to point that out.'

'I was bloody restrained,' said Featherlight. 'He kept all his teeth and was able to walk out. I merely connected with my customer in a meaningful way, like it says in my management book. That's all. What more do you want from me?'

'Just be careful,' said Hobbes. 'Now, I have a question for you.'

'If I get the answer right, do I win a prize?'

Hobbes shook his head. 'How many points were on the star you showed Andy?'

'Why don't you take a look instead of bothering me? Even a rank bonehead like Caplet should be capable of finding it.'

'He was, and we examined the scene, but it had already gone. Some youngsters may have taken it.'

'Shouldn't they have been at school?'

'Most schools are still closed because of the floods.'

'In that case,' said Featherlight, 'I'll tell you. It had seven points.'

'Are you absolutely sure?'

'Even after all these years, I think I can recognise one of their heptagrams when I see one,' said Featherlight.

Hobbes looked worried, which was worrying, because hardly anything worried him.

'So, they're back,' said Featherlight.

Hobbes shrugged. 'It would appear so. I'd already seen something on Hedbury Common that had made me wonder.'

'But what's so bad about a star made of twigs?' I asked.

'It's not just any star, Caplet, it's a heptagram, sometimes called a septacle,' said Featherlight in such a soft voice that I had to look again to confirm it was actually his.

'Umm ... what does that mean?'

'I don't know, but I fear it was made by the sly ones,' said Featherlight, 'and the last time I saw one of those there were deaths.'

'Whose deaths?'

'Public deaths, probably,' said Hobbes, 'though we never identified who they were because there was nothing left to recognise, and we failed to make any arrests.'

'Even though we knew who'd done it,' said Featherlight.

Hobbes nodded. 'However, it doesn't necessarily follow that history will repeat itself. It might mean nothing.'

'But, what about the murders?' I said without thinking.

'Enough, Andy,' said Hobbes sharply. 'We've got to go.'

He thanked Featherlight, turned and shoved me out into the street. I was apologetic, fearing I'd angered him, but he appeared merely thoughtful.

'I still don't understand about this star thing,' I said as we were walking along Mosse Lane.

'I'm not surprised,' said Hobbes.

'Umm ... could you tell me about it?'

'I could,' he said, breaking his stride to swing a boot at a plastic wheelie bin, 'if I knew enough.'

The bin resounded and he kicked it again and again before turning away as it split and fell, spewing out storm damaged rugs and cushions. I'd never before seen him display such violence against an inanimate object, and it scared me.

'Featherlight looked anxious.' I said when we'd moved on a bit.

Hobbes sighed. 'He may well have cause. The last time we saw a heptagram like that was in the fifties, and before that there'd been one at the start of the Second World War. Shortly afterwards, on both occasions, we noticed those he calls the sly ones around town and there were some nasty goings on.'

We turned up Vermin Street, which was busy, a number of shops having re-opened, though a few were still pumping out. Someone shouted, 'Thief!'

A tall, slim, hooded figure, all in black, burst through the doorway of Hound's Jewellers, pursued by the tiny rotund figure of Harry Hound. The hooded one, his head down, made the mistake of running in our general direction, though Hobbes was still so deep in thought I wondered if he'd noticed, and even considered taking action myself.

He had, of course, noticed and, stepping sideways, he held up his right hand. 'Stop!'

The thief, running full tilt, did stop, but only on impact. His legs swung up, his body levelled out, and he crashed to the pavement where he lay whimpering. Hobbes bent down and retrieved a gold necklace.

'Yours I believe, Mr Hound,' he said, handing it back. 'What happened?'

'Thank you, Mr Hobbes,' said the jowly jeweller. 'This young rascal came in, saying he wanted a gift for his girlfriend, and asked to see a number of items. He grabbed this and ran when I turned my back.'

'I see.' Hobbes hoisted the thief to his feet, where he stood, swaying slightly, head bowed. 'Push your hood back, and quickly.'

The bad man revealed himself as a youth of about seventeen, who might have been quite good looking were it not for his expression of wide-eyed terror, and the acne. His face reminded me a little of a pizza with added sweetcorn.

'Daniel Duffy,' said Hobbes. 'I'm surprised at you. Why d'you do it, Danny?'

'Wanted something for Angie for Valentine's Day. The necklace looked nice, only I couldn't afford it. I didn't want to disappoint her.'

'Pah!' said Mr Hound. 'As if the poor girl could be any more disappointed than having you for a boyfriend.'

'I'm sure the young man is not all bad,' said Hobbes.

'What are you going to do to me?'

'Good point,' said Hobbes. 'That largely depends on what Mr Hound decides.' He turned towards the jeweller. 'Any ideas?'

'The ruffian must be charged with theft, and I'd like to see him in prison,' said Mr Hound, who'd grown exceedingly red in the face. 'Hanging's too good for him. I don't know what young people are coming to. It was never like this in my day.'

'Was it not?' asked Hobbes. 'Perhaps you don't remember the laundry incident?'

'Oh ... er ...yes, maybe I was forgetting.' He grinned. 'Come to think about it, I won't press charges ... just so long as you have a word with the rascal. We were all young once.'

'I'll make sure I do,' said Hobbes, 'when I'm less busy.'

'That sounds fair enough,' said Mr Hound, chuckling and grinning for some reason that escaped me.

'Very good, sir,' said Hobbes.

'Am I going to prison?'

'No, Danny, not on this occasion, but I will be round to see you very soon, and then we will have a friendly little chat.'

'And then what?'

'Then you might wish you were in prison,' said Hobbes, with a sudden grin that showed his huge yellow teeth to their best advantage.

Danny cringed, looking more like a frightened little boy than a hardened criminal. His eyes bulged and his knees knocked so hard I could actually hear them over the street sounds.

'But for now,' said Hobbes, 'I have things to do, so let's have no more nonsense. How much is the necklace worth?'

'One hundred and fifty pounds,' said Mr Hound.

'Here you are then,' said Hobbes, drawing a fistful of notes from his wallet, handing them to the bewildered shopkeeper and turning back to Danny with the necklace. 'Take this, give it to Angie, and behave yourself from now on, if you know what's good for you. I will see you soon.'

He strode away, leaving Danny and Mr Hound open-mouthed and staring.

'That was an extraordinary thing to do,' I said, when I'd caught up, 'but why? He's a thief.'

'He certainly attempted to be one. However, I happen to know young Angie, who's a sweet girl and has been having a hard time. I wouldn't wish to make it any harder. As for Danny, his head is like an old empty barn – there's nothing in it, though his heart is in the right place. If I'd arrested him, he might have gone to prison, which would not benefit anyone. After we've had our little chat, I doubt he'll steal again. My way means he gets what he wants, Angie gets a nice surprise tomorrow, and Mr Hound gets his money. No one loses out.'

'Except you. You're a hundred and fifty pounds down on the deal. That doesn't seem right.'

He shrugged. I guessed he could afford it for he seemed wealthy enough, although few would have known, since he preferred a simple life, and rarely spent money on himself. Yet, he could be extraordinarily generous when the mood took him, as he had often been to me. However, the main thing I took from the conversation was a useful reminder that Valentine's Day was coming up, since with all the recent excitement it had almost slipped my mind. Even so, I was proud that I had remembered before Daphne left, and had secreted a nice card with a lovey-dovey message, along with a small box of her favourite chocolates from Chocolate Ears, a posh new shop on Rampart Street. I smiled to myself, thinking about what she'd say when she found them, and made a plan to head for Gollum's Logons in the morning and use one of its computers to send her a nice, soppy email. In fact, as I mulled it over, I decided there was nothing to stop me sending one right then while the idea was fresh in my head.

'I ... umm ... think I'll head to Gollum's Logons and send Daphne an email.'

'Good idea,' he said. 'I read your review of the place, but haven't looked in there yet. I'll come along and I might just try the coffee.'

We turned down Rampart Street, passing Chocolate Ears which, despite having been flooded, was doing a roaring trade, and headed for Goat Street, which had escaped the worst of the recent events. I'd been a little confused by my previous visit to Gollum's Logons, an unusual attempt at an internet café with a Lord of the Rings theme, and with pretensions to high class restaurant cuisine. Although the coffee had been pretty good, the wine acceptable and the service passable, my meal had been greasy, cold and tasteless and the broadband hadn't quite been adequate. It had taken me most of a week to get the right balance in my review of that one.

Somewhere, a woman screamed.

'No coffee for me I'm afraid,' said Hobbes and loped away at sprint speed.

How he could move so fast with his knuckles nearly scraping the ground was beyond me. When I'd experimented, I'd run headlong into a lamppost and given myself a fine head lump. The worst part, other than pain, had been trying to explain exactly what I'd been attempting to a passing American tourist who'd stopped to help me as I lay in the road. He'd listened patiently, thought for a moment, and called me a dumb-ass, an epithet I'd probably richly deserved. Hobbes, of course, never ran into anything he didn't mean to. As he turned out of sight, I considered following to see what all the fuss was about, but decided to attend to Daphne first.

15

There weren't many customers in Gollum's Logons, other than a couple of burly young guys I suspected were students on account of their Sorenchester University rugby shirts, and a strikingly good looking young woman with a rucksack by her side. I nodded at the little waitress, who was looking rather self-conscious, probably because she was dressed as a hobbit. She directed me to a computer and took my order for a cappuccino. It took me a while and a couple of attempts to remember how to logon to my email account, but I got there and felt quite proud of myself.

I scrolled through the list. The first two mails were suggesting remedies for my being tragically under-endowed, so I deleted them as probable spam. After that came eight from Daphne, which I started opening in chronological order. The first seven, her attempts to contact me, were filled with love and concern and were quite heart-warming, although part of me resented the implication that I might be incapable of looking after myself.

Then I opened the latest one. It was entitled 'Chocolate' and I grinned to myself, wondering what nice things she'd say. My complacent mood lasted until I clicked on it.

Andy, what the hell were you thinking? Were you actually thinking at all, or are you just an idiot? Whatever possessed you to do such a thing? (I'm assuming it was you – after all who else could it have been?) When I came back to my tent this lunchtime, I found it had been overrun by millions of little yellow ants. Millions! They were all through my luggage, in my clothes and even in my bed. Everywhere! And can you guess why? They'd been attracted by the sticky brown goo that was oozing from my holdall! When I opened it up, there was a box of chocolates that had melted and run through everything. It has completely ruined my smart dress which I needed for tonight, when I'm supposed to be meeting an important guest.

I'm really angry with you right now and I going to let my temper cool before I write again, which might take a while as it's nearly fifty degrees out here. I've got a headache and I'm tired and I can't lie down until I've got rid of all these ants. They bite, too, and I'm covered in unsightly itchy blotches.

Thank you so much and I hope you're satisfied.

That was all. There was no message of love, no indication that she was missing me, and no hope. She hadn't even signed off with her name. First I felt sick and confused, and then I became furious with myself.

'You really are a complete idiot,' I muttered, grinding my teeth. 'You're a total ass…'

'Excuse me, what did you say?' asked one of the students, who was close by.

'Umm …' I said, 'did I say that out loud? I didn't mean to.'

'You shouldn't even have thought it. I've never done anything to you, have I?'

'No, but …'

'Apologise.'

'But …'

'If you don't, I'll make you,' said the student, springing to his feet.

I couldn't help notice how tall and powerfully built he was. His face had taken on a similar tinge to the one exhibited by Featherlight in a rage.

'All right, but …'

As he walked towards me, bunching his fists, which, while not in the same league as Hobbes's or Featherlight's, were on the massive side, I kicked backwards, making my chair scoot across the floor. I bumped into something that screamed like a girl. Crockery shattered, and the hobbit, a tray still clutched in her hands, was sprawling among a debris of white plates, glittering cutlery and devastated confectionery.

'Sorry,' I said, getting to my feet and ducking under a straight punch from my assailant, who, to judge from his expression, was as unimpressed by my manoeuvre as I was by his fearsome breath.

'First you insult me ...' he said swinging again.

I blocked the punch with my left forearm, something I'd once seen Hobbes do, only he'd not squealed like I did. It really hurt, and my hand went numb and tingly hot at the same time.

'And then,' he continued, as I retreated, 'you attack that poor girl.'

His next punch, a real swinging clubbed effort, would probably have taken my head off, but I was on a roll – a cheese and onion one by the smell of it – and slipped. Missing threw him off balance and he lurched towards me as I fell backwards over the unfortunate hobbit girl who'd just got into a kneeling position. As my head went down, my feet flew up and booted him on the point of the chin. He collapsed as if poleaxed, going face-down into a sponge cake, which at least gave him a soft landing.

Apologising profusely to everyone who could hear, I got up. The other student was on his feet, looking furious, but dithering, clearly wanting to give me a damned good thrashing, but thinking he should first check on his chum, from whose face the hobbit girl was scraping jam and cream with a spoon.

The other woman, the attractive one, smiled. 'Cool

moves, dude,' she said in a strong American accent.

Making a show of nonchalance, I gave her my best devil-may-care grin, and sauntered towards the door. As soon as I was in the street and out of sight, I fled, congratulating myself on having got away unscathed. I'd just glanced back to ensure I was not being pursued when rough hands seized me. A coarse sack, stinking of garlic, was pulled over my head and my arms were pinioned to my sides, rendering me helpless, though I struggled and kicked as well as I could. The hands shoved me along, making me stumble up some steps. A door clicked shut and the muted sounds made me think I was indoors.

'I've got you now,' said a voice that, even accounting for the sack over my head, sounded muffled and strange. 'I'm going to teach you what happens when you don't show respect.'

Something hit me across my legs. I fell and, as I lay there writhing, I was pummelled all over. The only good thing was that whoever was doing it spared my face. The beating continued until I passed out.

When I came awake, I almost wished for oblivion again for my body was a mass of aches and I was shivering. It took a while, but I freed my arms and pulled the sack from my head to find myself surrounded by thick bushes and in semi-darkness. I had no idea where I was but, as I tried to rub life back into my hands, the church clock struck the quarter hour. To judge by the loudness, it was nearby. I rolled onto my hands and knees, groaning at the pain in my ribs, and crawled through the branches and twigs until I emerged onto a squelching lawn. I was in the old graveyard by Church Fields, right beside the tomb of the unknown worrier. Down the slope, the lake was still flooded, and a faint pink glow on the horizon made me suppose it was shortly before sunrise. I needed the support of a tree to stand up, and then staggered towards the gate, which, with its rusting steel bars, reminded me of a medieval portcullis, especially as it was shut with a heavy chain and a massive padlock. Outside, the streetlamps were still lit, and the streets seemed deserted. My watch had been smashed in the beating, and I couldn't see the church clock from where I was, but it was clearly next morning. Without expecting anything, I rattled the chain and tugged at the padlock. The result was just as expected.

I called for help, and even resorted to screaming, but no one was around yet, and kicking the gate did little to relieve my frustration, though the exquisite torment of my toes took my mind off the other aches and pains for a few moments.

Climbing over was an idea, though the barbed wire on top made it a poor one. However, doing nothing was not a great option either, because my clothes were damp, the sky was clear and there was a hint of frost. I feared I'd freeze to death before the good townsfolk were up and about.

Seeing no other possibilities, I made a bold attempt at scaling the gate, only to find the bars were covered in condensation and as slithery as wet fish. It was only luck that I didn't hurt myself as I slipped and fell. Since it seemed I would just have to endure and hope for release, I pulled my jacket closer, stuck my frozen hands into its pockets, and could have kicked myself in frustration. I might have, had I not already been too sore for such nonsense. Instead, I had to be content with calling myself an idiot, for only an idiot would have forgotten his mobile phone. I pulled it out and tried to figure out where Hobbes's number was listed. Finding it at last, I pressed to call.

It was answered almost immediately.

'Inspector Hobbes. How may I help you?'

'It's me, Andy,' I said. 'I'm sorry to wake you ...'

'I wasn't asleep. Are you calling to say you won't be back

for supper?'

'No, I'm stuck ... umm ... what do you mean supper?'

'I mean the meal we are accustomed to eat in the evening. You know that. Are you all right?'

'Not really. I'm locked in the old graveyard and can't get out. I've been here all night ... umm ... I think I have. Actually, what time is it?'

'Quarter past six, and you haven't been out all night. It's still Thursday. I'll come and get you. Are you at the gate?'

'Yes.'

'Well, don't go away.'

'I can't.'

Only a minute or two later, Hobbes came loping along Blackdog Street towards me. As he crossed the road, his grin changed into a look of concern. 'What happened to you?'

'I got put in a sack and I've been beaten up and I'm cold.'

'I'll have you out of there in a jiffy.'

On reaching the gate, he took the chain in his bear hands, stared at it for a moment, gritted his teeth and twisted until one of the links came apart with a groan like a man suffering a bad hangover. As he unwound the chain and released me, I stumbled out, and, like a maiden swooning in an old film, collapsed into his arms.

'Thank you,' I said, my teeth chattering.

'You're welcome.'

As I headed homewards, leaning on his arm, ashamed of my weakness, I explained what had happened as well as I could. He helped me up the steps into the house where Dregs, with a noticeably hangdog expression, looked up from his place on the mat, wagged his tail once and slumped.

'What's up with him?' I asked.

'I fear his courting went awry,' said Hobbes.

The air, besides the usual feral taint and a slight doggy odour, was filled with delicious savoury aromas that, despite my pains and shivers, set my mouth to watering. I would have been glad to go straight into the kitchen and eat, but Mrs Goodfellow saw me first and half-dragged, half-cajoled me upstairs and into yet another hot bath.

In all honesty, it was a wise decision, for, although my stomach and salivary glands might have disagreed, the warm water soon began to revive me, despite the embarrassment of having the old girl clucking over my collection of bruises and scrapes. After adding a curious minty-smelling green gunk to the tub, she called Hobbes, who appeared in the doorway and, much to my discomfiture, examined my collection of injuries.

'Somebody has certainly worked you over. Do you have any idea who did it?'

'No, not really. There was a sack over my head. I ... umm ... did have a bit of trouble beforehand, but I don't think it could possibly have been connected.'

Hobbes took another look at my back. 'It appears the attacker used a stick for a few blows, but most of your injuries are from boot or fist. Whoever did it must have unusually large hands and feet. Do you know anyone who fits that description?'

I shook my head and squawked as a pain stabbed between my shoulder blades. 'Only you and Featherlight,' I said.

'I can assure you it wasn't either of us. Enjoy your bath, but don't take too long, because I'm in need of my victuals.' He left us to it.

'Are you fit enough to bathe yourself, dear?' asked Mrs Goodfellow.

'I think so.'

As she left, I relaxed. I'd never felt comfortable with having no clothes on in front of her, despite her claims to have been a nurse and to have seen far worse than I'd ever showed. Still, feeling self-conscious didn't actually harm me, and her cooking and kindness had always led me to forgive her, even after she'd dunked Dregs and me together in the same flea bath when we'd become infested after hanging out with werewolves.

I wallowed for a while, contemplating my bruises while the warmth soothed away much of the pain. Unfortunately, it gave me time to think about the terrible thing I'd done to Daphne, as well as to remember that I'd never got round to sending her my Valentine's Day email. I was filled with a horrible fear that my thoughtless gift, though well-meaning, might mean I'd lost her, and the mere idea nearly made me feel sick.

The knocking on the bathroom door brought me back. 'Supper's ready as soon as you are,' said Hobbes, 'so you'd better get a move on. And quickly!'

A few minutes later, wearing neatly pressed, clean clothes, I headed downstairs, where the cooking smells encouraged me to believe that life was not so bad. Mrs Goodfellow started dishing up as soon as I appeared. Though the meal was only slow-cooked beans and bacon, a simple dish, it had been transformed by the old girl's golden touch into a delight fit for a king. I said as much when my plate was empty and my stomach was as full as was practical.

'It truly was a dish fit for a king,' said Hobbes. 'King George III instigated an annual bean feast after tasting it during a visit to Woolwich Arsenal.'

'King George III? Did you ever meet him?' My question was a cheeky attempt to get an idea of his age. I knew he was unfeasibly old, but how old?

'Of course not,' he said. 'I've rarely had sufficient time to meet royalty. Shall we go through to the sitting room?'

Thwarted, I nodded and followed him. I'd once asked

Mrs Goodfellow his age, but she hadn't known, other than that he'd been a police officer before the war, by which she meant the First World War. When I'd enquired if she thought he was immortal, she'd shrugged and said that he had been so far. Dying, she'd said, would be the last thing he'd ever do.

As we sat down on the sofa, a thought crossed my mind. 'When you ran off earlier, what was that all about?'

'A lady who works as a cleaner at The Italian Job was throwing some rubbish bags into the bins at the back when she was surprised by the wild boar.'

'In town? But I thought they were shy.'

'He is shy. As soon as he saw her he fled.'

'So, it's not dangerous.'

'I wouldn't go as far as that,' said Hobbes. 'Had she been in his path, and there was no other way out, he might have attacked. Fortunately, she wasn't, and, fortunately, she's not the sort that is easily cowed ...'

'Or do you mean boared?' I said with a chuckle.

'... cowed. She was keen to get back to work after a stiff brandy.'

'Good for her.'

'However, if the boar has taken to coming into town, the danger to the public has increased considerably. I'll have to do something about him, if there's time, because I do have a murderer to catch, and that business on Hedbury Common has not yet reached a satisfactory conclusion.'

'What did happen there?'

He sighed. 'Horrible things. I wish to interview somebody who might be able to assist me with my enquiries, but she has not yet turned up.'

'She?'

Hobbes nodded. 'The name she uses is Matilda Kielder.'

'Umm ... do you think she might be in danger?'

'No, I fear she is the danger ... but here's the tea! Thank

you, lass.'

Mrs Goodfellow set the tray on the table before us. Hobbes leant forward, filled two mugs, handed one to me, piled a pyramid of sugar into his and stirred it with his index finger, a trick that still alarmed me. How his finger wasn't cooked was beyond me, since the tea was volcano-hot. He raised his mug, quaffed it in one and poured himself another, as I sipped mine, protecting my lips and tongue. I'd barely wet my mouth when he got to his feet, drained his mug and yawned.

'I'm going to bed,' he said, though it was only seven-thirty. He loped upstairs.

Since there was nothing interesting or amusing on the television, I thought of going out for a lager, but didn't really fancy one, or want to risk any more trouble. Instead I just sat and thought. It had been another difficult day. Being on my own and staying with Hobbes and Mrs Goodfellow had been a pleasant change of routine, but I wanted Daphne back, and was desperately worried how she'd react to my thoughtless gift. Reason told me she wasn't likely to stay mad forever, but old insecurities kept sneaking in whenever I dropped my guard.

'Are you all right, dear?'

Mrs Goodfellow's question from just next to my right ear made me jump to my feet and crack my shin on the coffee table. My yelp of pain brought Dregs in from the kitchen to stare.

'I was,' I said, rubbing the bruised bit. 'Why?'

'You looked troubled.'

'I was just thinking ...'

'Ah, that would explain it.' She smiled.

'... If you must know, I was thinking about Daphne, and how much I miss her. You have no idea ...'

'I think I do,' she said.

'Umm ... yes ... I suppose you must do. I was forgetting.' I was ashamed of myself. Mrs Goodfellow's husband was still believed to be in Bali. 'How do you cope?'

'I keep busy. The old fellow takes a bit of looking after, and then there's my Kung Fu and marital arts classes. Still there are times ...'

I nodded and thought sad thoughts, until I recalled something Hobbes had mentioned. 'Do you know a woman called Kielder?'

'Matilda Kielder? I know of her but I only actually saw her once, and then only briefly.'

'Do you know anything about her?'

'Not a great deal, dear. She brought a lot of bother to the old fellow a few years ago. I gather she was something of a man-eater.'

'Do you mean she fancied him?' I'd always struggled to believe any woman, or at least any human woman, could have the hots for Hobbes. There was just something too feral about him. Besides, not even his mother would have considered him good looking, though, in fairness, there was a rough gallantry about him.

'No. She ate men. Really. Well, bits of them. Perhaps she was more of a man taster.'

'I suppose she couldn't eat a whole one, especially a whole Hobbes.'

'Not in one sitting, dear, and so far as I know, she never took a bite out of him.'

'How come I've never heard of her before? And how come she's not locked up?'

'I can't explain your ignorance,' she said with a gummy grin, 'but she's not locked up because she was never caught.'

'I thought Hobbes always got his man.'

'So he does, but Miss Kielder is a woman, and you know how he can be with them.'

I nodded, remembering how close he'd come to death

after trusting Narcisa Witcherley, my former editor's criminally insane wife, who'd shot him. I, too, had taken a bullet during those desperate hours, but had still acted heroically, at least by my standards. It served as a good reminder of the danger of getting involved, though, for reasons I couldn't quite understand, I rather enjoyed the excitement, or I did when I wasn't too terrified or in too much pain. Yet no one could have denied how much my life and my character had improved since I'd first met him, and the old girl, of course. The thought cheered me up a little, and when I eventually went to bed, carrying a cup of cocoa, I was in a far better frame of mind than earlier, despite lingering concerns. In all honesty, I had a whole litany of things to worry about beyond the normal background level, including the attacks on my person, possible consequences for having knocked out the student, blackmail, man-eaters and murderers. However, Daphne was foremost in my mind.

I suspected I'd enjoy little sleep that night, with all my anxieties, the bodily injuries, and a sore throat that was developing. However, just as I was starting to think I'd never drop off, I dropped off. On waking next morning to a dull grey day, I suspected the old girl had put a little something into my cocoa, and, not for the first time, I was grateful. My bumps and bruises didn't feel too bad when I tested them, so I got up and prepared for a new day.

16

Although I went downstairs looking forward to breakfast, I couldn't stop thinking about Daphne. I couldn't decide whether to call her as soon as possible or to give her more cooling-off time. Despite longing to be decisive, I sat and dithered and the result of my deep thought was that I had no recollection of actually eating, though I must have done. Hobbes, however, devoured a vast bowl of Sugar Puffs, a sure sign something was bothering him.

When he'd finished, I asked how his investigations were going.

He shook his head and looked glum, which was not a normal expression for him. 'Not well, I'm afraid. I've made little progress with the Septimus Slugg murder, and none with the earlier one, although Dr Ramage has given me a rough sketch showing an impression of how the skeleton's face might have looked in life. In addition, it'll be a chore to catch that boar, and I'll have to become a magic wielder to arrest Miss Kielder, if she really is back.'

'On the bright side,' I quipped, 'your poetry is improving.'

'I beg your pardon?'

'Chore, boar. Wielder, Kielder ... you're a poet and you didn't know it.'

'I see. I'm not convinced accidental rhyming counts as poetry, though it might pass as doggerel, I suppose. I would rather regard poetry as the interpretation of nature and the understanding of humankind written in a style that blends delicacy of words with grace of harmony and rhythm.'

'Really?'

'There are, of course, other opinions. I respect them, even if I can't agree with them.'

'I thought it was all about rhyming.'

'No, dear,' said Mrs Goodfellow. 'Poetry is when emotions find the right thoughts, the thoughts find the right words, and the words find the right form.'

'Is it?' I asked.

'It can be,' said Hobbes, 'but I must away, because, although I'd be happy to discuss poetry until the lowing herd winds slowly o'er the lea, I have interviews to conduct.'

'Eh? What lowing herd?'

'He means he could discuss poetry until the cows come home,' said Mrs Goodfellow. 'He's misquoting Gray.'

'Of course,' I said. 'Umm ... what's grey?'

'Thomas Gray the poet, dear, from his *Elegy Written in a Country Churchyard.*'

'Yes, I thought it was,' I bluffed.

'You can come along if you'd like,' said Hobbes. 'It might keep you out of trouble.'

'I'd love to, but ... umm ... I really should call Daphne. It is Valentine's Day, after all. Is that all right?'

'I'm in no rush. You can still come if you hurry up about it.'

'Thanks.'

'And hurry up now,' said Hobbes a few moments later. 'What's stopping you?'

'They've had a row,' said Mrs Goodfellow. 'Haven't you, dear?'

I nodded. 'How do you know?'

'It's written in your face, and your behaviour.'

'My behaviour?'

'It has been rather distracted, dear. You poured tea into the sugar dish instead of your mug and drank it, and you buttered two slices of toast, put them in a bowl and added milk and marmalade. Then you ate the mess without apparently noticing. You are showing classic symptoms of having fallen out with your beloved.'

'True,' said Hobbes, 'but your classic symptoms are more extreme than most. Go and make that call ... and quickly!'

I did as I was told. The only trouble was that nobody answered. After the third attempt, I slammed down the phone.

'Not in?' said Hobbes.

I shook my head.

'You could always text her.'

'I suppose I could, but I'd rather speak to her.' The truth was that, while I did know how to text, I had clumsy fingers and, anyway, I was suspicious that my phone had been possessed by imps since it had a tendency to put my words through the blender, changing them into utterly incoherent gibberish, or occasionally into downright insulting rudeness. My last attempt had been a couple of weeks earlier, when Daphne had texted to say she'd be back early, but would have to be heading out for a lecture on Egypt within an hour. When I'd replied, attempting to let her know that I'd prepare an early dinner, the imps had struck and I'd instead informed her that I'd preserve a warty donger. Subsequent attempts at correction had resulted in such a bizarre stream of balderdash that she'd come straight home, worrying I'd had a stroke.

'You know best,' said Hobbes. 'Are you ready now?'

'Yes.' I grabbed my coat and followed him out the door. 'Where are we going?'

'We are going to see Mr Godley.'

'Old Augustus or Kev the Rev?'

'Augustus. I want to show him Dr Ramage's picture.'

'Why? I know she's very pretty, but at his age?' Augustus Godley, having survived for over one hundred years, was the oldest human in town.

'I meant the sketch Dr Ramage gave me,' said Hobbes, striding along Blackdog Street, 'not a portrait of her.'

I kept up, though the effort cost me. The streets had

somewhat dried, though huge puddles still remained in places, and pumps were still pumping out. We crossed onto Moorend Road, where Mr Godley occupied the first of an impossibly cute row of alms-houses. Piles of sandbags against the wall suggested they'd been well protected against the deluge. Hobbes opened the garden gate, and we walked to the diminutive stone porch with its distinctive crust of lichens and moss. He rang the doorbell.

It was a long wait, for Mr Godley, though mentally acute, had physically slowed to sloth pace. After a few minutes, the door opened and he stood before us, his face as wrinkled as desiccated walnuts, his hair and bushy whiskers as white as vampire's teeth, his narrow shoulders stooped with age. His blue eyes, however, were sharp and alert.

'Sergeant Hobbes ... I mean Inspector Hobbes. How nice to see you. I suppose you want my help?'

'If you can spare the time, Mr Godley.'

'I was just getting ready for my parachute club, but I've got a few minutes. Come in and bring young Sandy with you. Where's your dog? Is he all right?'

'He's moping,' said Hobbes, following Mr Godley along the musty dusty and gloomy stone-paved corridor that led to his small, cluttered sitting room, where a coal fire burned brightly and dispelled any chills. 'He's been unlucky in love and wants to spend some time with his thoughts.'

'How very sad. He's a fine animal. Would you like a cup of tea?'

'No, thank you very much. We've just breakfasted.'

'Where's your budgie?' I asked, missing the little blue chatterer and fearing the worst.

'Taking a shower in the kitchen,' said Augustus, lowering himself into one of the faded velvet-covered armchairs and indicating that we should occupy the others. 'Now what are you here for?'

Hobbes pulled a sheet of paper from his pocket, unfolded

it and handed it to the old man, who smoothed it flat, and peered at it.

'Not bad,' he said after a minute or two, 'but, if you don't mind, I'd say it's not up to your usual standard.'

Hobbes chuckled. 'It's not one of mine.'

'Then why show it to me? The technique is adequate, but the face has no animation. Who did it?'

'A forensic pathologist,' said Hobbes, 'and you'll probably forgive the lack of animation when I tell you this is a rough impression of how a recently discovered skeleton might have appeared in life. I was hoping you might recognise him.'

'I don't.' Mr Godley stared at the sketch again and shook his head. 'Is that all? Because my taxi will be here any time now.'

'That is all,' said Hobbes, taking back the paper. 'It was a long shot, but worth taking. Thank you.'

As Hobbes and I were getting to our feet, Mr Godley raised his hand and frowned. 'Actually, there may be something ...'

'What?' said Hobbes.

'I remember there was this boy at my school, and it's not that your sketch looks much like him, or even as I imagine he might have been as an adult, but there's something.'

'Well done,' said Hobbes. 'What was his name?'

'Alas, that I can't remember. He was a couple of years younger than me, so a lower form of life to a ten year old ...'

Hobbes shrugged.

'... but there may be a record of him in the old school annals.'

'Which school?' said Hobbes, brightening.

'The Green Coat School. Do you remember it?'

'Yes, of course, but it must have closed over sixty years ago.'

'However, there may still be school records and

photographs in existence. I believe they went into the *Bugle's* archive.'

'I doubt it,' I said. 'I work there and there's no room for much of an archive. There's a small store room, but that's mostly full of ink and chemicals they used in the olden days.'

'I expect much of the archive is on those new-fangled computers,' said Mr Godley, 'but there may still be physical records. I'd ask the editor, or the owner.'

'That is very helpful. Thank you again,' said Hobbes, and we took our leave.

As we left the house, I had to ask a question that had been bugging me. 'He doesn't really go parachuting, does he?'

'Not anymore, but he's still a member of the club. He sometimes pilots their plane.'

'You're joking ... aren't you?'

'No. His body might have slowed, but his hands and brain are still quick, and he hasn't crashed since he was last shot down. He flew Spitfires in the war, you know.'

'I never knew that. He doesn't look very heroic.'

'Heroes don't on the whole. I think we should pay a visit to the *Bugle* and see if they do have the archive.'

'Yes, I suppose we should. Why was it called the Green Coat School? It's a funny name.'

'Because the pupils originally wore green coats as part of the school uniform. There's a statue of one in the church. Haven't you seen it?'

'Yes, I believe I have. I didn't know what it was, but it looked very quaint. Mr Godley didn't dress like that, did he?'

Hobbes shook his head. 'The statue represents how the pupils dressed in Victoria's day. He's not quite that old.'

As we turned onto Moss Lane I attempted to match his stride length while chatting, but caught my foot on a flagstone the flood had raised. I would have stretched my length in the gutter had he not grabbed my shoulder. For the rest of the walk, I kept quiet, concentrating on keeping upright and not entangling my feet, annoyed by my clumsiness, which I used to consider as the root of many of my problems, until Hobbes had pointed out that I was probably no more clumsy than average, but had a tendency to inflate any mistakes to the size of a hippopotamus. Since then, although not entirely convinced by his argument, I had frequently chastised myself for this failing, adding it to my ever-lengthening list of imperfections.

Swaggering towards us were five large young men, who appeared to belong to the rugby-playing tendency, an impression confirmed by their Sorenchester University Rugby Club hoodies. I recognised two of them, noting that the one I'd kicked had a sticking plaster on his chin. Butterflies took wing in my stomach when he pointed.

'That's the runt who kicked me in the face!'

'Let's scrag him and teach him to respect his betters,' said one, who was even bulkier than the first.

'I'm sorry about yesterday,' I said, 'but it really was just an unfortunate accident.'

They didn't seem to be in the mood for listening to reason and quickly surrounded us.

'There will be no scragging,' said Hobbes, smiling. 'What's all this about?'

'Stay out of it, old man,' said a third, probably the most thickset and burly of the lot. 'It's not your business. Back off, unless you want some, too.'

'Some what?'

'Some pain, granddad. Clear off. Your little chum attacked James, and we don't stand for that sort of thing.'

'Nor do I,' said Hobbes, pleasantly. 'What exactly did you do, Andy?'

'Nothing.' I squirmed, suspecting my face was turning red. 'Well, I did sort of knock that guy out, but I didn't mean it.'

'He insulted me for no reason,' said James, and when I remonstrated, he kicked me in the face. We're going to teach him some manners.'

'Everybody calm down,' said Hobbes, with a reassuring smile.

'Please don't hurt me,' I said, getting worried, as the pack drew in. 'I'm truly sorry for what happened. Let me explain …'

I never felt the first blow, or the next. In fact I didn't feel any at all. Hobbes blocked the lot.

'Stop it,' he said after a few moments. 'This is unseemly behaviour.'

The students, having retreated a step or two to rub bruised arms and shins, charged, front, side and rear. He never even raised a finger. Instead, picking me up by the shoulders, he ducked, dodged and weaved. Within a few seconds, which I saw mainly as a series of blurry images, four of the students contrived to collide, and lay in a moaning heap on the pavement. The last one standing, seeing the carnage, turned and ran. Unfortunately for him, he ran straight into a wall. Putting me down, Hobbes grabbed him as he fell and laid him to rest with the others.

'Thank you for that,' I said, still a little dizzy, and explained what had happened. 'So, you see, it really was an unfortunate set of calamities.'

'I see,' he said, checking no serious damage had been sustained by the students. 'I might doubt the story if others told it, but with you, Andy, it has the ring of truth. These hearty young fellows are clearly prone to aggressive behaviour, and I fear someone will get hurt, one of these days.'

To judge by their groans, they'd been hurt already, but I didn't point that out, just grateful Hobbes had been with me. He seemed thoughtful.

'What's up?' I asked.

'Well,' he said, 'although it's by no means unusual for some of the students to display arrogance and to be a little boisterous, they are not usually so much trouble, and physical violence is rare. However, these young fellows seemed overly belligerent, don't you think?'

I nodded, although I had provoked similar hostility in others before. Still, he was right. This lot had seemed a little unhinged.

'Another thing that interests me,' he continued, 'is why they were using an internet café, or rather an internet restaurant, when they almost certainly have their own devices.'

He dropped to his hands and knees, sniffing the bodies, which was puzzling to me as they smelled of changing rooms even from where I was. It reminded me of the school gym, where I and my classmates had spent many a miserable hour being tormented by the psychopathic games teacher. After a few moments Hobbes reached into one of their trouser pockets and pulled out a small plastic bottle. 'Aha!' he said.

'What's that?'

'It's a small plastic bottle.'

'Yes, but what's in it?'

He unscrewed it, poured a number of seven-sided pink pills into the palm of his hand and wrinkled his nose as if at an unpleasant smell.

'What are they?'

'Anabolic steroids.'

'The things that give you big muscles?'

'They can do, and sportsmen have been known to use them to improve performance and stamina. In high doses they can also increase irritability and aggression.'

'Well that certainly seems likely. Are they legal?'

'That rather depends on where they come from, what they are used for, and what the precise ingredients are.

Though some are legitimately prescribed by doctors, they are often sold on the black market, and if they're used without supervision and knowledge they can be dangerous, and not only to the users. Their use is certainly not permitted in sports.'

'What are you going to do?' I asked. 'Arrest them?'

'I'd rather not. The cells are already full.'

'I didn't know there'd been a crime wave.'

'There hasn't. They are temporarily occupied by members of the public whose homes have been flooded, since there's a scarcity of alternative accommodation. The church halls and other suitable locations are also full to bursting. Happily, more long-term arrangements are being worked out.'

'So, what are you going to do with this lot?'

'I'll confiscate their pills, and have a quiet chat with them when they are in a more receptive mood.'

'Like when they're fully conscious?'

'That would help.'

'But you can't just leave them lying here.'

'I can you know.'

'But shouldn't they be taken to the hospital?'

'The hospital is busy with flood casualties.' He squatted down, sorted the heap into individuals, examined them and rolled them into a neat line next to a wall. 'None of them has any serious injuries and I've made them comfortable enough. They'll wake up soon and may well have headaches and some bruising, but, being rugby players, they'll be used to that sort of thing.'

'Perhaps it'll teach them a lesson,' I said.

'I doubt it,' said Hobbes, 'but my little chat will. Let's go.'

As we walked away, they were all starting to sit up and were looking utterly bewildered. We carried on past the Feathers, where no violence was taking place, and crossed into The Shambles towards the offices of the *Bugle*.

17

Basil Dean was alone, keeping an eye on us while the other appeared to be checking the football scores. He nodded and stood up.

'Hiya. How may I help, Inspector?'

'Good morning, Mr Dean. Do you have the Green Coat School papers in your archive?'

Basil shook his head.

'Can't you check?' I asked.

'There'd be no point. The archive was here – we kept it in the basement for many years – but space is tight and we had a clear out. We removed a century of clutter. Some material was scanned and stored on computer, but I clearly remember Editorsaurus Rex taking the Green Coat School boxes away. He thought that, though they might have historical significance, they were unlikely to contain anything newsworthy.'

'What did Mr Witcherley do with them?' asked Hobbes.

'I imagine he chucked them into a skip, or took them down the dump, but I don't know for certain. You could ask him. Here's his phone number.'

Basil reached into his desk drawer and handed Hobbes a card.

'Thank you, Mr Dean,' said Hobbes. 'May I use your phone? Mine had a dunking and I haven't had time to replace it.'

'Be my guest. You can use that desk.'

Hobbes poked in the numbers.

'Good morning, Mr Witcherley,' he said after a short pause. 'Inspector Hobbes here ... Yes, I am fully recovered ... There are some scars, but nothing to worry about ... How is Mrs Witcherley? ... I'm sorry to hear that ... and she's still being treated? ... It must be a worry ... Yes, there is a reason. Can you recall what you did with the archives from the Green Coat School? ... In your attic? Excellent ... May I see them? ... When? ... I'll be with you within the hour. I'm mostly interested in records from the nineteen-twenties ... I'll be bringing Andy, if that's all right with you ... No, not Capstan, Caplet ... Yes, it is an odd name ... French I believe ... Goodbye, sir.'

I gulped for I'd always found the Editorsaurus intimidating. Yet, since he'd retired to look after his murderously insane wife, Narcisa, I'd had time to reflect on how he'd treated me back then, and had been forced to concede that he'd been far kinder and more forgiving than I'd deserved. I'd begun to recognise that I'd been lazy and almost useless when I'd first worked there. Besides, I'd had a bad attitude, stemming from resentment at being the longest-standing cub reporter the *Bugle* had ever employed, at never having had a pay rise, and because I'd rarely been assigned to any good, juicy news stories. My reporting back then had mostly been confined to dog shows, church fetes and whist drives, and, when I'd finally been given a proper assignment, the one that had introduced me to Hobbes, it had only been because no one else was available. Of course, it was largely down to Hobbes that I'd changed, that I'd met Daphne and that I'd got a job again. I actually had a lot to thank the Editorsaurus for.

'Stop dreaming,' said Hobbes, giving me a nudge that nearly flattened me. 'We need to get back to Blackdog Street, pick up the car and visit Mr Witcherley. Goodbye, Mr Dean.'

'Ta-ra for now,' said Basil, one eye looking up.

Hobbes bustled me from the office, down the stairs and onto The Shambles. Within ten minutes, we were in the car, hurtling towards Fenderton. I'd absent-mindedly taken the front seat, and, despite being fully aware of his driving record, still came close to screaming when I opened my eyes as he threaded the car through a line of speeding traffic into Alexander Court.

Halfway up the hill, hiding behind a thick yew hedge, was the Witcherley residence, an impressively large house even in a street packed with impressively large houses. Gravel scrunched beneath the tyres as we turned into the driveway. Hobbes parked by the garages, we got out and approached the front door. Despite the Editorsaurus no longer having power over me, I could feel flocks of butterflies beating against my insides as Hobbes raised his finger to ring the doorbell. Last time I'd been there, I'd been awed by the polished wood, the gleaming brass on the front door, and the glittering glass, but now the woodwork looked tired, the brass was dull, and the windows were smeary. I glanced into the porch, which must have been as big as the sitting room at Blackdog Street, and saw mud streaking the tiled floors, a pile of dirty boots in one corner, and a dead plant in the middle.

A few seconds later Editorsaurus Rex appeared, wearing a grubby white shirt and stained jeans. He'd lost weight and with it some of his imposing appearance. His skin looked greyish, and his bare ankles were thin and shocking as he crossed the porch and opened the door.

'Good day, and thank you for your help, sir,' said Hobbes, snapping off a sharp salute.

'I'm always pleased to help you, Inspector. Come in. You, too, Capstan.'

'Caplet,' I said.

'What?'

'Nothing,' There was little point in asserting my right to be called by my given name. He'd failed to get it correct during all my years working for him, and I just couldn't be bothered any more.

'Please excuse the mess. My cleaning lady's on holiday,'

said Rex, leading us to the lounge where he pushed aside a pile of old papers and magazines to reveal a sofa, and gestured for us to sit, while he went into the next room.

I was surprised to see layers of dust on the surfaces, and red wine stains disfiguring the deep-pile of the rich cream carpet. During my previous visit, I'd had the feeling that the house was too smart and neat to really be lived in.

Rex returned with a dusty old cardboard box and a musty tang.

'This one has the years you were interested in,' he said, handing it to Hobbes. 'You're lucky I've still got it, because Narcisa got fed up with the smell and stuck it in the attic. I had intended to take it to the dump sometime, but I sort of forgot about it, because of ... well, you know.'

I knew he was alluding to the events surrounding his wife's incarceration in a secure unit, after she'd turned from an efficient business woman into a wannabe vampire.

'Thank you, sir,' said Hobbes as he took the box.

It was full of yellowing papers and tatty books with faded covers. He leafed through them, piling them on my lap, until he emptied a manila envelope onto the carpet. The contents were a number of faded black and white photographs of the school's staff and pupils, with the teachers seated at the front and a mass of urchins standing behind in rows. He examined them closely.

'That's Mr Barry,' he said, pointing at a large, whiskered man in the middle, 'the legendary headmaster.'

'Why legendary?'

'Because he'd fly into rages and threaten to chop naughty children with his axe. They called him Barry the Hatchet.'

'But he never did, did he?' I asked, shocked.

'No. Even in those days dicing the pupils was frowned upon, but the mere threat stopped most bad behaviour. Those it didn't deter were caned, which was a popular pastime for teachers back in the day. Spare the rod and spoil the child was the thinking, but in Barry the Hatchet's case it was more like wield the rod and spoil the trousers. He was a vicious man.'

'I remember my grandfather talking of him,' said Rex. 'I thought he was exaggerating, like the old ones do.'

'All too true, I'm afraid,' said Hobbes, continuing to stare at the pictures. 'This one's got young Augustus in.'

I wouldn't have guessed the fresh-faced kid in the woollen jumper was the same person as the old man I knew, though there was something about him that made me accept the identification.

'Aha!' said Hobbes, holding up another photograph.

'What is it?' Rex and I asked in unison.

'This young fellow here,' he jabbed at it with his finger.

'What about him?' said Rex.

'He is of interest in regards to an inquiry.'

'But he probably died decades ago,' said Rex.

'Very probably,' said Hobbes, 'but he may still have living descendants.'

'But you can't blame them for whatever he did,' said Rex.

'Of course not, but I'm not investigating this young fellow.'

'Can I see?' I asked, feeling left out.

Hobbes was pointing to a small grinning lad in a tatty coat, who looked much like the other boys around him.

'What's so special about this one?'

'Something about him is remarkable, and it might be significant. Can you see it? Or I should say can you see them?'

I stared, but failed to make out what he was seeing.

'It's the ears, isn't it?' said Rex.

'That's right, sir,' said Hobbes. 'Now do you see, Andy?'

'Umm ... not really. The kid seems to have the requisite number, and they might stick out a bit.'

'But, they're unusually small,' said Rex, 'with tiny lobes.'

'I ... umm ... suppose they are, especially if you compare them to those on the other boys. Yeah ... I see what you mean, but so what?'

'I'll tell you later,' said Hobbes. 'In the meantime, let's see if we can identify him.'

Unfortunately, no one had bothered to record the pupils' names on any of the photographs, not even on the back. I thought we'd have to give up, but Hobbes began sifting through all the documents, muttering to himself on occasion. Rex and I sat back and waited and I'd just reached the yawning and fidgeting stage when Hobbes grunted.

'What?' I asked, sitting up.

'I've just found something interesting in the punishment book. There's a line here that, on January the fifteenth, Samuel Slugg received six strokes of the cane for fighting in the playground.'

'Samuel Slugg?' I did a swift calculation. 'Could that be Solomon and Septimus's father?'

'The age would fit.'

'Who are Solomon and Septimus?' asked Rex.

'They are ... umm ...' I began.

'... people who may be of interest in an enquiry,' Hobbes broke in before I could say too much. 'Let's take another look at that photograph.'

He examined it again, and checked the next three or four in chronological order. 'It would appear that young Samuel Slugg, assuming I've identified him correctly, was always shorter than the other boys in his class.'

'It wasn't his fault,' I said, 'and why does it matter how tall or short he was?'

'It might not, but, then again, it might,' said Hobbes, infuriatingly. 'Well, Mr Witcherley, I believe I've taken up enough of your valuable time. The information I have discovered may well prove useful. Thank you very much.'

'Always pleased to help,' said Rex. 'Drop in any time. You

too, Capstan.'

'Caplet,' I muttered.

Hobbes stood up. 'Come along, Andy. We'll see ourselves out.'

I got up, and shook Rex's proffered hand. It was large and soft, and a little moist. As we left I couldn't help feeling sorry for him; he seemed rather lonely and lost in his big house, with his wife locked up.

We were just about to drive away when a red sports car drove onto the drive and parked next to us. A smart and striking woman in her mid-thirties got out, smiled and, having taken a key from her bag, unlocked the front door and entered the house.

'I wonder who that was, and what she's doing here,' I said.

'It's probably his cleaning lady returned from her holiday,' said Hobbes.

I left it at that, and wondered whether my sympathy for Rex had been misplaced.

One of the things that still puzzled me about Hobbes was what he knew about sex, because sometimes he seemed a little naïve, though there'd been occasions when his knowledge and wisdom had struck me as incredible. Thinking about it, my main problem was that I doubted he could have a sex life, because I'd never seen an 'unhuman' woman of the right type, and I was convinced he was far too rough and ugly for any human woman. And yet, I wasn't entirely sure because Daphne's friend, Pinky, had once remarked, after a few glasses of chardonnay, that she found him rather sexy. Still, she was undoubtedly weird, being in a relationship with a gentleman of the vampire persuasion, albeit a charming one who had no inclination to suck people dry.

18

As we were driving away, I asked a question that had been bugging me. 'Was that really a useful visit, or were you just being polite?'

'It was very useful. I learned something I didn't know and have been reminded of a number of interesting facts that, taken on their own, might not mean a lot, but together are suggestive.'

'Like what?'

'That Septimus Slugg and the skeleton are almost certain to have been related to Samuel Slugg. I suspect they were two of his children.'

'Two of them? That suggests you think there were more. How do you work that out?'

'Septimus is from the Latin for seventh, which suggests at least six older siblings.'

'I didn't know you knew Latin.'

'It was compulsory at my school, like at many back then.'

'But there was more?'

'I was reminded of something. Many years ago there was a greengrocer's shop in Stillingham called Sam S Lugg's.'

'So?'

'Andy, if you don't mind me saying, you can sometimes be a little dense. If you think about it, being a Slugg in charge of lettuces might not be good for business, so, if someone had that name it might make sense to change it to Lugg, and ...'

'Might?' I said, peevishly, 'but there might really have been a Sam S Lugg, who had nothing to do with the Slugg family, and, besides, I can't see what an old greengrocer's shop in Stillingham has to do with anything anyway.'

'If you'd let me finish,' he said. 'Mr Sam S Lugg was

clearly the small boy in the photograph who'd grown up. And before you start, I know that because I recognised him. In those days I used to go over to Stillingham quite often to quell the cheese riots, and I distinctly remember asking a local hard case, named Brian Madde, to desist from hurling a brick through Sam S Lugg's shop window.'

'And did he?'

'He did. Unfortunately, he threw it at me instead and it rebounded off my helmet and smashed the post office's window.'

'Were you hurt?'

'No, but the point is that I remember Mr Lugg, as I thought he was called, having several children.'

'I believe you, but I still can't see what you're getting at.'

'If I recall correctly, and I usually do, all the family, except for his wife of course, had a certain look. I mean they all had small ears and were below average height.'

'Which means?'

'Think about it. The skeleton we found was of a short man, who had noticeably small ears.'

'Small ears? How on earth can you say that? Skulls don't have ears.' My doubts about this line of reasoning were growing fast.

'You should have been listening to what Dr Ramage was saying instead of staring at her bosom.'

'I wasn't ... was I?'

He nodded and continued. 'There were, of course, no ears on the skull. However, there was clay adhering to one side of it and the clay held a good impression of the ear.'

'Clay? Where did that come from?'

'The ground. And then we get to the body of Septimus Slugg who, again, was a man of short stature with small ears, which we can see, and which I remarked on.'

'Yes ... but ...' I floundered trying to think of an objection.

'What's wrong with Dregs?' said Hobbes, swinging the

wheel and sending the car twisting across the road onto the pavement beside the flooded meadows.

'What?'

'Over there, by the river.'

The dog was staggering through water up to his chest, his left back leg dragging.

'He's hurt himself,' I said, observantly. 'I wonder how?'

'That doesn't matter,' said Hobbes, leaping out as Dregs collapsed.

Before I could make another comment, he was sloshing towards the dog, who was paddling feebly, barely keeping his nose above water. Hobbes scooped him up and waded back, his face grim, and a crimson trail following. As he laid Dregs on the back seat, the dog whimpered and wagged his tail.

'What's the matter?' I asked. 'Did the boar get him?'

'Look at that,' said Hobbes, pointing to a bloody puncture mark.

'Is that all? It's tiny!'

'But it's deep. We'd better get him to the vet.'

'For that? Can't you just take him home? I'm sure Mrs Goodfellow could clean it up and put on a plaster. What caused it anyway? A bite?'

Hobbes shook his head. 'I once saw a similar injury to a cat in Pigton, so I'm fairly sure someone has shot him with an air rifle. It must have been a powerful one, or very close, or both, to break the skin and penetrate so deep.'

'An air rifle? I know just how that feels. Poor dog.'

Dregs looked mournful as Hobbes covered him with a rug and ran back to the driver's seat, where he crushed the accelerator, making the tatty old car leap forward like a stung bullock. Any supposed tolerance I'd built up to his driving was nowhere near sufficient when he was in a hurry, for whereas, normally it was merely terrifying, it became paralysing. I couldn't shut my eyes, or even gibber.

All I could do was to sit still, my hands clutching the seat, and let fate have its way. Of course, we reached the vets without injury to ourselves or anybody else, although the sparks that flew when we screeched round bends or landed after taking off over speed-bumps suggested the car might need some attention.

Hobbes was out and sweeping Dregs into his arms almost before we'd stopped.

'Lend a hand, Andy,' he said, as he sprinted towards the surgery door.

I gazed at him through unblinking eyes.

'And quickly!'

The last command, a roar, jerked me from my stupor and, having unlocked my hands and my seatbelt, I stumbled out and ran to open the surgery door for them.

'It's an emergency,' I shouted, bursting in, making the large man in the white coat by the counter jump, and causing a small ginger cat to break from its cage and circle the room at head level, apparently getting a grip on the wallpaper. 'Our dog's hurt.'

The man in the white coat, stared blankly, and I was on the verge of saying something rude, when the surgery door opened and a small girl in a dark green smock emerged.

'Bring him straight in, Inspector,' she said, 'and put him on the table.'

Hobbes did as asked, and I stood leaning against the door.

'Close it,' said the girl.

'Yeah, okay, but I'm holding it for the vet!'

'Hello, Mrs Collyer,' said Hobbes, interrupting. 'I believe he's been shot.'

'She's the vet?' I said as realisation and embarrassment struck together, making me blush, though no one was paying me any attention.

'So I see,' said Mrs Collyer, examining Dregs's leg and

poking about.

Dregs gave a muted yelp, raised his head, wagged his tail and flopped.

'I'll need the nurse,' said the vet, pushing me aside and opening the door. 'Nick. Can you come here at once, please?'

The man in the white coat looked around, but seemed far more concerned by the cat's antics. I was infuriated by his lack of urgency and dumb idiocy.

'Shift yourself,' I yelled, glaring. 'Can't you see it's an emergency?'

He pointed to his chest, looking gormless, shook his stupid head, and shrugged.

I was thinking of something really biting to say when another girl in a green smock appeared. 'I'm coming as fast as I can,' she said, grabbing the cat by the scruff of the neck and stuffing it back into its cage.

'Oh ... umm ... sorry ... I ... umm ...'

As the spring from which words normally gushed dried up, I was left red-faced and silent, trying to work out a form of words to explain my gaffe, or, to be honest, my gaffes, and to make the point that it had been the man's white coat that had confused me, and was not because I was sexist or anything.

However, no one was paying me any attention, so I just stood and cringed internally.

'I need to take this dog's blood pressure,' said the vet.

Nurse Nick, Nichola I assumed, nodded and fetched a trolley with electronic stuff on it and, after a glance at Dregs, reached into a drawer and pulled out a cuff. 'This one?'

Nodding, Mrs Collyer took it and wrapped it round Dregs's foreleg. 'His BP is low,' she said after several beeps.

'Is that because he's bled so much?' I asked, breaking my silence.

'Possibly, but shock is more likely ... I'm going to give him saline.'

Nurse Nick took a bag of clear fluid, a length of plastic tubing and a small plastic packet from a cabinet. When she removed a hypodermic needle from the packet, I began to feel weird and hot.

My brain was trying to work out why I was lying on my side on the floor. My eyes opened and focussed on a large rat that was watching me with interest. When I recoiled, I bashed the back of my head on what turned out to be a chair leg.

Rolling over, rubbing the bumped bit, I sat up. I was in the waiting room, but couldn't work out how I'd got there.

'Don't mind, Stanley,' said the man in white. 'He won't hurt you.'

'Good ... umm ... pleased to hear it.' My head cleared. 'Who's Stanley?'

'My rat. He's here with his piles.'

'So, you don't work here?'

'No, of course not. I'm a chef.'

'Where?' I asked, professional curiosity asserting itself.

'Gollum's Logons,' he said. 'Haven't you been one of our customers?'

'Yes.'

'I thought I recognised you.' He held out a big hand. 'I'm able.'

'Good ... umm ... able to do what?'

He laughed a long slow laugh as he engulfed my hand and shook it. 'My name is Abel. Abel Seaman.'

'With a name like that you should be a sailor.'

He grimaced. 'Used to be. I was cook on the QE3 until the company went under.'

'QE3? I don't know that one, but I do remember the old QE2. My parents sailed on it once, before they had me. It was their honeymoon, I think.'

He looked puzzled. 'That's odd. I didn't think the Quality

Export ships ever took passengers. I didn't catch your name, by the way.'

'It's Andy ... Andy Caplet.'

Abel nodded. 'I thought it might be. You're the critic who gave us a rotten review.'

'It wasn't all that bad. I said I liked the coffee, but I'm sorry if I caused any offence. I didn't mean to. The thing is I see my job as pointing out areas where things could be improved. It's all for your benefit in the long run.'

'Isn't it to sell newspapers?'

'Well, yes ... but if a restaurant improves as a result of something I've written, it's got to be better for the restaurant, and for the public, hasn't it?'

Had I not been so groggy, I might never have been so honest. Now I had, I began to worry what he might do, for he was a hefty man with meaty hands that looked capable of bunching into formidable cudgels, and I remembered Hobbes's comment that the man who'd beaten me had big fists.

He shrugged. 'Perhaps you're right. In fact, I did think the soup you described was rather inadequate, but it's all down to the ingredients, and, frankly, the boss is a cheapskate. Actually, the thing that most annoyed him was that you spelt our name wrong.'

'Did I?'

'Yes. There's only one "L" and no apostrophe in Golums. That was careless.'

'Sorry.'

I was about to ask the name of his boss when the surgery door opened and Hobbes appeared, with a huge smile and a thumbs up. 'Mrs Collyer has extracted the pellet, cleaned him up and stitched him. He'll be sore for a few days, but he'll soon be back to his normal self.'

'Great,' I said, my smile matching his. 'Can I see him?'

'Of course,' said Hobbes, 'but he's still sleeping. How are

you?'

'Better, I think, but I don't know what happened.'

'You keeled over when the needle went into him.'

'I've never been fond of them since Father used to practice on me.'

'Mr Seaman?' said the nurse. 'Mrs Collyer can see Stanley now.'

'Let's get out of here,' said Hobbes, stepping aside to allow Abel and his ailing rat into the surgery.

'It's time for dinner,' said Hobbes with a glance at his watch.

'Already? Umm ... how long was I out?'

'About an hour and a half. I've let the lass know what's been happening and I've asked her to get some bones in.'

19

Although the road conditions were reasonably good around town, our return to Blackdog Street was at a leisurely pace, which was alarming, since he normally only drove responsibly when there was a real danger to people, or when something was troubling him. I kept quiet, and vowed to stay clear of the sitting room after we'd eaten, because I had no need to guess what would happen then, and knew he'd put the fear of Hobbes into me if I was too close. It was an unfortunate and deeply disturbing quirk of his to release excess stress by crunching up a pile of raw bones. At such times, which were happily rare, there was something so feral and dangerous in his manner that it gave me the shakes, as if I were a helpless little lamb in a tiger's den, and, although he'd never actually done anything to hurt me, he'd given the impression of being out of control, of having cast off the veneer of civilisation. I'd seen the savage horror of his 'unhuman' self, and had been truly terrified.

On the plus side, there was lunch to look forward to.

The scent on entering 13 Blackdog Street, a heady mix of freshly baked bread and something rich and savoury, immediately set me drooling, though I had to endure a cruel wait while Hobbes updated the old girl about the dog's condition, and lingered forever over saying grace. Still, the wait was worth it when she presented us with a magnificent golden pea soup, so thick my spoon almost stood up on its own, with croutons that were so light and crunchy that I nearly wept for pleasure. It was served with warm, buttered freshly-made garlic bread that was so toothsome it drove the forthcoming dread from my mind.

For a short while.

As soon as we'd finished, a change came over Hobbes. Mrs Goodfellow, with a nod at me, a warning to stay clear, picked up a handful of old newspapers and took them through to the sitting room. Hobbes followed, growling and twitching, his dark eyes as cold as a shark's. She returned, took a blood-stained brown paper parcel from the larder, carried it to the sitting room door, and threw it in. I heard Hobbes snarl, and felt the thud as he pounced on the parcel.

Then, I blocked my ears so I didn't have to hear the slathering and the shocking cracks as his great teeth crunched through the bones as easily as mine did through digestive biscuits. I could only feel relief that the fit had not come upon him at the mortuary.

After a short while, Mrs Goodfellow handed me a mug of sweet tea and it was all over. I thanked her and sipped as Hobbes's footsteps clunked upstairs. Moments later he was roaring, only this time, there was pure exhilaration in his voice as the dangerous shower washed away the meat and bone scraps, and any residues of stress. I'd just started on my second mug when he returned, clean, in fresh clothes, and with a grin on his face.

'By heck, I needed that,' he said and accepted a mug of tea. 'Thank you, lass, for getting the bones in at such short notice.'

'You're welcome.' She smiled, looking at him as if she were an indulgent grandma who'd dished out a bag of toffees to a naughty but loveable child.

Hobbes heaped sugar into his mug, stirred it and drank. When he'd finished and poured himself another, he reached into his pocket and held out his hand. 'This is what Mrs Collyer dug out of Dregs.'

It was a small pellet, just like the one that had stung my bottom. I said as much.

'It is exactly like the one that hit you, in that it is the same calibre and from the same manufacturer.'

'Does that mean it was fired from the same gun?'

'Not necessarily. It's a fairly common type of ammo, widely used by shooters. However, as there have been very few incidents of crimes involving air rifles round here, and none to my knowledge, other than your misfortune, within the last five years, it would not surprise me. I'll get Dr Ramage to take a look and see if there is anything to confirm this.'

'But, if they were both fired from the same gun, does it mean someone shot Dregs to get at me?'

'It's a possibility,' said Hobbes, 'but I suspect a fairly remote one. Dregs can be annoying, too.'

'I suppose so … hey! What do you mean?'

He chuckled, reached out a long arm and patted me gently on the back, knocking the wind from my lungs.

As breathing and the power of speech returned, a thought popped into my head. 'Umm … when we were at the vets, I met the chef from Golums Logons. He thought I'd given the place a bad review, and he had big hands. Do you think he could have been the one that's been attacking me?'

Hobbes shrugged. 'Maybe. Did you catch his name?'

'Yes, I did … what was it … something nautical.'

'A strange name,' said Mrs Goodfellow.

Having forgotten she was still there, her unearthly cackle made me jump, bang my knee and groan. Dregs always loved this particular comedy routine, and the silence that followed showed how much he was missed.

'Actually, his name was Abel Seaman,' I said.

'I know Abel,' said Mrs Goodfellow. 'He's a kindly soul, always rescuing small animals and helping old ladies.'

'Yes,' said Hobbes, 'I'd heard he was back, but I would say that, unless going to sea has completely changed him, he's unlikely to have done you, or anyone else, any harm.'

'But what about his boss? Abel said he'd been annoyed, although that was mostly because I'd spelled the place's name wrong.'

'In what way?' asked Hobbes.

'I put an extra "L" in it. Apparently, there's only one in Golums ... I expect that's for copyright reasons or something. And there's no apostrophe.'

His expression instantly changed to one of quiet thought. 'Only one "L" you say? Now that is interesting.'

'Umm ... Good ... Why?'

'Would you get me a pencil and paper, please?' he asked.

Mrs Goodfellow obliged.

'Thank you,' he said, taking them and spreading the paper out.

'What are you doing?' I asked, getting up and trying to peer over one shoulder while Mrs Goodfellow tried the other. He leant back to let us see.

He'd written two lines, one directly above the other.

G O L U M S L O G O N S
S O L O M O N S L U G G

'I see,' said Mrs Goodfellow. 'That is interesting.'

'I don't see,' I said, feeling my usual confusion.

'Both lines have the same number of letters,' said Hobbes.

'I see that, but, so what?'

'Exactly the same number of letters.'

I must have looked blank for he took his pencil and drew lines, connecting the same letters on top to those below. At last, I got it.

'It's exactly the same number of exactly the same letters!' I said.

'Or to put it another way, Golums Logons is an anagram of Solomon Slugg.'

'I get it.' A wave of excitement washed over me, but still left me high and dry. 'Yeah, but what does it mean?'

'That remains to be seen,' he said, 'but I'd hazard a guess that Mr Slugg is the owner.'

'That's brilliant,' I said.

'Elementary, but it may not mean much. However, any little scrap of information may prove valuable to a detective.'

'How big were Solomon Slugg's hands,' I asked.

'About average for a man of his size.'

'Then it wasn't him that beat me ... unless he got someone to do it for him.'

Hobbes nodded. 'That is possible, although I didn't think your piece on Golums Logons was particularly scathing. I thought its tone was more encouraging and helpful, and it did make me think that I should look in some time for a coffee, or even a meal next time the lass is away.'

'That's what I was aiming for,' I said, delighted that, once again, he knew my work.

'Then you scored a bullseye.'

'Yes,' said Mrs Goodfellow. 'I always look out for your articles in the *Bugle.* They are most entertaining, and, Mrs Fitch at the newsagents says they are becoming quite influential in raising standards.'

Unused to praise, I found it hard to deal with and embarrassing, although I couldn't deny how gratifying it was to hear it. All I could do was to stammer out thanks and look bashful.

I was saved by the bell.

Hobbes went to answer the phone, and returned a few minutes later. 'That was Dr Ramage, with some interesting news.'

'Go on,' I said.

'She sent samples from the two more recent bodies for DNA testing, and has received the preliminary results.'

'That was quick.'

'I gather her fiancé works there and did her a favour.'

'She has a fiancé?' The news was disappointing, though I couldn't, or wouldn't, understand why.

'Yes. He's called Roger, and I gather he's nice and very intelligent.'

'Good for him,' I said, struggling to keep quite unreasonable jealousy from my voice, and to get back on track. 'But what were the results?'

'They indicate the two deceased individuals were closely related. In fact, they were probably brothers.'

'As you suggested.'

He nodded.

'But, what does it mean?' I asked, having taken up my familiar position of bafflement.

He smiled. 'It means I should do a little more investigation into the Slugg family.'

'Family? Umm ... but didn't Solomon Slugg say he only had the one brother?'

'He did and I've been wondering about that since.'

'Because Septimus should have been the seventh child. Are you going to arrest him?'

'Hold on there, Andy. I can't arrest someone for not telling the whole truth about his family when he wasn't even under caution. He claimed he'd been ashamed of Septimus, so perhaps he has the same opinion of the others.'

'True. Septimus sounded like a real liability.'

'He did,' said Hobbes, nodding, 'though we only have his brother's word for it.'

'D'you think he lied?'

'I have no means of knowing until I've established more facts. I'll start by investigating Septimus Slugg. I have his address, and the roads are dry enough now for a visit to Tode-in-the-Wold.'

'Can I come?'

'No,' said Mrs Goodfellow, from just behind my left ear.

'Why not?' I asked, when my speech returned.

'Because you have to talk to you wife, dear. Have you forgotten what day it is?'

'It's Friday.'

'It's St Valentine's day,' said Mrs Goodfellow, looking shocked.

'I know,' I said, 'but ... umm ... I don't think she'll want to talk to me. I covered all her clothes in chocolate and ants. It was an accident.'

'I know, dear,' said Mrs Goodfellow.

'How?'

'Because she telephoned when you were out.'

'Did she? Why didn't you tell me?'

'I just did, dear. I couldn't tell you earlier, because I know what you're like at meal times, and it didn't seem appropriate when the old fellow was ... busy.'

'I see. Thank you. Did she say anything?'

'It would have been a strange call if she hadn't, like the ones I used to get from that Gordon Bennett.'

'Was he the guy you arrested for flashing?' I asked Hobbes, who was heading towards the kitchen door.

'I did arrest Mr Bennett, but it wasn't for that, since I'd already convinced him that a cover up was required. Sadly, a few weeks later, he started making nuisance phone calls and I had to confiscate his phone. After that, he turned to car crime and I had to book him when he used violence against a member of the public. I'm afraid Mr Bennett is in prison now. Unfortunately, he appears to be one of those that can't help themselves. I gave him a second chance, and a third, but I fear he'll never break the habit. He gets it from his father and grandfather who were much the same back in their day.

'I'm off now, but the lass is right. You should call your wife as soon as possible. Goodbye.'

Despite knowing in my heart that he and the old girl were

correct, I just sat for a while and wondered what to do and when to do it.

'You can use our telephone,' said Mrs Goodfellow, who'd been observing my inertia with increasing annoyance, 'unless you want to Skype or send an email, in which case you'll have to go elsewhere.'

'Umm ... right ... thank you. What did Daphne tell you?'

'That it was very hot, and that Mahmoud had driven her to the nearest town, which is sixty miles away across the desert.'

'Mahmoud? Why?' Pangs of jealousy and suspicion stabbed through me.

'He has a car, and she needed new clothes, because of your little gift.'

The jealousy was replaced by guilt. 'Umm ... yes. I was a little foolish.'

'Only a little, dear?'

'Okay, a lot.' I admitted. 'I just hadn't thought it would be so hot in February, even in the desert. On reflection, chocolates were a pretty stupid idea.'

'But you meant well,' said Mrs Goodfellow, 'and she knows that. Now, call her.'

'Right,' I said, hoping I agreed with the old girl's assessment, 'I think I will.'

'Good lad ... well, what are you waiting for?'

'Nothing ... umm ... I was just wondering if she'd be around. What do you think? Wouldn't it be best to try later?'

'Since I'm not blessed with the second sight, I have no idea when she'll be around. What I do think, dear, is that you're prevaricating.'

'No, I'm not doing that. I was just starting to think I should wait a little. In the evening perhaps?'

Mrs Goodfellow gave me what I supposed was meant as a fierce glare. 'Call her now, or it'll be dry bread and water for your supper.'

Although I was almost certain she didn't mean it, the risk was too great, so I nodded. I would, at least, test the temperature by sending Daphne an apologetic email.

'I'm off to Golums Logons,' I said, grabbing my coat and fleeing into Blackdog Street, scurrying away, in case the old girl came after me.

My head was full of confusion, and I had to think, even though for some reason I seemed incapable of making a decision. Her absence was already disturbing my equilibrium. Part of me really wanted to talk to her, to tell her how much I loved her, and how much I was missing her. Another part feared she'd still be angry, and that any attempts to mollify her would make matters worse, leading me to say or do something that would be like the proverbial last straw and break the camel's back. I stopped that line of thought, for comparing her to a camel would not endear me. A final small but nasty part wanted her to suffer for her anger, though I knew a stupid attempt at punishing her might have terrible repercussions. Then I realised that if I didn't speak to her soon, she might think I didn't care.

Deep gloom gripped me as I turned onto Rampart Street, my feet finding their own way, since my brain had no room for ideas of navigation, or, as it turned out, road sense. The shriek of brakes brought me back, and I realised I'd just walked out in front of a car. The driver shook his totally bald head at me and mouthed something that looked rude, before driving around and speeding away. The volume of traffic appeared to be more or less what it was normally, but it took the horn of a white van to make me understand that I'd drifted off again and was still standing in the middle of the road.

'Sorry!' I mouthed, and ran to the pavement, where I stood awhile in thought in a clothes shop's doorway, getting my wits back, such as they were. And then, like someone switching on the light, I understood that I'd been on the verge of sabotaging my happiness because the negative part of my personality, the bit that believed Daphne was far too good for the likes of me, had briefly gained the upper hand. The knowledge helped me overcome it, and I hurried towards Golums Logons. When I reached it, I looked up and ascertained that it really did have one 'L', and no apostrophe.

I pushed open the door.

'Well done, dear,' said Mrs Goodfellow, making me jump as if she'd pricked me with a pin.

'You followed me,' I said, turning and getting smacked in the butt as the door swung back.

'I thought you might need some encouragement. Are you going in?'

'Umm ... yes.'

'I say, it's that runt again,' drawled a posh male voice as I entered, 'and this time he hasn't got the big bastard with him.'

Two of the rugby types stood up from their computers and stepped towards me with intent.

'Go get him, Guy! You and Toby can give him a damn good thumping,' said a third, who'd handed a wad of money to a vaguely familiar hooded man. The money looked tiny in his hands.

'Yeah, go for it,' said the hooded man, who had something a little foreign in the way he spoke, 'and give him one for me.'

As they advanced, Mrs Goodfellow thrust me aside and stood in front, her spindly arms folded across her chest.

'Oh look,' said Guy, 'he's brought his nanny!'

They laughed.

'You'd better stand aside, old woman,' said Guy, 'because we don't want to hurt you.'

'But we do want to hurt him, don't we?' said Toby.

'We certainly do. Would you care to join in the fun, James?'

The third one, having completed his transaction, strode towards us, nodding and grinning as the hooded man slipped away through a back door.

'Calm down, lads,' said Mrs Goodfellow. 'No one needs to get hurt.'

James tried to push her aside, which was a mistake. The old girl just took his hand turned it gently, and dumped him face first onto the carpet. His mates charged, no longer going for me, but for her. They failed most miserably, and, to judge from their cries, most painfully too. At a guess, I'd say the fight lasted five seconds, and ended with all three of them on the carpet, whimpering like kicked puppies.

Mrs Goodfellow drew herself up to her full height, which was about four foot ten, and wagged her finger. 'I want no more of this nonsense. Start behaving yourselves at once, or someone is going to get hurt.'

'I'm already hurt,' moaned Toby.

'No, you're not, my lad. It will pass in a minute or two. However, if I get to hear that any of you is mean to my friend, you will know what being hurt really is ... and that's not a threat, it's a promise. Get up, get your things, and get out.'

The three of them, looking sheepish and puzzled did exactly as she told them. I'd just been guided to a terminal by the hobbit girl, who appeared rather wary of me, when the door opened and James filled the doorway. I turned, expecting more trouble.

'We're very sorry, madam,' he said.

'That's all right, dear,' said Mrs Goodfellow, smiling gummily. 'Now, run along and be good.'

'We will. Again we are all truly sorry. Goodbye.' He turned and walked away.

'A nice, polite, well-brought up young lad,' said Mrs

Goodfellow.

'Then why does he keep attacking me?'

'That is a very good question. Now sit down and talk to your wife.'

'Yes,' I said, and logged into my account.

Daphne had sent me an email. Since it was entitled *Sorry,* I hoped it was a sign that she'd forgiven my stupidity. Then again, what if it meant 'I hope you are sorry for what you did'? Or even 'I'm sorry the marriage didn't work out'. Or ...

'Aren't you going to open it, dear? There's nothing to worry about.'

I nodded.

'When?'

'Now ... but ... but ...'

'No more buts, dear. Open it. I promise I won't look.'

'Okay.' I took a deep breath and clicked.

Dear Andy,

I'm ever so sorry, and hope you can forgive me for my bad temper yesterday. I was just too hot and too tired, and an ant had bitten me on the eyelid, and seeing all the mess in my things was the last straw. I hadn't remembered it was Valentine's Day today, and I now understand why you put the chocolates there. It was a nice idea, and you weren't to know it would be unusually hot here for the time of year. And thank you for the lovely card, too. It's a bit chocolatey, but it's lovely. I hope you're not feeling too neglected and think I didn't get you one, because I did. I hid one in my bedside table, and planned to tell you today, but I suppose it must have been destroyed.

Have you made any progress with the insurance claim yet? Or found anywhere to live?

I really miss you, and would love to hear your voice. I rang earlier, but you were out.

Love, Daphne

I released the breath in a long happy sigh.

'There you are, dear. I told you there was nothing to worry about.'

'Yes ... and you also promised not to look!'

'I didn't, dear. She'd already told me what she'd written.'

I was feeling so much better that, had I been somewhere less public, I would have let loose a mighty whoop, or even burst into song. As I wasn't, I restricted myself to a grin.

'You do have lovely teeth, dear,' Mrs Goodfellow remarked. 'I'm so glad you look after them well.'

She'd long ago put in a request that when I had no further use for them, they would go to her collection. Although I'd agreed at the time, being in a panic, I wondered whether Daphne might want a say in the distribution of my body parts, should anything untoward befall me. Of course, I'd naively assumed my teeth would be safe from falling into the old girl's clutches, because, being so old, she would almost certainly die long before me, but she seemed so fit, that I'd developed doubts. Not that it would bother me if I was dead, but I'd sometimes wondered if our verbal agreement was legally binding, and suspected Daphne might not like it.

'You'd better reply, dear, or you could call her now you know there's nothing to worry about.'

The truth was that there were many things to worry about, such as putting in an insurance claim, and finding a new flat, but I'd had little chance to do anything so far, and there seemed to be no immediate rush. In addition, and potentially more serious, the photographs of me and Sally were bound to turn up sooner or later, and I was on tenterhooks, not knowing if my unknown and known assailants might strike again. In fact, I had a host of worries jostling for attention at the back of my mind, but they would just have to wait their turn.

'I'll send her an email now,' I said, resolute for once, 'and I'll ring her later, if you're sure you don't mind me using your phone.'

'Of course not, dear, and you can always use your mobile. Daffy says you keep forgetting you've got one.'

'That's true. I'd got so used to being without one that I just can't get into the habit.' I took it from my pocket. 'It needs recharging.'

'Use ours then.'

'I will later, after I've emailed.'

'Good lad.' She left me to get on with it and I composed a reply.

Dear Daphne,

Happy Valentine's Day!

It was great to receive your email. Don't worry about losing your temper, because it really was all my fault. I hadn't thought it through properly. I hope your new clothes are wonderful, and I hope your bite is getting better. I wish I could have found your card, but I imagine it's still in what's left of the Elweses' flat. I haven't been able to do much about that, because everything has been really difficult here with the floods, but they aren't quite so bad now. I've also been helping Hobbes with a double murder, and with looking after Dregs who got shot by someone with an air gun, but he will be all right, according to the vet.

I will talk to you soon. I'll be going back to Blackdog Street and Mrs Goodfellow says I can use their phone while my mobile recharges.

I love you and miss you,

Andy

P.S. When I say I'm helping Hobbes with a double murder, I don't mean helping him commit them, I mean we are investigating them.

I sent it, paid for my session and, feeling as happy as I could be when she was thousands of miles away, walked into the street and turned homewards.

That was when I saw the first one.

20

A poster, about the size of a paper-backed book, had been stuck on a lamppost in Rampart Street, and my unfortunate little dalliance with Sally was now made public. Although I'd been expecting something, it took my breath, chilled my blood, set my heart racing and made my chest hurt. I felt sick, convinced every passer-by was staring at me, seeing my apparent infidelity and judging me a rotter. My legs trembled so much I dropped to my knees, staring up at the image as if through a long dark tube. It was me, and though little of Sally was recognisable, she was clearly not Daphne.

'You praying to that lamppost, mate?' a man asked. He laughed and walked on.

I had to endure what felt like an aeon of shaking, sweating and blackness before I could force my legs to stand on my own two feet. Though I tore the poster down, there was another further on, and as I lurched towards it, I spotted the next, and the next, and the next ... all along the street. My image seemed to be everywhere, and it was unmistakeably me, despite the face I was pulling, a weird mix of elation, incomprehension and (I hoped) reluctance. I was convinced people were pointing and smirking.

Cringing, avoiding eye contact, I hurried homewards, tearing down any posters I saw. As I turned into Goat Street, Featherlight's harsh voice broke into my nightmare, almost as a welcome distraction.

'Oi, Caplet! Unless my eyes mistake me, and they don't, that lady is not your wife. What've you been up to, you dirty dog?'

He lumbered towards me, one of the posters in his hand, one of his bellies protruding beneath his greasy singlet.

'Oh, hi,' I said, and failed to pull off a nonchalant smile.

'It's not what it looks like.'

'What are you playing at, you idiot? You've got yourself a fine woman – far better than you deserve – and yet as soon as she's out of sight you fling yourself at a floozy. What's wrong with you, knucklehead? I've a good mind to teach you a lesson.'

'Please don't,' I whined. 'It was a set up and now it's a complete nightmare. Do you really think I ... umm ... wanted to kiss her?'

'I can't see you putting up much of a fight.'

'A camera doesn't always show what really happened. She took me by surprise.'

'Several times by the looks of it,' said Featherlight, scowling. 'If I had a woman like Daphne, I wouldn't go snogging any young doxy who crossed my path. Are you trying to mess up your marriage?'

'I wasn't. It was all just a horrible mistake, and I'm scared Daphne'll find out and not understand. I don't know who's been sticking these things up, or why. Who'd hate me so much they'd do something like this?'

'Anyone who's met you, I expect,' he said, shaking his head and making his chins wobble. 'Look, Caplet, if it was just you I'd let you flounder in your own mess, but since I have a great admiration for your good lady wife, except for her poor taste in husbands, I'll tell you that I saw the bloke who's posting them turn down Vermin Street about five minutes ago.'

'Who was it?'

'A bloke.'

'Could you describe him?'

'He was a bloke wearing a black hoody ... average height ... quite muscular ... bit of a belly ...'

'Is that all?' It didn't seem much to go on.

'... and he had hands like a mole.'

'What? Muddy?'

'Big.'

'But you didn't recognise him?'

'No, but you might, if you hurry.'

'What?'

'Use what passes for your brain. He might still be around, mightn't he?'

'Umm ... yes ... I suppose so ... Vermin Street? Thanks.'

I scurried away, hoping to spot the fiend, while hoping he wouldn't spot me, for I'd not forgotten the size of his hands, and had already linked them to the bruises from my beating. Fighting to overcome a sense of terror, my hunting instincts buzzing, I kept my eyes skinned, but other than posters on lampposts, there was no evidence of him. I even asked a number of passers-by, but no one admitted to having seen anything. I rushed around town like a mad thing, tearing down poster after poster, but never spotted him. The horror was immense and my panic was growing. I leant against a wall and clutched my head, despairing until a heady, spicy fragrance surrounded me, renewing hope that things might work out.

'Good afternoon, Andy,' said the soft, honey-coated voice of Hilda Elwes. 'I see you've been enjoying yourself. When the cats away, eh?'

'Umm ... hello.' I turned to face her, and forced myself to be normal. 'It's not that. It's all a big mistake ... honestly.'

'I'm not judging you,' she said. 'Everyone has their own little foibles and weaknesses.'

She was wearing a flimsy purple dress and high heels, looking so stylish and summery among the drab winter clothes that she might have been modelling for one of the fashion magazines I'd flicked through in doctors' waiting rooms. Her smile was comforting, and her jade eyes were soft and forgiving. For a moment I wondered if she might be trying it on, having seen evidence that I was such a soft touch, and I made up my mind not to succumb to her charm, although it was immense. However, I must have misread her, for she continued on an entirely different tack.

'I'm told the engineers have made the flats safe, so, if you want to see if anything can be salvaged, I'd report to the council. They'll give you a pass to get on-site.'

'Thank you,' I said. 'I will ... when I have time ... umm ... how are you managing?'

'Managing, Andy?'

'I mean since that night. Have you found anywhere to stay?'

I realised how lucky I was to be back with Hobbes and Mrs Goodfellow, and how little thought I'd given to my neighbours who'd had no such friends.

'Oh yes.'

'Where?'

'Over that way.' She waved her hand vaguely in the direction of Ride Street.

'With friends?'

'No, just the two of us.'

'Good ... umm ... Good.' My conversational skills having dried up, I resorted to an inane grin, and thought desperately. 'Someone shot Hobbes's dog.'

'Was he mad?'

'He wasn't happy about it, but the vet took an air rifle pellet out and reckons he'll be all right. What kind of person would shoot a dog? I mean ... he's a big daft brute, but he's good natured.'

Hilda's uncanny gaze was still fixed on me. 'I don't know, but Aubrey saw a man with an air rifle shooting at rabbits in Ride Park last night.'

'You think it might be the same person?'

She shrugged. 'Who knows?'

'Umm ... how could he be shooting in Ride Park? It's closed at night. I know because I nearly got locked in once.' I shuddered, recalling a terrifying walk through dark woods, with a big cat on my tail.

'So I've heard. Colonel Squire doesn't like plebs in his park at night.'

'But he lets your husband in?'

'Not as such, but Aubrey likes a moonlit walk. So do I ... and he's not my husband ... he's my cousin.'

Her smile made me feel like a puppy dog, desperate to ingratiate himself. There was something enchanting about Hilda Elwes.

'I see.' For a moment my suspicion that she was coming onto me returned, though her eyes suggested she merely found me amusing, but she was so charming and lovely. With an effort, I got back to the subject in hand. 'Did he see who was shooting?'

'No, he kept well out of the way.'

'Oh ... never mind ... thank you ... umm ...'

'I mustn't keep you, Andy, I'm sure you are very busy. Farewell.'

She walked away, leaving a hazy cloud of fragrance and a feeling of total confusion. I thought her an alluring woman, although I wasn't entirely sure. She was certainly elegant, or probably was, but oddly I couldn't picture her. However, I was sure I didn't fancy her ... and yet, she did something to me, and when she was around I wished I had a tail to wag. Now she'd gone, I felt suddenly tired and drained.

I found myself back at 13 Blackdog Street, where the steps up to the front door felt like climbing a mountain. As I opened the door I sneezed. Then I sneezed again and again as if my head was exploding.

Mrs Goodfellow appeared. 'Are you all right, dear?'

I shook my head and shivered.

'You look very pale.'

'I feel very pale.' I sneezed. 'And my throat hurts.'

'You'd better go upstairs and lie down. You've probably caught something. It's not surprising after all the soakings and the dirty water.'

I forced myself upstairs, stripped and fell into bed, where I lay shivering until Mrs Goodfellow appeared with a hot drink. She put her hand on my forehead.

'You're a little feverish. Never mind, drink this.'

It was hot and tasted of honey and lemon combined with something I couldn't quite place, though I didn't care, for it was warming and soothed my throat.

'You should sleep, dear,' she said, closing the curtains.

'But I've got to call Daphne,' I said, remembering and making a feeble attempt to get up.

Mrs Goodfellow pushed me back. 'Stay where you are. I'll call her, and say you're ill.'

'All right. Say I'll try later.'

I was soon in a deep sleep that was, as far as I could remember, dreamless. At some point, I think I came awake and staggered to the bathroom and back. At another point, Mrs Goodfellow fed me chicken soup, but after that I knew nothing until morning, when I sat up with a slight headache and a nose that was as well stuffed as a marrow. I had breakfast in bed, lunch in bed and even dinner in bed and only got up for calls of nature. The rest of the time I slept.

21

The following day, my headache was better, the stuffiness was gone, and the sore throat was almost a memory. I bounced from bed, washed, dressed and went downstairs where I was greeted by Dregs, who, if not quite his usual self, and who looked unbalanced with his left back leg shaved and in a white dressing, was delighted to see me. The feeling was mutual.

Hobbes was already at the table. 'Glad to see you back on your feet.'

'Me or Dregs?'

'Both of you.' He grinned.

'I thought he'd be wearing one of those plastic lampshade things, so he can't pull his dressing off,' I said, remembering the time Granny Caplet's wicked orange cat, having got himself into a brawl, had needed stitches. They'd left him even more bad tempered than usual, and when I'd laughed at his stupid plastic cone, he'd upped and scratched me on the nose, which Granny had said served me right.

'Mrs Collyer thought he should have one, but I had a quiet word with him and he knows to leave the dressing well alone,' Hobbes explained.

Mrs Goodfellow presented us with creamy scrambled eggs on thick buttered toast, the toast somehow staying crispy, and the eggs as fluffy as only she could make them. My appetite was as hearty as that of the proverbial condemned man, and I followed up with more toast, this time with a new batch of marmalade, a perfect melding of sweet and sour with just a hint of smokiness. The latter flavour was something of a mystery because I'd watched her at work and the only ingredients had been Seville oranges and sugar.

'It's good to see you back to normal,' said Mrs Goodfellow as I finished off the last crumbs. 'That was a nasty bug.'

'I think it might have been flu,' I said, 'but that stuff you gave me worked wonders. What was it?'

'Honey and lemon, dear.'

'And?'

'And a secret ingredient.'

'And some of my best Islay malt whisky,' said Hobbes, looking grumpy.

'Just a drop,' she admitted.

'Well, it was good stuff. Thanks.'

'You're welcome, dear. Now, I'd better get on with the washing up and get the dinner in the oven before I get ready for church.'

'It's Sunday is it?' I said, pleased to have spotted the clues.

'It is,' said Hobbes.

'I should telephone Daphne. I was going to do it yesterday ... no ... on Friday. She'll be worried.'

'No, she won't,' said Mrs Goodfellow, 'because I told her you were under the weather. But, yes, you should call today.'

'I'll do it now, if I can use your phone?'

Hobbes nodded, and I hurried through to the sitting room and, after a bit of thought, poked in her number. I got through.

'Hello,' I said. 'Daphne?'

'No, buddy,' said a deep voice with an American accent. 'Mike Parker. Mrs Caplet is busy with the professor, and he said they should not be disturbed until they've finished.'

'The professor?'

'Professor Mahmoud El-Gammal.'

'Him again,' I said, flushed with jealousy. 'What are they doing?'

'They're in the bedchamber, making out ...'

'What?'

'... making out an inventory.'

'I see. Just the two of them?'

'Yep.'

'Why?'

'Why what? Excuse me, but who are you?' asked Mike.

'I'm Daphne's husband.'

'Thought you might be. How you doing, buddy?'

'I'm fine.'

'Great, because I heard you were sick.'

'I was. Umm ... why are she and the professor working alone?'

'Because there's no room for anyone else in there.'

'There's usually space for more than two in a bedroom,' I said.

He laughed. 'It's not actually a bedroom. It's a chamber where we found a bed and some other artefacts.'

'I don't get it. What's the difference?'

He laughed again. 'Daffy said you're a dude who'll always choose the wrong end of a snake to poke. I'll explain. When we were investigating what might prove to be a tomb, we came across a small chamber that just happens to have a bed in it.'

'Like in Tutankhamun's tomb?' I asked, trying to show how switched on, intelligent and knowledgeable I was.

'Nothing like that. That was a magnificent piece, fit for a pharaoh, but the one we got is a piece of worm-eaten junk.'

'So, why are you interested in it?'

'We may not be.'

'Why not? It's old isn't it?'

'Oldish, and that's as much as I'm willing to say, because anything else would be speculation. I'll let Daffy know you called, and ask her to call back, or d'you wanna leave a message?'

The answer was yes. I wanted to tell her how much I

loved her and missed her, and how much I wanted her back, but I couldn't bring myself to say these things to Mike, who seemed far too familiar with her. Besides, I really didn't like her being alone with Professor Mahmoud El-Gammal.

'Umm ... no. Just say I'll try later.'

'OK, buddy, I'll do that. Ciao.'

'Chow?'

He hung up, and I was just about to sit down when the phone rang. Excited, I picked it up.

'Daphne, how are you?'

'Bonehead,' said Featherlight. 'If you had an identical twin, the pair of you wouldn't have the brains to make a whole idiot.'

'Sorry,' I said. 'I thought you were her, because ...'

'If you've started to think I'm your lovely wife, then you've got even more problems than are obvious.'

'I didn't know it was you until you spoke. Sorry, Featherlight.'

'It's Mr Binks to you, Caplet, and I don't want you calling me Daphne again. Got it?'

'I won't. Now, how can I help you?'

'You can't even help yourself. Just tell Mrs Goodfellow that Billy was having a tidy up and came across a bag of mixed teeth which no one has claimed. She can have 'em.'

'I'm sure she'll be delighted,' I said with a grimace.

He hung up, and I went into the kitchen, only to find Mrs Goodfellow wasn't there. How she wasn't there was a puzzle, because she couldn't have got by me without my noticing. I looked out into the back garden, where Dregs, all alone, was enjoying a good sniff, his breath curling like dragon's smoke. As I watched, he turned his head as if intending to lick his wounded leg, but paused, and resumed sniffing. I returned to the sitting room as the old girl came downstairs dressed in her Sunday best, a long green winter coat and a longer turquoise skirt, the effect a little spoiled by the tatty black Wellington boots. She beamed when I passed on Featherlight's message.

'Thank you, dear. He's such a thoughtful man, isn't he? I'll pick them up after church.'

Although he was not at all a thoughtful man in my opinion, there was still something about him that was weirdly disarming. That was the reason, I supposed, why there were so many regular customers at the Feathers, even though there were far nicer pubs in town. Thinking about it, all the other pubs were nicer, but they didn't have Featherlight. According to Hobbes, he meant well, though it wasn't easy to tell, especially for those who got on his wrong side and felt his fists, which, like his bellies, were big, but which, unlike his bellies, were as hard as granite. Happily, his temper rarely lasted more than a minute, though it was a minute too long for most. Another peculiar facet of his personality was the old-fashioned courtesy he always extended to women, even though few ventured into the Feathers to experience it, being repelled, so I'd been told, not by the smell or the dirt, but by the customers. However, the few who did enter had nothing to fear since he'd swiftly sort out any man who stepped far out of line, and most of us – them, rather – did not dare explore how far that might be.

As Mrs Goodfellow left for church, Hobbes came downstairs, and I wondered why he wasn't escorting her, which he normally did unless snowed under with work. He was poking at a rather smart new mobile he must have acquired when I'd been afflicted and didn't appear too busy, despite the murders and the boar.

'I'm going to take Dregs for a walk,' he said.

'Is that wise? With his leg?'

'With all of his legs. The vet said he should take exercise, so long as he doesn't overdo it. Are you fit enough to go out?'

'I think so,' I said, having checked it wasn't raining.

'Well, if you want to come, get yourself ready while I fetch him.'

I grabbed my coat, and, realising I was wearing slippers, rushed upstairs for my boots. When I returned Hobbes was ready and the dog, unusually, was on his lead.

'Why did you put that on?' I asked.

'I don't want him rushing off at the moment. He knows he should take it easy, but there are too many distractions. Let's go.'

We headed up Hedbury Road towards the side entrance of Ride Park. Just as we approached Keeper's Cottage, Dregs tucked his tail between his legs and bristled.

'What's up?' I asked.

He said nothing, but growled and bared his teeth.

'Interesting,' said Hobbes.

'Yeah,' I agreed, putting on a spurt to keep up. 'Why?'

'Because he's not happy, and this is where he left us to go courting.'

'So it is. D'you think she rejected him?'

'A big, handsome fellow like Dregs? I doubt it.'

'Well, something's upset him,' I said as we passed the cottage.

'But he's over it now,' Hobbes observed.

Indeed, Dregs, his tail wagging again, was marching in front, straining against his lead, eager to reach the park despite his injured leg. Hobbes released him as soon as we got there, and though I expected him to run off like the mad thing he usually was, he walked with us, obviously heeding the vet's advice, even when a squirrel ran across the path. As I huddled into my coat against the bitterly cold wind, I'd have liked to question Hobbes about what he'd been up to, but, since he appeared to be in deep contemplation, I reined in my curiosity.

The park wasn't quite as deserted as I'd first thought, though only a handful of people were out and about, mainly walking with dogs. I guessed it was too raw for most. Still, after a day in bed, I was delighted to be in the open, and to feel so well, since my previous bad cold had left me bedbound for a week, and lethargic and drained for a further week. Admittedly, I might have made a little more of it than had been strictly necessary, since I'd rather enjoyed Daphne fussing over me.

I wondered what she was doing all alone with that professor, and why she hadn't mentioned Mike, who sounded like a big, confident kind of guy, the sort any woman would want to have around. For some reason the world became tinged with green, and for a moment I thought it might be a side effect of jealousy. It turned out we'd walked into a small copse festooned with ivy and almost enclosed by holly.

Hobbes stopped and stared at the ground.

'What's up?' I asked.

He held up his hand in warning and stepped into the dense undergrowth, Dregs on his heels, while I stayed put, scared in case he'd discovered something dangerous, like, for instance, a wild boar's nest. However, Dregs's body-language, ears up, tail up, wary but calm, suggested interest rather than alarm. I still held my breath as Hobbes dragged aside a curtain of bramble and ivy, but since nothing horrible appeared, I relaxed.

He stood to the side to let me see. 'Someone's been camping here.'

Hidden deep in the vegetation was a small hut made of sticks, woven twigs and grass, with stones around the base. He pushed aside a woven screen of sticks and ivy and revealed the interior, a snug space, lined with moss and dry leaves. A pair of hammocks, again cunningly woven by nimble fingers from whatever grew around, had been stretched between the walls.

'I wouldn't have wanted to sleep out in this with all the rain we've had,' I said.

'I suspect you'd have been fine,' said Hobbes, looking around, 'though it appears, in fact, to have been built since the storm. These twigs have been cut very recently.'

'Who would make such a thing? Kids?'

'It's far too well built for children. Whoever made this knew precisely what they were doing, because I reckon it would keep out even the heaviest weather. It looks nearly windproof, and it's well insulated and is just about as well put together as it could be without timber and nails.'

'I still wouldn't want to live here though,' I said.

'Maybe not if you had a choice, but this place, although it clearly lacks modern comforts, would be acceptable. It's not so long ago that most people round here had to live much like this, though in more permanent structures. I'd guess it's only a temporary dwelling.'

'You didn't answer my question. Who could have done it? I mean, who would have the right skills and knowledge?'

'I don't know, but I have some suspicions.'

'Go on.'

'Do you remember the heptagram?'

'The star thing? Of course.'

'Well, whoever made that probably made this. The handiwork is very similar to ones I've seen before.'

'Yeah, I suppose it's possible, but since you don't know who made the star, it doesn't really help, does it?'

'I don't know their names, and I may not need to. It's not a criminal offence to live in this manner, although Colonel Squire is hot-headed enough to do something against the law if he finds someone using his land without permission and without paying rent. I'm inclined to think the people who built this shelter may have come here after being flooded out.'

'Or maybe their flat was demolished by a tree,' I said as a couple of random thoughts came together and stuck.

'Do you know something?'

'I might do. You see, the Elweses, the couple whose flat ours fell on, weren't home at the time, which was lucky for them, though I thought it strange, because ... well ... I mean to say, it was a rotten night to be out in, wasn't it?'

Hobbes nodded.

'And when I bumped into her earlier, we had a chat, and she said something ...'

'It would have been rather one-sided if she hadn't.'

'She said her cousin, Aubrey, had seen a man with an air rifle in the park last night, and I wondered about that because ...'

'Because the park is locked at dusk,' said Hobbes, nodding. 'I don't suppose he recognised the shooter?'

'I asked the same question, because I thought it might have been the bloke who shot Dregs and me, but she said Aubrey hadn't seen him clearly.'

'Thanks,' said Hobbes. 'You may well be right about this being their accommodation.'

'Thanks, but ... umm ... thinking about it again, I'm not so sure. She, Hilda that is, was really smartly dressed, at least I think she was, and she didn't look like she'd been sleeping in a hut.'

Hobbes shrugged. 'If she's what I suspect she is, she could easily appear smart to one such as you.'

'What d'you mean "one such as me"?'

'A member of the public,' said Hobbes. 'Let's put their screen back and get out of here. By the way, have you noticed anything unusual about this place?'

'Not really. What do you mean?'

'Something is missing.'

As he picked up the screen, I took a last look around inside and stepped out into the open.

'Umm ... a bathroom?'

He fitted the screen and turned away. 'They could do their business in the woods, like bears are reputed to do, and there are facilities in town. No, I mean something fundamental.'

'Umm ... wardrobes?' I hazarded, following as he marched away.

'No. Let me put it this way. If you were building a shelter at this time of year, besides making it weatherproof, what would you want to include?'

I screwed up my face with the effort of thinking while Hobbes rearranged the undergrowth so that no one would know there was a hidden shelter.

'Yeah,' I said at last, 'I've got it ... somewhere to cook!'

'Well, yes, it could be used for that, but I was thinking more generally of a fire.' He sniffed the air, dropped to his knees and crawled towards a small holly bush. When he pushed it, it fell to reveal a shallow pit with stones around the top and charred wood and ash at the bottom. 'I thought so. Most folk would want some sort of fireplace. It gets dark at night, and cold.'

'It's not so warm now,' I said, shivering as he replaced the holly.

'A brisk walk will warm you up, and give me time to think.'

A brisk walk for him and Dregs was close to a fast jog for me, and as I followed them around the park, gasping for air, I reflected that my fitness was not as good as when I'd been staying with them full-time, and yet I reckoned I was already fitter and a little slimmer than I'd been when Daphne had left. I hoped I could pleasantly surprise her when she came back, whenever that was. Soon I hoped, and nearly choked – not too soon would be better, since I needed to sort out my little problem with the compromising photographs first. I would have liked to ask Hobbes for advice but was too embarrassed and ashamed, and, anyway, he had two murders to solve, though he seemed not to be doing very much about them.

And yet, there'd been other occasions when I'd not noticed him doing anything, when in reality I just wasn't following the process. It would have been nice if he'd chosen to let me know more of what he was thinking, though, in fairness, he had discussed some cases with me. In fact, there'd been occasions when he'd thanked me for my help in resolving them, although, in all honesty, I'd entirely failed to grasp the significance of what I'd said or done until much later. After one instance, when I'd felt frustrated by his thought processes, I'd asked Mrs Goodfellow how he did it.

'Well, dear,' she'd said, after a good cackle at my vexed expression, 'to make a cake, you have to mix all the ingredients together, put the mixture in the right pan, and put it in the oven at the correct temperature for the correct time. If you're impatient and take it out too soon, you end up with half-baked goo that is no good to anyone. You've got to wait until it is ready.'

Although I'd not entirely grasped her point, my brain being confounded by thoughts of cake, the outcome had been pleasing, since the analogy had inspired her to bake the lightest, fluffiest, richest, most delicious English sponge I'd ever tasted.

I was so much into my own thoughts that I failed to notice Hobbes had stopped until I walked into his back, which was about as soft as a brick wall. Getting back to my feet, a little stunned, I realised we'd left the park and that Dregs was growling and bristling. Once again we were outside Keeper's Cottage.

22

'There's something about this place that upsets him,' said Hobbes, 'which, together with the information you gave me earlier, makes me think I should have a bit of a nose around.'

'What information?' I asked.

'The man with the air rifle.'

'I see … umm … possibly. Do you think he lives here?'

'I think it's a distinct possibility since it gives him easy access to the park.'

'So do a lot of places,' I pointed out.

'True, but Dregs only reacted to this one.'

'So what?'

Hobbes sighed. 'So, it's possible the man with the air rifle in the park, is the individual who shot him.'

'That's what I thought! Are you going in?'

'Not until Dregs is away from here. He's not happy, so you'd better take him home.'

Though I would have preferred to stay and watch the fun, the dog was evidently in so much distress that I nodded and led him away. As soon as we were past the cottage, he perked up and headed for home at a sedate pace, in keeping with his invalid status. Unfortunately, this didn't last. After a couple of minutes he seemed to forget he was an invalid and broke into a run, overcoming my attempt to restrain him, and dragging me towards Blackdog Street at a speed I would once have described as breakneck, but which, since my neck remained intact, could more properly have been described as traumatic.

It was busy in town, and despite having to exert an immense amount of concentration on merely staying on my feet, I couldn't understand people's reactions. I was not used to inspiring shock, fear, and horror. Many fled as we approached, some of them screaming, and by no means all of them women. Realisation dawned appallingly slowly that they weren't actually looking at me or Dregs, but at something following us. This left me with a dreadful dilemma since I couldn't look back without losing my balance, unless I released Dregs's lead first, in which case I would slow down and whatever was behind would catch up. I still hadn't solved the problem, when Dregs made it academic by swerving around a red pillar box, a manoeuvre inertia would not permit me. Releasing the lead, I made a desperate attempt at a leapfrog, getting one leg over, but catching the other. For a moment I straddled the top, and then, as gravity took over, flopped back, and landed astride something that was large, bristly and muscular. It had huge, erect hairy ears, fearsome tusks, and squealed like a pig. A man in my position has two choices: to try to hang on, or to fall off. I chose the latter, or rather the boar chose for me, when after a number of steps that caused immense grief to my groin department, it executed a series of pirouettes that sent me spinning into the gutter.

All the breath was knocked out of me, and it seemed ages before I was able to re-inflate my lungs. As breathing returned, I asked my brain what I could do should the boar attack, and, for once, it responded really quickly; I could do nothing at all, except squeal, which was exactly what I did when something touched my shoulder.

'Are you all right?' asked Hobbes.

'Umm ... yes. At least I think so.'

'Good. Now, what made you decide to ride the boar?'

'I didn't actually decide. It was an accident.'

'Oh well, it was entertaining while it lasted.'

'Great, but ... umm ... where's it gone now?'

'Away. It turned left at the end of the road, so I expect it's heading towards the river, or Church Fields.'

'Where did it come from?' I asked as he helped me back to my feet.

'Keeper's Cottage. When I hopped into the back garden, there he was. My arrival must have spooked him, and he leapt the wall like a show jumper and fled into town. I must say I was impressed by your turn of speed when you realised he was behind you.'

I nodded modestly, but said nothing. We turned into Blackdog Street.

'However, your attempt at hurdling the pillar box was less impressive. Ah! Here he is.'

Dregs, looking around suspiciously as if expecting attack from every shadow, was trotting towards us, dragging his lead and, other than a slight limp, appeared unscathed. He gave us an enthusiastic greeting and seemed keen to get home, where he enjoyed a noisy drink before settling down in his basket for a well-deserved rest.

'Are you going back to Keeper's Cottage?' I asked Hobbes.

He shook his head. 'Not until later. It's nearly dinner time.'

I glanced at the clock, surprised it was already half-past twelve, though the aroma of roasting pork ought to have alerted me. 'But where is Mrs Goodfellow?'

'Good question,' he said. 'She should be back by now.'

'She did mention going to the Feathers after church to pick up a bag of teeth.'

'Oh dear,' he said.

'Why? They're lost teeth no one wants anymore and she'll give them a good home.'

'Yes, I'm sure she will, but I was thinking more of our dinners.'

'She hasn't gone far. She'll be back soon ... won't she?'

'Possibly not. There's the sherry you see.'

'Sherry? What sherry?' I asked. 'Where's she going to get sherry from?'

'Featherlight will offer her a glass.'

'Sherry? At the Feathers? You're having me on.'

'I wish I was,' said Hobbes looking gloomy. 'He keeps some in for his lady customers.'

'He gets lady customers?'

'Not often,' he admitted, 'but he always keeps some in on the off chance, and the trouble is that the lass has a bit of a weakness for it. She'll occasionally take a sip of other drinks, but sherry ...'

'You think she'll drink too much?'

He nodded. 'And she can't hold it.'

'At her age, she should know her limits,' I said.

'She knows them well enough, but ignores them.'

At that moment, the front door bell rang. Dregs looked up and barked, and decided he was still too much of an invalid to go charging around. Hobbes answered it.

It was Featherlight, wearing the old girl across his shoulders like a cape. He ducked his head and she rolled into Hobbes's arms.

'I know who you are,' she said opening her eyes, looking up and burping. 'Pardon me!'

'Sherry?' asked Hobbes.

Featherlight nodded and treated us to his broadest grin, which was not pleasant on an empty stomach. 'I'll leave her to you,' he said. He started to turn away and paused. 'I had a customer in last night ...'

'Amazing!' I said, and was rewarded with a glare.

'... who said something interesting.'

'About what?' said Hobbes, cutting me off before I could make a facetious reply.

'About a wild boar. He was reading about it in the *Bugle,* and said he'd delivered one to a smallholding near Fenderton a couple of months back. He was a bit vague because he'd had a few drinks, mind.'

'Do you think it's the same boar?' I asked.

Featherlight shrugged.

'Thank you very much,' said Hobbes. 'I don't suppose you caught the gentleman's name? Or asked the address where he'd delivered it?'

Featherlight shook his head. 'I'm not a copper any more. I leave that kind of stuff to you. He was just a van driver.' He paused. 'I think his name was 'arry, but he was heading for Birmingham today.'

Then he glared at me. 'There's more of those posters gone up. It looks like you've been a naughty boy, and if Hobbes wasn't here I'd give you such a clout that'd teach you to treat your marriage vows with respect.'

Featherlight turned away, raising a hand in farewell and leaving me to panic again.

'Posters?' said Hobbes.

'Oh ... umm ... they're nothing much, but they're ... umm ... a little embarrassing. I'll deal with them.'

'All right then,' he said and shut the front door.

I was by no means convinced I could do anything sensible, but it was my problem, and I was too guilt-ridden to talk about it. Besides, it could hardly be his priority, and hopefully it would sort itself out.

'I need to give some thought to that boar,' said Hobbes, 'but first I'd better put the lass to bed.'

'I'm not a bore and it's not bedtime,' said Mrs Goodfellow, yawning. 'I'm not tired.'

'Why would somebody want a boar?' I asked as he carried her upstairs. 'I reckon they'd be a bit fierce for a pet.'

'Who knows,' said Hobbes. 'Some folk like fierce things. I once knew a chap in Hedbury who kept a crocodile as a pet. He said it was friendly and only gave him love bites. One day it bit his head off.'

'My granny had a mad bad cat,' I said, 'but he was only fierce to me.'

Having carried the old girl to her room, he laid her on her

side on the edge of the bed. 'You'd better get her a bucket,' he said.

I fetched a heavy galvanised bucket and set it on the floor beneath her face and we left her, snoring.

'What about lunch?' I asked as we went back downstairs.

'The pork will be fine, but we'll have to manage the vegetables between us.'

'What should I do?' I asked when we were in the kitchen.

'Fetch some spuds up from the cellar, and make sure they're the starchy ones. While you're doing that I'll start on the greens and take the meat out to rest.'

He grabbed the hugest knife in the rack, one that reminded me of a cutlass, and selected a pointy cabbage, leeks and broccoli from a box. I headed into the cellar, and since I had reason to be nervous of things that had lurked in the dark down there, I was relieved the light was working, as well as being pleased the rickety old steps had been replaced by sturdy new ones. Although occasional and usually carried out just before whatever he was working on entirely turned up its toes, Hobbes's handiwork was effective and reliable. He was the only person I knew who could drive nails into wood with his knuckles, or turn a screw with his fingernails, though I suspected Featherlight might be capable of similar feats, should he ever feel the need to repair anything, which, going by the state of the Feathers, he didn't often.

The flood was evidenced by dark, dank puddles, a stagnant stench, and a watermark a third of the way up the walls, but the old girl's roots, like Hobbes's wines, were safely stored on wooden racks above the high tide mark. There were baskets of parsnips, turnips, swedes, carrots and some long, weird vegetables I didn't recognise, but I had a bit of trouble finding potatoes. I eventually spotted some on a rack in the corner. They were, perhaps, a little on the small side, and had a few too many roots sprouting, but they felt firm, and I reckoned they looked starchy enough, whatever that meant. I selected a generous handful of the bigger specimens and carried them upstairs.

'Peel 'em, cut 'em into quarters and boil 'em for fifteen minutes with a pinch of salt. Then drain 'em, mash 'em with a masher, add a knob of butter, and serve 'em,' said Hobbes, who was hacking cabbage into tiny strips.

The task was fiddly and hard going, even though I'd selected a knife almost as massive as Hobbes's. However, I finally triumphed and placed the peeled, chopped spuds in a saucepan, with sufficient, but not too much, water and a pinch of salt. Hobbes, having poked the resting pork, lit the gas under the saucepans.

'Keep an eye on those,' he said, 'while I check on the lass.'

He left me to it, and I discovered the truth in the old adage about watched pots never boiling. Getting bored, I picked up the *Bugle* and read about the boar, only to be disappointed that the article contained less information than I already knew. At some point, I was vaguely aware of a sort of hiss but I didn't register what it was until I smelt gas. When I glanced up, all the pans had boiled over and dowsed the burners, leaving the top of the cooker awash. I got up, took a match from the drawer, and struck it as I approached the cooker.

The flash and the heat took me by surprise, but left me unhurt, though I wondered about the unpleasant sulphurous smell as I tried to calm Dregs, who was barking and excited. Hobbes burst in and, to give him credit, ascertained that neither of us had been hurt before laughing long and loud. It was by no means the first time I'd come close to disaster in there.

'What is it with you and kitchens?' he asked, when his guffaws had subsided into grins.

'I don't know. I do my best, but this one seems to have it in for me. I'm sorry.'

'Never mind,' he said. 'No real harm's been done. I'm sure it'll all grow back.'

'What will?'

'Your eyebrows and the hair at the front.'

'Oh, no ... how long?'

'As long as it was before, but it'll take a few weeks.'

I ran upstairs, peered in the mirror, and groaned. The frizzed hair on my forehead, coupled with the blank canvass where my eyebrows should have lived, left me looking like an alien. I just knew people would point me out in the street and laugh, that dogs would bark at me and that little children would flee in horror. And what would Daphne say when she saw me?

I returned to the kitchen where Hobbes, having brought the cooking back under control, was carving the meat, and to be fair, not making a bad job of it. The pan with the meat juices was simmering nicely, emitting pleasant aromas, and I began to hope we'd managed without the old girl.

'How can I help?' I asked.

'Mash the potatoes, please.'

I did as he asked, draining them and pummelling them with the masher, although the task, and the spuds, were much harder than I'd anticipated. As soon as I'd thrown in a little butter, Hobbes began plating up.

I took my place and waited while he said grace. It looked like we'd done a reasonable job, though the vegetables were perhaps a little watery. Hobbes shovelled a fork-load of mashed potato into his mouth, and looked puzzled.

'What did you do to this?' he asked.

'Nothing I shouldn't have.'

I sampled a little. The texture was all wrong and the taste, though not exactly unpleasant, was exactly unlike what I'd been expecting, being a curious mixture of carrot, celery and water-chestnut.

'I don't believe this is potato at all,' said Hobbes with a

chuckle.

'Umm ... it must be. What else can it be?'

He laughed again.

'What's so funny?'

'Where did you find them?'

'In the cellar, like you said.'

'On the vegetable racks or the one in the corner?'

'The one in the corner. That's where they were, and it's not my fault they taste funny.'

'They taste of what they are.'

'What?'

'Congratulations, you have prepared a fine dish of mashed dahlia roots. The lass stores them down there ready for planting out in the spring, and she won't be happy we've eaten them. I'd make the most of this dinner if I were you, because you'll be on dry bread and water when she sobers up and realises what you've done.'

Although I knew he was joking, the thought of missing out on her cooking made my stomach lurch.

'They're not poisonous are they?' I asked, as he helped himself to a large fork load.

'No,' he said when he'd swallowed. 'The Aztecs cultivated them for food.'

'But didn't they die out?'

'Their culture did, and many of the people, but, don't worry, it wasn't dahlia tubers that killed them. I believe it was smallpox.'

'How do you know all this stuff?'

'I read – you should try it, but in this case, I was told when I was in Mexico.'

'I didn't know you'd been there ... when?'

'Long ago.'

'Why?'

'They asked me to police an outbreak of chupacabras.'

'What?'

'Dangerous beasts.'

I would love to have probed more, but a deep frown dissuaded me and I left him to his dinner, which, all things considered, wasn't too bad, and was far better than many pub meals I'd enjoyed before I'd acquired a gourmet's palate.

Afterwards, I cleared the dishes and, feeling extremely virtuous, washed up while Hobbes made a pot of tea. We were reasonably successful at both tasks; I only chipped one plate, and the tea was drinkable. We repaired to the sitting room and sat down.

'So, apart from the boar, did you see anything else of interest at Keeper's Cottage?' I asked, as he stirred sugar into his mug.

'I believe I met Dregs's love interest, a sweet Samoyed bitch, who, to go by the tag on her collar, is called Mimi.'

'What's a Samoyed?'

'A breed of dog,' said Hobbes.

'I guessed that. I mean what are they like?'

'Medium-sized, white, fluffy and doggy. The breed was once used for pulling sleds in Siberia.'

'So, a bit like a husky?'

'A bit, but smaller and fluffier. Her behaviour worried me.'

'Why?'

'She was scared.'

'I'm not surprised with that boar around.'

'No, by me. She seemed quite relaxed with the boar.'

'That's unusual,' I said, for Hobbes had something about him, his feral odour I suspected, that dogs seemed to like. I'd once thought of analysing it, bottling it, and selling it to postmen and the like, but hadn't quite got round to it.

'It is, and it's also unusual to keep a timid dog on a heavy chain. I suspect she's being ill-treated, so I intend to make a further visit.'

'When?'

'When I've finished my tea.'

The phone rang. Hobbes put down his mug to answer. 'Inspector Hobbes, how may I help you? ... Good afternoon, Derek ... Mr Marco Jones? Are you sure? ... I see ... and did you find out the other thing? ... Now that is interesting ... What about Golums Logons? ... Yes, I suspected so ... Thank you very much indeed.'

Having replaced the receiver, he returned to the sofa, looking thoughtful.

'Who was that?' I asked.

'Constable Poll. He's been doing a bit of investigation for me.'

'That's nice. So ... umm ... who is Marco Jones?'

'The tenant of Keeper's Cottage.'

'You sounded really interested. Why?'

'Because Derek found out who actually owns the cottage.'

'And?'

'It's Mr Solomon Slugg.'

'Him again? It's probably just a coincidence?'

'Possibly. Coincidences happen all the time, but not so often that I wouldn't check them. According to Poll, Mr Slugg also owns Golums Logons, and has a majority holding in Big Mama's Canteen, where Mr Marco Jones works.'

'Well, he is a local businessman. Wouldn't you expect him to have an interest in a few local concerns?'

'Of course,' said Hobbes. 'However, Mr Slugg is really starting to interest me.' He drained his mug and poured himself another.

'Because of Septimus?' I asked, 'Or is there something else?'

'During my visit to Tode-in-the-Wold, I asked a number of people about Mr Septimus Slugg and it turned out that he was quite well known there. However, no one I spoke to suggested he might be a wastrel or a drunkard. He was, in fact, the town librarian, and though he used to enjoy the occasional pint in the Green Dragon and often took part in its pub quiz, he was never known to be drunk or to cause trouble. I confirmed that he had no police record.'

'That doesn't fit in with Solomon's account,' I observed.

'Certainly not,' he agreed. 'Furthermore, Septimus was indeed the seventh and youngest child of Mr Samuel Slugg, also known as Samuel S Lugg. Two of his brothers have died, but the other siblings, two sisters and a brother, are alive and well in Australia, to where they emigrated in the sixties. According to his phone records, Septimus kept in regular contact, and his passport showed he'd visited there about three years ago. So, it seems to have been a happy family, other than Solomon. I contacted his sister Emily, who is now Mrs Boon, and informed her of Septimus's death. She was understandably upset, though she'd suspected something was amiss since he hadn't been in contact, which was unlike him. In addition, she gave me some interesting information about Solomon.'

'What?' I asked, agog, my tea cooling.

'She said he was nearly a recluse. He lived alone, rarely left the house, and was financially dependent on a trust fund set up for him by his late father. The family sent him birthday and Christmas cards, and occasional letters, but he never responded and hardly ever allowed them to visit. None of them had actually set eyes on him since nineteen ninety five.'

'Except for Septimus,' I pointed out. 'She must have been lying for some reason, because we've met Solomon who's rather a charming gentleman, and not at all reclusive.'

'No,' he admitted. 'He didn't give that impression.'

'So you could discount her evidence.'

'I could, but I won't. I can think of no reason for her to lie about him.'

'In that case, he must have changed, though isn't it more usual for people of his age to become set in their ways rather than to suddenly decide to go into politics and business?'

'It depends on the individual,' he said, 'but I have a suspicion that whatever has changed, it was not Mr Slugg's personality. There's a numerical element to this case that is intriguing.'

'You've lost me now. We know what he's like, and, if you believe what his sister says, he must have changed considerably, which doesn't make sense.'

'I think it might,' he said, grinning in the infuriating way he had when he was trying to get me to think.

I was spared by a thump and a clang from above.

'What was that?'

'The lass falling out of bed, I expect,' he said, standing up, and loping to the rescue.

I followed, nearly getting bowled over by Dregs who, fully restored by his nap, was keen to see what was happening.

Mrs Goodfellow's normally pale face held more colour than was usual; it was green. She was sitting on the floor, groaning.

'I think I may have imbibed a trifle too much sherry, dear,' she said as Hobbes helped her up. 'Take me to the bathroom. Now!'

He took her at a gallop, and shut the door behind her, which at least muffled the horrible retching and splashing. After a few minutes, she tottered out and he helped her back to bed.

'How are you feeling?' I asked.

'A little delicate.'

'Can I get you anything?'

She nodded, groaned, and held her head. 'Could you go to my drawer in the kitchen and fetch my tonic? And I'd like a glass of water too, if it's not too much bother.'

I hurried away, filled a glass and found the bottle she wanted beneath her set of nunchakus. Instead of pushing them aside and leaving them well alone, I thought it might be fun to give them a quick whirl, like Bruce Lee in the movies. I was mistaken. When I'd recovered enough to stand up straight, I vowed never to touch the things again. I took her tonic and water upstairs.

'You've been playing with her nunchakus,' said Hobbes as I reached the old girl's room. 'I can tell by the way you're walking.'

'Those things are dangerous.'

'Not when they're in the drawer, dear,' said Mrs Goodfellow, taking the glass and shaking in a few drops of her tonic, which was thick and red, like tomato ketchup, but which smelt of unwashed feet. She gulped down the contents in one, and lay back with a groan.

A moment later, she performed a vertical take-off, crashed down and went rigid, the manoeuvre making Dregs bound around the room, barking like a mad thing.

'Is she all right?' I asked.

Hobbes held up his hand.

She sat up, blew her nose on a tissue and smiled. 'Thank you, dear.' Then she fell back unconscious.

'She'll sleep for a couple of hours now,' said Hobbes, 'and will wake feeling better, after which she'll swear off drink, and adhere to her pledge. Until next time.'

'Does she do it often?'

'About once a year.' He covered her with a blanket and opened the plastic bag she'd been clutching. 'Let's see what she got.'

'That sounds like teeth,' I said, horribly familiar with the rattle.

He nodded and showed me. There must have been a hundred, in all shades from snow white to slush brown:

molars, premolars, canines and incisors. Once the sight, and the knowledge of why they'd left their owners in the Feathers, would have made me sick, but I'd grown into sterner material and a slight shudder sufficed. Even so, when one fell to the floor and I bent to pick it up, I recoiled.

'You can't handle the tooth,' said Hobbes, who had no such qualms.

'That's a good haul,' I said as he dropped it back into the bag. 'Do you think Featherlight is putting dentists out of business, or is keeping them busy repairing the damage?'

'That is a question to which I suspect we'll never know the answer. Right, I'm heading back to Keeper's Cottage, where I hope to have a word with Mr Jones.'

We left her bedroom. Then Hobbes turned, went back, and retrieved Dregs, who'd been attempting to sneak onto the bed.

'Can I come with you?' I asked when we were heading downstairs.

'Yes, but Dregs had better stay.'

The dog's tail drooped as he heard the fateful word 'stay', and he looked up at Hobbes with a pleading expression.

'No,' said Hobbes. 'You might find it upsetting.'

Dregs whined, wagged his tail and twisted his mouth into a passably endearing grin.

'Oh, all right then. Just behave yourself.'

23

A minute or two later, suitably clad against drizzle so fine it was almost mist, we started towards Keeper's Cottage. A man in a hooded mac was walking ahead, and although I thought there was something familiar about him, it took a few moments to work out why, by which time he'd turned towards Keeper's Cottage and gone inside. Dregs started growling again until Hobbes reminded him to behave.

'I saw that man in Golums Logons when Mrs Goodfellow sorted out the students,' I told Hobbes. 'He was taking money. Quite a lot of it, I think.'

'Thank you,' said Hobbes, walking up to the door and ringing the doorbell. The door opened almost immediately and the man stood there. Although he was of less than average height and rather thick around the waist, he looked powerful, like a body-builder.

'Who are you?' he asked, frowning, his accent an odd mix of local with a smidgeon of Welsh and a pinch of something foreign.

'Mr Marco Jones?' asked Hobbes, showing his ID card.

'Maybe. What do you want?'

'I want a world of harmony and peace ...' said Hobbes.

'You what?' said Mr Jones, looking confused. When he saw me, he bit his lip as if my presence alarmed him, which was not an effect I normally had on people.

'... and I'd like to see your dog, sir.'

'I don't have a dog.'

'In that case, I'd like to see the dog in your garden.'

'Which one?'

'The one at the back of your house.'

'Why?' asked Mr Jones.

'Why not?' asked Hobbes with a smile.

From the bafflement on Marco's face, I suspected he might not be overly endowed with brains.

'Er ... Because she's dangerous,' he said after a long pause.

'All the more reason for me to see her,' said Hobbes. 'If she's dangerous, it might mean she's a threat to the public, and we can't allow that sort of thing, can we? It's bad enough having that wild boar running about.'

'Have you seen one?' asked Mr Jones, looking suddenly interested.

'Why? Have you lost one, sir?'

'Er ... no ... of course not ... er ... what would I be doing with a boar? They can be dangerous, and I wouldn't keep a dangerous animal.'

'Apart from your dog?'

'It's not mine.'

'I trust you haven't stolen her, sir,' said Hobbes with a stern expression.

'No ... I'm ... er ... keeping her for ... a friend ... because his smallholding is flooded. Yes, that's it.'

Having had some experience of Hobbes's interviews, I was growing suspicious of Marco Jones.

However, Hobbes merely nodded and smiled. 'A friend in need is a friend indeed, sir. Just to satisfy my curiosity, could you tell me your friend's name and address?'

'His name is ... er ... er ...'

'One of the Gloucestershire Er-Ers, I presume. Does he have a first name?'

'Eh?'

'So, Mr A Er-Er. Quite unusual, sir.'

'No,' said Marco, squirming. 'You've got it wrong and you're making fun of me. I don't like it.'

'Sorry, sir. Your friend's name?'

'It's on the tip of my tongue ... it's ... John ... er ... Johnson ... and he lives in ... that place that got flooded ...'

'Atlantis?' I suggested.

'No, Fenderton.'

'By the Soren, I expect,' said Hobbes, nodding. 'I know the area well, but I'm not aware of any Mr John Johnson. I wonder why?'

'Er ... that's because he's ... er ... only just moved there. ... Yes, that's right.'

'Have you known him long, sir?'

'A few years.'

'Very good, sir.'

Marco blew out his cheeks, as if he thought he'd just sailed unscathed through the hazardous straits of thought. But Hobbes was not finished.

'Where did you first meet?'

'At the Bellman's Arms. Do you know it?'

'Indeed, I do, sir. It's on The Shambles, near to the *Bugle's* offices ... but, hold on a minute, that sounds a little strange. Are you quite sure?'

'Yes.'

'Then perhaps you could enlighten me how you met Mr Johnson at the Bellman's a few years ago, when he's only just moved here, and you yourself have not been in town for very long?'

It was a good point that Marco failed to appreciate. 'Are you calling me a liar?'

'No, of course not, sir, but I am suggesting you may have got a little confused.'

It may have been a trick of the light, but Hobbes appeared to have grown both in height and breadth, and was looming over Marco like a thundercloud over a picnic. Marco was suddenly as pale as the snowdrops that had recently emerged from their long sleep, and was as twitchy as I'd been when infested with werewolf fleas.

'Yes, I am a little confused.'

'It can happen so easily,' said Hobbes. 'I suppose you

must be flustered because you're not used to being asked questions by a police officer. I am right, aren't I, sir?'

'Yes.'

'And I suppose you would like me to leave you in peace?'

'Yes.'

'But you'd be happy to let me see the dog first?'

'Yes ... er ...'

'Thank you, sir. Is this the way?'

Not forgetting to wipe his feet on the doormat, he squeezed past Marco, who looked utterly bamboozled.

'Come along,' he said.

Dregs and I followed, with Marco clumping along at the rear, apparently lost for words, though he was making a strange whimpering noise. Dregs never took his eyes off Marco. The cottage itself, though weather-beaten Cotswold stone on the outside, had been modernised within so that, although it still retained much of its rustic charm and character, it was warm and comfortable, with varnished floorboards, fine furniture and cream plastered walls. It was discreetly lit by small strategically positioned lamps, was neat and tidy, and smelt fresh and citrusy. It was not as I would have expected, had I got around to expecting anything.

'Very nice, sir,' observed Hobbes, looking back over his shoulder. 'Is this the way to the back door?'

Although Marco nodded, his mouth moved as if it wanted to say something, if only his brain had managed to think of anything.

Hobbes led us through the kitchen, past a polished plank table and wooden chairs painted a pale blue, between a tall dresser covered with plates and other crockery on the left, and, on the right, a cream Aga range with a row of gleaming copper saucepans above. He opened the back door and we entered the back garden, where a beautiful, long-haired white dog was tethered to a stake by a heavy chain padlocked to a steel collar. She cringed and whimpered on seeing us, until Dregs burst past and ran towards her, whining and wagging his tail, like she was an old friend. She relaxed, and allowed us to stroke her, though she flinched if a hand went close to a small scab on her neck. Whenever Marco moved, she cringed.

'She's a fine looking dog,' said Hobbes, 'but I fail to understand why you have her chained up like this, especially without food, water or shelter. I would like an explanation, and one that doesn't have any reference to the fictional Mr John Johnson.'

'He's not fictional, he he ...' Marco began and stuttered to a halt, stunned, I imagined, by Hobbes's inter-continental scowl.

'No more untruths, sir. It'll be so much better for you if you start answering honestly while you have a choice, rather than later when I get angry. You wouldn't like it when I'm angry.'

'No, you really wouldn't,' I said as Marco looked to me for guidance.

I shuddered, recalling those rare occasions when I'd been caught in the fallout of Hobbes's rage, which although not directed at me, had been dreadful. He could be amazingly lenient with petty offenders, if having to endure one of his little talks could be described as lenient, but would come down harder, heavier and faster than a concrete slab on those he suspected of cruelty or of abusing positions of authority. Of course, when he allowed himself to get in a rage the recipients were no longer mere suspects, but definites.

Marco, wide-eyed and rubber legged, stared around, as if searching for sanctuary. None was available.

'Speak to me, Mr Jones,' said Hobbes, towering over him.

'He's fainted,' I observed, as the man went down like a punctured airbed.

'So I see,' said Hobbes with a wicked grin, 'and, since an unconscious man is clearly incapable of caring for a dog, I feel I ought to take charge of her.'

He carried the casualty to the white-leather sofa in the sitting room and, having ascertained that his vital signs were okay, returned to the garden and picked up the dog's chain. Expecting a demonstration of his phenomenal strength, I was disappointed when he simply unbuckled her collar. The released dog bounded around us, nuzzling and playing with Dregs, and Hobbes sent me into the kitchen to fetch her some water. I returned with a brimming copper pan which she lapped dry as soon as I put it down.

'I'd like to get her out of here as soon as possible,' said Hobbes. 'Would you take her home?'

'Yeah ... why? What are you going to do?'

'I am going to ensure Mr Jones is comfortable, and I might take the opportunity for a bit of a nose around.' He tapped the side of his rather large hooter and chuckled.

'You planned this, didn't you?'

'How could I plan for Mr Jones to faint?'

'I don't know,' I admitted, though it had struck me as odd that so many of those he was interviewing passed out at the most convenient moment.

'You'd better put her on Dregs's lead, because she may not be very good in traffic, or meeting people.'

'But her collar is still padlocked to the chain.'

'So it is,' said Hobbes and took the padlock in his great fist, squeezing until there was a crack. He handed me the collar.

'Thanks,' I said, taking it. 'Come on, Mimi.'

She looked up on hearing her name and trotted towards me, allowing me to refit her collar, and to clip on the lead. I said goodbye to Hobbes, who was on his knees and sniffing in the kitchen, and headed home with Dregs who, though normally a connoisseur of police work, chose to join us, walking at Mimi's side, his thick black tail wagging as if he might take off like a helicopter.

When I reached home, Mrs Goodfellow, looking bleary and wan, was at the kitchen table, splitting hairs with the enormous cleaver she used for slicing tomatoes.

'Hello, dear,' she said, giving me a toothless smile. 'Who's the bitch?'

'Mimi,' I said. 'Hobbes thinks we should look after her, because the man who's supposed to have been doing it is unconscious.'

The old girl nodded, groaned and clutched her head. 'I'm never ever going to drink sherry again,' she announced, fulfilling Hobbes's prophecy.

'Can I get you anything?' I asked, sympathising, for I, too, had over consumed alcohol on occasions, and had been glad of any small kindness.

'No thank you, dear. My tonic is working and I'll be fine after a cup of tea.'

'I'll put the kettle on,' I said.

'Thank you, dear. I'd better feed Mimi. She looks like she needs something.'

'You're probably right. She was very thirsty earlier, and Hobbes thinks she's been mistreated. Umm ... what can we give her?'

'There are a few dog food tins in the cupboard. We can open one of those for now, and after that there's some venison in the cellar that needs using up.'

'Is there? I didn't see any and I was down there at lunchtime.'

'Billy brought it round a few minutes ago. That's why I'm awake already.'

'Where did he get it from? The shops only seem to be selling basics at the moment.'

'Off Pigton Road.'

'Road kill?'

'Mercedes kill, if the mark on the poor beast's flank is anything to go by.'

'Is it all right to eat?'

'It's fresh and has been tenderised.'

'Umm ... okay ... shall I go and fetch it?'

'I thought you were putting the kettle on, dear.'

'I am,' I said, picking up the old copper kettle, filling it and putting it on to boil. 'I'll get the venison now.'

'No, dear. It's a little heavy, so you'd better leave it to me. You can open a tin for Mimi.' She got up, groaning, and headed for the cellar.

There had been a time when my manly ego would have insisted on lifting heavy things for her, but I'd learned to look past her frail appearance and advanced years and see the strength within. Leaving her to get on with it, I patted Mimi, who acknowledged the gesture with a thump of her tail and went back to nuzzling Dregs, who was a most smug-looking dog.

'You're a lucky fellow,' I told him.

Wagging his tail, he whined and woofed, and, from the way she snickered and glanced in my direction, I could only believe he'd told her something about me that wasn't entirely complimentary. It might merely have been my paranoia talking, but I think it was Dregs.

I opened a tin, popped the meat into a bowl and set it down. Both dogs came up, and though Dregs merely sniffed at it, Mimi wolfed the whole lot down within seconds. As soon as she'd finished, she lay down and licked her lips.

Now and again a bump sounded from below. After a particularly loud one, I thought I ought to check.

I headed for the cellar door. 'Are you all right?'

'I'm fine,' she gasped, and came into view, hunched under a massive carcass.

'Bloody Hell!' I exclaimed, 'What on earth is that? Are you

sure it's a deer? It's as big as a cow!'

'It's a red deer, dear, and mind your language.'

'Sorry ... but it can't be ... where are its horny things? I mean its antlers? Shouldn't it have them if it really is a deer?'

'The males drop them this time of year ...'

'Very careless,' I said.

'... but this is a doe, dear, and so never had any.'

'I see. Do you want any help?'

'No, thank you.' She continued upwards, moving the carcass far more easily than I would have. Always helpful, I got out of her way.

When she reached the middle of the room, she dropped her right shoulder and twisted her scrawny old hips, depositing the deer onto the table. Both dogs watched with interest, but only Mimi approached for a sniff. I wasn't surprised, since Dregs had developed an aversion to meat unless it had been prepared and cooked to his satisfaction. In this regard he was more civilised than Hobbes. Mrs Goodfellow stood upright and stretched.

'Now what?' I asked.

'Now we butcher the carcass. First we skin it, and then we cut it into joints.'

'We?' I said.

'Only if you want to, dear.'

Accepting this as my cue to exit, I fled to the sitting room, for although I didn't believe I had a weak constitution, I was concerned the smell would turn my stomach as easily as I could turn a door knob. It made me wonder how a charming young woman like Dr Cynthia could cope with the sights and stinks she must meet on a regular basis, and I could only marvel at her fortitude. Her job was not one that appealed, although I could understand she might get some sort of intellectual thrill from uncovering hidden secrets, much like Daphne must have been finding with her tombs and bedchambers.

I flopped onto the sofa, overcome by the weight of thoughts in my head: Daphne, the murders, the bones, the poster vendetta, the boar, the dog shooter, the psychopathic rugby players, what Hobbes suspected about Solomon Slugg, my getting syndicated in *Sorenchester Life,* and what I ought to be doing about the flat and contacting the insurers. Although it seemed reasonable to deal with the insurance first, it was the least interesting on the list, though Daphne would struggle to understand why I hadn't done it, and I would struggle to explain myself. It was clear I ought to contact the insurers soon, and afterwards that I should search for accommodation. Yet, I couldn't stop thinking that, if I failed to deal with the posters and the threat of blackmail, Daphne might not want me any longer. Before she'd left, and after hard reflection, I'd concluded that the best thing I'd brought to the marriage had been loyalty, and, although I still was loyal really, albeit I had briefly allowed myself to be flattered by a beautiful face, she might not see it like that.

Every now and then my thoughts were punctuated by thuds, and occasional cries of 'get down, Mimi' from the kitchen. The distractions meant that I hadn't quite come to a conclusion about my next move when Hobbes returned, looking rather pleased with himself.

'How did it go?' I asked.

He hung up his coat and sat beside me. 'Firstly, I believe I have confirmed why Dregs was upset in the vicinity of Keeper's Cottage.'

'Go on.'

'When I was nosing around I came across an air rifle and ammunition hidden at the back of a wardrobe. There's nothing wrong with that as such, though the pellets match the one taken from Dregs's leg.'

'So, you think it was Marco who shot him? I thought the

pellets were common.'

'So they are, and they would mean little had Mr Jones not volunteered a confession when he came round and was shown the evidence.'

'Volunteered?'

Hobbes had the grace to chuckle. 'He volunteered the information when I pressed for an answer as to why he possessed such a weapon. It is possible that he formed the impression that possessing a powerful air rifle was illegal, and confessed to spare himself more distress, but I don't know where he got that idea from. It would not be unreasonable to suggest that he is not conspicuously intelligent.'

'Did you charge him?'

'No, I negotiated with him, and since he was worried how his mother would react to his being arrested, he was inclined to be helpful.'

'He has a mother?'

'Everyone has, or had, one. His runs the restaurant where he works. I suspect few others would employ him.'

'She's Big Mama?'

'Indeed. She is a formidable lady.'

A series of thuds came from the kitchen.

'What's the lass doing?' he asked.

'Butchering a dead deer for the dogs.'

'Well, she would hardly butcher a live one,' he said, a little uncertainly.

'I would hope not.'

'So would I. I think I've put a stop to that sort of thing, but she can be a little forgetful.'

'I suppose she is getting on a bit,' I said.

'So she is, but her memory is better than when she first came to stay.' He sighed, and shook his head. 'Anyway, to return to Mr Jones, he did confirm that Mr Solomon Slugg has a controlling stake in the restaurant and is often there.'

'Him again? But, isn't it confirmation that his sister's comments were just wrong?'

'Only if we accept Mr Slugg at face value,' said Hobbes.

'What do you mean?'

'I mean I have strong suspicions about him.'

'I don't see why. He's charismatic and charming, and yes, I understand he's a bit of an oddball, but there's nothing wrong with being eccentric, or owning a restaurant, or even in being a politician.'

'You are essentially correct,' he said, 'though some might quibble about the latter.'

'But, you can't really suspect him of killing his own brother?'

'I don't believe he killed either of his brothers.'

'Either? And aren't you sure the skeleton was Solomon's brother?'

'Quite sure.'

'And ... umm ... didn't you say his surviving brother is in Australia?'

He nodded.

'Then that can't be right ... unless his sister lied.'

'She didn't,' he said, grinning.

'All right, I'll accept that for the moment,' I said, my brain hurting with the effort. 'The important thing is, if you don't think Solomon killed them, who do you think did?'

'If you stop to think about the numbers here, you might begin to suspect he did.'

'You just said he didn't!'

'No, what I said was that I didn't think he'd killed *his* brothers.'

'Now you're just confusing me.'

His smile was infuriating. 'I'm going to see whether the lass needs any help. I'll leave you to mull it over.'

He headed into the kitchen, and I sat back, scratching my head and hoping I hadn't picked up fleas again. It turned out to be just the one and I quickly caught and crushed the little perisher, suspecting Mimi as the source, since Dregs had learnt that Mrs Goodfellow wouldn't allow that sort of thing in the house. Freed from the itch, I was able to devote myself to deep thought. The problem, as I saw it, was that Hobbes suspected Solomon of the murders, and at the same time didn't suspect him. Perhaps he'd meant it philosophically, in that he suspected everybody in general, but nobody in particular, and yet I reckoned he'd meant more than that. It was an impossible conundrum. How could he have murdered the two brothers and, yet, not have murdered his brothers? I'd almost convinced myself that Hobbes had been talking nonsense, when I became aware of a thought at the back of my mind, just out of reach. I forced myself to think outside the box, as Phil had often encouraged me.

The facts were that two brothers had been murdered, one of them being Septimus, the seventh and last of his family. Two others had died long ago, one lived in Australia, and there were two sisters. I counted them up. Seven. That was right. I wondered what Hobbes had been getting at with his talk of numbers. There'd been seven siblings in the family, and I'd accounted for them all.

I slapped my head in frustration, which caused the thought to come loose. As it drifted closer, I snatched at it and held on.

I'd got it! At least I thought I had.

I'd forgotten to include Solomon. That meant there were seven plus one: eight siblings. So, assuming the sister wasn't lying, there appeared to be an extra brother.

The problem was starting to resolve itself. What if the charming man who'd identified himself as Solomon Slugg wasn't really him? Wouldn't that explain why he'd been so different to his sister's description? Despite his beguiling personality, he could be an imposter. That thought opened the possibility that he had killed two brothers, but they were not actually *his* brothers because he was not Solomon. It was a simple solution to what had seemed a crazy conundrum, though why he'd done it was a question to answer later.

Elated by my triumph, I got up and ran to the kitchen to check my answer, quite failing to notice Dregs stretched out in the doorway. Tripping over him, making him yelp, I fell, splatting into the kitchen floor, skidding over the red bricks, and coming eyeball to anus with a sleeping Mimi, who, clearly a dog of delicate sensibilities, leapt to her feet with a yelp, and tried to clear the table at a single bound, just as Mrs Goodfellow's heavy, gleaming cleaver swung down. It would have split Mimi in two had Hobbes not flung himself into harm's way. The cleaver missed the dog, but struck the top of his head with a horrible crunch like cabbage being chopped, and, as I looked in horror at what I'd done, I was showered in hot blood. I got up, trying to help, but found my legs had turned to mush.

24

When I came to, I was staring at Dregs between my legs and the legs of the chair I was sitting on. Seeing my eyes were open, he wagged his tail. I pulled myself upright, still feeling groggy, and wondered why my face was so sore.

'Are you all right, dear?' asked Mrs Goodfellow who was still hacking, though the carcass had been mostly reduced to joints of meat.

'I think so.' I nodded, trying to shake my brain back to life, vaguely aware something had happened.

'Good, but you're still very pale.'

'Did I faint?'

She nodded. 'You went out like a light and fell face first into a chair. You've got a lovely pair of shiners, but I've put a little of my tincture on them, so, in a day or two, they'll be as right as reindeer.'

'Thanks.' I became more my normal self and remembered. 'Hobbes! Is he all right?'

'He's fine.'

'But he can't be ... I saw you chop him ... didn't I?'

'Yes, dear, but he's a tough nut.'

'But, I'm all covered in his blood!'

'Then you'd better wash it off, and change your shirt as soon as you feel up to it.'

'Right. Where's Mimi?'

'In the back garden with the old fellow. The poor bitch is very nervous after what you did to her and he's calming her down. Dregs tried, but what he had in mind didn't suit her, so he's confined in here for now. Would you like a glass of water?'

I nodded, and after washing her hands she handed me a drink. The coolness soon made me feel better, and I sluiced it down, washing away an unpleasant metallic taste, and trying not to think where it had come from. I'd just finished when the garden door opened and Hobbes entered, his head turbaned in white bandages.

'Feeling better?' he asked.

I nodded. 'You?'

'I'll be fine. It's not the first time someone's tried to scalp me. On the other hand, poor Mimi was distressed by the whole incident. She's a highly strung creature.'

'What are you going to do with her? Are you going to take her back to Marco?'

'No, but I would like to find her owner.'

'Surely that'll be easy? A pedigree like her is bound to have been microchipped. You just need to get her scanned.'

'It probably would have been easy had her chip not been cut out.'

'That nasty scab on her neck?' asked Mrs Goodfellow, taking a break from hacking.

Hobbes nodded.

'Well,' I said, 'what about her tag?'

'It's new,' he said, 'and the address on the back is Jones at Keeper's Cottage.'

'That means Marco really did lie about her belonging to John Johnson. That was well spotted.'

'It was obvious, and it's possible she's not really called Mimi.'

'You think she was stolen, but why?'

'I suspect she was taken to be used as a breeding mother. According to Constable Poll, who knows about such things, pure-bred Samoyed puppies go for a lot of money – three thousand pounds each or more. They usually have four to six puppies at a time, and can have two litters a year.'

'So Marco could easily make thirty-six thousand pounds every year. That's not a bad sideline.'

'It wouldn't all be profit, because he'd have to feed her,

though I'd imagine he could do much of that with scraps from the restaurant, and he'd need a male Samoyed, at least for a short time. Of course, if he was intending to breed pedigrees it would be a reason for shooting Dregs. He wouldn't want a dog whose ancestry is obscure hanging around her. However, I don't actually believe the scheme was concocted by Mr Jones.'

'No,' I agreed, 'he didn't strike me as a man of ideas, but we know he's working for someone. His mother?'

Hobbes shook his head. 'I have a better candidate.'

'Who?'

'Mr Solomon Slugg, or whatever his real name is.'

'So, I was right,' I exclaimed. 'I worked out that he wasn't who he said he was. But are you sure? He can't be behind everything.'

'No, not everything. However, I've often found that someone I arrest for committing one crime later admits to many others.'

'Maybe, but you don't really see the guy as a one man crime wave, do you?'

'I do.'

'But he doesn't seem the sort. He's a respectable businessman and a politician. What evidence do you have?'

'Firstly, he's not who he says he is, and secondly, he owns a controlling share in Big Mama's Canteen, and I suspect is responsible for leading Mr Marco Jones into bad ways.'

'That'll not convince a jury.'

'I'll admit the evidence is circumstantial at the moment, but it'll be fun finding proof, and there are other things to consider ...'

'Like what?'

'Such as how the boar came here, the intruders at Mr Slugg's house, why he was so evasive, and who has been supplying the steroids to the rugby players. I would very much like to know the true identity of the man claiming to be Mr Solomon Slugg.'

'So, what are you going to do?' I asked.

'The cryptic crossword.'

'No, really.'

'Really. It's a fine way of clearing the mind of other problems, and creating space for thoughts to grow. You should try it. After I've finished that, I might pay another visit to the Slugg residence.'

He headed to the sitting room, picked up the *Bugle* and a pen, and sat down on the sofa.

'Do you mind if I try calling Daphne again?' I asked before he became engrossed.

'Hmm? Daphne? Of course I don't mind.'

As I reached for the phone, it rang. I grabbed the handset. 'Daphne?'

'You what, mate? Have I got the wrong number? Who are you?'

The voice, though distorted by the phone, was familiar.

'Is that you, Bob?'

'I think so, but I wanted Inspector Hobbes. Have I used the right number?'

'You have.'

'You don't sound like him. Are you sure?'

'I'm not.'

'You're not sure? Are you winding me up?'

'No, I'm not Inspector Hobbes.'

'Why did you say you were?'

'I didn't.'

'You bloody well did.'

'No, I said you had the right number for Inspector Hobbes.'

'I know I've got the right number for him – it's on the card he gave me, but I wanted to know if I'd dialled it right.'

'You did. Would you like to speak to him?'

'I wouldn't have gone round to Mr Custard's house and

used his telephone to call Mr Hobbes if I didn't want to speak to him, would I?'

'No, I suppose you wouldn't ... umm ...' By this point I was confused, and relieved when Hobbes took over.

'Inspector Hobbes. How may I help you? ... Yes it is me ... The idiot? ... Oh, that was Andy ... yes, his telephone technique could be better ... now what do you want, Mr Nibblet? ... I see. When? ... And it's still there, is it? ... Well done ... I'll be round as soon as I can. How are the floods? ... Goodbye, Mr Nibblet.'

'What's happening?' I asked.

'Bob's caught the boar,' he said, putting the phone down.

'Really? How?'

'He turned up looking for food and Bob trapped him in Crackling Rosie's pen.'

'But that had a big hole in it. How can he keep it inside?'

'I gather he's persuaded Mrs Nibblet to guard it. Apparently, she's very handy with a piece of plywood and a stick.'

'But that huge beast is really dangerous.'

'That's no way to talk about Mrs Nibblet,' he said. 'I'll grab my coat and go straight there. Are you coming?'

'Yes, please ... but ... umm ... what are you going to do with it?'

'I thought I'd wear it.'

'Not your coat, the boar.'

'I suppose I'll have to arrest him.'

'And then what?'

'Put him in secure accommodation, until I can determine where he's come from.'

'Where?'

'That's a good point. Sergeant Bert gets upset when I keep livestock in the cells, and, besides, they are still filled with displaced members of the public, though I hope not for much longer.'

'Where then?'

'He'll have to stay here.'

'I feared you might say that. Umm ... you're not thinking of bringing the creature back in the car, are you?'

His expression told me that he was. 'Actually,' I said, 'though I'd love to go with you, I really must phone Daphne. Do you mind if I give this one a miss?'

'Of course not.'

He left me to feelings of relief that I wouldn't have to share the car with such a fierce and powerful animal, and disappointment that I'd miss seeing Fenella Nibblet's pig wrangling.

I phoned Daphne and after three rings someone answered.

'Daphne?'

'No, sir,' said a deep American voice. 'Mike Parker. Are you Randy?'

'That's none of your business ... Oh, I see ... my name's Andy.'

'My mistake, Andy. How may I help?'

He sounded tired.

'I'd like to speak to my wife, Daphne.'

'You can't, she's in bed with the professor and half the others ...'

'What?' I snapped, my jealousy rising like a hungry trout to a mayfly.

'Let me finish. They are all in bed ...'

'I don't believe you!'

'... because they've gone down with a bad case of gippy tummy – that's what you guys call it, isn't it?'

'Oh, I see ... sorry.'

Mike chuckled, a deep resonance in my ear. 'Don't worry yourself, buddy. I might have phrased it better ... my bad.'

'Is she all right?' I asked, jealousy standing aside to allow worry through.

'No, not really. A doctor's on his way from Cairo, but he won't be here for a few hours.'

'What's wrong with them?'

'It's likely something they picked up from unwashed dates. The cook bought some in the market and they were shared round before he could rinse them. I'm only okay because I don't like them, but those that do are quite ill. I hope it is just gippy tummy.'

'Why?' I asked, fear upwelling, and my stomach churning. 'What else might it be?'

'Someone suggested it might be amoebic dysentery. That's bad.'

'How bad?'

'Pretty bad, but it is treatable. At the moment those of us who are still fit are making sure they get enough to drink. Dehydration can be a big problem out here.'

'Is there anything I can do?'

'Not from England, buddy. Call back in a couple of hours and maybe I'll have better news.'

'Right ... yes ... umm ... thanks, Mike.'

'No problem, Randy,' said Mike, hanging up before I could correct him.

I slumped onto the sofa and worried, and the worst part was that, for all my fretting, there really was nothing I could do.

A sharp rat-a-tat shocked me from my gloom. I went to the front door and opened it. Billy Shawcroft was looking up at me.

'Wotcha, Andy, I'm back again. I like what you've done to your face. Is Hobbesie in?'

'No, sorry. He went out a few minutes ago to arrest the boar. Can I take a message?'

'I suppose so, matie. It's from Featherlight.'

'What does he want?'

'He asked me to tell Hobbesie that he spotted a pair of them hanging around in Ride Park.'

'A pair of what?' I asked.

'He didn't elucidate. He said Hobbesie would understand.'

'Do you have any idea what he meant?'

'Not really, except that he looked worried, and when he gets that look, there's usually something to worry about.'

'In that case I'll make sure to tell Hobbes as soon as he gets back. Umm ... would you like to come in for a cup of tea, or something?'

Billy glanced at his watch. 'I'd love one.'

'Great. Mrs G will be pleased to see you. She's been hacking up that deer so she can feed the dogs.'

'Dogs?' said Billy, stepping inside.

I shut the door and explained about Mimi as we headed towards the kitchen, where Mrs Goodfellow, having finished hacking, was simmering something in a jumbo-sized copper saucepan, and unleashing delicious aromas into the world. Mimi was far more interested in the cooking smells and only spared Billy a short glance, as he took a seat, but Dregs was delighted to see him and to act as a rest for his little legs.

We drank tea and engaged in trivial banter for a pleasant twenty minutes, until, feeling relaxed and convivial, I accidentally mentioned Solomon Slugg.

'Solomon Slugg?' said Billy, looking interested. 'Is Hobbesie interested in him?'

'Yes, because he seems to think Solomon might be involved in a couple of murders and other stuff ....'

Mrs Goodfellow frowned.

'Umm ... I shouldn't have said all that. Don't tell anyone, please.'

'Don't worry. I know the ropes,' said Billy. 'It's just that the name stuck in my mind, because it's unusual, and because I remember seeing his picture in the *Bugle* and thinking he looked familiar. I reckon I used to know him years ago ...'

'His sister says he was a recluse, but now he runs businesses and has tried his hand at politics.'

'The man I knew was never a recluse, worse luck. He was charismatic and plausible, but underneath he was a nasty piece of work, always causing trouble in a mean sort of way. Of course, he went by a different name back then.'

'So, how come Hobbes doesn't recognise him?'

'Probably because the guy I knew didn't live here. He was a drifter, but often hung around Tode-in-the-Wold when I lived there.'

'I didn't know you lived there.'

'Yes, well, I don't often talk about that part of life. You see, I was a bit of a bad lad then. I was a conman, and my trick was to pass myself off as a psychic, using it as cover for collecting information from my customers, which I'd then use to make money. To cut a long story short, it all went badly wrong one day, and I had to go on the run.'

'There was an article in the *Bugle,*' said Mrs Goodfellow, stirring the pot. 'It had that funny headline. What was it?'

'"Small Medium at Large."' Billy grimaced. 'It was a bad period in my life and who knows what would have happened if I hadn't run into Hobbesie when I did.'

'How did that happen?' I asked.

'I jumped on a bus and fled to Sorenchester, hoping no one would know me here, but a copper spotted me and I scarpered down the alley by the church and literally ran headfirst into Hobbes. Anyway, I came round in hospital, and he had a long talk with me, after which I gave up being a crook.' He shivered and looked thoughtful for a few moments. 'It wasn't easy, because it had never really been about the money, but more about the buzz, and when I went straight, I took to drinking too much. Hobbesie saw what was going on and now he kindly involves me in some of his work, so, along with all the bother at the Feathers, I still get some excitement, but don't have to spend all my time in courtrooms and with lawyers.'

'The old fellow's always said there's much more to policing than upholding the law,' said Mrs Goodfellow.

I nodded, realising again how little I knew of him, though I was sure I knew much more than nearly everybody else. I really wished he'd give me permission to write his life story, but I doubted he ever would because, for him, the past was dead, buried and best forgotten, except when he needed to exhume a memory pertinent to a case.

'I really must go,' said Billy, with another glance at his watch. 'Thank you for the tea.'

'You're always welcome, dear,' said Mrs Goodfellow.

As I let him out, I had a thought. 'I was just wondering how you ... umm ... manage to reach the door knocker?'

'I have an extendable tool.'

'That must be handy,' I said as he went down the steps. 'By the way, you don't recall the name used by the bloke claiming to be Solomon Slugg, do you?'

'No, mate ... not really ... maybe it was something like Elvis ... but I can't quite put my finger on it ... and the name I knew him by might not have been his real one anyway. See you.'

'See you, Billy. Take care.'

I watched the diminutive figure wander away along the drizzly street, before heading back inside and stumbling over Dregs again, to the evident delight of Mimi, who'd temporarily abandoned her kitchen watch to observe my antics. Hearing Dregs's snicker as I hit the deck made me suspect he'd done it on purpose. Perhaps it was his way of showing Mimi how harmless I was. Whatever, from that moment, she became very friendly, although she took to staring at my face with an embarrassing intensity, as if she saw something hilarious there.

As I got back up, an alarm bell started ringing in my brain, a warning that something wasn't right. It took a moment to work it out. Then I rushed back to the front door, opened it and looked up and down the street. Another poster had appeared on the nearest lamppost, and I knew what it was without even having to take a look. I ran outside and tore it down. It showed a different photograph, one in which I appeared to be gazing at Sally with big, soulful eyes while holding her hand, which just went to show how a picture could lie. Other lampposts were similarly decorated, and I tore down two more on Blackdog Street and a further half dozen on Ride Street before giving up and retreating to the warmth and dryness of number 13.

'What have you got there, dear?' asked Mrs Goodfellow as I shut the front door behind me.

'Nothing,' I said, hiding the crumpled sheets behind my back.

'Then why are you blushing?'

'I'd rather you didn't see them. They make me look bad.'

'I'll be the judge of that,' she said. 'Let me see.'

I tried to escape, but should have known better.

Darting forward with cobra speed, she grasped my upper arm between finger and thumb and squeezed gently. I found myself helpless as she took the posters from my paralysed hand and released me. I regained control of my body, but it was too late. She'd already seen enough.

'I see,' she said, giving me her stern look.

'It's not what you think.'

'I think it is what I think.'

'It isn't!'

'What do you think I think, dear?'

'That I've been messing about with other women when Daphne's away.'

'I don't think that, dear. I think there's only been the one.'

'There was, but I didn't mean for anything like that to happen. She was the one who saved me when I was nearly run down. I only went for an innocent coffee with her and before I knew what was going on she was all over me, and then a man with a camera turned up. I guess I was unlucky.'

'No, dear, I guess you were lucky ...'

'How?' I asked. 'I didn't want the attention at all.'

'But it could have been so much worse.'

'I don't see how!'

'Maybe not yet, dear, but, then you don't know who she is ...'

'She's called Sally.'

'But she's also known as Matilda Kielder.'

'The one Hobbes has been after?'

'Yes, dear. It's a much nicer picture of you than on those other posters.'

'You saw them?'

'Of course. They were all around town.'

'Why didn't you warn me earlier?'

'To be fair, dear, the others didn't show much of her that was recognisable, and she's changed her hair colour since I saw her. You were lucky the cameraman turned up when he did, or she would have lured you away to a terrible fate. Did I mention she was a man-eater?'

'You did. I sort of thought you were joking. I know I'm gullible at times – Daphne said so. I'm quite worried about her because she's poorly after eating some bad dates.'

I explained what had happened, enjoying the ensuing sympathy and gratified the old girl cared about my wife, though I might have wished Mimi wasn't sitting on my foot and staring into my face.

'She seems to like you,' Mrs Goodfellow observed, turning towards the kitchen, 'I wonder why? Right, I'm going to get back to supper.'

'Great. What are we having? Venison?'

‘Not tonight, dear. I’m cooking beef, slow braised in Hedbury stout, with creamed potatoes and glazed carrots.’

‘That sounds great,’ I said, anticipating true greatness. Then, since I didn’t wish to just sit and drool until suppertime, I decided to take a look around town.

25

Having put on my coat and escaped from Mimi, I left Blackdog Street and wandered aimlessly around, brooding on my luck and quaking every time I thought about myself having been on Matilda Kielder's menu. I happened to pass Travis's, an estate agent's at the top of Vermin Street, where I was struck by how useless I'd been at finding somewhere to live. The window was filled with photographs and details of properties of all sizes and locations, and it was depressing how few were in our price range. To be completely honest, I suspected that none of them was in our price range, unless we won the lottery or something. It was clear we'd have to rent unless we moved somewhere cheaper like Pigton.

Bowed beneath a weight of gloom, I walked away from Travis's and stumbled over a broken broomstick on the pavement. Being a good citizen, I picked it up and looked around for somewhere to dispose of it.

My mobile rang and I answered, surprised to see it was on.

'I've arrested the boar,' said Hobbes. 'I'll bring him home and he'll have to go in the back garden for now.'

'Good,' I said, wondering why he'd felt the need to call me.

'I expect you're wondering why I called,' he said, 'and the answer is that I need you to ensure both dogs are out the way. I suggest putting them in my bedroom while I get the boar through the house, because I'm not sure how they'll interact. Can you be back at Blackdog Street in ten minutes?'

'Yes, I expect so. How did you know I wasn't at home?'

'Because you sound as if you're outside. I can hear the drizzle ...'

'That's well heard,' I said, impressed.

'... and I've just spoken to the lass, who said you'd gone out.'

'I'm starting back now. I'll see you soon.'

As I turned for home, a dented black Mercedes drove past and stopped just outside Big Mama's. A sturdy man, undoubtedly Marco Jones, got out and walked into the canteen. Again I forgot to note the car's number plate.

I was almost certain it was the same car that had taken away the man who'd punched me, and, other than its damaged front, it could easily have been the one from which I'd been shot. Besides, Marco was a strong man with big hands who owned an air rifle. Then I remembered his strange reaction at the door of Keeper's Cottage. Had that been guilt? I wondered who owned the Mercedes, because whoever it was must have known what was going on. Perhaps it was Marco's mum – Hobbes had said she was a formidable woman. There again, the evidence for someone else being involved was purely circumstantial, and it could easily just have been Marco who had it in for me, though I couldn't think of anything I'd done to upset him. My review of Big Mama's had been generally favourable, since the food there had been good and wholesome and I'd marked it as one of the best in the Cotswolds for informal friendly dining.

I was within sight of home when Hobbes's little car drew up by the kerb. He leapt out, grinning. I wondered why he'd phoned me for help, when Mrs Goodfellow could just as easily move the dogs. Perhaps she was too busy cooking.

'I'll unleash the beast!' he said, walking round to open the passenger door.

Fenella Nibblet, carrying a huge white sports bag, emerged like a balloon squeezing from a box and stood up, wheezing and groaning.

Aghast at his lack of manners, I'd already opened my mouth to tell him off when I found myself staring into a pair of piggy eyes in a long hairy face. The boar was sitting on the back seat.

As Hobbes let it out, I noticed it was not restrained by anything other than a red ribbon around what I imagined was its neck. It turned towards me, flicking its tail like Granny Caplet's mad cat used to before it bit me. I eyed up the distance to the front door, estimating my chance of getting inside before I was run down and tusked – somewhere between slim and fat, probably. Running down the street, screaming my head off, was pointless as I'd already experienced its pace. I dithered, and stood still. It trotted towards me, stopped, and sniffed. For some reason, I dropped my hand and stroked its bristly head. It responded like a big friendly dog.

'He likes you,' said Hobbes, walking up the steps to 13 Blackdog Street. 'It seems he's friendly and that he's quite used to being in people's company.'

'I'm almost sorry to lose him,' said Fenella. 'Robinson's rather a lovely pig, and not at all vicious like that horrible Rosie, despite what Bob would have you believe. Well, I'd better be on my way. Thank you for the lift, Mr Hobbes, and I hope your head is better soon.'

'You're welcome, Mrs Nibblet, and thank you for looking after Robinson so well, and, of course, for the nettle tea. I hope you enjoy your Zumba class.'

'Robinson?' I said as she rolled out of earshot.

'That's what she's been calling him. Are you going to help get him in?'

'Of course ... umm ... how?'

'Say "heel" in a commanding voice, and walk towards me.'

'OK. Will he follow?'

'Maybe. Let's see.'

'Heel!' I said, in my firm voice, the one that Dregs ignored unless it suited him. Taking one end of the ribbon firmly in my left hand, I started walking. To my astonishment, he came with me.

A couple of elderly passers-by gaped.

'That is the ugliest guide dog I've ever seen!' the old man announced in a loud voice. 'Almost as bad as his owner.'

'Shh!' said the woman equally loudly. 'He's blind, not deaf. Don't be rude.'

'Why did they think I was blind?' I asked Hobbes as they walked away.

'I'd suggest it was because of your stick,' said Hobbes, 'and because your black eyes could be mistaken for sunglasses at a distance and when seen with failing eyesight.'

Until then I hadn't realised I was still holding the broomstick. I must have had a vague idea it would come in handy.

'What I want you to do,' said Hobbes, 'is run inside and ensure Dregs and Mimi are out of the way, so I can allow Pig Robinson through to the garden. I expect things would be fine, but interactions between animals can sometimes get a little out of hand. In addition, please ask the lass to go to her room. Have you got that?'

'Yes, but ... umm ... why does she have to go to her room?'

'Because pigs are scared of her. I don't know why.'

'What does she do to them?'

'Nothing normally, but for some reason they take one look at her and flee, though they're usually fine once they get to know her. The initial meeting can be ... messy.'

I nodded, despite not understanding how a powerful boar could be frightened of a skinny old lady. Perhaps it was pheromones or something. I handed the boar's ribbon to Hobbes and headed inside. Mrs Goodfellow was cleaning the kitchen, removing the evidence of butchery, while Dregs and Mimi rushed me as I entered, knocked me down and gave me a right good licking. Though part of me was gratified, the outside parts were wet and sticky. It must have taken a good two minutes before I shook them off and got to my feet, with a chuckling Mrs Goodfellow being of no assistance whatsoever.

'Are you ready yet?' asked Hobbes looking in at the front door.

'Not quite,' I said.

Mimi was entirely relaxed about the situation and seemed pleased to follow me upstairs to Hobbes's room. I expected trouble with Dregs, but he charged up with her and allowed himself to be locked in. It was Mrs Goodfellow, pouting and stubborn, who had to be coaxed.

'It's not my fault I frighten them,' she said.

'No, I'm sure it isn't, but he asked me to ask you to go to your room until he's got Robinson in the garden.'

'Robinson, dear?'

'No, Robinson Pig. Mrs Nibblet named it.'

'After the Beatrix Potter character, I presume,' said the old girl.

'She was a writer, yes?' I said, displaying my literary gem like a medal.

'Well done, dear. I suspect that was the last book Fenella read.'

'Can I bring him in now?' Hobbes yelled from the front door.

'Not quite. I still have to move something.'

'All right, dear,' said Mrs Goodfellow and sighed. 'I'll go.'

I went to the front door as soon as I heard her in her bedroom, and in burst the boar. Then came Hobbes and between us we managed to steer a course to the kitchen, without any mishap, other than when I trod in Dregs's water bowl. My squelching feet seemed to amuse the boar, and we got him through the back door into the garden.

'That was easier than I thought,' said Hobbes, strolling

out after him.

'It certainly was,' I said, standing in the doorway, watching as Robinson started to explore his new home.

'That's a fine animal,' said Mrs Goodfellow, leaning from her window.

Robinson squealed, a sound like a knife on a shiny plate but much louder, did an about turn, and rushed towards me, trying to get inside. Unable to shut the door in time, I tried to block him. He brushed me aside and I had a horrible thought that the front door was still open and that we'd lose him again. Acting on impulse, I grabbed his tail, there being few other handholds on a pig, but his momentum was far too much, and he jerked me off my feet onto my front. I slid easily across the kitchen floor, feeling, I assumed, the warm glow of friction on my belly as Robinson, clearly under the illusion that he was still a dainty little piglet, ran straight for the kitchen table, apparently believing he could fit beneath.

He couldn't. His ridged back hit the table hard. For a moment it skittered in front of us until, snagging against a chair, it toppled onto its side. Squealing, Robinson kept going, the table in front like a bulldozer, scooping chairs and the kitchen bin towards the sitting room. How he knew where to go was a puzzle since the table must have blocked his vision, but, fortunately, the whole lot wedged in the kitchen doorway. Hobbes vaulted over us, miraculously not braining himself on the door jamb, and slammed the front door shut.

'Well held, Andy,' he said, 'though you clearly find pig handling is a drag. You can let him go now, and I'll take it from here.' He dropped to his knees and whispered into the pig's ear, while stroking its back with unusual gentleness, until it quietened down.

I was very glad to let go, for my shoulders felt as if they were about to pop from their sockets, and my hands were tired and stiff. Although I hadn't been bitten or trampled, I suspected I'd picked up any number of bruises to add to my tally. Still, I was pleased with myself, until I became aware of a pungent new aroma that was overwhelming the cooking smells and the normal odour of Hobbes.

'Could you clear up in here?' he asked, 'while I take him outside again.'

'All right,' I said, thinking it would be a small job, just putting the kitchen furniture back where it had been.

The smell was getting stronger, my shirtfront was feeling clammy, and I realised the warm glow I'd experienced had not been the result of friction, but Robinson's lamentable lack of bodily control. I was horribly plastered and a smudged brown trail crossed the kitchen, charting our progress.

Despite trying to convince myself that he'd only meant for me to clear up the furniture, I knew what I had to do, and could have kicked myself for having agreed so readily, though I felt it would be some re-payment for all his generosity. Drawing a deep breath, which was a mistake in the circumstances, I gritted my teeth and set to work with bucket, rags and cleaning materials, making occasional forays to the back door for fresh air. Most of the time I spent on my knees, scrubbing and rubbing, and it took me about twenty minutes before I was reasonably satisfied. When I'd finished, I stood up to admire my work, hoping it would be good enough for Mrs Goodfellow, and wondering where she'd got to.

'Well done, dear,' she said, from the stove, where she was stirring something in a pot.

'You were upstairs,' I pointed out when my voice came back under control. 'Now you're here. How?'

'I came to check on the dog meat,' she said, which was no answer at all.

'Robinson is settled,' Hobbes announced, walking in. 'I've given him some water, but he'll need feeding soon.'

'What would he like to eat?' asked Mrs Goodfellow.

'Acorns,' I said, vaguely remembering something I'd seen on telly.

'Where am I going to get acorns from at this time of year?'

'Wild boars do indeed eat acorns in the autumn,' said Hobbes with a smile, 'but they're omnivorous, so they'll eat nearly anything. At the moment, I would suggest a large bowl of porridge.'

'Do they prefer it with salt or sugar, or both?' asked Mrs Goodfellow, pulling a sack of oats from a cupboard.

'Neither, I think,' said Hobbes. 'We can also feed him bread and vegetables and meat scraps, which should keep him going until I can sort out where he's going to live.'

'So, he's not going to be here permanently?' I asked, relieved.

'No. He needs space, and it won't be long before I have to start preparing the soil for my spuds and aubergines and flowers. He'll have to be gone by then, or he'll dig the lot up when he's rooting around, and I wouldn't like that. Besides, I suspect he belongs to someone. He's nervous around people, though he's clearly used to them. I suspect ill treatment.'

'Like with Mimi?' I said.

He nodded. 'You'd better change your shirt, and you can let the dogs out now.'

I ran upstairs, opened the door and found the pair of them in a rather compromising position. Dregs glared, until, muttering profuse apologies, I retreated and shut them back in.

'They're not ready yet,' I announced, when I returned downstairs, washed and in a fresh shirt and trousers. 'I'd give them another few minutes.'

'I see from your delicate blush what they were up to,' said Mrs Goodfellow. 'Do you think Dregs will make a good father?'

'Umm ... I don't know.'

'I don't suppose Mr Marco Jones and his boss will be best pleased,' said Hobbes. 'Whatever Dregs's merits might be, he is by no stretch of the imagination a pedigree Samoyed.'

'You mean the pups won't be worth anything?' I said.

'Well, they won't fetch anywhere near as much money, though I'm sure they'll be fine dogs.'

'Assuming there are any,' said Mrs Goodfellow. 'For all we know Dregs is firing blanks.'

'What makes you say that?' I asked. 'He seems fit and well in every other respect.'

'Yes, dear, but he hasn't fathered any other pups, though I suppose that may just be because he's incredibly ugly.'

'He's not that bad,' I said, defending him, and wishing the conversation would move towards other matters.

The dogs joined us, Dregs smug and Mimi looking extraordinarily coy. How they'd let themselves out of Hobbes's room was beyond me. It was possible I hadn't shut the door properly, but I reckoned Dregs had been showing off.

Mrs Goodfellow put down some stewed venison for them. Dregs, ever the connoisseur, ate slowly as if savouring every bite; Mimi gulped hers down within seconds and then started on his, growling and snarling when he attempted to regain possession of his bowl. He sat back on his haunches, pained by her ill manners, and then sighed as if realising that allowances had to be made for her previous privations, and lack of education. Fortunately, he wasn't hungry for too long since she soon retired to the blanket Hobbes had laid out for her, and seconds were served.

26

After a really beefy supper, feeling gloriously full and slightly drowsy, I was sipping tea while Hobbes browsed a book on pig management.

'Billy asked me to tell you something,' I said, having just remembered.

'Go on,' said Hobbes, looking up.

'He ... umm ... said to tell you that Featherlight told him to tell you that he'd seen a pair of them in Ride Park. He said Featherlight said you'd know what he meant.'

'When was this?'

'Earlier.'

'Clearly,' he said. 'Today?'

'Yes.'

'Morning or afternoon?'

'Afternoon.'

'Thank you, though you should have told me earlier. I'm going to see Featherlight. Are you coming?'

He dropped his book on the coffee table, slurped his tea, and stood up, reaching for his raincoat. As I got ready, he removed the bandage from his head, revealing a wound as long as the cleaver. Though the surrounding hair was bristly with congealed blood, it seemed to bother him less than a paper cut did me.

'Come along,' he said and opened the front door.

Dregs joined us, looking keen, which I suspected was only because Mimi had gone to sleep. Then, our breath steaming like old-fashioned locomotives, we stepped into the night.

'There's going to be a sharp frost tonight,' said Hobbes, sniffing the air and yomping towards the Feathers.

'That'll be fun with all the standing water,' I said.

He nodded. 'The problem is that some people will always try to skate on ice, no matter how thin, and there'll be accidents. I've already got enough bodies to deal with, though I've seen no recent sign of Matilda Kielder, which might be good news.'

'Oh, her.' I felt a blush develop and spread. 'Umm ... you know I mentioned a girl saving me?'

'I remember.'

'The thing is ... umm ... there was a bit more I should have said. We went for a coffee and she started kissing me, though I didn't want her to, and since then someone's been putting up photographs of the two of us. I've been tearing them down, but Mrs Goodfellow saw the last lot, and she reckons the girl in the picture was Matilda Kielder.'

'Actually, I've seen some of them. You were very clear, but not much of her was showing.'

'Yes, but this last lot were different. You could see her face and my ... umm ... embarrassment.'

'Interesting,' said Hobbes, continuing to walk at an uncomfortable pace.

'The old girl recognised her right away. She said she'd seen her once.'

'She did, maybe thirty years ago, when ... when there was some trouble. The lass actually stopped her murdering a man, by hitting her with a mouldy grapefruit before too much harm was done. I think, Andy, you had a lucky escape.'

'Thirty years ago? No, that can't be right. She must be thinking of someone else. The girl I kissed, umm ... I mean the girl who kissed me ... couldn't have been more than twenty.'

'The truth is, Andy, that there's something about them that confounds the senses.'

'Them?'

'People of her type.'

'Which people? Who are they?' I asked, putting on a

spurt to catch up.

'I don't know.'

'Well they must be called something.'

'I suppose so,' he said, 'but putting a label on a group of people doesn't help much since they're all individuals with their own stories and behaviours. Featherlight, however, has all sorts of names for them, some of them mythical, many of them unrepeatable.'

'He called them the sly ones.'

'Sly may be apt, though it has connotations,' he said, looking troubled. 'Perhaps he's right since the word encompasses cunning and covert as well as sneaky. What I know about them is that individuals and small groups turn up every now and then, and there's often trouble when they do, though not every time, and it's not always them that start it. I've found that, while some of them have carried out the most dreadful acts, others are quite decent.'

'You mean they're good law-abiding citizens?'

'Absolutely not.' He shook his head. 'I don't think any of them have regard for our human laws. The one known as Matilda Kielder is, unfortunately, of the dreadful sort. I suspect she ate someone on Hedbury Common recently, but there wasn't enough left to identify him, not even for DNA testing. She'd sucked him dry.'

'I know what you mean. She was all over me, and I couldn't do anything about it,' I said, though thinking back to that morning in Café Nerd, I wasn't absolutely sure I couldn't have done a little more to get her off. However, such was my story, and I intended sticking to it.

'I'm sure you tried,' said Hobbes, 'but if you hadn't been interrupted when you were, she'd have taken you somewhere quiet and ...'

'I don't want to know any more,' I said, shuddering, although I was sweating, despite the falling temperatures.

'It's probably best not to,' he said.

Since, according to Mrs Goodfellow, even Hobbes, with his hippopotamus-thick skin and years of police experience, had been appalled by whatever Matilda Kielder had done, I was starting to believe I really had been lucky. Yet I was puzzled, since he seemed to know more about her people than he was willing to divulge and I found his attitude worrying. He seemed nervous, if not scared, and that was almost unheard of. Normally he relished danger and enjoyed pitting himself against any villainy, the bigger the better. That, and the thought that she was still out there, and might be anywhere, left me with churning guts and a dry mouth.

A light came on in a window across the street, and I glimpsed a woman's face before she pulled down the blinds. She didn't look anything like Sally, yet how could I be sure now? I caught myself staring at every passer-by, just in case I saw anything to alarm me, which had the effect that everything alarmed me. Even so, part of me could only think of her as sweet and pretty, and I struggled to dislike her, even as Matilda Kielder.

I was twitching and starting like a nervous rabbit by the time we reached the Feathers, where a chalked sign on the door announced it was quiz night, which was odd, as Featherlight didn't believe in entertainment that involved him handing out prizes. As we entered the warm fug, his voice was booming out from the bar on which he was sitting, a chipped pint mug wedged between a couple of his bellies. 'What do you mean there's no such country? I assure you there is. I've been there.'

'But it hasn't been called that for decades,' said a familiar posh voice, the middle-sized one of the rugby playing students. The one called Guy.

'Well, aren't you a clever dick,' said Featherlight, 'but the country is still there even if the name's changed, and the question is the same. What's the capital city of Upper Volta?'

'It's Burkina Faso now.'

'Wrong. It's Ouagadougou.'

'That's the capital of Burkina Faso and you've just told us the answer,' said Guy, shaking his head.

'You're an overweight idiot!' the one known as James sneered.

Featherlight twitched, his face darkening like the evening sky before a storm.

'You can't even run a proper quiz, never mind this so-called pub of yours,' James continued. 'You couldn't even organise the proverbial in a brewery. What a retard!'

'Absolutely right,' said the one called Toby, and deliberately poured his beer onto what had once been the carpet. 'This place is the pits, your customers are swine, and you,' he pointed at Featherlight, 'are an absolute ar ...'

But we never heard the pearls of wisdom Toby intended to cast before us, for Featherlight lurched to his feet, the mug popping from his belly folds like a cork from a champagne bottle and arcing across the room with a beery comet tail. Billy, who was already sporting the helmet he'd taken to wearing when trouble was brewing, caught it as Featherlight, snorting like an enraged bull, lunged in a blur of swinging arms. He demolished all three students before they'd even managed to get to their feet. Then, one by one, he lifted them by the seat of their trousers and the necks of their shirts and hurled them into the street, where they lay, groaning and spurting blood from flattened noses. Although Hobbes frowned, he did not intervene.

'Quiz Night is cancelled,' Featherlight announced, his words evidently a relief to the regulars who could return to their normal pastimes of serious drinking, darts, and incoherent arguing about darts and drink.

'What can I get you gentlemen?' asked Billy, removing his helmet and walking beneath the flap to behind the bar.

'A pint of your best bitter for me,' said Hobbes, a pint of lager for Andy, and a shandy for Dregs, who's still an invalid. Have one for yourself if you'd like, and one for your boss.'

'Thank you,' said Billy, reaching for a bowl with his tool.

Featherlight came back grinning, his big brown teeth a dental horror show. 'Before you start, I'm still giving my customers what they want, and I left those students with a couple of questions to answer.'

'What questions?' I asked.

'Where am I? And what hit me?'

'Still they were correct in saying that Upper Volta is now known as Burkina Faso,' said Hobbes, accepting a glass from Billy, and putting the bowl of shandy down for Dregs, who lapped it up noisily and messily.

'I know,' said Featherlight, 'but those blockheads have been trying to provoke me since I started running the quiz, and I just needed an excuse to rid myself of them.'

'Do they come here often?' asked Hobbes.

'They've been visiting now and again since last year, and, as students go, they weren't too bad at first. However, since their blasted rugby team started doing well they've become increasingly arrogant and aggressive, and they've taken to throwing their weight about and causing trouble.'

'I thought you liked trouble,' I said, and took a slurp of lager.

'Only if it's fair trouble, and I won't have them pushing the old timers around.'

Once again he'd taken me by surprise. Beneath his horrible exterior, there were traces of something decent, though they could only rarely be glimpsed. His bad temper had vanished like a gust of wind, unlike the gust of wind he released on sitting down, which hung around like a smog cloud.

'It's interesting that their behaviour changed when they became successful,' said Hobbes.

Billy nodded, handed a glass to Featherlight and began pouring a beer for himself. 'I've seen that sort of behaviour in body-builders when they started taking anabolic steroids.'

'I reckon you're right,' said Hobbes. 'I confiscated a bottle off them, and when I've got time I intend to ask them politely who their supplier is.'

'No need,' said Billy. 'It's that thick bloke from Big Mama's. He came in here, trying to sell his stuff, but the boss kicked him out.'

'And it was a good kick,' said Featherlight, laughing. 'He must have flown ten feet through the air, and I had to buy a new pair of boots.'

'I suspected it might be him,' said Hobbes. 'Still, I'll have to get proof and some other witnesses ... or perhaps he might be inclined to confess.'

'Actually,' I said, 'I might be a witness. I think I saw him taking a wad of money from one of those students in Golums Logons. I didn't know who he was at the time, and it didn't cross my mind that it might be for drugs.'

'A mind as sharp as a banana,' said Featherlight. 'It amazes me he can walk and breathe at the same time.'

'He has his lucid moments,' said Hobbes with a laugh. 'He did remember to tell me your message ... eventually. He said you'd spotted a pair of them. Is that correct?'

'Yep. They were in Ride Park this morning. One male and one female. There'll be trouble, mark my words. There always is when the bloody sly ones turn up.'

'Who and what are they?' I asked.

'As to who, I don't know,' said Featherlight, scowling. 'As to what they are, all I know is they're dangerous troublemakers.'

'Umm ... what sort of trouble?'

'Big trouble,' said Featherlight, banging down his glass on the bar with such force that it shattered and beer and blood spilled. 'Dammit! I've just mugged myself.' He held up his hand and glared at the gore dripping from his thumb as if he could cauterize it with a look. 'Give me a towel and make it fast.'

Billy wrapped one of the filthy rags that served as bar towels around Featherlight's hand.

'Thanks,' he grunted.

'At least your glass was half-empty,' I remarked.

'It was more like half-full. Pour me another. These sly ones make me nervous.'

'You're bleeding through,' Hobbes observed, as blood dripped onto the floor. 'You need to get that cut stitched. Have you got a needle and thread?'

'There's some by the till. Shall I do it?' said Billy. He pulled a black cotton reel from a canvas bag and threaded a needle.

'Make it sew,' said Featherlight.

'You'll feel a bit of a prick,' he said, taking Featherlight's massive paw in his own little hand.

'No more than I do now,' said Featherlight with a grin. 'It was a stupid thing to do.'

Although I had to look away as Billy went to work, the sound of sewing still reached my ears and travelled all the way down to my stomach. I had to put my drink down and concentrate very hard on not jettisoning my supper. Featherlight never made a sound throughout the procedure, and Hobbes merely commented on the neat job Billy was making. I took his word for it, studiously looking away, even when it was all over and Billy poured a tot from a bottle of what Featherlight laughably claimed was whisky over the wound.

Featherlight grunted his thanks, and continued talking. 'If I've seen a pair of them, I'll bet there are others.'

'You'd win your bet,' said Hobbes. 'Andy had a run in with the one that calls herself Matilda Kielder. She's his poster girl.'

'The one Caplet was snogging? He's lucky to have escaped intact.'

'Very lucky,' I said, quivering, and still a little queasy and faint.

'If you'd gone with her,' said Featherlight, 'she'd have got you alone somewhere and then she would've taken your ...'

Shortly afterwards, cold water splashed across my face, and I sat up spluttering, wondering why I was on the floor with an audience of grinning faces. Featherlight was laughing, and when I remembered what he'd been saying I came close to passing out again.

He turned back to Hobbes. 'So, this Matilda Kielder has eaten someone again, and has escaped justice so far by using her feminine wiles. Is that correct?'

Hobbes, looking as grave as I'd ever seen him, nodded.

'There's something strange in this,' said Billy.

'Stranger than man-eaters?' I asked, trying to stand, but finding my legs were still infirm.

Billy shrugged. 'It's just that I'd assumed the photos were taken to blackmail Andy and that she was part of the plot, but she doesn't sound the sort of girl who'd do that.'

'You're right,' said Hobbes, 'but don't mistake her for a girl. I've known of this one since the Hedbury Horror of 1956.'

Featherlight creased up. 'Caplet's been snogging pensioners. I always knew he was weird.'

'I didn't know she was that old,' I said, 'and, what's more, I didn't snog her. She snogged me.'

'Poor innocent little lamb,' said Featherlight. 'She took advantage of him.'

'She did, and I can't see why that's so funny.' I scowled at the grinning faces, although it caused hysteria throughout the pub.

I stood up with all the dignity I could muster in the circumstances, though the effect was somewhat marred when my feet slipped in Featherlight's spilt beer and I came as close as I ever could, and far closer than I'd ever wanted, to doing the splits. The laughter would have been unbearable pre-Hobbes, but I'd developed a sort of immunity. I knew I had a tendency to being a clumsy oaf, but I wasn't always, and it didn't always matter, and when I realised I hadn't torn anything, I found I was laughing with the rest of them.

'Was there anything else?' asked Hobbes when order had been restored.

'Only that I reckon they might be living in Ride Park, and I reckon that heptagram was a declaration of war or something like that,' said Featherlight.

'There again, it might just have been a warning, like Keep off the Grass,' said Hobbes, 'or, for all we know, it was a message to one of them.'

There were times when I was confused, and this was one of them. Danger was close, and both Featherlight and Hobbes were worried, yet they wouldn't, or couldn't, say who these sly ones were or why they were such a danger. Since the pair of them could look after themselves, I felt it reasonable to be alarmed. I found one possible atom of comfort: it seemed unlikely that Sally, or Matilda Kielder, or whatever she was really called, had come after me specifically. Yet, the posters were still going up, and I had no idea who was behind them. Was the photographer responsible? Unlikely, since I hadn't recognised him. It seemed more probable that he'd been a hired gun, sent out to catch me doing something embarrassing, but by whom? And what about the man with the big hands, and, more to the point, fists? Was he the same one who'd punched me, or had that been yet another hired goon? As I thought, I came to suspect the Mercedes driver might be behind it all, but why?

One thing remained certain; I was in a mess and really did have to extricate myself before Daphne returned, though, if I couldn't, I retained a hope that Hobbes and Mrs Goodfellow might persuade her I'd been brave and lucky to have escaped Matilda Kielder's clutches.

Hobbes was saying goodbye. I supped up my lager and, having nodded my farewell, followed him out.

'What now?' I asked as we strode into the night.

'I'm going after them.'

'The ones Featherlight saw?'

He nodded.

'Why are they so dangerous?'

'They might not be, since not all of them are malicious, though I doubt I could persuade Featherlight of that, since one was responsible for the death of his wife and unborn child.'

'Featherlight was married?' I gasped, half assuming he was joking, even though his mood was grim.

'He was, and he only took to the drink after losing them. Before then he'd been a fine police constable. One of the best.'

'What happened?'

'Murder, and that's as much as I'm prepared to say.'

'Did you catch who did it?'

'No, but some of the killer's people did, and carried out their own form of justice.'

'But who are they?'

'Hidden people ... an ancient people ... cunning people ... they're outside the law.'

'Outlaws?'

'An outlaw was formerly someone declared outside the protection of the law, but these folk don't recognise our laws and have always been outside them, though they apparently have some sort of code that most adhere to. I understand the term outlaw is now used for anyone who consistently violates the law, but these people are simply not a part of it.'

'I don't understand,' I said, catching up as Hobbes and Dregs waited on the kerb for a car to pass.

'Nor do I. All I know is that certain populations in this land have always been here and have always gone about their business with little or no regard for humans, whom they treat as upstarts. Normally, fortunately, there is little interaction, and when there is it usually turns out badly for us.'

I was surprised and a little touched that Hobbes, for all his 'unhumanity', regarded himself as one of us. It was reassuring that he was on our side.

'And yet on the whole they don't seek conflict,' he continued, as we crossed towards Goat Street. 'Problems begin when one or more turn renegade and live among us. You see even the best of them have traditionally regarded humans as little more than animals, while the renegades have tended to treat them like vermin.'

'But what about you?' I asked. 'I mean to say, you're ... umm ... not exactly human. How do they treat you?'

'Much the same. Now, what do you want to do? Come with us? Or would you prefer to go home?'

'Where are you going?'

'To Ride Park.'

'It'll be locked.'

'Probably, but that's no problem.'

'I'll ... umm ... think about it,' I said.

'Be quick then, for here is where you must decide. You can either turn right and go home, or turn left and follow us. It might be dangerous.'

'I want to ... go with you ... I think.' I said, certain my decision was not rational, but too intrigued to turn away, even though my brain kept reminding me of all the important things I should have been doing.

'Good,' said Hobbes. 'Now, follow, and keep quiet.'

27

We hastened along Hedbury Road, Dregs hard on Hobbes's heels, me puffing along behind, already regretting my foolish curiosity. Keeper's Cottage was all in darkness. I assumed Marco was working in Big Mama's. The park gate was locked, and the park was apparently secure behind its stone wall.

Hobbes and Dregs stopped. So did I, though only in my head. In practice, my feet slid from under me, and I went down with a thud and an oath.

'Careful,' said Hobbes, 'it's icy.'

'I noticed,' I whispered, trying to divert Dregs from licking me where I lay.

'Get up,' said Hobbes, 'and keep quiet.'

I got to my feet, trying to stay away from slippery bits, which wasn't easy. 'What are we going to do now?'

'Go in.'

'How?' I asked, though I should have known better.

'Like this,' he said, grabbing me round the waist and hurling me skywards.

Had I not been accustomed to this type of treatment, and had I not been warned to keep quiet, I would have shrieked. Instead, I kept my mouth clamped until I landed atop the wall, when a sound somewhere between oof and a whimper escaped.

'Shhh!' he hissed.

Looking over my shoulder into the park, I could make out little, though a silvery glow filtering through trees on the horizon suggested the moon was on the rise, and the coal black sky scintillated with myriad stars. Their beauty was reassuring and calming.

'Catch!' said Hobbes.

There was a muted yelp, and Dregs was in my arms, the impact coming close to knocking me backwards from my perch, but before I could think of complaining, Hobbes was squatting by my side, sniffing the air.

'What now?' I asked.

'We jump down, of course.'

'Umm ... it's too dark to see. I'll hurt myself.'

'I'll lower you. Keep a tight grip on Dregs.'

I started to point out that, since Dregs was a born wriggler, I'd need both arms to hold him, and, in consequence, had nothing by which I could be lowered. However, my hypothesis was disproved by his picking me up by my coat collar, dangling me like a rag doll, and lowering me to the ground. He was at my side before I could even put Dregs down.

'Follow me,' said Hobbes, 'and quickly.'

'Of course, but, please, not too quickly, I don't want to get lost.'

'You can't possibly get lost in Ride Park. It's far too small.'

'It's nearly four thousand acres!'

'Exactly.'

As someone who'd gone astray in many places, I wasn't convinced. A particularly traumatic incident from schooldays came to mind when, engrossed in desperate last minute revision, I'd walked into a storeroom instead of the classroom two floors below where I was due to take a maths exam. Although it shouldn't have been a problem, the door handle had come off in my hand, and by the time anyone heard my cries for help, the exam was long over. The worst part had been trying to explain to Father why I'd failed maths, despite two terms of after-school tutoring.

'Hurry up,' Hobbes hissed.

I followed the darker darkness ahead. The park walls and trees blocked virtually all light and, although I had no fear of the night as such, I was nervous of things that might be out in it.

A scream, as if someone was being cruelly murdered, nearly stopped my heart, and I blundered blindly forwards, only to run headlong into something as solid as a tree.

'Careful, Andy,' said Hobbes softly, as I held my head, 'or you'll hurt yourself.'

'Did you hear that?' I whispered, pushing Dregs's shaggy head away from my groin, and thinking it a stupid question. Of course he'd heard. So, why was he not rushing to help the poor victim?

'D'you mean the fox?'

'Oh. Sorry. Umm ... where exactly are we going?'

'Towards the shelter we found.'

'Are we nearly there yet?'

'Nearly. Keep up.' He walked away, quieter than a flying owl.

I did keep up, refusing to become distracted by the churning sea of thoughts that kept vying for attention, some of which were actually most important, but not just then. We weaved through trees for maybe twenty minutes before I heard something.

'What's that?' I whispered, feeling strangely disoriented, and putting it down to the lager. Perhaps Featherlight had stopped watering it down.

'Singing. Now, keep quiet.'

As we continued, I began to make out two voices. Their song was soft and sad and beautiful, though the words, if any, meant nothing to me.

There was a flicker of orange light ahead. I gasped.

'Shhh!' said Hobbes, holding out an arm to stop me. 'It's just a fire. Stay here with Dregs, and I'll see who it belongs to, though I suspect we know.'

Handing me Dregs's lead, at the far end of which Dregs was alert and bristling, he slipped away into the darkness, invisible and silent. We waited nervously. Well, I was nervous, with any unexpected sound setting my heart rate to overdrive, and there were many unexpected sounds. I regretted my rash decision, wishing I was warm and safe with a cup of tea back at Blackdog Street rather than shivering in Ride Park. Yet, maybe it wasn't quite as dark as it had been, for the edge of the moon, only a couple of days past its fullest, was peeping through the branches and the utter blackness was replaced by a faint silvery twinkle. It might have eased my stretched nerves, had it not enabled me to make out dark shapes, walking on two legs, like twisted little people with wedge-shaped heads, their sharp teeth glinting in narrow mouths, their eyes gleaming black voids. They were about the size of cats, and there were dozens of them, not actually close, but not so far away that I could watch with detachment. Dregs, however, did not react in the slightest, not even when one, approaching much closer, nearly brushed the tip of his nose.

'Come along, Andy,' said Hobbes, his voice seeming to come from a great distance.

Although I was feeling disconnected from my body, I followed, shaking my head, trying to clear it.

'What are they?' I asked at last, my voice slow and slurred.

'What are what?' asked Hobbes.

'The small walking things with the teeth!'

'I didn't see anything. Perhaps they were rabbits, or maybe you were dreaming.'

'I wasn't ... I don't think,' I said, though I dimly recalled similar childhood nightmares after my sister died.

'Well, whatever you saw, they're not here now are they?'

I looked around, but it was still too dark to see much, and there was nothing I wouldn't have expected. 'No.'

'Good. Now, shift yourself and come and say hello. I'll introduce you.'

I followed him into the light with some trepidation.

'Andy,' said a honeyed female voice. 'How nice of you to drop in. The no eyebrow look really suits you.'

'It is indeed a great pleasure,' said a deep, cultured male voice.

'Mr and ... umm ... Miss Elwes!'

'Aubrey and Hilda, please,' said Aubrey. 'We're old friends now.'

'So, you do know each other,' said Hobbes, nodding.

'Of course. Aubrey and Hilda were our downstairs neighbours, until that horrible night.'

'Which is no doubt why you're living out here,' said Hobbes. 'Does Colonel Squire know?'

'I very much doubt it,' said Hilda with a musical laugh.

'But why in the park?' I asked. 'Couldn't you find somewhere warm and comfortable? It's cold out here, and scary.' As if to emphasise my point, I shivered.

'We're fine,' said Aubrey. 'Come on in, pull up a chair, and warm yourself at the fire.'

I did as he suggested, sitting down on a most comfortable and enticing armchair, which part of my brain registered as being a little out of place, and warmed my hands at the blaze. Dregs lay in front of me, and we basked in the warmth and the light and the night. The little horrors felt a long way away.

'Can I get you a drink?' asked Hilda, her voice as rich and sweet as melted fudge.

Her eyes were sparkling like starlight. I gazed into them and nodded. 'Yes, please.'

'What would you like?'

'Umm ... if you've got it, I'd like a sweet hot chocolate ... umm ... please.'

'Such beautiful manners in this one,' she remarked, making me smile, as I remembered smiling when Miss Morgan, my favourite ever teacher, used to say nice things to me when I was seven. 'I'll fetch your drink.'

Hobbes and Aubrey were talking, and although I could have reached out and touched them, their voices came to me as if from some distant place, and for a moment I could have sworn I saw them on some ice-clad mountain, frozen under starlight. Yet, when I shook my head and looked again, they were sitting at my side by the fire. Hilda, her smile as bright as a full moon, handed me my drink, and I took it eagerly, mumbling thanks, feeling even more like a child.

'I hope it's not too hot or too sweet,' she said.

I sipped and it was perfect: warm without scalding, sweet without being sickly, and it was as fragrant as spring flowers and as delicious as ... Before I could put my thoughts into words, I was drinking it, almost oblivious to anything else, except for Hilda's beauty, and Aubrey's majesty. Hobbes, his voice as harsh as a crow's, looked like a deformed ape, and I knew I was just a silly little boy, with scabby knees and runny nose, who was only tolerated because they were so kind. I tried to listen to the grown-ups' spellbinding conversation, as I had in church when the man in the black dress would talk about things my young mind couldn't comprehend. The names Solomon Slugg, and Matilda Kielder came up now and again, amongst others that meant little to me. Aubrey spoke of his family, and Hilda of laws and punishment, while I listened, spellbound by the beauty of their voices that rose and fell harmoniously like music. I was glad Hobbes only rarely spoiled it by interrupting. The fire was hot, the drink heady, and the night blurred into dreamscapes of strange lands and alien skies.

I became aware of Hobbes's voice and found we were walking under streetlights. Dregs was at my side.

'Are you all right now, Andy?' Hobbes asked.

I thought for a moment and nodded. 'Umm ... where am I?'

'Walking along Hedbury Road. I'm glad you're back, and I'm sorry I exposed you to that. I hadn't realised they had so much power.'

'What happened?' I asked, some of the fuzzy heat in my head dispersing, leaving me shivering and disoriented. Everything felt wrong, as if I'd fallen asleep as a child in my bed and woken as an adult in a cold street.

'You fell for their charm,' said Hobbes.

'What do you mean?'

'You were enthralled. I've seen it affect people before, but never quite so strongly. Perhaps it was the moonlight and music.'

'I thought I was somewhere else. Did she put something in my chocolate? Some sort of drug?'

'You were gone before that, and she only gave you cold water.'

'No, it was definitely hot chocolate. Wasn't it comfortable in the woods? It was so much better than I could ever have imagined. That armchair was so soft.'

'Imagined is the right word,' said Hobbes. 'You were sitting on a log.'

I shook my head but, if I concentrated really hard, part of me knew he was right. As so often in my excursions with him, I was bewildered, so I just kept walking, while the sense of being detached, of being intoxicated, faded slowly.

'Were they trying to harm me?' I asked, as we turned into Blackdog Street.

'I don't believe so,' he said, 'but you just happen to be sensitive. According to what they told me, they have no desire to cause any mischief to the general public, and I have no reason to doubt them.'

'Okay ... good, but ... umm ... does that mean they do wish to cause mischief to somebody?'

'They are hunting two individuals of their sort.'

A glimmer of their conversation returned. 'Solomon Slugg and Matilda Kielder?'

'Yes, though those aren't their real names. They never use their own.'

When we reached home at last, Dregs bounded up the steps and waited impatiently to be let in. Whether that was because he wished to escape the frost or because he wished to reacquaint himself with Mimi wasn't clear.

By the time Hobbes opened the door, I was yawning my head off, and went straight upstairs, flopping face-first onto the bed as soon as I reached my room. I was probably asleep before I landed.

28

When I awoke, I was tucked up in bed and wearing pyjamas. My mouth was dry and tasted as if I'd been eating compost. Memories of the previous evening, or at least the bit after we arrived in the park, were vague and elusive, and it took me several minutes to grasp any of them; huge chunks had slipped away for good, or ill. One thing was crystal clear – there really was something fascinating about Hilda Elwes, who I remembered as sparkling like spring flowers in sunshine after gentle rain, and yet I couldn't quite picture her, and was uncertain whether she was tall, or petite, blonde or brunette, fair skinned or dark. I couldn't envisage Aubrey either, though I didn't try so hard. Even so, the nobility and dignity he exuded had the power to make me feel small, and grateful he'd paid any attention to my unworthy presence.

Fortunately, the scent of frying sausages had sufficient power to bring me back to Blackdog Street. I hurried through my ablutions, dressed, and headed for the kitchen, where Mrs Goodfellow was turning delicately spiced Sorenchester Old Spot sausages in an enormous cast-iron frying pan. A pan of mushrooms simmered alongside and, awaiting transformation was a saucepan of beaten eggs. Though I was nearly always hungry in the mornings, that particular morning I was ravenous and could barely wait.

'Good morning, dear.'

'Good morning,' I replied. 'That smells delicious. Umm … where's Hobbes? And the dogs?'

'Out for a walk. They'll be back soon.' Turning the gas on beneath the eggs, she stirred the pan gently, as I sat, fidgeting and drooling, hoping they wouldn't be long.

They returned with just enough time for Hobbes to wash

his hands and sit down before the old girl started dishing up. I had to fend off twice the normal quantity of dogs' tongues before they allowed me to tuck in. Not a word was spoken until we'd finished.

'Last night was interesting,' I said when Mrs Goodfellow was clearing away our plates, 'but I can only recall odd bits.'

'I'm surprised you remember anything at all,' said Hobbes. 'You were in a most peculiar place. They really dazzled you, didn't they?'

'I think so. I saw things that weren't there, even before I met the Elweses, and way before I drank the hot chocolate. It tasted delicious last night, but this morning my memory is only of cold muddy water.'

'They do that to humans, and I don't think it's something they can control, but at least the Elweses, as they call themselves, don't appear to have any malicious intent.'

'I'm confused, because ... umm ... you say Matilda Kielder is one of them, whatever they are, but she looked nothing like them. I don't think she did, anyway.'

'Of course not,' said Mrs Goodfellow. 'She'd appear to you just as she'd want to appear.'

Hobbes nodded. 'And, unless you normally cavort with strange women as soon as your wife is out of sight, her perceived glamour fascinated you.'

'I ... umm ... see what you mean. I've never done anything like it before, and I tried to resist, though I didn't do very well. Who, exactly, is she?'

'As far as I can understand, she is what we'd call the Elweses' cousin. They were keeping her under restraint after what she did thirty years ago and before, but she escaped last year. When Aubrey and Hilda tracked her down, they coincidently discovered the one we know as Solomon Slugg, who is another cousin.'

'He's one of them as well? But he looks nothing like the Elweses or Matilda.' Even as I said it, I realised how foolish it was.

'You see him how he wants to be seen. I wonder how he'd appear if you had a clear mind?'

'Do they influence you? Or other animals?' I stopped, realising what I'd just implied.

He shrugged. 'To an extent they do, but I've met them a few times and nowadays I can largely maintain control when they do their thing. At least I can, if I know what I'm going into. However, I was taken unawares, and may have been somewhat deceived by Alvin Elwes, though I had suspicions about him.'

'And who is Alvin Elwes?'

'He's the one we've been referring to as Solomon Slugg.'

'How do you know?'

'The one calling herself Miss Hilda Elwes told me last night, when you were sitting on that log with an idiot smile on your face and burbling about burbots.'

'What is burbots?' I asked, wondering if he was making a joke at my expense.

'They are a type of freshwater fish and are regarded as extinct in this country, though I know a few deep lakes where they still thrive.'

'But I've never heard of them, so how could I have been saying anything?'

'I don't know, but you sounded very familiar with preparing, cooking and eating them,' said Hobbes. 'You recited several recipes.'

I shook my head, but he appeared to mean what he was saying.

'What are you going to do about our visitors?' asked Mrs Goodfellow from just behind my right ear.

'Firstly, I'll question Mr Alvin Elwes, aka Solomon Slugg, since I believe he has committed at least two murders.'

'Has he really?' I asked. 'Who?'

'Septimus Slugg and the real Solomon Slugg.'

'What? No! I thought he was just a bit of a rogue, and an unfortunate politician. How can you tie him to the murders?' Even as I spoke, I had a strong feeling of déjà vu, and knew he was telling the truth, though I couldn't remember why.

'I'll tell you later. Do you want to come and see the fun?'

'I'd like to, but can I make a phone call first? I need to check how Daphne's getting on.'

'If you're quick,' he said. 'I intend taking both dogs, so there won't be much room in the car.'

'You're not planning on arresting Alvin, are you?' I asked as I stood up.

'I might be.'

'But where would you put him if the car's already full?'

'I'll think of something, should the need arise. Now, call your good lady wife, and quickly!'

I hurried to make my call.

The deep, resonant American voice of Mike Parker answered. 'Hi, how can I help you?'

'It's Andy,' I said, wondering why he'd sounded so down.

'Hiya, buddy. I'm afraid we've had some bad news today ...'

I was instantly transformed into panic-stricken Andy. 'What's happened? Is it amoebic dysentery? Is she all right?' I felt as if cold strong hands were twisting my guts into knots.

'Daphne's on the way to Cairo.'

'Cairo hospital?' The panic was rising.

'No, it turns out she only had a nasty tummy bug and she's over it now. She's gotta call in at the university.'

'But why?'

'Because Professor Mahmoud has cancelled the dig – that's our bad news. What we found wasn't what we'd hoped for. It seems to be some sort of nineteenth-century junk store.'

'Not a tomb, then?'

'The prof thinks it might have been built as a tomb, but there's no evidence it was ever used for that purpose. As it happens, there were one or two interesting items among the crap, but it's not even clear whether they're genuine.'

'So, what's happening with Daphne?'

'She'll be heading home soon, and I guess she'll call you when she knows more. There's some paperwork she needs to deal with first, but she should be with you in a day or two, when she can get a flight. I'm in the process of winding down the camp, and paying off the local staff.'

Panic had mutated into euphoria. She was coming home! However, I felt I should say something appropriate, and feeling every bit the hypocrite, injected a tone of sadness into my voice. 'I'm so sorry to hear that.'

'So are we,' said Mike. 'I need to get on now. It's been good to talk to you. So long.'

'So long, Mike. All the best.'

I put the phone down and was in the process of punching the air when panic struck again. I still hadn't sorted out the problem with the posters ... and then there was finding somewhere to live ... and getting the insurance sorted out ... and ...

'Ready?' asked Hobbes.

I nodded, and before I could say anything he'd bundled me and a tangle of dogs from the house, and towards the car, which was white with frost. He scraped the windows with his fingernails, ploughing deep furrows in the ice until they were clear. Since Dregs and Mimi were happy to be together in the back, I was allowed the privilege of riding up front, which, although it felt like a promotion, also meant there was far less in front to crumple and cushion me should we smash into a lamppost. He started the engine.

'Seat belt, Andy.'

I obeyed, and the car sprang forward like a greyhound

from a trap, hurtling along Blackdog Street while I closed my eyes and clung on, one hand gripping the door handle, the other the edge of my seat. It was something to do, though it didn't divert my mind from the imminence of oblivion as the journey, taken at his normal breakneck speed to the usual accompaniment of angry car horns, was unusually terrifying, because of the icy road, which, combined with his sharp braking, mad acceleration and cornering, caused us to skid several times. At some point, I'm sure we careered backwards around a bend.

'Here we are,' said Hobbes at last. 'You can wake up now.'

'I wasn't sleeping, I was resting my eyes,' I said, blinking and looking around.

We were outside the home of Solomon Slugg, or, as I'd now have to think of him, Alvin Elwes. Hobbes and the dogs seemed entirely unconcerned by the ride, and, although I was shaking, I forced myself to appear nonchalant, an act that was growing easier with practice. One day, if I survived long enough, I hoped it would no longer be an act.

Dregs was alert, leaning forward between the seats and blowing dog breath into my face. Mimi looked nervous.

Hobbes glanced back at her. 'It looks like she's been here before. I suspected she might have.'

'Does that mean you think Marco Jones stole her from here?' I asked.

He shook his head. 'I think it more likely that Mr Jones stole her on behalf of his boss, Mr Alvin Elwes.'

'Right. I get it ... umm ... actually I don't. Why?'

'I had Constable Poll check a few things, and it appears Big Mama's Canteen was in deep financial trouble after Little Papa ran off with the waitress and the cash. Mr Elwes, in the guise of Solomon Slugg, invested in it and, although it undoubtedly saved the business, it left the Joneses heavily in his debt. Marco, who was brought up to be obedient and was heavily under the man's charm, felt he had to do whatever he was told to do, even though he knew some of it was wrong. He kept it from his mother. I think, in his way, he was trying to protect her.'

'That's reassuring.'

'Perhaps, though he still shouldn't have done what he did. However, he is beginning to realise and is already somewhat repentant. He's not a villain at heart, but he will feel a lot more repentant when I have my next little chat with him. At least he now accepts that he's done wrong and I've convinced him that I'm his only chance of staying out of prison, so I expect further cooperation. In addition he admitted to the attacks on you, though he says they were not intended to cause any serious harm.'

'I see ... umm ... sort of. But why?'

'Later. There's work to be done.'

'So, what are we going to do now?'

'I'm going to have a quick look in there.'

He got out of the car, walked towards the garage, peeped in through the window, and beckoned me over. Standing on tiptoe, I looked. Inside was a Mercedes with tinted windows.

'Do you recognise that?' he asked.

'Umm ... I think it might be the one that picked up Marco after he'd hit me, and it could be the one that shot me, if you see what I mean, but it's got a dent in now.'

Hobbes nodded. 'Which I suspect was caused by running into the deer. See how its badge is bent?

'And now, let's have a talk with Mr Alvin Elwes.'

'Do you think he'll even open the door when he sees who it is?'

'The door will open.'

'And then what? Are you going to arrest him?'

'An imminent arrest is certainly a possibility.'

'And then are you going after Sally ... Matilda Kielder ... umm ... Elwes, or whatever her name is?' I asked, feeling that if anyone had a legitimate interest in keeping her off the streets and away from vulnerable young men, it was me.

'If I can find her. She's possibly even more dangerous than her cousin Alvin at the moment, and I might need help. Right, I'm going in. Come along if you want, and bring the dogs if they wish.'

He loped towards the house and rang the doorbell while I released the dogs, who sniffed around in the hedge, their breath smoking. Having no wish to get my head bashed in by Alvin's leaded stick, I stayed back with them and shivered, wondering if he'd used the same weapon to bludgeon the real Solomon Slugg. Yet, even then, I had doubts, for, despite everything I'd been told and seen, I couldn't see him as a killer; he was far too charismatic and pleasant. A distant part of my brain suggested that perhaps he was still exerting an influence, though I had no idea how, since I didn't believe I was the sort of weak-minded individual who could easily fall under someone's spell when I'd been forewarned.

There again, perhaps I was. Who could say what was true with these people? And why did I believe what Hobbes told me? Could it be that he was the one exerting the influence? If so, it certainly wasn't through his charm, though it might explain why I was following him around when I should have been sorting out my own problems.

Hobbes rang again and knocked, shaking the door on its hinges. Neither Alvin Elwes nor his big stick appeared.

'Now what?' I asked.

Hobbes scowled, his features hardening from ugly to gargoyle. He knocked a third time and, after waiting a minute, leant forward and struck the door with both fists. It cracked and burst open, a number of locks and chains hanging uselessly from the jamb.

'Stay here until I tell you it's safe,' he said, charging in, his face unusually grim, and although I feared for Alvin's wellbeing should he be home, I felt in no danger.

I stood in the front garden, keeping an eye on the dogs, until I heard a door crash shut from the back of the house. A moment later, Alvin was running towards me, and I smiled, pleased to see an old friend, though something didn't feel quite right. Perhaps it was because he was wielding a billhook, or was it because his noble features were distorted by murderous rage? It was interesting to speculate, but at the last moment I registered that a maniac was bearing down on me, and my animal body overrode my brain. I fled, despite knowing he was already too close and too fast, and that I'd left it too late. Any moment, I expected to feel the blade bite into my head or back, but I'd reckoned without Mimi.

Until that moment, I'd regarded her as little more than a fluffy bundle of fur. I had to revise that assessment when she transformed into a seething mass of muscle and snarling white fangs and sprang. She knocked me aside as if I were an empty bottle, and Alvin shrieked like a trapped rabbit. Mimi, growling like a furious bear, struck him in the chest, flattening him. His left hand struggled to hold her off, her teeth inches from his face, but his right hand groped for the billhook he'd dropped. As his fingers closed around the handle, Hobbes strolled from the house and trod on them, a remarkably effective, if painful, technique for disarming a man. Alvin screamed again and, to add insult to his injury, Dregs, who'd been watching the performance with interest, swaggered forwards, cocked a leg and widdled on his face.

'That's enough,' said Hobbes. 'Drop.'

As Mimi released her grip, Hobbes picked Alvin up by the collar and let him dangle. His left forearm was punctured and bloody and his right hand hung uselessly. As he moaned and writhed in Hobbes's grasp, I was amazed I'd ever considered him good looking. In fact, he was sharp faced, looking a bit like an old rat, and though the pain was evident in his expression, it did not override the fury and cruelty in his eyes. His long hair had fallen in such a way that one of his ears was revealed. It was large and pointed, most unlike the tiny Slugg family ears. I wondered what Matilda's ears looked like beneath all that long, golden hair.

'Are you going to call him an ambulance?' I asked, shaken, and not trying to hide it.

'Later, perhaps,' said Hobbes.

He dragged Alvin, half-walking, half-stumbling, and moaning piteously, into the house and nodded, which I took as an invitation to follow. I felt no sympathy for Alvin, thinking that it served him right, and though the thought was callous, the look in his eyes made me think I was thinking right. The dogs and I entered the house, where Alvin, who was trying to cradle both arms at the same time, was sprawled on the sofa in the lounge.

'This is police brutality and entirely uncalled for,' he said, his voice soft and sad, as if he'd been cruelly wronged, but sought no vengeance.

'I merely prevented you from re-acquiring a potentially lethal weapon, sir,' said Hobbes, 'and I used the minimum amount of force I deemed necessary in the circumstances.'

'You set your dog on me!'

'I did no such thing and she's not my dog, sir. I suspect you know much more about her than I do.'

'That's slander,' said Alvin. 'I've never seen her before in my life.'

'Yet, she appears to know you, sir.'

Mimi, her hackles high, her teeth bared, was growling at Alvin, while Dregs was staring at her, looking puzzled.

'Get that brute away from me,' Alvin's voice was harsh again.

'She won't hurt you, as long as you stay where you are,' said Hobbes, with a glance at Mimi who sat down and relaxed, though without taking her eyes off Alvin.

'She's already hurt me. Call me an ambulance.'

'Very good, sir. You're an ambulance.' Hobbes smiled. 'Mr Godley told me that one.'

'Who the hell is Mr Godley?' asked Alvin, his mellow voice cracking, so the end of his question came out as a squawk.

'An old fellow who knows a lot, Mr Elwes.'

'That's not my name. I am Solomon Slugg. I don't know anyone called Elwes.'

'We'll see about that,' said Hobbes. 'Perhaps I'll fetch your relations here and have them identify you.'

'My brother is dead and my sisters live in Australia.'

'But, didn't you tell me your family was just you and Septimus, sir?'

'Er ... yes... maybe ... I'd forgotten about them ... because of the distress caused by his death.'

'Solomon Slugg's brother is dead,' said Hobbes, 'because you killed him, with, I suspect that billhook, which is a fearsome weapon in the right hands. And, by the way, when we had our earlier chat, you let slip that Septimus Slugg was killed by one, which I hadn't known until then. I took that as an indication of your guilt.'

'He was going to use it on me,' I said, 'and would have, if Mimi hadn't bitten him.'

Mimi broke off trying to outstare Alvin to give me a big adoring glance. It was getting embarrassing.

'I had no intention of using it on you, young man,' said Alvin, smiling through his pain, his words dripping sincerity and good intentions. 'I was rushing out to protect you from that ferocious dog.'

I almost believed him ... and yet, was that a sly look in his eyes?

'She's not ferocious,' I said, struggling against his beguiling manner. 'She only became that way when you showed up.'

'Let's give you the benefit of the doubt for now, sir,' said Hobbes. 'Perhaps you could inform me what it was about Mimi that made you believe she was a threat to Andy.'

'I know that breed of dog. They are highly aggressive, and had I been elected, I would have done my utmost to ensure they were muzzled at all times when out in public.'

'How do you know this sort of dog, sir? Did you have one once?'

'No, never. I did, however, know of someone who owned one. One day, it turned on him, and he had to get rid of it. It had become a grave danger to people.'

'Exactly where did it bite you, sir?' asked Hobbes sounding and looking sympathetic.

'On my ... on his calf.'

'Yours or his, sir?'

'His of course. You confused me for a moment.'

'Yes, sir, I understand how a perfectly straightforward question might be confusing.'

'Damn you!' said Alvin, springing from the sofa, the rage taking over. 'I'm going to phone my solicitor.'

'I won't stop you, but first I need to check something, and I apologise for what I'm about to do to you, sir.'

His next move certainly took me by surprise.

Stepping forward and squatting, Hobbes grabbed the waistband of Alvin's trousers, tugged them down, tore them off and tossed them into the corner, where Mimi, growling ferociously, pounced on them.

'What do you mean by this outrageous behaviour?' Alvin shrieked. 'I'm going to have words with your superintendent, and I can tell you, Inspector, you're in a heap of trouble.'

I must admit to thinking that he might be right, for Hobbes had surely gone too far this time. He was staring at Alvin's spaghetti-thin legs.

'Those are impressive scars, sir,' he said, shoving Alvin

back onto the sofa. 'They look just as if they were the result of a recent dog bite.'

'So what?' asked Alvin, whose face was red, and whose voice was drained of all its honey, leaving only sharp ill-humour. 'I got bitten by a dog. That's all.'

'This dog, I suppose,' said Hobbes, with a glance at Mimi, who was shaking the trousers as if she'd got hold of a rat.

'Not at all. I was attacked when taking my morning constitutional three weeks ago. It's nothing to do with that bitch.'

'And yet, I'd make a bet that her teeth match your wounds. Shall we try them for size, sir?'

'Certainly not. I am injured and in pain and demand immediate medical attention.'

'Of course, sir. How remiss of me. Where are your first aid supplies? In the bathroom? I'll have a look.'

'You can't search my house without a warrant. You are only making things worse for yourself.'

'I'm not searching your house, sir. I am merely looking for your medical supplies. You do have some, don't you?'

'It's no business of yours. Call me an ambulance!'

'I've already done that, sir,' said Hobbes as he headed upstairs. There were a few bumps and bangs and other noises, suggestive of rummaging.

Alvin glared. 'What's he doing up there? He has no right.'

'Looking for your first aid kit, I expect,' I said, keeping a wary eye on him, though I felt surprisingly relaxed.

'Who the hell are you?' he asked, his glare reaching near-Hobbesian power.

'I'm ... umm ...Andy.'

'And what do you do when you're not helping that brute harass law-abiding citizens.'

'I'm a food critic ...'

'What?' He spluttered, his bafflement almost concealing the rage on his face. 'Why are you here?'

'Umm … he asked me if I wanted to come.'

'Do you get a sick thrill from seeing a gentleman in difficulties and in pain?'

'No … umm … not as such. Seeing Hobbes at work can be very educational and …'

'Shut up a moment,' said Alvin. 'Andy, you said?'

I nodded, unable to look away.

'I know who you are now. You're that snotty food critic from the *Bugle.* I just wish he'd hit you harder.'

'How do you know about that?' I asked.

'None of your damn business. Yes, I know you. You were trying to ruin Big Mama's, which I have an interest in. How could you write that it was appalling? The food there is not, by any stretch of the imagination, fiendish, and the wine is definitely not minging – I chose it myself.'

'I never wrote anything like that.'

'Liar. Marco showed me your text. That's what it said.'

'It didn't. I gave it a very good review. I said it was appealing, and that there were fine dishes and that the wine left my palate singing.'

Alvin snorted. 'I know what I saw. Don't lie. You deserved what you got and you should have got more.'

I started to argue, and stopped, realising I'd again been a victim of predictive text. That and clumsy fingers.

'What a useless parasitical occupation you have,' Alvin continued. 'It's so easy to criticize and lambast hard-working people when you don't have to do it yourself, and couldn't if you tried. You remind me of one of those horrid boys who pull the wings off butterflies for sport. I've a good mind to finish what Marco started.'

He made a move as if he was going to get up, but a growl from Mimi changed his mind. Having torn the trousers to shreds, she was bristling again, while Dregs gazed as if amazed.

'Get that animal out of here,' Alvin demanded.

'Certainly, sir,' said Hobbes, reappearing. 'Please, leave the room, Andy.'

'What?' I said, jerking like a sleep walker awaking.

'I meant the blasted dog,' said Alvin.

'But, I'm sure she means no harm,' said Hobbes, 'though she would appear to bear a grudge against you. I wonder why that would be.'

'I have no idea.'

'And I suspect you're going to claim to have no idea why there is a dog cage in your back garden.'

'You've been tramping all over my garden as well, have you?' said Alvin. 'My solicitor is going to have so much fun putting you in your place.'

'Actually, sir, I glanced out the window when I was looking for your first aid kit.'

'Did you find it?' I asked.

'I did, and I've taken the liberty of removing some bandages, a dressing and a bottle of TCP. If you'd allow me, sir?'

He opened the bottle, took Alvin's wounded arm and poured a drop of the pungent liquid into the punctures.

'That stings,' Alvin moaned, writhing and trying to break away.

'That shows it's working,' said Hobbes with a pleasant smile, 'and suggests there's no nerve damage. Isn't that good news, sir?'

Having torn open a couple of packets, he dressed the bites and then examined the hand he'd stepped on.

'It's bruised, that's all. Stop whining and give me an explanation for these.' He reached into his pocket and pulled out a handful of small bottles.

'What are those?' I asked.

'A handful of small bottles. However, they are full of pills and I'd like Mr Elwes to explain why he was keeping them in the recess under his bath.'

'They're nothing to do with me,' said Alvin. 'You must have planted them. I've done nothing wrong, but you've attacked me, ransacked my home and planted illegal amphetamines on me. I want my solicitor.'

'Are they illegal amphetamines, sir?' asked Hobbes innocently.

'Well, I ... er ... think they must be, otherwise you wouldn't have planted them. I don't know what you suspect me of, Inspector, but I'm innocent ...'

'I don't suspect you, sir.'

'Then get out of here, and take your savage dogs and that idiot food critic with you.'

'Not when we're getting on so well,' said Hobbes in a light, conversational tone. 'The fact is, Mr Elwes, that I don't suspect you, because I know what you've done. You murdered Solomon Slugg and Septimus Slugg, and used Solomon's identity, you stole one Samoyed bitch for the purposes of breeding and selling the pups, you stole a wild boar ...'

'Well, you got that one wrong, smartass. I paid for that boar fair and square. I have the receipt. It's just that he escaped.'

'So, you admit the rest?' asked Hobbes.

'I admit nothing, and I'm saying nothing more.'

'That is, of course, your right, sir. In the meantime, I am arresting you for the murder of Solomon and Septimus Slugg. Other charges may be brought later.'

'You can't arrest me without reading me my rights.'

'I can, sir, but, if you like, I can caution you to start telling the truth or your situation will become even worse than it is already.'

'Worse? What do you mean?'

'I might become angry.'

'Which is not a pretty sight,' I said.

'Thank you, Andy. Now, Mr Elwes, are you going to come

to the police station quietly?'

'Yes, but when I get there, I intend to kick up such a fuss that you'll regret ever being born.'

'That is your right, sir.'

'And I warn you that I know your superintendent, and the chief constable.'

'So do I, sir,' said Hobbes, and jerked him to his feet.

'I'm not leaving the house without trousers.'

'Of course not, sir. It's awfully chilly out there, and I wouldn't want you to catch a cold. Shall I fetch you a pair, or would you prefer to get them yourself?'

'I'll do it myself. Just keep that damned hellhound away.'

'Andy,' said Hobbes, 'would you mind holding Mimi's collar?'

I did as asked while Mr Elwes headed for the stairs. Hobbes's grin suggested he was up to something, though I had no idea what.

'Stay here,' he said, walking from the room.

A moment later, I looked through the window and saw him heading up the drive.

'What's his game?' I asked.

The dogs didn't say, though Dregs snickered, and I could have sworn there was a knowing expression in his dark eyes. Mimi, having exhausted the possibilities of trousers, made herself comfortable on the sofa, exuding an element of defiance, as well as of fear, as if she believed she was being a bad dog, but didn't care. I let her settle, wondering how long Alvin would take to get dressed, and hoping Hobbes would be back before then, since I didn't fancy facing a murderer on my own.

29

A window creaked open upstairs.

'He's trying to get away!' I yelled, but there was no sign of Hobbes.

I ran and looked out the front door. Alvin was climbing down the trellis.

'Stop!' I said.

There was a triumphant grin on his face as he prepared to jump the last bit, but as he let go, Hobbes's car, its engine revving madly, screeched backwards down the drive with its boot wide open. Alvin dropped right in. Hobbes, grinning, sprinted round before he could move and shut him in.

'You were wondering how we'd all fit in the car if I arrested Mr Elwes,' said Hobbes. 'I found a solution.'

'Umm ... did you plan that?'

'No. I merely went to collect my handcuffs, because his sort is dangerous. Get the dogs and we'll head back to town.'

Alvin kept kicking and cursing, which, although annoying, was a distraction from the driving.

'I can't breathe!' he screamed after about five minutes.

'Shouldn't you let him have some air?' I asked.

'There's plenty,' said Hobbes, his voice booming. 'At least there will be if he doesn't waste it.'

Alvin quietened down for the rest of the journey. I hoped he hadn't snuffed it, for even Hobbes would struggle to get away with asphyxiating a suspect. Not that Alvin was technically a suspect by then; he was a definite in Hobbes's eyes.

After parking outside the police station, Hobbes opened the boot and Alvin sprang up, trying to make a run for it.

'Stop messing about,' said Hobbes, seizing him by the collar and making him squeal. 'I need to get you booked in. Andy, would you mind taking the dogs home? I'll be along as soon as he's safely in a cell. I'll not be long, because I want my dinner.'

A glance at the church clock showed it was nearly lunchtime and that the morning had passed really quickly. I intended to stroll home, but it wasn't long before the wind had bitten through my coat and forced me to adopt a brisk, hunched walk, with the dogs bounding about, seemingly pleased to have seen the back of Alvin. Without a lead, I'd had some worries about Mimi, but she appeared to have acquired Dregs's traffic sense, which he'd picked up from Hobbes. I reflected that it hadn't been so long ago when he'd been a wild and potentially dangerous animal. Dregs that was. Hobbes was still wild and potentially dangerous.

I led the pack back into 13 Blackdog Street and took off my coat, enjoying the feeling of warmth and wondering what we'd have to eat. Besides food, I had two further reasons for being cheerful: Daphne was coming home, and I hadn't spotted any more embarrassing posters. There were down sides to both points, since she would want somewhere to live, and the posters might reappear, but I still hoped to deal with both situations in time. I checked my mobile, but there were no new messages.

The old girl was in the kitchen, stirring magical aromas from a gleaming copper pot. 'Hello, dear. Dinner's nearly ready. Did you have a good morning?'

'Not bad. Hobbes arrested Solomon Slugg, who's also Alvin Elwes, and, who is apparently, my neighbours' cousin. It was him that murdered them.'

Mrs Goodfellow looked baffled. 'Alvin Elwes murdered your neighbours?'

'No.'

'So, who did murder them?'

'No one did. They are both well.'

'I don't quite follow. Was it your neighbours that murdered someone?'

'Umm ... no ... not as far as I know. I'll start again.' I took a deep breath, thinking myself lucky that my job involved writing rather than speaking. 'What I was trying to say is that Alvin Elwes killed Solomon Slugg and pretended to be him, and then murdered his brother ... umm ... that is to say he murdered Solomon's brother, Septimus.'

'Then I'm not surprised the old fellow arrested him, and that sounded like the front door. Go and wash your hands, and I'll start ladling out the soup.'

Hobbes had returned and three minutes later he and I were enjoying a rich and hearty soup, made with winter vegetables, basil and chunks of Italian sausage. Together with freshly-baked crusty bread and primrose-yellow butter, it was a feast made in heaven, and one to drive away all vestige of winter's chill.

We were nicely full and sipping tea in the sitting room when a mobile rang and I pulled mine from my pocket, hoping it was Daphne. I stared at it baffled for a moment, wondering when I'd turned it off.

'Good afternoon, Billy,' said Hobbes on his new phone. 'What's happening? I see ... Thanks ... I'll be with you as soon as possible. I'll bring the dogs, and would you ask Featherlight to keep close, but not too close, and to be ready on his mobile?'

'What's up?' I asked.

'The game is afoot.'

'Is it? What game?'

He was already up and putting on his mac. 'A dangerous one.'

'Can I come and watch?' I asked, and, on seeing his grim, worried face, wished I'd bitten my tongue off instead.

'No. It would be better if you stayed here out of harm's

way. I'm going out and I may be some time.'

I sat for a while after he'd gone, my brain a battlefield between two conflicting thoughts. The first was the sensible reasoning of a sensible married man with responsibilities that he ought to be dealing with. However, just when it seemed sense would triumph, the idiotic part of me launched an attack, using notions of excitement and bravery, and swept aside all opposition before it could be reinforced. I grabbed my coat, and rushed out, jealous that Billy, Featherlight and the dogs were part of whatever was going on, and I wasn't invited.

Although Hobbes was out of sight, his car was still parked at the kerb. Surmising he was on foot, I ran to the end of Blackdog Street and into The Shambles where I glimpsed him on Vermin Street. He turned down the alley towards the police station.

I ran, my legs like pistons, my lungs burning, my breath steaming, and my heart thumping, as the good shopper folk of Sorenchester parted before me. Sweat trickled down my back, as I reached the chemist's shop and turned into the alley. A few steps later, I stopped and backed into the shadows. A twitching in my stomach suggested all was not well, though my brain could not identify any specific reason.

My position gave a good view of the back of the police station, where all appeared quiet and normal, apart from Hobbes who was squatting by a skip, apparently mumbling to himself. He nodded and scratched his chin as if in deep thought, and I wondered if something might have moved high up on the edge of vision. I craned my neck, hoping for a better sighting, but whatever it had been had gone. The sensible part of me rallied, wanting to get the hell out of there, but idiocy, or something, had control of my will. I stayed where I was, watching, and reassured to hear people walking up the alley behind me. Then their voices dropped, their footsteps faltered, and they hurried back the way they'd come, though they couldn't possibly have seen anything.

The back door of the station opened and the lanky figure of Constable Poll staggered out as if he'd been punched. He would have fallen had Hobbes not leapt up, caught him and lugged him over his shoulder. As he did so, a small dark shape moved from the shadows by the skip and I tried to call out a warning. Only a cracked croak escaped. For a moment, I feared it was one of the things I thought I'd seen in the park, but it was only Billy in his ninja outfit. After a quick word with Hobbes, he slipped back into the shadows.

A strange confusion began to cloud my brain, and a terrible feeling of dread was growing. Then I heard a voice.

'I thought I told you to stay at home,' said Hobbes, looming above me.

'Umm ... you did ... but ... I ...'

'Didn't do as you were told,' he said and sighed. 'Well, since you're here, you'd better look after Derek.'

He swung Constable Poll down and sat him with his back propped against the alley wall.

'What's wrong with him?'

'He appears to have been dazzled by her charms.'

'Her charms?'

'Matilda Kielder's. She is inside the station, doing what she does best.'

'Why? Is she going to eat somebody?' I shivered, reflecting on my own lucky escape.

'Possibly, but I suspect she's here to release Alvin.'

Hobbes turned back towards the police station.

'She's so beautiful,' Constable Poll murmured, staring with wide, unfocussed eyes as I leant over him. 'You're not, though. What have you done to her?'

'It's me, Andy,' I said. 'Andy Caplet. Snap out of it, man.'

'Take me back to her.'

'Her? Do you mean Matilda?'

'The angel lady. She's so beautiful, and her perfume is …'

'That's nice, but she's a man-eater? You'll get over her.'

'Won't.'

'I bet you will. I have, I think. She wanted to eat me.'

'You filthy lying swine,' said Poll, making a feeble effort to punch me but keeling over and sliding onto his side. He lay still, burbling to himself, a stupid grin on his face, his enormous pupils obscuring the blueness of his eyes.

'What about the others in there?' I asked, but he was in a happy world of his own, and I wondered if I'd been in a similar state that day in the café. It seemed so long ago, though it was only about a week.

Hobbes was walking towards the back door of the police station, something in his hunched movement reminiscent of a desperate gun fighter in one of the old westerns he loved. I wished I knew what he was planning, and what he was up against, because, although normally he could cope with anything life threw at him, there'd been occasions when he'd seemed incredibly vulnerable. The way the chills were running down my spine suggested this might be another of them. I wanted to help, to be the trusty sidekick who saves the day, but I was held back by fear, almost like a physical barrier. In addition, an unhappy thought came to me that, all too often, it was the trusty sidekick who got gunned down.

Trying to focus, I reminded myself that I wasn't in the Wild West and that a gunfight was unlikely. Although I'd never been keen on guns, I'd grown even less enamoured of them after the Editorsaurus's wife shot me in the leg. Admittedly I'd not been the target – she'd been trying to shoot her own trusty sidekick – and the bullet that hit me had ricocheted and was nearly spent, but it had stung and broken the skin, and I fancied I could still make out the scar under bright lights. Daphne had agreed when I pointed it out, though I suspected she might have been humouring me.

Constable Poll giggled as if drunk.

'Are you all right?' I asked.

'It's all too beautiful,' he said, making a feeble attempt to get to his feet, but slumping face down onto the moss-encrusted pavement.

'What are you doing?' I asked. 'It's cold, damp and filthy down there.'

'I'm resting my eyes in shades of green,' he said, and snored.

Since he seemed quite relaxed and there was no sign of immediate danger, I thought I could safely leave him for a short time. The main threat to him seemed to be the biting wind, so I covered him with my coat and wondered whether my next move would count as one of my finer moments, or would just increase my tally of stupid ones. Despite every better instinct, despite the fear, I was going in.

'Don't go away,' I told the sleeping policeman, and scurried towards the station.

It was only a few steps away, though it felt longer, as if I was running into a strong, cold wind. Gritting my teeth, I butted forward, swaying as if the earth was shaking, and I was making reasonable progress until a small dark figure darted out, grabbed my legs and squeezed them together. I crashed down right in front of the door.

'What do you think you're doing?' said Billy, rolling me over and sitting on my chest. 'Hobbesie didn't want anyone else involved, and you should be safe back at Blackdog Street. It's really dangerous in there.'

'I'm ... umm ... worried about him and came to help.'

'I'm worried too, mate, but you're not going to be any use if something happens to you.'

'What could happen? Derek Poll's all right, other than being completely out of it.'

'You think being completely out of it is all right?'

'No ... I suppose not, but I'm feeling kind of strange

myself. What about you?'

'Yeah, a little.'

'But why?'

'I wish I knew, mate. It's just something these people do.'

'But who are they?'

'Dunno. I'd never heard of them before, but Featherlight reckons they just turn up and cause trouble. He's banned them from the Feathers, though that doesn't mean much. He's banned most people, including me a few times, and I'm the only barman who'll work there.'

I got an impression of movement.

'I think someone's on the roof,' said Billy.

'Yes, I thought I saw something when I got here.'

He scanned the roof line. 'I can't see anyone now. Get out of here while you can.'

He rolled off me and dived back into the shadows while I retreated to the alley, where Constable Poll was snoring and occasionally giggling. My desire to get inside the police station had become a compulsion, and, although I was still worried about Hobbes, that was not the reason. It was as if something like a magnet was drawing me in, weakening my sense of fear.

I lost control and sprinted for the door. Billy, cursing, dived out and got a grip on my ankle, but I kept going, dragging him with me.

'Stop!' he cried. 'Don't be stupid!'

I shook my head, unable to understand why I was doing it, and trying to kick him off. He proved a persistent little sod, but eventually I caught him a good one, and left him clutching his ribs, though he still managed to block the back door. I felt myself drawn round to the front entrance, feeling a bit like a fish must feel when hooked and being reeled in. When I scuttled inside, Sergeant Dixon, a youngish man built like a docker, was lying on his back by the front desk, grinning and chuckling like Poll. His outstretched legs were propping open the door to the inner station.

'Are you all right?' I asked, stopping briefly.

All I got by way of reply was a soppy grin that reminded me of something, though it took a few moments to remember that it was the same goofy expression I'd worn in our wedding photographs, and, I suspected, when I'd been with Violet, the lovely woman who'd taken an unexpected shine to me, and who had then, even more unexpectedly, turned out to be a werecat.

There was no sign of Hobbes.

30

Despite fear building up, something was drawing me further in. I stepped over Dixon, who waved and giggled, and entered the main corridor. On my right was the main office, where everything appeared much like the last time I'd been there, though some desks had a neglected look as if they were no longer regularly used. One thing was decidedly different; the officers, civilian and uniformed alike, were sprawling on the floor, smiling and helpless. A skinny, grey-haired little woman in brown slacks held out her arms.

'Love me,' she demanded.

'Umm ... what?' I said, maintaining my ability to communicate in awkward situations.

My voice seemed to take her aback. 'You're not him. You're an imposter!'

'Not who?'

'Not the beautiful one.'

'You don't mean Hobbes, do you?' I asked, astounded, though I'd noticed with huge mystification that some women seemed at least half-attracted by his feral Hobbesness.

'Don't be silly.' She shook her head and smiled as she lay back down, her eyes glazing over. I walked past her and looked inside the canteen, which, other than vending machines, Formica-covered tables and orange plastic seats, appeared empty, though an enchanting feminine fragrance made me linger.

'Why, it's Andy,' said a sweet voice that reminded me of Daphne and Violet and every other charming woman I'd had a crush on, though it was softer, gentler and more alluring.

A beautiful young woman with huge, emerald green eyes

full of desire and delight gazed at me from the doorway that led into the kitchen.

'Sally!' I cried and took a clumsy, lumbering step towards her, my arms held out like a clock stuck at quarter-to-three.

Deep down I had an inkling that something was terribly wrong. I fought to regain control, trying to resist her charms, reminding myself that I loved Daphne, and that so much beauty was unnatural. For a moment I held back. Then she smiled and I was lost. I lurched forwards, shaking as if I were about to attempt a tight rope walk over a ravine, and my heart filled with desire and love for this wondrous apparition.

'Come to me, you delightful man,' she said, her voice sweeter and thicker than honey. 'I love your new frizzed hair, and not having eyebrows really suits you.'

'Thank you,' I murmured, and, like a fly about to ensnare itself hopelessly in a honeydew plant, I went to her, enraptured by her perfume, her voice, her loveliness.

'Andy, no!'

A harsh, high-pitched squawk grated on my nerves. I looked down at the diminutive black-clad figure who was standing between me and my heart's desire and shoved him aside.

'Well done, darling,' said Sally. 'Come to me. We were meant to be and should never have parted. Come to me now. I'm so hungry for love.'

'I'm coming,' I said.

'No,' said Billy, but I ignored him.

'Come to me, my own true love.'

I nodded, my eyes fixed on the spellbinding vision, my head pounding.

'It's a trap, Andy,' Billy cried, his voice muffled by the blood rush through my brain. 'She's not what you think she is, and you know it.'

'Be quiet, little man,' said Sally, her voice cold and sour.

'Get out or expect a bitter fate.'

I couldn't have said the spell was broken, yet for a second I was more myself, and able to take in my surroundings. Billy was on his hands and knees, blood dripping through his ninja mask, though what had happened to him was beyond me.

'You've been warned,' Sally snarled. 'Get out or I'll introduce you to my cousin, and he's not as nice as I am.'

Something must have gone wrong with my eyes because for a moment she looked nothing like my lovely Sally, and there was something about her that made me think of the praying mantis from the wildlife park.

Then she smiled again and beckoned, and despite my body shaking with terror, I was drawn to her, and in those moments, though they felt as long as hours, I would willingly have died for her. The mix of terror and ecstasy and being entirely out of my own control was most peculiar, and reminded me of when someone had slipped something into my beer at a party and I'd come awake in a park where an electric-blue gorilla was playing bagpipes.

'Andy!' Her call was that of the Siren.

'Sally,' I cried.

'That's not who she is,' said Billy's voice, as if from a great distance. 'She's Matilda Kielder, the man-eater.'

'She can eat me whenever she likes,' I murmured, though I so much wanted to run and save my life, and Billy's.

I was intensely aware of all my flaws: frizzed hair, bald eyebrows, a slightly misaligned front tooth, a chin that might have been better shaved, breath that stank, a nose that was too big and had a tiny pimple, and the clumsiness of my lumpen body. It was clear I was unworthy of the vision before me, and, though I really ought to crawl away and die, grateful for having glimpsed such perfection, her compassion was so vast that she could love even a wretch like me. I dragged my hopeless ungainly body towards her welcoming arms, and though an image of Daphne, the woman I loved, flashed before my eyes, it did not deter me.

What might have happened next had I not been such an uncoordinated oaf is something I never dared dwell upon. My huge, disgusting feet became entangled and, instead of flinging myself into her arms, I tripped, lunged forward, and head-butted her in the midriff.

Her screech, more the bellow of an enraged and ferocious animal than a woman's cry, scared me, making me desperate to get away, but I was still falling, going down on her as she clawed at me with astonishing strength. There was no softness in her body as we hit the floor. She gasped, a weirdly primeval noise that made me stare into her face, which had become dark and desiccated, like a mummy's. Her mouth was a nightmare of shark-like teeth, and a repulsive stagnant smell was all around.

Though winded and fuzzy headed, I leapt up and tried to flee, only to be brought back down by a grip like contracting steel around my ankle. She was dragging me towards her, despite my attempts to crawl away; no traction was to be had on the smooth linoleum flooring. I screamed for help, but Billy was curled up against the wall, not moving. When I turned to look at the woman, I saw no beauty, and she now reminded me of one of the prehistoric bodies that occasionally turned up in peat bogs, deflated, leathery, and half-rotten. How I'd ever seen her as the least bit attractive was beyond me. The spell fell apart, and even in my panic and despair, I felt relief.

'What do you want with me?' I asked, my voice quavering. I was hoping she'd explain herself and that my brilliant ploy would, at worst, buy me some time, and, at best, would end with her changing her mind and letting me go.

She was not in a talkative mood.

She leapt on me, her scent overly sweet and repulsive, like the stink of slow decay. Her sinewy limbs were unnaturally strong and there was nothing wrong with her teeth so far as sharpness went, though Mrs Goodfellow would have found fault with the bubbling grey film coating them.

'Help!' I cried, and she giggled, sounding for a moment just like my darling Sally.

'Kiss me!' she breathed, her mouth a hideous pucker.

'Shan't,' I said, closing my lips as tight as I could and turning my head aside.

Kissing, I feared, was not what she had in mind, and those sharp teeth served to remind me, if I could have forgotten, that she was a man-eater.

She leaned forward and I was drowning in her breath, my head spinning, losing all hope and wondering how I'd explain my death to Daphne.

A massive thud shook the room and made her look up, giving me an opportunity to escape, though I was in no condition to take it. All I could manage was a feeble wriggle, like a maggot on a hook. Another thud, booming even louder than the first, stirred up dust that twinkled and scintillated for a moment in a stray beam of sunlight.

'What's that?' said Matilda.

There was a third massive bang and the wall burst inwards in a whirlwind of debris with Hobbes at the centre. He landed on top of her. Only he stood up.

'Oof!' he said, and grinned. 'I always thought a door would come in handy there. All right, Andy?'

I nodded and coughed as plaster and flakes of paint showered us, giving him the appearance of a white-haired old man with appalling dandruff. He shook himself like a dog, and returned to his more normal appearance, such as it was.

He poked the unconscious monstrous thing sprawled at his feet with the toe of his boot, but she didn't respond. In her stillness, she, if that pronoun applied, looked even more like a bog body.

I sat up, shaking. 'I was wondering when you'd blow in. Where were you? She was going to eat me, I think.'

'I only knew you were here when I heard your cry for help. You were supposed to be looking after Derek.'

'Oh, yes, well ... umm ... I thought he'd be all right where he was ... I did cover him up ... He wasn't himself though.'

'No, he got a full blast of Matilda's charm, but, like you, he's tougher than he appears, and managed to get out on his own.'

'I'm tougher than I appear?' I wasn't sure whether to feel pleased or insulted.

'You resisted more than some, though you'd had prior experience.'

I nodded, the fuzzy headed feeling clearing a little. 'But where were you? I saw you come in ... I think ...'

'I was on the roof, negotiating with Aubrey and Hilda Elwes. It took some time, so I only got away a few moments ago.'

'Aubrey and Hilda? What are they doing up there?'

'They were planning to bust Alvin out.'

'Bust him out? But I thought they were the good guys ... sort of.'

'Perhaps they are ... sort of.' Hobbes half-smiled. 'They intended taking him into their own custody and I've not yet decided whether to grant their wish.'

'But you can't. He's a double murderer.'

'It's true that he's killed at least twice.'

'You think there may be others?'

He shrugged. 'Maybe. Anyway, the point is moot since Matilda got to him first, and freed him. His current whereabouts are unknown, though he can't have gone far.'

'That's worrying.'

He nodded and glanced towards Billy. 'What happened to him?'

'I ... umm ... don't know.' I had a vague memory of violence, but was nearly certain I wouldn't have hurt my friend.

Hobbes went towards him, but paused. 'Maybe I should restrain her before anything else. She may still present a danger.'

He pulled a set of old-fashioned handcuffs from his pocket, looked at her inert form for a few moments, and put them back. 'Maybe not. She doesn't look as if she'll cause any more trouble for a while.'

'Are you sure?' I asked, but he was already looking after Billy.

When he turned him over, I gasped.

'He's been beaten up,' said Hobbes, removing the little fellow's ninja hood. Blood was oozing from his nose and mouth.

'Is he all right?'

He checked Billy's vital signs. 'He's got a strong pulse and he's breathing well.'

'Umm ... who could have done such a thing?'

'Come here.'

I hobbled over, drained and dizzy as if I'd been drinking long and hard.

'Kneel down and make a fist.'

I knelt, clenching my fingers and wrapping my thumb around them tightly, as Mrs Goodfellow had once shown me, and tried to work out why my knuckles were skinned and bruised. He took my fist and fitted it to one of the bruises on Billy's face.

'But I only pushed him away,' I said. 'He was being really annoying and trying to stop me going to Sally... ' I hesitated. 'I don't remember hitting him ... and she was just an illusion, wasn't she? He was trying to save my life and if he hadn't slowed me down ...'

Hobbes wiped blood from Billy's face.

'Sorry,' I said. 'I must have done it, but I don't remember. I didn't know what I was doing.'

'Do you ever?' said Billy and sat up with a groan.

'How are you feeling?' asked Hobbes.

'As well as anyone who's just been bashed by a maniac,' said Billy and wiped a fresh trickle of blood from his nose, which was bent far enough that he'd be able to sniff around corners.

'I'm sorry,' I repeated, feeling as thoroughly ashamed of myself as anyone who'd just beaten up an innocent dwarf should feel, though all I could recall was giving him a bit of a shove. I wanted to deny everything, but the evidence was compelling.

'Forget it, mate.'

'Thank you,' I said, and turned to Hobbes. 'Does he need an ambulance?'

'He don't need an ambulance,' said Billy. 'I'll be fine.'

'But, your nose!'

He touched it, grimaced, and pulled it straight with a sickening scrunch that nearly made me faint.

'Ouch,' he said, as if reading my mind. He grinned, and mopped his face with a black handkerchief.

'Good. All's well as ends well,' said Hobbes, and helped him to his feet.

'What are you going to do with her?' I asked, jabbing a thumb in the general direction of Matilda, who, other than twitching slightly, had not moved. 'Are you going to sling her in the cells?'

'I ought to find her cousin,' said Hobbes, 'but I suppose I should lock her up first.'

'Yes, and then we can hunt him down,' I said, elated to have survived another horror. 'And he'll be easier to deal with.'

'What makes you think that?' asked Billy, his voice rather nasal.

'Well, you know what they say, don't you? The female of the species is more deadly than the male.'

'So I've heard,' said Hobbes, 'but, I don't know who they are that say such things, and I'm not sure it's true. Both genders of these people can be equally dangerous, depending on circumstances.'

'Even Aubrey and Hilda?' I asked. 'They seem rather nice, and she's awfully pretty.'

'You still haven't quite worked them out, have you?' said Hobbes. 'If they so chose, Aubrey and Hilda could be at least as dangerous as their cousins, and you can't judge by their appearances.'

I nodded, feeling utterly confused, which was at least within my comfort zone. 'You mean she doesn't look like what she looks like?'

'I mean, she does look just like she looks like, but it's all a mirage, and the same goes for him. However, these debates, though clearly fascinating, can be left for later. In the meantime, I'd like to put Matilda somewhere safe,' said Hobbes in a loud clear voice.

The canteen door flew open and smacked against the wall.

'Oh no, you don't,' said a familiar voice.

It was Solomon Slugg. That is, it was Alvin Elwes.

'Shift yourself, Knuckledragger,' he said, giving a glance over his shoulder.

Marco Jones, looking dazed, followed him into the canteen, a double-barrelled shotgun in his big hands. He pointed it at Hobbes, and occasionally at Billy, but clearly did not consider me a threat. I suppose I should have been insulted, but I wasn't, because it meant I wasn't in immediate danger. Even so I thought it wise to step away from them as I tried to figure out how long it would take him to reload if he shot at Hobbes and Billy, and whether that would give me sufficient time to get out of there in one piece. Given the volume of adrenalin surging through me, I reckoned I'd be halfway up Vermin Street by the time he was ready. I hoped it wouldn't come to that.

Alvin looked at us, smiling sadly, and it struck me how much we'd wronged him, because there was no way such a noble man could possibly murder anyone, and it was obvious that all his business interests were entirely legitimate. I wondered if he might become my friend, since he was evidently a far superior kind of person to Hobbes, and way above Billy, though everybody was way above that little runt. I stared at them, finding it unbelievable that I'd never noticed just how ugly they both were. Of course I'd known Hobbes was no oil painting, but I'd never before been struck by how hideous and uncouth he was. There were gargoyles and grotesques on the church with better features, and more social graces. As for Billy, small, and stubby, I couldn't believe I'd ever considered him a friend. What had possessed me to believe I wanted to hang around with such freaks, such monsters? Hobbes nodded at Billy and I was sickened by how lumpish his every movement was. I was soothed by Alvin's voice. How beautiful were his words, like lyrical poetry. How gentle and charming was his voice.

Something about the word charming triggered a warning. I shook my head and blinked, trying to disperse a fog of confusion and found I'd drawn closer to Alvin, whose brilliant eyes were fixed on mine. He really was a fine looking man, honest and decent, and yet, if I concentrated and my eyes were shut, I knew it was all deception. Hobbes, was standing still, his shoulders hunched, looking defeated. Billy held a mobile phone in his hand. As I watched, he pressed a button.

'Throw that down, little man,' said Alvin, his voice sweet, yet not at all wholesome, and containing something of sickness and decay.

Billy dropped the phone, and gave a barely perceptible wink to Hobbes, whose lips twitched into a quick smile. Feeling more myself, I took a step towards my friends, towards Hobbes and Billy, though it took such an effort of will that I almost cried with the pain.

'Welcome back from the dark side,' Billy whispered.

'Fool,' said Alvin, addressing me. 'I thought you were the clever one. You could have joined me, to both of our benefits. I could have done so much for this town, and you could have helped me and risen high in the world. Never mind. It's clear you belong in the gutter with those freaks.

'Now, give me back my cousin, if you'd be so good. It's time for us to go.'

'I'll not stop you,' said Hobbes, standing aside to allow him access to Matilda, 'but are you sure you want to leave us? Aubrey and Hilda are waiting outside.'

'Liar!'

'I never lie,' said Hobbes. 'They've been looking for you. I've persuaded them to wait, but if they see you making a run for it they will have you, and I won't be able to help.'

For a moment, Alvin sagged, looking like a bog body in a business suit. Then his fine-chiselled chin jutted defiantly and he looked heroic, distinguished and thoroughly admirable. 'They won't get me. Was it them that broke into my house?'

'So they said,' said Hobbes, 'but you ran away.'

'As I'd already seen their heptagram asking for news of Matilda, I suspected they'd tracked me down too, so I made a strategic withdrawal.' He glanced at Marco. 'Pick up the telephone.'

Marco looked around stupidly at the tables. 'What telephone? There isn't one.'

'The one on the floor next to the dwarf.'

'The mobile phone?'

'Yes, Marco, the mobile phone. Pick it up and give it to me.'

Marco did as he was told, his body as slow as his mind.

Alvin took the mobile, poked a few buttons, shook his head and laughed. 'What sort of message is that?' he asked. 'Dogged by misfortune, release the hounds."

Billy shrugged. 'It was a joke.'

'I don't get it.' said Alvin. 'It's not very funny.'

'No,' admitted Billy, stone-faced.

'Why don't you give yourself up, sir?' asked Hobbes. 'It will be better for you.'

'Because, Inspector, I have no intention of going to one of your prisons. They used to be a piece of cake to escape from, but I'm not so sure these days.'

'Modern times, sir. I don't suppose even you can charm an electronic lock,' said Hobbes sympathetically. 'But, tell me why you murdered Solomon Slugg.'

'I didn't murder him. It was self-defence, and it's something I regret, though it was necessary.'

'I wish I could believe you, sir. Perhaps you can convince me. Where did you defend yourself?'

'In the house. He wanted me to leave it and I wasn't ready. He manhandled me.'

'And you unfortunately killed him.'

'Yes. He wouldn't keep quiet.'

'Fair enough,' said Hobbes. 'I can see why that might have been annoying.'

I could see that too and Alvin's case seemed convincing, and one no reasonable person could argue against.

'I do have a question, though,' Hobbes continued. 'What were you doing in his house?'

'Taking possession of it.'

'And he objected, sir?'

'Indeed he did. Violently. In the subsequent fracas I accidently hit him on the head.'

'That seems clear,' said Hobbes. 'You broke into his house ...'

'I didn't break in. I entered through an open window.'

'That obviously makes a difference, sir, but would you confirm the sequence of events? You entered his house via an open window, he objected to your presence ...'

'Strongly objected ...'

'And in the ensuing struggle you accidently bashed him over the head repeatedly with your lead-weighted stick.'

'Correct, Inspector. Well done.'

'And how did Mr Septimus Slugg die?'

'Oh, him. He came to visit when I was gardening and refused to accept my explanation of why I was there. He said he was going to tell the police, so I dissuaded him with my billhook.'

'And you disposed of both bodies in the culvert by the church. Why there, sir?'

'It was deep and old, and no one knew about it.'

'Thank you, sir. That was useful. You'd have got away with it too had it not been for the flood and Andy's luck.'

'I will still get away with it, Inspector. You won't profit from what I've told you, since I have the upper hand.'

'In what way, sir? You're in a police station, and, despite your protestation of innocence I am not convinced, so I intend to re-arrest you for the murders of Solomon Slugg and Septimus Slugg, to which you have admitted in front of witnesses. I rather think I have the upper hand.'

'Not while I have Marco with me. I find a shotgun trumps all arguments.'

'But Marco won't use it.'

'He damned well will when I tell him to.'

'I doubt it, sir.'

'Why, Inspector? He's a useful idiot and does what he's

told.'

'Not anymore. He'll put the gun down and walk away.'

'Why would you think that? His will is mine.'

'You may think so, sir, but if he doesn't put the gun down I'll tell his mum.'

'Enough!' said Alvin, his face ugly with rage as he glanced at Marco. 'Shoot him, and then shoot the homunculus.'

'But he said he'll tell ma,' said Marco, his eyes wide. 'And I don't know what a homunculus is.'

'Just do as you're told. Shoot the big one and then the little one!'

'Put the gun down, Marco,' said Hobbes gently, 'because if you don't, I really will tell her, and she'll be ever so cross. Can you imagine what she'll say if I have to tell her you've shot us?'

Despite a lingering and persistent fuzziness in my head, I wondered if Hobbes's logic might be flawed, but no such doubts seemed to afflict Marco.

'Please don't tell, Mr Hobbes. I don't mean any harm. I'll put it down.'

He bent and placed the shotgun carefully on the floor.

'Thank you, Marco,' said Hobbes. 'You may go now, if you wish.'

Looking dazed, Marco nodded, turned and ambled away, humming to himself.

For a moment Alvin seemed nonplussed. Then, as swift as a foraging ferret, he sprang forward and grabbed the shotgun. 'If a job's worth doing,' he said, 'do it yourself.'

'I really wouldn't if I were you, sir,' said Hobbes, shaking his head.

'Don't tell me what to do, you freak. I'm in charge here.'

'You're really not, sir. Please put the gun down. I don't want you to get hurt again.'

'It's not me who's going to get hurt,' said Alvin, raising the shotgun.

Hobbes shook his head. 'OK,' he said. 'Get him.'

'What?' said Alvin, turning towards the sudden scrabbling from the corridor.

It was dogs' claws accelerating on lino. Dregs barged in, closely followed by Mimi. Alvin screamed as they leapt, knocking him flat onto his back, while Hobbes, diving forwards, caught the shotgun. Dregs, knowing police business, stepped off Alvin, and stared at his face, alert and ready for action. Mimi, however, was a dog possessed and, her hackles up, her teeth bared, she went for any bit of Alvin she could get her teeth into, and there turned out to be lots of bits.

'Drop!' said Hobbes and passed the shotgun to Billy.

Mimi glanced up, and, clearly unused to being spoken to in that way, resumed her attack, getting a firm grip on Alvin's ankle, which she was trying to shake as if it were a scrawny rat, while he shrieked, his voice sharp and harsh, lacking any of the honeyed sweetness of a few seconds earlier. I could see why Hobbes had entrusted the shotgun to Billy rather than to me; I might have been convinced to use it against the wrong targets. In fact, I was still feeling ridiculously amiable towards Alvin, who had never done me any harm, so far as I knew, whereas Hobbes kept putting me into the firing line, and Billy had hurt my knuckles on his face ...

Hobbes gently tried to prise Mimi off Alvin's groin, to which she'd become quite attached, having had her fill of ankles. I shook my head again, and had to keep reminding myself that Hobbes and Billy were my friends, and that Alvin was a sick and twisted individual, whose ugly interior was now mirrored by his ugly exterior. As he lay there, screeching and groaning, with skinny tea-brown limbs, a narrow, leathery face, stained teeth and pale, sunken eyes, he really did look like something dragged into the daylight after millennia festering. He smelt that way as well.

'Get the savage brute away from me!' Alvin yelled.

'I'm doing my best, sir,' said Hobbes, lifting Mimi to one side, and holding her still as she wriggled, bristling and snarling, clearly convinced her task had only just begun. To be fair, parts of Alvin remained unbitten.

Despite his desiccated appearance, Alvin appeared to be rather talented at leaking blood, and, despite my improved ability to cope with gore (so long as it wasn't my own) I was becoming increasingly light-headed and wobbly. Billy must have noticed, because, having laid the shotgun carefully in the corner, he came across and helped me to a chair. I plumped down heavily, my head lolling, and tried not to faint.

'I'll get you a glass of water,' he said and trotted into the kitchen.

31

Hobbes, with a little assistance from Dregs, wrestled Mimi out into the corridor, and shut the door behind them, leaving me alone with Alvin. I wasn't concerned, because he clearly was in no state to do anything, except moan and groan, at which he was proving himself an expert. I shut my eyes, fighting a sense of increasing confusion, until something hard and cold jabbed under my nose.

I flinched and gasped, looking up into the face of the woman I'd have died for a few minutes earlier. Somehow I'd forgotten about Matilda, or Sally, or whatever her real name was, or rather, I'd just assumed she was no longer a threat. Sadly she still was, especially now she had the shotgun.

'Did I wake you, Andy?' she said, and the allure was back in her voice, though I fought it.

I trembled, watching how the shotgun followed my every movement.

'Did you do that?' she asked, pointing at Alvin, who was groaning and writhing.

'Umm ... no ... It was a dog.'

'A dog, Andy? I see no dog. Do you mean that uncouth inspector?'

'No, and he's not uncouth. Well, he is a bit, but he doesn't go round biting people ... not often, anyway.'

'Stand up!'

I got to my feet, confusion overridden by fear, for, although I could occasionally catch a glimpse of my lovely Sally, I could mostly see scrawny, leathery Matilda, who bore scant resemblance to a living woman, and who, to judge from the dark emptiness in her eyes, would have no compunction in blasting me into eternity.

'What are you going to do?' I asked.

'Get out of here with my cousin.'

'Good plan. You won't need me for that, will you?'

'I think I might. Firstly, you'll make a good hostage, in case anyone thinks about doing something stupid, and secondly, you will assist my cousin, who needs a supporting hand. Help him to his feet, Andy, like a good lad.'

Although repulsed and almost sickened by the dry parchment feel of his skin that seemed to crackle over his bones, I helped him to get up, trying to ignore his blood on my hands.

'Take him into the corridor, and don't think of running away or you'll get a blast of hot lead.'

Despite his emaciated appearance, Alvin hung like a lead-weight on my arm as I dragged him towards the exit.

'Here's your water,' said Billy, walking back through the kitchen door as I was struggling to lug Alvin into the corridor.

Dropping the glass, he ducked back into the kitchen and slammed the door behind him. Although I couldn't blame him, for he was only a little guy and the shotgun was big and in the hands of a merciless killer, I couldn't help but feel disappointed. I'd been hoping he'd do something amazing. Still, I wasn't despondent, certain that Hobbes would get me out of the predicament.

Neither he nor the dogs were in the corridor, or anywhere else to be seen.

'Take Alvin out the front,' Matilda commanded, 'and don't think of doing anything silly.'

'I wasn't thinking of anything ... and ... umm ... what are you going to do when we're out? He won't get far like this.'

'We'll take a car. You can drive.'

'No, I really can't,' I said, gasping under Alvin's weight as I man-handled him to the front desk, where Sergeant Dixon was still propped against the wall, grinning and singing to himself.

'I don't believe you,' said Matilda.

'It's true. I've never learnt, and last time I tried I knocked over a tree ... it was in the *Bugle.*'

'In that case, I'll drive,' she said.

'That would be wise and then ... umm ... then you wouldn't want me, would you?'

'You will still be my hostage, until you have no further use.'

'And then you'll let me go?'

'Of course,' she said, smiling.

I wanted to believe her.

'Now what?'

'Get me to a car,' said Alvin, his first articulate sound for some time. He returned to groaning, and continued dripping blood from any number of punctures.

'Shouldn't we give him first aid?' I asked.

'That will have to wait,' said Matilda, opening the front door and stepping out. 'We need to get away from here before that big bruiser comes back. Now move!'

That was the moment when I saw my chance to escape. All I had to do was throw Alvin at her, slam the doors behind them, and barricade myself in the kitchen with Billy. Unfortunately, just before I acted, Sergeant Dixon muttered something about truth and beauty, and I realised I'd be leaving him, and the others, in danger. I couldn't do it, and my chance had gone.

Matilda made a gesture with the shotgun that removed any lingering idea of escape, and I did as she demanded, helping Alvin through the door, bearing his weight while she peered up and down the street.

'It's all clear,' she said, with a smile that allowed me another glimpse of Sally. 'Come along. Let's find a car.'

I looked around for Hobbes, but there was no sign of him, and the whole area was quiet. In fact, it appeared to be deserted, and I began to feel very much abandoned, fearing he'd taken the dogs back home after they'd done their bit, and that he was sitting there, probably with his feet up and with a mug of tea in his hand. However, it would be wrong to suggest it was then when I began to feel sorry for myself, since I'd been feeling that way since I'd first bumped into Sally, and yet part of me was almost enjoying my new role as tragic hero, who, rather than leave a helpless police sergeant to a dreadful fate, was bravely marching to a martyr's death. It was a far, far better thing that I was doing, than I had ever done, though I wished Alvin wasn't so heavy.

Then everything went heavy, and the only possible direction of movement was downwards. I hit the ground, with Alvin at my side and Matilda just in front. Despite struggling, I was helpless, as were the others, though perhaps if Matilda had put as much effort into trying to move as she did into screaming obscenities, she might have got away, for she was only just beneath the wide-meshed net that had entrapped us. As for me, the more I fought it, the more entangled I became until all I could move was my head.

There was nothing else to do, so I tried to relax as much as was possible when flat on my back on an icy cold pavement with my legs bent beneath me. I stared at the sky, by then a pleasant pale blue without a hint of cloud, and waited for something to happen. Then I glanced down my body. The shotgun was pointing at my crotch, and Matilda's finger was still on the trigger. She was face down and furious, but when she saw what I'd seen she grinned. No charm remained.

'Inspector Hobbes,' she shouted, 'get me and my cousin out of this net, or I'll ruin Andy's day.'

I waited, hoping.

'I mean it.' Her finger twitched.

'Please, don't!' I cried, but there was no response from Hobbes.

But there was a response.

'You might as well give up now, dear cousin,' said the smooth voice of Aubrey Elwes.

Matilda's hiss made me even more nervous.

'He said they were here,' said Alvin. 'I didn't believe him.'

'Both of them?' asked Matilda.

'Yes, cousin dearest,' said Hilda her voice sweet, like a honeyed-up bee with a sting in its tail.

'Let us go, or I'll blow the hostage in two.'

'No, don't,' I said, though I doubted anyone was listening.

'You must know your threat means nothing to us,' said Hilda. 'Whether he lives or dies is irrelevant.'

'No, it isn't!' I said, for although I'd been in plenty of uncomfortable situations, this was possibly the most terrifying, and besides, I'd thought Hilda and Aubrey were my friends. However, in those desperate moments, disappointment was not my main concern.

'Liar,' said Matilda. 'You two were always soft on these upstarts. Let us out, or I'll blast him.'

'Do what you want,' said Aubrey, 'but it won't help you. All you'll get is his gizzards splashed on your nice frock.'

'I'll do it.'

'She really will,' said Alvin, leaving off moaning for a second.

'So what?' said Hilda. 'Do it if you must, but we'll still catch you. And then we will take you to Auntie, who is already angry that you two have turned out to be killers.'

'I'm not a killer,' said Alvin.

'Yes, you are,' I corrected him. 'You killed Solomon and Septimus Slugg.'

'I admit it, but, I'm not a killer. I'm someone who has killed. There's a difference.'

'Umm ... I'm not sure there is.'

'Of course there is. I admit to having killed two people. I didn't want to, I didn't enjoy doing it, and I don't make a habit of it. I merely did what had to be done. Now, my adorable cousin ...'

'Shut up,' said Matilda.

'... gets a kick from killing ...'

'Shut up.'

'And she likes to chew the fat of her latest sweetheart.'

'Shut up,' said Matilda.

'No, go on,' said Aubrey. 'Your account is most illuminating.'

Matilda, hissing like a maddened snake, was fighting furiously and I really hoped she was being careful with her trigger finger, for I couldn't even move my legs together, which might have been a small comfort. All I could do was raise my head slightly and watch as she finally freed herself with a convulsive heave. I hoped Hobbes would turn up, but he didn't. I hoped Aubrey or Hilda would disarm her, but they didn't. Matilda got to her feet, holding the shotgun with a casual menace that wouldn't have looked out of place in the old gangster movies Hobbes loved to watch.

She pointed the double barrels at my head. I wasn't sure this was an improvement.

'Let my cousin go,' she yelled, 'or we'll find out whether lover-boy here has any brains in his thick skull. My bet is that he doesn't.'

'You'd lose,' I said. 'I had a scan and ...'

'You talk too much. Just shut up.'

I shut up and she checked the streets and rooftops.

'You'd better show yourself, Inspector Hobbes, because my beloved siblings seem strangely unmoved by your friend's plight.'

Nothing happened, but at least Aubrey and Hilda refrained from encouraging her.

'Get me out of here,' said Alvin.

'Leave him there,' said Hilda.

'Get lost,' said Matilda. 'Remember, there's two barrels in

this gun, so there'll be one left for you.'

'Why waste one on me?' I asked. 'I'm no threat to you, but they are. You might need both barrels.'

'I'll shoot whomever I want,' said Matilda. 'If your precious inspector doesn't show himself within ten seconds, and release my cousin from this net, then you're going to get it.'

'By it, I don't suppose you mean the net?' I said.

She laughed. 'I'm going to miss you, Andy.'

'I really hope you do.'

She laughed again, sounding almost like my Sally, but when she spoke her voice was harsh and shrill. 'Ten seconds, Inspector. The countdown starts now. Ten ... nine ... eight ...'

'Help!' I cried.

'Seven ... six ... five ...'

There was no sign of Hobbes, and Aubrey and Hilda were just lounging by the police station wall, smiling.

'Four ...three ...'

'Two and three quarters,' I hinted.

'Two ... one ...'

'Please don't,' I pleaded.

'Too late, Inspector,' she said. 'You had a chance to save your foolish friend, but you blew it, and now I'm going to blow his head off.' She stood over me, her leathery face cracked into a malicious leer.

Still there was no sign of Hobbes.

'I don't know what I ever saw in you,' I said, hatred momentarily getting the best of fear. 'You're hideous.'

'Shut up! You're no oil painting yourself with that stupid frizzed hair and no eyebrows ... and the rest. What did you do?'

'It's a long story,' I said. 'It all began when I was a child ...'

I was hoping to buy time. It didn't work.

'Enough. I've really had enough of you,' she said. 'I

reckon I'm doing the world a favour.'

Her finger tightened on the trigger and I stared death in the face. It was no less horrible than her.

32

I was lying on something soft, and swaying slightly as if I was on a boat. My knuckles were sore. There were voices nearby, and, since they didn't sound at all angelic, I concluded I wasn't in the afterlife. As consciousness crept back, they began to sound very much like those of Hobbes and Billy. I opened my eyes. The sky was blue and cloudless.

'Ah, Andy, you're back,' said Hobbes.

'Wotcha, Andy,' said Billy, sounding as if he needed a handkerchief.

'What happened?' I asked, struggling to sit up. 'She was going to blow my head off.'

'She would never have shot you,' said Hobbes.

For an instant my mind took me back to smiling, lovely Sally. 'You mean she still liked me?'

'Of course not.'

'Then ... umm ... why?'

'Because I'd already taken the shells from the gun,' said Billy, pulling them from his pocket.

'I didn't know that!'

'I don't suppose you did,' said Hobbes.

'I thought I was going to die.'

'Sorry,' he said, and I was gratified that he did look a little shame-faced. 'However, you shouldn't have been there. It was a dangerous situation, which was why I told you to stay away.'

'I thought I could help.'

'Actually, in a way you did,' said Hobbes with a grin. 'It's possible that if you hadn't got yourself into such a predicament, I would have relented and taken the pair of them into custody.'

'Pleased I could help, but are you saying they're not in

custody. You mean you let them go? They're killers. Well, Alvin reckons he isn't exactly, and Sally ... umm ... Matilda can be quite charming and lovely ...' I stopped, still confused, but relieved to find it was mostly my normal confusion, and not the confusion they'd put in me.

'They are both killers,' said Hobbes. 'When I arrested Alvin I intended charging him and putting him before a jury.'

'But why didn't you?' I was outraged. 'They're really dangerous.'

'They were,' said Hobbes, his expression shifting from grin to grim.

'What have you done?' I asked, fearing something awful. It wasn't the first time I'd suspected him of murder, though last time he'd been entirely innocent, other than possibly having bent a few laws in the cause of real justice.

'Let me explain,' he said. 'I was going to ensure they had a fair trial, even though they would not have recognised the court.'

'So why didn't you?' I asked, feeling let down.

'Because when I saw how they charmed you and the others, I realised just how easily they manipulated people, even a roomful of people.'

Light began to dawn. 'So you reckoned they'd do their charm thing on a jury and get off?'

'No. I suspect they would have charmed their way out of the cells well before any trial. It has happened before.'

I thought about this for a moment, and it made sense. They'd really messed up my mind, and I'd been by no means the worst affected. 'So where are they now? What did you do?'

'He left them to their cousins,' said Billy.

'Hilda and Aubrey, but why?'

'Because, they can deal with their own without distractions. I doubt Matilda and Alvin will trouble us again.'

'What will they do to them? Sal ... umm ... Matilda seemed scared. They both did.'

'I don't know,' said Hobbes.

'It might be best not to,' Billy suggested, and wiped a smear of blood from his nose.

I nodded, and then stared at him. 'What happened to you?'

'You did, mate. Don't you remember? You laid into me with your fists when I got in your way.'

'I didn't—' I started, and fell silent, struck by an overpowering sensation of déjà vu. Had I been in a similar conversation not so long ago?

'You did, mate.'

'I don't remember ... I've got fractured images in my head, but they're like those weird bits you remember from dreams in the morning ... umm ... sorry for what I did. I didn't mean it.'

'It's all right,' said Billy. 'You weren't yourself.'

'Who was I?'

'You'd fallen under their spell, particularly under Matilda's,' said Hobbes. 'At least, that's how I understand it. Alvin had almost completely beguiled you before, of course. Remember how you found it difficult to believe him a villain, even when the evidence was right before your eyes? And when you met her, you were enchanted because in your eyes she was a beautiful young woman. You've always been susceptible to a pretty face, haven't you?'

I nodded unhappily.

'But if it's any consolation, you stood up to her better than all the lads in the station. Derek put up some sort of resistance but even he crumbled quickly.'

'It is some consolation,' I said, 'but there's just one thing I don't understand ...'

'Just one thing?' said Billy with a lop-sided smirk.

'... among the many things I don't understand is that

there were women in there, and they, too, were completely out of it.'

'That was Alvin,' said Hobbes. 'Dr Ramage seemed particularly spellbound.'

'Spellbound?'

'The word seems appropriate.'

'Will everyone recover?' I asked. 'Will I?'

'Those affected seem much better already,' said Hobbes, 'and you are nearly back to what passes for normal.'

'Thanks ... umm ... what do you mean passes for normal?'

'The phrase seems appropriate.' He grinned, and it was clear his natural humour was back.

'Now what?' I asked.

'If you're feeling well, you can get up, and get on with your life.'

I made a move, realising too late that I'd been resting on the net that had been strung between two lampposts like a hammock. As my legs swung round, the whole thing swayed and tipped me face first into the gutter. Typically, the street was busy again, so I had a small but appreciative audience.

Holding out his huge hairy paw Hobbes yanked me back onto my feet.

'Right,' said Billy, 'I'm off. I need to clean up and change into my work clothes. I'll let the boss know you didn't attack me on purpose. See you.'

'Thanks for your help,' said Hobbes, 'and thank Featherlight for letting the dogs go on cue.'

'Sorry I beat you up, Billy,' I said as he walked away.

It was typical that one of the passers-by was the blue-rinsed Mrs Nutter, whose gorgon glare, focussed though horn-rimmed spectacles, would have turned me to stone had I not fled for sanctuary inside the police station. Sergeant Dixon and Constable Poll were standing by the front desk, comparing notes on what had just happened to them.

‘The coast is clear,’ said Hobbes, grinning round the door a moment or two later. ‘All right, Reg? All right, Derek?’

The two police officers, looking sheepish, nodded.

‘Good,’ said Hobbes. ‘I’m going to get the dogs and then I’m off home for a cup of tea. Coming, Andy?’

After we’d released the dogs from internment in his office, we walked home, for once at a relaxed pace. The cool fresh air cleared my head with every breath and I was able to appreciate a beautiful afternoon, and, though it was still cool, it felt like spring might not be far away. As if in confirmation, the first shoots of crocuses and daffodils were showing in their planters around Pansy Corner. All of this added to the elation of having survived yet another crisis, and I felt fantastic.

It didn’t last, because, by the time we reached Blackdog Street my limbs were heavy and I couldn’t stop yawning. I barely stayed awake long enough to drink a cup of tea, before tottering upstairs and crashing out.

33

I awoke with bright morning light filtering through the curtains. Beneath the mouth-watering scent of frying bacon I noticed an earthy animal odour as well as a pleasantly fresh feminine scent. However, a pressing matter had to be attended to before anything else, so I sprinted to the bathroom. Afterwards, as I was washing my hands, I realised I'd slept right through the night, and had missed my supper. It was a bitter disappointment, though much mitigated by the prospect of breakfast. I shaved, washed, and, having dressed with extreme haste, headed downstairs.

There were women's voices in the kitchen. I assumed Mrs Goodfellow was entertaining some of her friends, a mob of cheery and disreputable old ladies, whose eccentricities were legendary. They always liked to fuss over me, and I just hoped they wouldn't interfere with my eating.

It wasn't them. Two younger women were at the table. The one with her back to me was tanned, with short brown hair and a trim figure. The one facing me was blonde, blue-eyed and breathtakingly beautiful in pink.

'Hi, Pinky,' I said, wondering what she was doing there, and fearing I'd done something wrong again.

The other woman turned and my heart leapt at her lovely smile and soft dark eyes, though the surprise of seeing her knocked my brain out of gear.

'Good morning,' she said, laughing at my impromptu impression of a goldfish.

Unable to find words, I ran towards her, just as Mimi appeared from nowhere and tripped me, making me fling myself into Daphne's arms.

'He's still keen,' said Pinky.

I didn't respond, being locked in a kiss that I wanted to continue forever.

Eventually, though, we both had to come up for air.

'When did you get here?' I asked.

'About an hour ago. I got a late flight yesterday, but it was delayed, and we only landed at about six this morning. After that, I took a coach and came straight here. Mrs Goodfellow has been looking after me.'

'Fantastic,' I said, as I fought off Mimi, 'but why didn't you wake me?'

'We tried,' said Mrs Goodfellow, 'but you were determined to get your beauty sleep. Not even Pig Robinson could rouse you.'

'You put that creature in my bedroom?'

'Yes,' said Daphne. 'Isn't he sweet?'

'Is he? I suppose he is in his way, though we thought he might be dangerous to start with.'

'He seems quite safe to me,' said Mrs Goodfellow. 'He's certainly never come close to blowing up my kitchen, unlike some folk I could mention.'

'Which explains the frizz and the bald eyebrow look, I expect,' said Pinky.

'I ... umm ... was a bit careless with the gas.'

'It'll soon grow out,' said Daphne, holding my hands and gazing into my face.

She looked thin and tired, though her face had tanned to the colour of toffee.

'I expect you'll be wanting your breakfast?' said Mrs Goodfellow.

'Yes ... I expect I will,' I said, though Daphne's return had driven hunger away.

It came back with a rush when the old girl set a plate of bacon and eggs and fried bread and toast before me.

'Excuse me,' I said, 'but I'm famished. I didn't have my supper.'

'Go ahead,' said Daphne. 'Mrs Goodfellow's been telling me some of what you've been up to. You've been busy.'

'I'd better be off to work,' said Pinky, glancing at her pink watch. 'It's great to have you back, Daffy, and nice to see you Mrs G. Goodbye.'

I ate well, though without pigging out, while Daphne told me about the dig. It was only when I'd finished that I wondered where Hobbes was.

'He and Dregs went to have a word with those students you fell out with,' said Mrs Goodfellow as she cleared the dishes.

I had to explain to Daphne what had happened.

'These things could only happen to you,' she said, laughing.

I laughed too, and stopped abruptly as a horrible thought swooped into my mind; I still hadn't sorted out the posters, and she was going to be so upset when she saw them. A ridiculous notion of taking her away someplace where no one knew me came into my head, though I doubted it would work. Sooner or later she'd see one, or someone would talk. Unable to come up with a better idea, I decided to confess.

'That wasn't the only thing that happened,' I admitted, hot faced and ashamed. 'There was this woman, well, it turned out she wasn't actually a woman ... but nothing happened anyway, and it wasn't my fault ...'

'You'd better tell me all about it,' said Daphne, looking straight into my eyes while I squirmed.

'Well ... umm ... what happened was that a car tried to run me down and this woman warned me and saved me ... and then we went for a cup of coffee ...'

'I see. Was she pretty?'

'Umm ... no ... well ... I thought she was at the time, but ...'

'Carry on,' she said, frowning, and folding her arms – a bad sign if ever I saw one.

'Right ... umm ... when we were in the café she sort of

threw herself onto me and, though I tried to get her off ...'

'I bet you tried really hard,' she said, her frown deepening, her eyes teary.

'I did actually, but she'd cast some sort of spell on me ...'

'Well, that's original. Go on.'

I stared at the table, and forced myself to speak. 'Then she made me kiss her ...'

I cringed at her sudden intake of breath, expecting a tearful outburst, and, maybe the beginning of the end of our marriage.

'I'm truly sorry,' I said, forcing myself to look her in the face, fearing the worst.

She chuckled once, opened her mouth as if to say something, and fell into a long fit of helpless laughter. Every time it looked as if she was regaining control, she'd look at my puzzled face and her giggles restarted. At last, wiping her eyes, she overcame the paroxysm.

'What's going on?' I said.

'Assuming you mean the woman on the posters, Mrs Goodfellow has already told me about it. You are talking about that one, aren't you?'

'Yes,' I said, still feeling apprehensive and guilty. 'I don't know what came over me.'

'Nor do I. She looks like something dragged from a bog.'

'On the posters?' I asked, confused.

'Where else? And, since I once helped excavate a bog body, I know what I'm talking about.'

'Excuse me a minute, I need the bathroom,' I said.

I ran upstairs and stared at the poster I'd hidden beneath the handkerchiefs in the bedside table. Daphne was quite correct. Now Matilda's spell was broken, she looked like what she was, a hideous skeletal, leathery-skinned thing who barely even looked female. I tore the poster into tiny bits, flushed them down the toilet and went back to be with my wife.

We stayed with Hobbes and Mrs Goodfellow while we sorted ourselves out, filling in forms, and searching for a new flat. In truth, Daphne did most of the difficult stuff while I helped Hobbes clear up a few things, including locating Mimi's real owners, a retired couple from Stillingham. Handing her back was rather traumatic since I'd grown fond of her, and had half hoped I could keep her. However, her evident delight at the reunion gave me reason to believe she'd be happy.

We also found Pig Robinson a good home. Skeleton Bob, on the explicit instructions of Fenella, adopted him and, since he turned out to be a champion truffle hunter, he provided a massive boost to the Nibblets' income.

The university rugby team's fortunes took a nose dive after their supply of anabolic steroids dried up, though the lads who'd had it in for me, after experiencing one of Hobbes's little talks, became model citizens. Except for the one called Guy, who dropped out of his course and switched to dentistry.

I never saw any of the Elwes family again, which was probably for the best, though I wouldn't have minded seeing Hilda. She'd been so charming.

A few weeks later, when life had settled down again, I entered the Bear with a Sore Head, a town pub that had recently gone upmarket. I was combining business with pleasure, since I intended reviewing the menu for my new syndicated column while enjoying lunch with Daphne. She'd just started her new job, which was excavating and cataloguing the medieval charnel house I'd discovered, and had texted to say she'd be a few minutes late.

I passed the time with a pint of lager, and was trying to get a sense of the pub's ambience and clientele when I noticed a stout balding, sleazy-looking man in a long grubby mac sneaking up on a couple at a table in the corner.

'What are you doing?' I asked.

The man spun around. He was holding a camera, and his fingers were yellow with nicotine.

'You!' I said.

He looked puzzled for a moment, and then smiled as if at an old friend. 'Why, it's Mr Caplet! How nice to see you again. Did you like the photos? I thought you came out really well.'

'No, I didn't, but why did you take them?'

'It was a job. Nothing personal.'

'Really? Well, then ... umm ... who do you work for?'

'Anyone who pays me.' He reached into his pocket and handed me a card. 'If you ever need my services ...'

'Victor Ludorum, private detective? But why me? I'd done nothing wrong.'

'As I understand it, my client believed you were trying to ruin his restaurant and wanted some ... leverage. Unfortunately, he seems to have disappeared and still owes me. Now, if you'll excuse me, I'm working ...'

He turned back, but the couple he'd been sneaking up on had already escaped. Mr Ludorum, if that was his real name, shrugged. 'Never mind. I'll catch up with them later. Jealous husbands can be strung along with snippets for weeks, and it doesn't pay to peak too early.'

'Sorry I'm late,' said Daphne, walking towards me.

'Another beauteous woman,' murmured Mr Ludorum with a wink. 'How do you do it?'

'Pure charm,' I replied.

The private detective hurried away.

'Who was that?' Daphne asked.

'A chance acquaintance, of no importance. Let's get something to eat.'

Continue Your Unhuman Journey

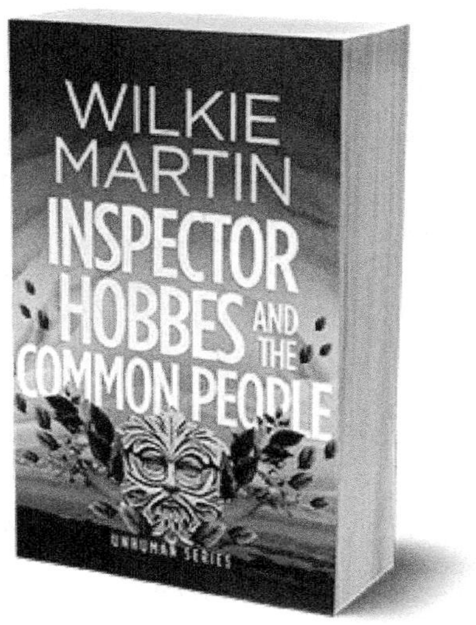

Inspector Hobbes and the Common People
unhuman V

Wilkie Martin

Start reading here:

go.wilkiemartin.com/hobbes-commonpeople-book2look

Join The Unhuman Readers

FREE ON SIGN UP

Sign up for Wilkie's Readers' List and get a free download copy of *Sorenchester Book Maps,* and see where everything takes place. You can also download a free copy of *Relative Disasters* – his little book of silly verse and *Hobbes's Choice Recipes* by Wilkie as A. C. Caplet.

Be amongst the first to hear about Wilkie's new books, publications and products and for exclusive giveaways.

Join here
go.wilkiemartin.com/join-readers-list

WILKIE MARTIN

Wilkie Martin's first novel *Inspector Hobbes and the Blood*, also published by The Witcherley Book Company, was shortlisted for the Impress Prize for New Writers in 2012 under its original title: *Inspector Hobbes*. As well as novels, Wilkie writes short stories and silly poems, some of which are available on YouTube. Like his characters, he relishes a good curry, which he enjoys cooking. In his spare time, he is a qualified scuba-diving instructor, and a guitar twanger who should be stopped.

Born in Nottingham, he went to school in Sutton Coldfield, studied at the University of Leeds, worked in Cheltenham for 25 years, and now lives in the Cotswolds with his partner of 30 years.

wilkiemartin.com

Wilkie Martin Author Page facebook

A Note From The Author

I want to thank you for reading my book. As a new author, one of my biggest challenges is getting known and finding readers. I'm thrilled you have read it and hope you enjoyed it; if you did I would really appreciate you letting your friends and family know. Even a quick Instagram or Facebook status update or a tweet really can make a difference, or if you want to write a review then that would be fantastic. I'd also love to hear from you, so send me a message and let me know what you thought of the book. Thank you for your time.

Wilkie

Share Inspector Hobbes and the Bones

go.wilkiemartin.com/hobbes-bones-book2look

Acknowledgements

Once again, I would like to thank the members of Catchword for their support, guidance and encouragement: Liz Carew, Gill Garret, Derek Healy, Richard Hensley, Pam Keevil, Sarah King, Dr Rona Laycock, Jan Petrie and Susannah White.

I would like to thank Natasha Wagner for proofreading, and Stuart Bache of Books Covered for the series covers.

Writers in the Brewery and the members of Gloucestershire Writers' Network have also provided much appreciated support.

Finally, a huge thank you to my family, to Julia, and to The Witcherley Book Company.